STORMFORCE

Book Three of The Last Legion

Chris Bunch

A ROC BOOK

ROC
Published by New American Library, a division of
Penguin Putnam Inc., 375 Hudson Street,
New York, New York 10014, U.S.A.
Penguin Books Ltd, 27 Wrights Lane,
London W8 5TZ, England
Penguin Books Australia Ltd, Ringwood,
Victoria, Australia
Penguin Books Canada Ltd, 10 Alcorn Avenue,
Toronto, Ontario, Canada M4V 3B2
Penguin Books (N.Z.) Ltd, 182–190 Wairau Road,
Auckland 10, New Zealand

Penguin Books Ltd, Registered Offices:
Harmondsworth, Middlesex, England

First published by Roc, an imprint of New American Library,
a division of Penguin Putnam Inc.

First Printing, October 2000
10 9 8 7 6 5 4 3 2 1

PUBLISHER'S NOTE
This is a work of fiction. Names, characters, places, and incidents either
are the product of the author's imagination or are used fictitiously,
and any resemblance to actual persons, living or dead, business establish-
ments, events, or locales is entirely coincidental.

For
The Langnes:
Stacy, Glenn, Michaela, Annalee

CHAPTER
1

Cumbre/D-Cumbre

The clerk looked over the top of her fashionably antique glasses at the rather odd couple in front of her, odd even for a spaceport's operations section.

One was human, but about two and a half meters tall, with a weightlifter's build, prematurely balding, wearing a flight suit with the rank tabs of a Confederation Forces *Cent* and the name tag DILL.

The other was even bigger than Dill. He was an alien, one of the Musth who'd been defeated in the brutal war half an E-year gone. He was fur-covered, his banded coat light to dark brown in color, with black tips on his feet and tail. His neck was long, head pointed, round ears cocked. Strangely, he wore a weapons harness in the blue/white colors of the Confederation.

The woman's expression hardened. "You wish?"

"*Cent* Ben Dill," the big man said, holding out a requisition slip. "To pick up the navigational material requested by the Force. YAG Nine-three-X is the number on the requisition slip."

"I'm not sure I know where it is," the clerk said. "Besides, my superior's out for the day. Perhaps you'd come back later, after I have time to look. By tomorrow certainly."

"By tomorrow I'm one long gone goose," Dill said. "And it'd be the one right over there. In the security case."

The clerk sniffed, put the case on the table, then slid the form back to Dill, trying to land it on the floor. Both the Musth and Dill reached. Dill's hand was on the form, the Musth's double-thumbed paw atop his.

"Still faster'n you, Alikhan," Dill said cheerfully. He dug a pen from his flight suit, signed, picked up the case.

"Half a nice half-life," he said, and the two went out.

The clerk watched them walk toward a lifter, took a small box from her purse, lifted her com, touched sensors. There was a click on the other end.

"Mar Eleven," she said. "Scrambling." She touched a sensor on the box.

The answering voice was synthed, neutral.

"Scramble acknowledged. Report."

In the lifter, Alikhan looked back at the office. "That one does not like me." The son of the late Musth War Leader Wlencing, he had been captured near the beginning of the war, and been instrumental in bringing peace.

Since the Confederation Strike Force, called the Legion by its members, had begun using the superb Musth fighter craft, Alikhan had been offered a pilot's commission. He, and a scattering of other Musth combat veterans, not sure of what they wanted but knowing they didn't want the drabness of peace, became Confederation mercenaries.

"Probably not," Ben Dill said. "Lot of people don't like uniforms."

"That was not it."

"Hokay," Dill said. "Go ahead and take it personally. She doesn't like Musth. Maybe you guys ate her lover or something."

"We would not eat a member of another species, especially one that probably tastes as rank as you."

"Couldn't prove your secret tastes by me," Dill said. "Just 'cause we hiked half a planet together once upon a time doesn't mean you weren't repressing your anthropopopawhatevergagous tendencies. Look at that rotten meat you get loaded on."

"Will your people always hate us?"

"Probably," Dill said as he took the lifter off, heading toward the bay and across to the Force's base on Chance Island. "At least until you fuzzy bastards are as good-looking as I am. Or until they've got something newer to hate."

"Humans are strange."

"And of course you Musth are paragons of frigging logic and sense, who never get pissed at nobody for no particular reason or other."

Alikhan showed fangs, and hissed from the back of his throat. That was the Musth sign of amusement.

Chance Island, home of the Legion's central base, sat in the middle of Dharma Island's huge bay. Camp Mahan had been completely destroyed in the Musth War, and gravlifters were still scooping up rubble and taking it out to sea. They regularly found a Forcewoman or -man's entombed body, killed during the fighting, and work stopped for a burial ceremony.

The Force, slowly rebuilding to its ten-thousand-strong authorized strength, was now scattered across D-Cumbre, with only Headquarters and Fourth Regiment at Camp Mahan, living and working in temporary prefabs.

They had been assigned to the Cumbre system some nine years earlier, as a stopgap against any intentions the equally expansionistic Musth might have on the Confederation Empire. Out there on the fringes of the Empire, the Force was also intended to keep the peace among the class-ridden Cumbrians themselves.

As usual, nothing ever happens as predicted, and four years after the Force—then grandiosely called Swift Lance—deployed to Cumbre, the Confederation disintegrated.

No one on Cumbre quite knew what had happened,

since they'd had more than enough troubles of their own, first with the uprising by the 'Raum, the "underclass" of Cumbre, and then with the Musth.

That war was over, but there would be new troubles, most likely "Protector" Alena Redruth, the tyrant who controlled the systems of Larix and Kura, blocking the normal navigational tracks between Cumbre and the Empire. He'd already offered his "protection" to Cumbre, with only the Musth attack keeping him from taking over that system as well.

War with Larix/Kura was inevitable. The Force's new commander, *Caud* Grig Angara, had cleverly conned Planetary Government into passing a special tax, while everyone was still feeling warm and loving about the military. Part of the special tax was for shipbuilding, to give the Force an interplanetary/interstellar capability.

The problem was, no Cumbrian shipyard had much experience designing or building warships, especially on an assembly-line basis, and construction was proceeding slowly. The Legion had therefore been forced to contract with their former enemy for starships.

Parked in the ruins of the Force's huge landing field was one of the Musth destroyer-class *velv,* all weapons station bulges and strange finning. It had been delivered by a Musth shipyard that month, after being modified to human standards. Other Musth ships were coming in-system as fast as the alien yards could work.

The *velv*'s hybrid modification was made even more strange by the two *aksai,* the Musth open-crescent-shaped fighting ships, mag-coupled to the top of the *velv*'s hull.

Workers scurried around the *velv,* in a final loading frenzy. Dill landed the lifter and took the case with the nav-data for the presumed-enemy systems of Larix and Kura to the ship, Alikhan bouncing beside him like a curious puppy.

*   *   *

Ab Yohns decided he'd never get used to reporting to a machine.

"Our agent also reports the Confederation officer said he would be departing this system within the next two days. Have no data on mission intent or other details. Clear."

The transmission was compressed to a blurt, spat into space to a transceiver on K-Cumbre, the system's last planet in a regular orbit, then sent into hyperspace, bouncing three more times before reaching its destination on Larix.

The transmitter beeped that the signal had been received, and Yohns shut it down. He went up the cellar stairs, came out in the rear of a tiny closet, closed the trapdoor behind him, and pushed past hanging coats into one bedroom of his villa.

He added an unknown amount to his credits waiting on Larix, wondered how many millions awaited the day when the hounds got too close or his nerve cracked and he called for extraction. He decided to reward himself with one drink, mixed it strong, and strolled out onto the veranda overlooking the tiny mountain village of Tungi.

Yohns was heavily tanned, looked younger than his forty-plus years, and played the role of an independently wealthy, mildly reclusive offworlder, living on his investments. He certainly didn't match anyone's idea of what a contract spy looked like.

Far distant across the bay was Chance Island. Yohns decided he'd put a motion detector and a camera in place to record the Legion ship's liftoff, and if the time differed significantly from his original report, he'd file a backup, even though it'd most likely arrive in the Larix system at the same time as the ship.

He, like his master Alena Redruth, had been expecting a move by the Force.

"I don't want any flipping heroics," *Haut* Jon Hedley, the gangling Force executive officer, said quietly.

"I rather resent that," Ann Heiser said. She and Danfin Froude, one a physicist, the other a mathematician, were two of the three civilians in the floodlit bustle around the *velv*. They were the recently added Scientific Analysis Section that Froude had convinced the Force CO he needed.

"I've never thought of myself as Horatia at the Bridge," Heiser added.

"I wasn't talking to you as much as to your esteemed colleague, who's been known to be a little flipping suicidal in his investigations," Hedley said. "But you can listen, too. I never trust civilians not to do something dumb like getting killed."

"I have a quite sensible regard for my own skin," Danfin Froude said.

Hedley snorted in disbelief.

Caud Angara, CO of the Legion, a smallish, intense man in his early fifties, smiled. "Don't mind him. He's just angry I won't let him go."

Hedley, about to say something, broke off as *Mil* Garvin Jaansma, Legion Intelligence Section commander and *Cent* Njangu Yoshitaro, head of the Force's Intelligence and Reconnaissance Company, approached, saluted.

Garvin was blond, muscled, stalwart, in his midtwenties, and looked like a recruiting poster.

Njangu was slender, dark, two years younger than Jaansma. His name, in Earth's ancient ki-Swahili, meant "bad," "dangerous." No one argued that Njangu was well named.

"Everything's aboard except the people," Jaansma said.

"No problems?" Hedley asked.

"Just one," Jaansma said.

Njangu looked a bit surprised.

"We're taking another civilian along besides these two," Jaansma said.

"Like who?" Yoshitaro puzzled.

"Like you."

"Oh for . . . stop trying to be funny."

"Not being funny," Jaansma said. "According to records, your enlistment's expired. Four years you've been a-soldiering, and now it's time to pay you off and let you go out and try to find a job worthy of your talents. Shoveling shit, I should rather imagine."

Yoshitaro gaped, recovered.

"Boss," he said to Hedley, "tell him we don't have time for this crap."

"Not at all," Angara said, hiding a grin. "It's the attention to details that makes a good soldier better. Guess we'll have to devolunteer you, eh?"

Njangu stood in silence. Hedley looked closely.

"What's the matter?"

Yoshitaro didn't answer for an instant. He was realizing that he was now legally a civilian, that he could tell them to shove this job and all the rest, like he'd been threatening for about 3.99 E-years, since being forced into uniform by a vengeful criminal court. So he could be a civilian. And then?

"Ah hell," he said. "Do you want me to stick up a paw and swear again?"

"Not if you really don't want to," Garvin said. "I guess we'd miss you and all."

Hedley checked a watch finger. "We're still short of the tick," he announced. "So we've got a few more minutes to screw around, being cute and building flipping morale."

"Consider me sworn," Njangu said to Garvin, his nominal superior. "Sir. Now go say good-bye to your honey."

"With your permission, sir?"

"Go, already," Hedley said.

Garvin went to the side of the bustle, where the only other civilian waited. She was Jasith Mellusin, head of Mellusin Mining, a billionaire, and someone who'd let the Force use her resources whenever necessary.

Jasith was a few years younger than Garvin, model-slender, and still wore her dark hair long. She and Garvin had been lovers for a time, then, after her father's death, she ended her relationship with him, for a reason neither of them quite understood, and married another member of the rich set, the Rentiers. That brief marriage had exploded during the Musth War, and she'd returned to Garvin, neither of them quite sure where their relationship was going.

"Well," Garvin said awkwardly.

"I suppose," Jasith said, "I should be grateful you just keep going out doing dangerous things, instead of having a drug habit or screwing around on me."

"This isn't dangerous," Garvin said. "We're just going out, all quiet, and have a look at things."

"You're a crappy liar. Now kiss me, so I can get out of here and not have anybody see me acting like a twiddle in a romance."

Garvin obeyed, and they held each other tightly.

"You be sure and come back now?"

Garvin nodded, didn't say anything.

Jasith kissed him again, broke away from the embrace, and hurried to her exotic speedster. She got in, and seconds later lifted off. Garvin watched her nav lights flit across the water toward her mansion on Leggett Island.

Yoshitaro, some meters away, watched. Beside him was First *Tweg* Monique Lir, senior noncommissioned officer of I&R.

"See what happens," he said, "when you go and get entangled? Gets harder to say good-bye every time."

Two months earlier, Yoshitaro and his politician lover, Jo Poynton, had split for the second and seemingly final time, as she'd resigned her position with PlanGov to go to another island and try sculpting. Lir didn't respond to that.

"I'm still pissed, boss," Lir said. "Hedley's let both of you go. What'll happen to I&R if you don't come back?"

"I guess you'd have to take that commission everybody keeps shoving at you and become an officer, wouldn't you?"

Monique Lir growled like the somewhat humorless carnivore she was.

"Come on, Njangu," Garvin said. "We're the only ones still a-dragging." He saluted Angara, and they, and the two scientists, went up the ramp, into the *velv*.

There were four pilots aboard the *velv:* Ben Dill, recently certified as trained on the Musth ship; Alikhan; another Musth, Tvem, to fly one *aksai;* Jacqueline Boursier for the other. Another ten Legionnaires, including another Musth, almost all technicians, crewed the *velv*.

"A strong team," Angara said.

"Strong enough to flipping come back and have what we need, I hope," Hedley muttered.

Minutes later, the *velv* whined to life, lifted from the tarmac, and, without ceremony or clearance, climbed for space.

CHAPTER
2

N-Space

"I think," Dr. Danfin Froude said, "I might have a theory on why the Confederation has forgotten us."

"You're assuming the whole damned thing hasn't just fallen apart, which is reassuring for somebody like me who's on the Imperial Payroll," Yoshitaro said.

He, Alikhan, Froude, and Heiser were in what passed for the *velv*'s wardroom. Dill and Jaansma had the watch.

"Is that truth," Alikhan asked, "or are you being metaphoric? I ask, because, if I have become one who fights for pay, should I be concerned with my own wages?"

"He's being cute," Ann Heiser said.

"Then," Alikhan continued, "why is it our duty to concern ourselves with the fate of the Confederation?"

"Wouldn't you give a damn," Njangu asked, "if all of a sudden your loveletters home weren't getting answered?"

"You mean, if all of the worlds of the Musth appeared to have vanished?" Alikhan was silent for a moment. "At first, I think not terribly, since obviously you are talking about the government, not the people themselves.

"As you know, we Musth pride ourselves on our independence, our solitary thinking. But we are deceiving ourselves, at least to a degree.

"So of course, if I heard nothing from my own worlds, I would want to know what happened."

Froude was about to say something, when Alikhan held up a paw.

"Bear with me for a moment," he said. "For my thinking is not complete.

"There would be more than just curiosity. To think I, or any of my race, would deny that we care about the many generations that have put us where we are, made us what we are . . . that would be the thinking of a savage."

Froude nodded somberly. "We know that we still have some order, some civilization. Therefore, it devolves upon us to accept the responsibility of investigating the disaster and, if possible, rectifying the situation.

"Though thinking that we're the only ones in the galaxy who care sounds rather egocentric, or possibly I'm using the wrong word, and I should be saying we're veering close to solipsism."

"Words," Yoshitaro said. "Let's go back to your grand theory, Doctor. That'll pass the time until the next jump, and make me forget about my stomach bounding around."

"The problem is not only ships from Cumbre bound for Confederation ports not returning, but no ships from Centrum or other Confederation worlds arriving at all, as well as a blackout on all subspace communications, correct?

"Consider this," Froude continued. "There are a certain number of navigational points that are convenient to reach the Cumbre System. Most of those pass close to or within the twin systems of Larix and Kura.

"It's certainly well established that Protector Redruth would like to add Cumbre to the two systems he controls."

"I think you're belaboring the obvious," Heiser said.

"Whuppin' up on a dead horse is how we'd put it," Yoshitaro said.

"Let us consider our problems," Froude went on, unruffled. "First, coms from the homeworlds. Easy to black out, since the transmission points *all* pass through Larix/Kura. I looked that up, by the way. One problem solved. Ships bound for the Confederation are seized by Larix/Kura. That's already known. We have tapes."

"Which leaves only one other question, which is the one that screws the goat," Heiser said.

"Very vulgar, Doctor," Froude said. "But that's easy enough. Suppose the Confederation is having its own set of problems."

"That's obvious, too," Yoshitaro said. "Garvin and I saw that when we were raw recruits, just passing through Centrum."

"Suppose our dear friend Redruth has informed the Confederation, oh what a pity," Froude said, "the Cumbre System appears to have fallen into chaos and anarchy. Would the Confederation bother sending anyone out to check?"

"Maybe once, maybe twice," Yoshitaro said. "Maybe not at all."

"And those ships Redruth could easily destroy," Alikhan said, "since the Confederation would still think of him as an ally."

"Just so," Froude said. "Now doesn't that conveniently account for our isolation?"

"Which means," Njangu said, "we've got to tromp all over Redruth before we can find out about the Confederation. Which we knew a long time ago."

"Still," Froude said, "it's nice to have a few good theories on our side."

"That may be," the Musth said. "However, in my mind, it raises a rather terrible thought, at least for you humans. Assuming that your Confederation is as large and powerful as we Musth believed it to be, does not that mean the Confederation's woes must be rather greater than anyone can easily imagine?

"Does not that also mean if we manage to deal with Redruth, and then proceed into the Confederation, we well may be biting off a great deal more than is swallowable, since problems an empire cannot solve most likely would be impossible for a mere solar system?"

The three humans sourly considered each other.

"I think," Froude said, "Alikhan's logic is un-assailable."

"Thank the Bouncing Baby Buddha," Yoshitaro said, "a low-ranking ossifer like I am's only gotta worry about one disaster at a time."

The intercom beeped.

"Stand by for Second Jump."

"All right," Garvin said, having been replaced on the bridge by Alikhan, "why aren't you getting out? You couldn't be that goddamned absentminded as to forget your termination date."

"I sure was," Njangu said. "Not that I especially liked you reminding me of it back there."

"Sorry," Garvin said. "I was trying for a little joke."

"Little laugh. Ha."

"No, I mean I really am sorry."

"Forget about it," Njangu said.

"All right. So you went and swallowed the shilling again, or however the phrase goes, whatever the hell a shilling is," Garvin said. "I thought you were the balls-out hater of the little blue machine that used to be part of the big blue machine."

"Yeh, well, it still looks like the only way to go, at least for right now," Njangu said, uncomfortably. "I don't see anything having changed since the last time we talked about sleazing quietly offstage.

"Which brings up something. *Your* bustout date's what, two E-months after mine? What're you going to do?"

Garvin looked at his friend. "Now I see why you got assed at me back there. Damned uncomfortable question, isn't it?"

"Why?" Njangu asked. "You've got a bootiful lady, gazillions of credits just sitting around waiting to be spent. Hell, if you lust after danger, you could always go a-mining and get your head squashed down one of her shafts . . . sorry, don't take that the way it seemed to come out . . . or go exploring for minerals on one of the ice giants."

"It's still an uncomfortable question."

"Which means you're going to reenlist?"

"Probably."

"Why?"

"You expect logic from a goddamned soldier?"

Again the intercom sounded: "Stand by for Third Jump."

"Here's the sitrep," Ben Dill said briskly. A system projection swung lazily in the air between him, the other pilots, Jaansma, Yoshitaro, and the two scientists. "We've got four possible exit points into the Larix System. Here, which is the logical point for landing on the fifth planet, Larix Prime, here, which is the alternate, here, which is way the billy-blue-blazes out in nowhere, or here, sneakily hidden just quote above endquote Five.

"I'd suggest we use that one, then sort of leisurely slither down, maybe take a polar synchronous orbit waaaay out, and put our snoopers back to work."

"That's what we theorized back on Cumbre," Jaansma said. "We've had nothing that'd suggest we were wrong, have we?" He looked around. " 'Kay. Make the final jump."

"Emerging from hyperspace," the synthed voice announced.

"All *right,* and here we are," Dill announced. "Mrs.

Dill's favorite son's provided a nice view of Larix down there and SON OF A BITCH!"

He slapped sensors, and hyperspace blurred around them again. Garvin had time enough to see a single blip on a screen, a subscreen showing a familiar ship in detail, the bigger screen suddenly show two blips, and the subscreen show a missile launch.

"Now we get cute," Dill said. "Alikhan, gimme two random jumps."

Garvin keyed the throat mike. The crew was already at action stations.

"All stations, stand by. A Larix patrol ship was waiting for us when we came out of N-Space."

"I've got a tentative ID on the sucker," Yoshitaro said, from a weapons station. "I think it was one of those flashy-ass Nana-boats Redruth stole when he highjacked us."

"Class confirmed," a technician reported. "Nana-class it is."

An alarm shrilled.

"And the bastard was fast enough to put a tracer on us and make the jump, too," Dill said. "Ho-kay. Hang on to your belly buttons." He turned to Alikhan. "Gimme a point on . . . better, behind, one of Larix frigging Five's moons. We'll duck and consider.

"Coming out . . . YOW!"

"I have a launch," a technician said, tonelessly, as she'd been trained. "On target. Impact one-zero. Counterlaunch ready . . . ready . . . fired. Three-missile spread . . . missile closing . . . closing . . . hit! Missile destroyed."

"Jump!" Dill said, and the *velv* shuddered, went in, out of hyperspace, and Larix was on screen again, partially obscured by a moon. "Awright. *Aksai* pilots, man your stations."

The com crackled. "Already there," Boursier said quietly. "Bolted down and ready to launch."

Another, heavily accented voice came. "Tvem in placcce. Ssstanding by, ready to fight."

"And here those frigging weasels come again," Dill said. "Two of 'em, this time. *Aksai* pilots, launch."

He ran fingers across controls. Magnetic grapples released the *aksai,* and they darted away from the *velv,* toward the two Larix patrol ships.

One Nana patrol ship launched a missile, which had its guidance system scrambled by a tech aboard the *velv.*

"Nice," Yoshitaro said, "to be fighting somebody using the same frequencies you've got."

Dill jinked the *velv* again, then again as the two *aksai* slammed in against the patrol craft. One launched from head-on, the other from center high. The Nana launched a single countermissile that went wide, both Cumbrian missiles slammed into the ship, and there was nothing but incandescent gas.

The other ship went for hyperspace, just as a second launch exploded just to the Nana's rear.

"I do not know if I ssstruck that ssship," Tvem said.

"If you didn't," Boursier said, "you shit-sure worried it some."

"Alikhan," Dill ordered, "set up for a jump, back the way we came. One jump, then a blind jump, then back on track."

"I obey."

"I have two other ships on-screen," a tech said.

"Launch stations," Dill said. "Stand by."

"Standing by, sir."

"*Aksai,* get your little heinies back aboard."

"But boss—"

"That's a frigging order," Dill snarled. "I don't want those waggly-ass Goddards to make a mistake and blow you into smithereens. Move, move, move, or I'll leave you for the vultures!"

Obediently the two *aksai* swung close to the *velv,* and dull thuds sounded as the couplers reconnected.

"Weapons, do you have those buggers in your sights?"

"Affirm . . ."

"Locked in, Ben."

"Launch one . . . launch two . . ."

The Goddards were six-meter-long shipkillers normally carried by the Force's Zhukovs, although they were originally built for deep-space war. Launch tubes had been added by Force machinists after the *velv* was purchased, and the missiles' Target-Acquisition systems modified for longer range.

"Homing . . . homing . . . homing . . . miss!"

"Stand by to jump," Dill said.

"Hang on a second," the second Goddard technician said. "I'm almost—"

"Jump!" Dill ordered, and Larix, moons, missiles, and patrol ships vanished.

"Aw, Ben," the tech complained. "I coulda got me a little gold star on my control panel."

"Countdown to Second Jump, seventy-four seconds."

"You take it," Dill told Alikhan, swinging away from the control panel to Garvin's station. "That was about a big fat bust."

"To put it politely," Garvin agreed.

"You know what I think?"

"You know what I frigging *know?*" Garvin said. "Those bastard were laying for us."

"Sixty-three seconds to jump."

"Njangu," Garvin said. "Somebody's leaking like a sieve. Somebody on D Cumbre."

"No shiteedah, boss," Yoshitaro said. "Let's get on back home, so I can start pulling people's toenails out and find out who."

CHAPTER
3

Cumbre

One jump short of the Cumbre system, Yoshitaro sent a coded message EYES ONLY to Jon Hedley, requesting all com units scan for transmissions from out-system. He hoped he'd get lucky.

An inbound signal was picked up. The recipient retransmitted it on another frequency, but there the trail ran cold. The Force cryptoanalysts weren't able to break the code.

At least they'd located the first reception point, on a moon of J-Cumbre's.

"I am not one for Electronic Intelligence," Yoshitaro complained. "Hard to backstab a computer, which doesn't sound like much fun, anyway."

"We've got more than enough who are," Hedley soothed. "Your trade's murder from a ditch, which is a rarer specialty."

"Thanks, I think. Then I'd like to borrow a couple-three techies, and me and a few I&R crunchies're on our way back out to J-Cumbre."

"Plus one," Hedley said. "You'll need Rumbles."

"Rumbles? What kind of frigging name is that?"

"No worse than Njangu Yoshitaro."

"You racist bastard. Sir."

Rumbles poked one eye over the rocks, scanned the area. Nothing moved. He moved forward, found cover behind a hillock of frozen oxygen.

"There it is, sir," Rumbles's operator said. "See, on the infrared scan, we get a little blip. Probably from its solar charger, or maybe battery." The operator was named Tanya Felder, held the rank of *Finf,* and looked more like a ballet dancer than a robot wonk.

She, like the other soldiers, was suited against the moon's unbreathable and mildly corrosive atmosphere. Felder's head and upper body were hidden by Rumbles's operating center, something that looked entirely too much like the front half of a coffin, but kept Felder from being confused between real and artificial input. Inside the box were screens, sensors, and controls, all linked to the robot, a few hundred meters away.

Rumbles was a new addition to the Force. He was half a meter high and wide, and about a meter long. He had variable binocular lenses front and rear, sensors in every range his builders could think of, ran silently on padded tracks. Extendable claws capable of lifting or pulling over two hundred kilos were folded, crablike, across his bow. "He" had a range of about three kilometers, and was armed with a stubby blaster below his forward eyes. The robot could be fitted with a host of accessories, depending on its mission.

"You want us to take it from here, boss?" Monique Lir asked. She and the other five I&R soldiers were sprawled on line near Felder, weapons ready.

"Uh-uh," Yoshitaro said. "I love you all too much to find out if that mother's booby-trapped. Stand by. Tanya, you want to run Rumbles in a little closer? We're still in the exploratory stages of the operation."

"Yes, sir." Felder still wasn't used to the I&R practice of calling superiors by their first names or simply "boss."

Rumbles moved out of cover, followed the low ridgeline.

"Here," Felder said. "I've got a better view now, straight visual. Patching to you, sir. The transmitter's about twenty-five meters from Rumbles."

The small screen below Njangu's faceplate swirled, showed a nondescript section of the frozen world, clicked to a higher power, then again. Njangu saw a gray semicylinder almost hidden in a rock outcropping.

"No sign of any attendants," Felder said.

Yoshitaro considered. "Can you tell which end of that transmitter's the front?"

"No, sir."

"All right. Hung for sheepsies, hung for lambsies, and all that. Go in, slow. Record everything."

"Already am. Sir."

"Sorry."

The cylinder grew larger on Yoshitaro's screen.

"Any transmission from the station? I'm assuming it's completely automatic."

"Nothing, sir."

"Stop at about three meters, while we figure out how we're going to grab it."

"Four meters away, and ready to—"

Yoshitaro's screen went blank, and Felder's legs jerked. A ball of red fire flashed ahead of the team, and the shock wave came, then, a few seconds later, the rock under them shook.

"Tricky bastards, aren't they?" Yoshitaro said. "Felder, did it get your robot?"

"Y . . . yes. I'm getting no vital signs."

"All right, troops." Yoshitaro got to his feet. "I don't think there's anything worth looking at, but let's wander forward and take a gander. Don't get close to anything. Booby traps can go bang more than once."

Felder slid out of the control compartment. Njangu gave her a hand up, unplugged the commo line into her leg.

"Sorry about Rumbles."

Felder snuffled. A bit surprised, Yoshitaro glanced in her faceplate, saw tear streaks on the woman's face. He didn't say anything as they headed for the destroyed transmitter.

*   *   *

"So we know a transmission came in from Larix . . . nobody else in the Universe cares enough about us to send even a birthday card," Jaansma told Angara. "That box on J-Cumbre picked it up, bounced it somewhere else.

"There wasn't anything to salvage when the bastard blew but a handful of fragments. I've got those out for analysis, and I'll bet all we get is that the transmitter was made from materials not common in the Cumbre system."

"What next?" Angara asked.

"Things are going to be flipping sticky from here," Hedley said.

Garvin and Njangu nodded glumly. "I'm assuming what we're looking for is one head agent, and a bunch of little guys, who may be double-flagged and not know who they're really working for," Garvin said. "I'll also bet that transmission we intercepted was telling that agent about the oops there off Larix, and that, well, they sort of missed the intruders, but thanks for the tip anyway and keep us posted."

"If I were the spy, who I think needs a name, call him Snoopy," Njangu said, "I'd get my young ass into a nice safe hole and pull it up around me until the smoke blew away. Jon's got intercept operators riding that frequency the initial signal came in-system on, with zed results so far, and I'll bet more big fat zeroes to come."

"Ideas?" Angara asked.

"One," Garvin said. "And it's not a good one. The problem is, we've got no goddamned clue as to how we're leaking, or where. We were sloppy the last time we went to Larix, and there were too many people in the know."

"*Very* flipping sloppy," Hedley agreed. "We should have nailed Snoopy a long time ago. Let's make a probably valid assumption that we're talking about one Snoopy, not a dozen or so. My flipping justification for that is I believe we can be dumb-ass enough to miss one superspy, but I flipping refuse to countenance the idea there's more underfoot.

"So let's consider that he goes at least back to those guns that Larix/Kura shipped in back during the 'Raum rising. We didn't get him then, were mostly lucky we were able to grab the bangsticks.

"Next, how much you want to bet Snoopy was somehow involved with that flipping explosion that took out Aesc, and started the Musth War?"

"No takers," Angara said. "Especially since not one single freedom fighter bigot has claimed credit for killing that Musth. Two big operations, one perfect, one stopped by accident, and we've got to assume he's been feeding Redruth everything we do for a long time. We've got to nail him before we can do a full-scale move against Larix/Kura.

"You said you had a rotten idea, Jaansma."

"We set up another sortie, this one for Kura. But this one should look real only till the ship lifts off. We watch in every direction while we're putting it together, hoping to snag our boy.

"The problem is, of course, is that it'll put everybody around Kura on full alert for a while, which'll queer any attempt to really do a sneak against them for the near future. Plus, if we don't get Snoopy, what's the follow-up? I'm blank."

"This is the third time I've heard you boot that idea around since last night," Njangu said. "I don't like it any better than you, or than I did the first time. But maybe there's a way to make it nastier, so our friend doesn't catch on.

"The only problem is it'll screw somebody's life up for a good while, and there'll always be those who don't get the correction later. We nail an innocent, loudly shout we've got Snoopy, and hope the real agent relaxes enough to get careless."

Hedley thought, then pulled at his nose.

"That's definitely shitty, Njangu. I think we ought

to try it. But let's not just screw up one guy's flipping life. Let's go for half a dozen."

From *Matin*:

Force Breaks Spy Ring
Scandal Rocks Legion Ranks

By Ron Prest'n

Leggett City—Six ranking officers of the Confederation Force were arrested early this AM by the military's internal counterintelligence section, and charged with espionage and high treason. The six, whose ranks range from *Haut* to *Alt,* are accused of being members of a deep-cover spy ring, working for an unnamed extrastellar government.

Matin, however, with its usual skill, learned from confidential sources that the government is almost certainly that of Larix and Kura, once considered one of Cumbre's closest allies, but now regarded as having imperialist designs on our system.

Mil Jon Headley, head of the Force's Intelligence Section, told Loy Kouro, *Matin*'s publisher, that this ring has been operating for some time. "We estimate these agents have been working against us since at least the Troubles with the 'Raum, and further are likely involved with the assassination of Musth Leader Aesc, which began the recent misunderstanding with that culture.

"We've suspected the existence of such a network for some time," Headley continued, "but continued our investigation until we were sure we had discovered all agents. We then made our arrests, and have all suspects in custody at a remote location, where full debriefing will be made."

Confessions are expected, and the trial will be public, and is expected to be held within the next three months, as soon as the military judicial system finishes preparing its case . . .

"Son of a bitch couldn't even spell my name right," Hedley complained.

"It could be worse, boss," Garvin said. "He could've asked for pictures of those poor bastards we've got hiding out in the boonies until the heat goes down."

"Why couldn't we have just arrested Kouro?" Njangu said. "He makes a pretty good enemy agent, from where I sit."

Loy Kouro was Jasith Mellusin's ex-husband, an abuser, and a longtime enemy of Garvin's. He also had been one of the most eager collaborators during the recent Musth War, and had been jailed after the Musth defeat by the Force. Criminal charges hadn't stuck, but there were several megacredit civil suits pending.

"That's what I like about you," Garvin said. "Every now and then, you *do* stick up for your friends."

"Have to. You owe me too much money."

"Awright, you two," Hedley broke in. "Phase I is under way. Now, let's . . . oh shit. Forgot to tell you. Both of you are due at sixteen hundred hours on the parade ground. Full dress."

"What for?"

"Reenlistment ceremony. You're going to provide an awesome example for the new blood."

Garvin and Njangu stared at each other in horror.

"No way out?"

"Not a chance," Hedley said firmly. "This is the old man's idea."

"Aw, shit! Can we at least get drunk afterward?" Njangu moaned.

"You have my permission to go drinking this evening, and the Legion'll pick up the tab," Hedley said. "Just be able to function by dawn, or thereabouts."

"You see," Garvin said. "The Force never takes

away with one hand but what it gives with the other. I'll go call Jasith for transport."

"I thought you boys were very pretty out there, marching around and saluting everything from flags to lapdogs," Jasith Mellusin said as she zigged around a shuttle lifting off, ignoring the horn blast, and dropped her lim neatly into the valet parking area of the Shelburne Hotel. "Still are, in fact."

Garvin started to preen a bit, then saw Jasith's tongue sticking well into her cheek.

"So why didn't you let us change?" Njangu complained. "You think I *like* going out in this costume? Makes a man too noticeable when he might want to slide out in an unobtrusive manner."

"But you're with me," Jasith said. "Which means you're not only going to be pretty, but well behaved, too." She slid out of the lim's pilot compartment as she spoke, hand automatically extending a bill to the attendant with the casual arrogance only the very rich knew.

"Good *and* pretty, both? How goddamned dull," Njangu said. "I coulda called a shuttle and had a lot less hassle."

"But not the company of somebody as lovely as I am," Jasith said. "Besides, one of my friends may be here and lonely."

"Jasith Mellusin," Garvin said. "Pimp to proper patriots."

She kicked him accurately in the shins, then yelped. "That's why sojers wear boots," Garvin said smugly. "Heavy boots."

"C'mon, you two," Njangu said. "Alcohol calls."

The Shelburne was D-Cumbre's most exclusive hotel, the social center for politicians and Rentiers. Oddly enough, the management also welcomed the Legion's Intelligence and Reconnaissance section. Or, if welcome wasn't precise, no one from I&R had been barred so far, as long as her or his credits clinked.

The main entrance was a sweeping semicircular drive, with low steps leading into the main reception area, with walls of tiny antique glass panes.

As Garvin, Jasith, and Njangu went up the steps, the door slid open, and Loy Kouro came out, walking with the precision of the very drunk. Flanking him were two very large men. All three wore evening dress.

The following happened very quickly:

Kouro noticed Jasith and Garvin, and his face reddened.

Jasith and Garvin pretended Kouro didn't exist.

As the two parties passed close, Kouro leaned over and said something in an undertone to Jasith.

Her eyes widened, her face went white, and her hand came up to backhand Kouro.

Kouro pushed her away, and she went to one knee.

Garvin had Kouro's arm, spun with it, twisting. The bone snapped loudly, and Kouro howled, clutched it.

One of the large men hit a stance, launched a knife-hand strike at Jaansma. Garvin wasn't there, turning away toward the second man.

The second man lifted his hands into guard as Garvin stepped inside them, headbutted the man in the face, hit him hard in the gut with both hands, was away as the man went down, vomiting over himself.

The first man snapkicked toward Garvin, was well wide of his mark, and Yoshitaro had the man's foot in both hands and lifted high, brought his own foot up, and kicked the first squarely in the crotch.

The first man howled, stumbled back into Kouro, who was intent on his broken arm, who screeched at the impact, stumbled back, bounced off the glass-paned wall.

Kouro saw Yoshitaro, face in a grimace, a meter in the air above him, legs curled. Njangu lashed out in a flying-mare kick and smashed Kouro through the glass wall, landed on his hands, and rolled to his feet.

Glass tinkled, and hotel employees scurried.

"Son of a bitch," Garvin said. "What'd he say to you, anyway?"

"It doesn't matter," Jasith said.

"Nope," Njangu agreed. "I suppose it doesn't. Not now." He surveyed the damage. "Guess press-military relations have just hit a new low, hmm? Who the hell, by the way, were those two bruisers?"

"Damfino," Garvin said. "Rent-a-goons, maybe. Or sports journohs." He kicked a bit of glass. "Good thing the Legion's picking up our tab. I'll bet this one'll be expensive."

"It surely relieved my tensions and anxieties better than a simple old drunk," Njangu said dreamily. "Pity the son of a bitch appears to be still breathing."

"Brawling in public," *Caud* Angara growled. "In dress uniform, to boot. Savagely attacking, without any reason, and hospitalizing the publisher of the biggest holo on Cumbre. Plus two of his aides."

"Yessir," Jaansma said. He and Yoshitaro were at rigid attention in front of the *Caud*'s desk.

"Any explanation?"

"Nossir," Yoshitaro said.

Angara considered them, picking up a piece of paper from his desk.

"Mister Kouro has declined to press charges against you. His com said he preferred to let military justice deal with you two miscreants, since he considers it to be far more severe." Angara grunted. "I am not fond of civilians expecting us to do their jobs for them."

He sighed. "Knowing Mister Kouro and his, shall we say, personality quirks, and certain . . . personal matters about you, *Mil* Jaansma, I can theorize about the actual course of events."

He tore the paper in half, deposited it in his wastecan.

"I'm taking no official response to this matter, either as far as punishment or reprimands in your file.

You will, however, be held responsible for the repairs to the Shelburne, which seems fair.

"Also, both of you are on my unofficial villain list. I don't want to have any other problems from either of you until I tell you it's authorized to be rowdies. Understand?"

"Yessir," the two chorused.

"I'll also suggest you can get back into my good graces the quicker you catch that damned spy. That's all. Dismissed."

Garvin saluted, and the two, moving like clockwork figures, left-faced and went to the door.

"Jaansma!"

Garvin stopped. "Yes, sir?"

"After the hoo-raw, did you two ever get your reenlistment drink?"

"Nossir. We didn't figure it was a good night for boozing."

Angara nodded, and the two went out. After a moment, he shook his head, grinned, and turned to other matters.

Yoshitaro looked at screens. "Okay, here's my theory on our agent. Since Redruth hasn't spent much time on Cumbre, he must've hired him out-system. I'd guess Snoopy is either a native of Larix/Kura, or maybe a Cumbrian native who spent some time on those planets, long enough to get bought or subverted."

"Sounds logical," Hedley said from where he sprawled on a couch.

"It'd be a lot simpler if everybody on Cumbre had an ID card," Yoshitaro said. "We could just look up anybody who's been around Larix and Kura, haul 'em in, and take out the thumbscrews."

"Hell of a note, hearing you say that," Garvin said. "Considering your background."

Hedley looked curious. Yoshitaro decided this might not be the time to tell the boss about his background as a professional thief, lock-breaker, forger, arsonist, strongarm man, and general layabout.

"Actually," Hedley said, "you'd have a problem even if you could roust everybody in who knows anything about flipping Larix/Kura. Before you two got shipped out here, that was the main shopping vacation for the Rentiers. If we hauled all of those rich pigs in and started asking, you know they'd gossip, which I'll assume would go straight back to Snoopy."

"So everything stays at ground zero until we nail him," Garvin said. "All right, *Cent* Yoshitaro. Let's hook the snake."

"Right," Njangu said. "We've hopefully got Snoopy relaxed with our phony spies all locked up. Now I think it's time to begin our operation against Kura."

Hedley scanned the printout.

"We're sure . . . as sure as we can be . . . this includes everybody who had any knowledge of our penetration attempt against Larix?"

"We were sloppy, boss," Njangu said wearily. "But not *that* sloppy. We did try to keep a need to know on things."

"And you trust the Force enough to be assuming the leak to Snoopy was from a civilian source?"

"Not me," Yoshitaro said. "I mistrust everygoddamnedbody. But Garvin said we can't spread ourselves too thin."

" 'Kay," Hedley said. "Now, get your ass out there and talk to all participants again, and make sure they didn't just happen to forget anybody."

"Slave driver." But Yoshitaro said it with grudging respect.

"Hey, Njangu," Ben Dill said. "I got a small confession to make."

"Don't tell me the baddie we're looking for is you?" Since Dill had been party to the blown mission into

Larix, nobody had bothered to run the cover story about the phony Kura operation past him.

"Yeh," Dill said, and bared his fangs. "Went and bribed me for two honeys and a roast *felmet* under glass."

"I should've known that was why your breath smells the way it does. What's the confession?"

Dill told him. When he finished, he spread his hands. "Sorry. But we were in a hurry."

"You *just* remembered that?"

"No." Dill looked shamefaced. "Alikhan had to remind me."

"Fine," Njangu snapped. "Now be sure and remind me if you happen to remember anything else, like you've got an aged aunt who's head of Redruth's security."

"You mean I didn't mention her already?"

"*Cent* Ben Dill to pick up some charts," Dill said. "Requisition YAG One-Nine-Eight." The Musth beside him didn't speak, but his head darted back and forth.

The clerk took off her glasses, scowled at the alien, then lifted a security case from under the counter, set it down, a little too heavily.

"Thank'ee," Dill said, scrawled a signature, and the pair left.

The clerk looked around the airfield office. Her supervisor and another clerk were still working.

"Could you take the desk for me, ma'am, for a couple of minutes?"

The supervisor nodded, taking her folder to the desk. The clerk picked up her belt pouch, and headed for the bathrooms.

"Bingo," the tech said. "The scan picked it up right away. We've got 'Eleven' and 'Scrambling.' The rest of the transmission's coded."

"Enough?" her *tweg* asked Yoshitaro.

"More than," he said, turned to the four military policemen in the back of the Grierson, parked a few meters from the spaceport's administrative building. "Take her. Don't let her use an L-pill, and make sure you grab all of her possessions. Get in and out, fast. She's got no rights. No talking to anybody, no lawyer, no nothing."

"We've got an agent," Hedley said. "I've got our analysts looking for others. But so far, this Pon Wrathers is all we've got."

"Bear down," Angara said. "The clock is running."

The room was very big and felt like it was far underground. An air conditioner was running somewhere, just loud enough to be annoying. Pon Wrathers stood in a pool of light. There was a desk in front of her. Sitting behind it was a man, hidden in the shadows. There was a small box on the table.

"I wish a lawyer."

Silence.

"Who are you?"

"My name is Njangu Yoshitaro."

"What are you? Some sort of policeman?"

Again, silence.

"Why am I being held?"

"Who do you suppose you're spying for?" Njangu asked.

"I'm not a spy!"

"Then why did you make a coded transmission just after giving some officers of the Force classified navigational data?"

"I made no transmission! That scrambler was planted on me by one of those thugs who arrested me."

"You're either naturally quick, or well trained," Njangu said. "Did you realize you were working for an agent of an extrastellar government?"

Wrathers jerked just slightly. "I did no such thing! I want a lawyer!"

"Let me apprise you of something, Wrathers. You don't know who I work for, what agency of the government. Perhaps I'm not working for *any* government. The Rentiers used to run their own police and death squads, remember?"

Wrathers blinked.

"If that were the case, your asking for a lawyer is a joke," Njangu went on. "You ought to be more concerned about what could happen to you, here, alone, in a strange place, when no one on the outside knows anything about where you are."

"Who are you? What are you doing to me?"

Njangu waited silently for a moment. It was interesting being on the far end of techniques he'd experienced as a youth on Waughtal's Planet.

"I'm doing nothing," he said calmly. "Not yet. All I want is my questions answered. Why were you transmitting data in code?"

"I already told you, I wasn't making any transmission!"

"Who is Eleven?"

"I know nothing about any Mar Eleven." Wrathers realized she'd slipped, but Yoshitaro seemed to take no notice.

"You weren't scrambling?"

"For the thirty-third time, I wasn't scrambling anything! Look, I'm a citizen of Cumbre, and you, whoever you are, army or what or secret police, you can't just grab me like you did, and then take me somewhere without even making charges against me or anything and leave me in a dark cell for hours, and ask the dumbest questions over and over!"

A red light on the box lit.

"We've got enough."

"Good," Njangu said. "Keep it running, just in case. And send in somebody to take her out."

Yoshitaro stood.

"What are you going to do to me now? You'd better not torture me or anything, or else I'll sue you, when I'm free." Wrathers realized she was getting hysterical, couldn't seem to stop herself.

"What now?" Yoshitaro said. "We're going to keep you around for, oh, a day or so if things go well. Then you'll be released, with no charges being filed. You can go back to doing things the way you did, although I sort of suspect your job with the Air Traffic Department might be eliminated shortly. Even bureaucrats don't like spies."

"You just grabbed me, and took me here . . . and . . . what did you want? I didn't answer your questions!"

"You didn't have to," Njangu said.

"Take it, Mister Yoshitaro," *Caud* Angara said. "You did the footwork, you deserve the glory."

Njangu took a very deep breath. This was the largest operation he'd ever been in charge of, and it didn't help that there was only one chance of success.

The night air around Chance Island swarmed with Griersons, civilian-appearing lims, lifters, all carrying armed and ready soldiers, all on a single frequency. In space, satellites were listening, as was every passive sensor the Force had access to.

A technician punched numbers into a com. It buzzed twice, then a click came. A second technician fingered a sensor.

Pon Wrathers's voice, recorded in the interrogation room, then synthesized, said:

"Mar Eleven. Scrambling."

The first tech hit another sensor. Garbled words, still recognizable as Wrathers's voice, came through speakers, then stopped.

Other techs at a control bank worked hurriedly. One grinned, lifted his thumb.

Two moments of silence, then: "Did not translate. Resubmit."

Again the transmission roared. There was no error in coding—the 'cast was nothing more than garble.

Njangu, not knowing what setting Wrathers's scrambler should be set on, had been afraid to get trickier.

The receiver went suddenly dead.

"Got him," a tech said. "The transmission went to somewhere around Lanbay Island, then got bounced back to the main island. The response was from right . . . here."

His finger touched a large-scale map. "Tungi. And I've got a precise DR." His mike was open to all Force units. He touched a screen, and a large-scale photo projection of the village came up. "Right here. On this mansion."

Njangu keyed his own com.

"Garvin, you've got that. Take him out. I'll take care of the backup around Tungi."

A mike double-clicked, and blacked-out Griersons dived toward the mountain village.

Ab Yohns stared at his transceiver. Hair on the back of his neck and wrists prickled. He hesitated, then leaned over, and twisted a key in a slot. He went to the stairs, to a large switch sealed in a plastic box. Yohns snapped the cover off, hit the switch, then went up the stairs hastily. Behind him, the smell of burning insulation and charring circuitry grew.

Yohns went out of the villa. Toward the ocean, high in the sky, he could make out black dots diving on Tungi. Then he heard their drives, getting louder.

Yohns grinned, thought, *A little late, fellows,* and ran into the jungle, to where his small lifter was hidden.

"I have a transmission from Tungi," the technician reported.

"Track it!" Njangu ordered.

The first Grierson landed half a dozen meters from the sprawling villa above the village. Other I&R craft slammed down nearby, blocking all exits from Tungi. Garvin and a squad of troops doubled out of the rear ramp of the Grierson and leapfrogged toward the villa, blasters ready. No fire came to meet them.

"Sir," a soldier said. "I smell smoke. Something's burning!"

Garvin sniffed. "Sure is." He keyed his com. "Get the fire brigade in here. The quarry's self-destructing!"

Njangu buckled himself into the high-speed lifter, once a civilian lim, listening to the 'cast on a belt transceiver. Beside it, he had two holstered pistols.

"Sibyl Base, you got a location on that cast from Tungi?" he asked. Waiting, he turned to the pilot.

"Running Bear, get us in the air. Like yesterday."

The lim's drive whined, and it jumped forward, airborne even as the com crackled a response to Njangu's question.

"Sybil Base," Garvin said. "This is Janus Six. The whole goddamned house is going up, and there's no firemen here yet. We're losing everything, over."

"This is Sibyl Base. Fire response still one-zero away. Do what you can, over."

Another transmission overrode it.

"Janus Six, this is Sibyl Six Actual. Screw the house and get back in the air." Njangu gave coordinates. "And haul ass. The game's afoot."

Ab Yohns took his lifter into the clearing, pushed his way into brush, and grounded. It was about two hours after dawn. He got out, took a small sender from his pocket, pressed it again.

Dirt shifted, and a square section of the clearing lifted, slid aside. Inside was a thirty-meter yacht, drive already warming, nav position set for one of the asteroids off G-Cumbre, all accomplished by his first transmission after fleeing Tungi.

From the asteroid he'd signal for pickup, then wait for Redruth to come get him.

Yohns took a moment to admire his cleverness.

Years ago, he'd had work crews dig a wine cellar in his villa, the crew imported from Leggett City. He'd done the finishing work and installed the electronics himself.

Similarly, he'd had another crew of workmen, these picked up from the city's casual labor pools, excavate the foundations and storage for a hunting camp here on the shore of Mullion Island east of Chance Island.

The prickling that'd sent him into flight was gone. In half an hour, he'd be beyond Confederation reach, and on his way to being a very rich man in Alena Redruth's empire.

Behind him, Njangu Yoshitaro lifted out of cover, aiming a long-barreled pistol. He pulled the trigger, and the dart spat across the clearing, taking Yohns in the neck. Yohns had a second to slap a hand to what might've been an insect bite, then dropped bonelessly. Njangu holstered the dart gun, drew his blaster.

"Let's roll him up, Running Bear."

The big AmerInd stood, stretched. "Damned glad I'm not one of your I&R folks. I think a snail ate my balls off while we were waiting."

They went across the clearing to the slumped Yohns.

"We'll strip him down, check everything, including his mouth to make sure he's not loaded with a lethal pill," Njangu said. He took plas cuffs from a pouch. "Then we'll wrap him like he was for the roasting.

"Which he is."

CHAPTER
4

The two guards escorted Ab Yohns into the room, went out, and closed the door. The compartment was comfortably fitted, and might have been a living room, except there were no windows or coms.

Sitting, very relaxed, were Njangu Yoshitaro and Jon Hedley.

"Sit down," Hedley said. "There are drinks over there. Nothing with alcohol in it."

"I'll decline."

"If you want," Njangu said, "I'll have a drink out of any of them. They're not drugged."

Yohns smiled, sat down.

"I assume the effects of the knockout shot have worn off," Hedley said. "The doctor assured us you've had normal functions for some hours now."

"I'm fully functional," Yohns said. "This is most civilized."

"Why not?" Hedley said. "We're professionals, and assume you are, too. My name's Hancock, and this is Dexter, by the way. He's the one who came up with the scheme that trapped you."

"Ah?" Yohns inclined his head. "Well done."

Njangu nodded.

Hedley stood. "I wanted to introduce myself, reassure you that you're in the hands of the Confederation, and will be dealt with according to all legal considerations, or as many as circumstances permit."

"Thank you, *Mil* Hedley," Yohns said. "I recognized you from the holos."

"Alas, how flipping fame spreads," Hedley murmured. "Dexter, you may take it from here." He smiled, and left.

"I don't believe I recognize you, however," Yohns said.

"As the boss said, the name's Dexter."

"Very well . . . Dexter."

"In Tungi, you were known as Ab Yohns," Njangu said. "Your real name?"

"Frankly, I'm not sure I remember what my real name is. People in my profession frequently find cause to use aliases. Let's leave it at Yohns, since I've been comfortable with that label for quite a number of years.

"What is in store for me, if I might ask?"

"Like the boss said, you'll be taken care of, if you give us what we want. Which I assume you already figured out."

"Which is?"

"Everything you've got about Larix, Kura, Protector Alena Redruth and his forces."

"I'm afraid you're in for a surprise."

"How so?"

"Have *you* ever seen Redruth in person?"

"I even had a chance to shoot at him once," Njangu said. "Missed."

"You're far ahead of me. I doubt if you'll believe me, but I've never met the man."

"No belief is a nice, comfortable way to put it," Njangu said.

"But no more than the truth. I was hired, through a third- or fourth-hand party a long time ago, back on Centrum, by the Protector. I gave him good service, was well paid for it. When the situation loomed toward intolerable, I decided to depart the Confederation and spend some quiet time on the frontiers until things settled out.

"I looked in the area of my employer's worlds. I wasn't sure I wanted to live on either Larix or Kura, because, as I'm sure you know, kings fear their spymasters. I thought it might be well to be a little distant from his attentions.

"Redruth himself suggested I emigrate to Cumbre, where I could continue to provide services, since he has a strong desire to add this system to his holdings.

"Perhaps I will chance a glass of water."

Njangu poured a glass, sipped, then gave it to Yohns.

"I came to Cumbre with no more than an earth-hour's layover on Larix. I could perhaps give you my memories of the spaceport, but not much more. As for his worlds, what I know is from holos and gazetteers. You certainly know more about his military than I do.

"I'd planned eventually to flee to Larix. That's where the monies he's paid are deposited, so I'll hardly be desperate for work. He would have found a place for me if for no other reason than to keep me from mischief."

"There are drugs to check what you're telling me," Njangu said, still skeptical.

The corner of Yohns mouth twitched.

"There are, indeed," he said, a bit of a rasp in his voice. "But they'll do no more than confirm what I just said. I'm afraid I'm a bit of an empty vessel.

"But that isn't to say I want to be thrown into a dungeon with the rats, and have whatever tortures, psychic or real, wreaked on me. I despise pain.

"As your commander said, I *am* a professional. I'm more than content to be tucked in whatever comfortable prison you have on some distant island, and give as much help as I can while you pursue your venture against Redruth. That should ensure my continued survival, in a measure of comfort."

His voice suddenly sounded a bit unsure. "Do you think such an arrangement might be possible?"

Njangu, carefully blank-faced, stood.

"I'll discuss this with my superiors. I'm afraid we

can't leave you in this room, by the way. It's not as secure as others. Someone will escort you back to your previous compartment in a few minutes. Tomorrow we'll continue our discussion, and perhaps in the meantime you'll think if you don't remember a bit more than you said about Larix and Kura."

Yohns was on his feet, holding out a hand.

"I'm sure we'll work well together."

Yoshitaro didn't want to take his hand, but did.

He went out to where the guards waited. "Take him back to the clank. Oh yeah. Put him on a suicide watch, round the clock."

"Yes, sir, *Cent.*"

Njangu rolled to his feet, the pistol always under his pillow in hand as a fist thundered at the thin door.

"Yeh?"

"*Cent* Yoshitaro!" It was the Bachelor Officer Quarters' Charge of Quarters. "It's an emergency!"

Njangu had the door unlocked and open in a second.

"Sir," the CQ said, "II Section says you're to go to what they said was the prisoner's quarters at once."

"That's a hard way to go," *Mil* Hedley said, looking down at the bloody corpse. "Damned if I think I'd have the flipping guts to chew through my own tongue and then just quietly bleed to death."

"I don't understand why he killed himself," Njangu said.

"Who knows?" Hedley said. "Spies aren't the most stable people. Maybe he didn't believe us when we said we weren't gonna toss him in an iron maiden just for laughs.

"More likely, he started thinking about how an oh-so-clever agent got his flipping ass trapped by a bunch of infantrymen with dirt under their fingernails, and his ego told him it couldn't handle things."

"I had a suicide watch mounted," Njangu said, holding back his anger. "He asks for some fresh water, and both guards go out of the cell. I know two troopies who're going to be mounting suicide watch on each other on the smallest frigging reef on this frigging planet." Promise made, he forgot about the two for the moment, looked back down at Yohns.

"All this goddamned work," he hissed. "To end up with—"

"With nothing," Hedley said. "Except he won't be hanging over our shoulder, watching, anymore. But he could've been so much, much flipping more," he said.

Yoshitaro remembered the extent of Yohns's claimed knowledge.

"Maybe. Or maybe not." An idea came. "Or maybe we can still get some miles out of his sorry ass."

"Like how?"

Njangu turned a profile to Hedley. "Don't I make an utterly lovely Ab Yohns?"

CHAPTER
5

Asteroid Glyph-Hander

The yacht belonging to the late Ab Yohns matched orbits with the dumbbell-shaped asteroid, then landed. A *velv* held position about three kilometers away from the asteroid.

"Finished with engines and all that nautical rot," Ben Dill said.

Njangu Yoshitaro got up from the copilot's chair. "Damn. I was sure you were gonna stack it up on that rock on final."

"You see your problem?" Ben asked. "You're in the hands of the finest pilot humanity has produced since, oh, mebbe Orville and Wilbur Lilienthal, and do you show proper respect? Hah! I say again, hah!

"Your biggest problem, Yoshitaro, is that you've never learned to fly, so you have no method of judging a natural birdman like myself." Dill caught himself. "Yoish, but I'm a dolt."

"No kid."

"No, I mean I went and volunteered to fly you out here for your rendezvous with destiny, and it never occurred: You're playing Ab Yohns. Who was a spy. And a pilot, or else he wouldn't of had this here yacht."

"Don't remind me of the holes in my cover."

"What's gonna happen if somebody asks you to spin a few fast orbits around Larix?"

"I'm going to develop the worse case of vertigo

you've ever seen." Yoshitaro went to the passenger compartment, opened the hatch. "All right, gentlepeople. You can sweep in here now." Four sterile-suited technicians went to work on the pilot's compartment as they'd done the rest of the ship. Every surface had been cleaned twice of all fingerprints. After that, prints from three or four hands, most blurred, were strategically placed. Then Yoshitaro's prints went everywhere. Now Dill's fingerprints were scrubbed from the controls, and Njangu, on command, touched and pressed things here and there.

Dill made his farewells, clambered into a suit, and jetted up from the yacht's skin toward the waiting ship. The technicians made sure there were no stray hairs, spittle, or waste in the yacht's cycling system, then followed him out.

Yoshitaro was alone, half a system from anything.

"The stage is set," he muttered. "The musicians have tuned up. The spotlight's on the goddamned podium."

He crossed into the fresher, looked at his semi-new face not for the first nor the fifteenth time since the doctors had finished. His hair now had a gray streak at the temple, and his skin had been weathered, aged. Yohns had supposedly been in his late forties. Yoshitaro thought he could pass for mid-thirties, maybe a bit older, and hoped Redruth didn't have Yohns's birth certificate handy. He also hoped that the medicos could, as promised, reverse their craft when he came home.

"The maestro comes into the spotlight. Taps his baton. There's silence in the hall."

Yoshitaro punched a sensor, and Yohns's bleat for help spat toward Larix.

"The maestro lifts his baton, and goes ass over teakettle into the orchestra pit as the first kazoo begins playing.

"Shit, I need a drink. I hope I like what Yohns drank. And, come to think, Njangu ol' buddy, you better start worrying about talking to yourself when you've only been by yourself for an hour."

Dill hadn't needed to point out the problems with Yoshitaro playing Yohns. First was the assumption that just because Yohns had never met Redruth, there wasn't a handy photo somewhere in Larix's files that'd doom Njangu. Second, Yoshitaro knew almost nothing about the spy, so any bio data Larix had could be equally deadly.

Even if he carried off his deception, he wasn't exactly the best-equipped spy in history. Just for openers, there'd be a problem, if he got in place, in reporting.

The only reason Angara approved the mission was the assumption that Larix/Kura probably had Confederation coms, as did Cumbre. So all, in theory, that was necessary was for Njangu to acquire one and make slight modifications with one of the four carefully hidden chips he carried. In theory.

But brooding wouldn't accomplish much, any more than drinking. Yoshitaro looked for something to fill the hours, found a dozen holos, mostly the basic tracts of various religious sects. He wondered how Yohns had managed to reconcile his profession with these tracts, most of which were somewhat opposed to dishonesty and treason.

Maybe the spy had been curious about how the other half thought. Or maybe he believed in some hereafter, and was trying to get in the good graces of somebody, everybody.

In any event, the holos weren't to Yoshitaro's taste, although he read them carefully, and found a measure of delight in tracking the myriad contradictions.

He worked out hard, remembering every *kata* he'd been taught, developed a few sequences of his own.

Fighting, you idiot? he thought. *Better you think about zen running.*

Njangu didn't suit up and explore the asteroid, for

fear he'd miss an incoming signal from his rescuers, or that he'd manage to lock himself out as well.

Deep down, he wasn't sure if he didn't hope Redruth would abandon him to the "enemy," so he could just go back home and figure out something a deal safer.

Time, more time passed.

Finally, his com beeped. Yoshitaro touched a sensor, responding in the same code he'd asked for extraction on.

"Stand by," the return came, automatically decoded by his com. "You're located. Pickup in twenty-three E-hours."

The com went dead.

Less than a dozen minutes from the ETA, a warship closed on the asteroid. Njangu's *Jane's* identified it as the old *Corfe,* a Confederation destroyer leader that had been Redruth's flagship when he attempted to take over Cumbre. Two Nana-boats gave "high" cover to the *Corfe.* Its missile tubes and close-range chainguns were unmasked, ready.

A hangar port yawned, and a small ship darted out, grounding on the asteroid. Five suited men came out. Two took defensive positions close to the yacht, the other three approached the ship's lock, blasters ready.

The outer door buzzed open, closed, and pumps let air into the airlock.

Yoshitaro touched an intercom sensor. "Come on in."

"Stand clear of the door," a metallic voice answered. "Do not move when we enter."

Yoshitaro spun in his control chair, his hands in plain view as the airlock door opened. One man came in quickly, looked back and forth, said something into his suit mike, and a second entered. The first cleared the yacht's other compartments, came back, and a third man entered the compartment. The first two kept their weapons on Njangu.

The third man opened his faceplate, and Yoshitaro recognized him.

"Ab Yohns, I might assume," the man said. "My name is Celidon. I command Larix and Kura's armed forces."

Celidon was an officer with a reputation for efficient brutality. Cashiered from the Confederation, he'd ended up working for Redruth as a mercenary. He was tall, with a scarred forehead. His expression was coldly amused.

"I'm very damned glad to see you," Njangu said. "I'd clap hands, but I don't want to get shot by your cronies."

"I'll take the welcome as having been expressed," Celidon said. "Get your possessions and come with me. I want to be out of the Cumbre system this E-day."

"I don't have much of anything," Yoshitaro said. "That bag there, no more. I left in a bit of a hurry."

"Suit up then," Celidon ordered. "Suit frequency thirty-six. My man will carry your things." Yoshitaro obeyed, noticing that one of Celidon's men searched the inside of his suit before letting him put it on.

The man escorted Njangu into the lock and cycled them out onto the asteroid. Moments later, the second man came out, then, after a bit, Celidon. He cycled the airlock door shut.

"Are you going to destroy my ship?" Yoshitaro asked.

"No," Celidon said. "The blast might attract attention, and you've set enough wasps buzzing already. But I did leave a little present for anyone who discovers the boat and opens the lock."

Njangu hoped no one decided to recover the yacht anytime soon, at least not anyone he knew.

They transited to the *Corfe,* and Njangu was told to unsuit, then led to a bare room, efficiently searched by a crew member, and left alone.

The *Corfe*'s drive activated, then, sometime later,

the ship made its first N-space jump. Njangu, having nothing else to do, lay down and tried to sleep.

An unknown time later, an armed man and woman took him to a large, spartanly equipped stateroom. Celidon sat behind a desk and motioned Yoshitaro to a seat. On the desk were Yoshitaro's bag and a heavy, rather old-fashioned blaster.

"Is this the only weapon you brought?" Celidon asked.

"No," Yoshitaro said. "May I?"

Celidon nodded.

Njangu slid one hand inside his belt, down behind his scrotum, and took out a small, flat pistol, a projectile weapon firing explosive charges.

"My men didn't find that, obviously."

"Obviously."

"Protector Redruth is very particular about those whom he allows to carry weapons," Celidon said. "But since you'll almost certainly be invited to join our government, there should be no problem. Thank you for your honesty."

Yoshitaro held out his hands. "I haven't forgotten whom I work for."

"Good," Celidon said. "I'll have the louts who failed to find that weapon punished. One thing I might suggest. Don't carry any weapons, not even a knife, into the Protector's presence. He becomes . . . nervous."

"Thank you for the warning."

Celidon went to a sideboard, slid it open.

"A drink?"

"Whatever you're having."

"This is a triple-herbed tea," Celidon said, pouring two glasses from a metal pot. "I find it improves my thinking." He handed one glass to Yoshitaro.

"You've certainly served the Protector . . . and his worlds . . . well, over the years."

"And I've been rewarded," Yoshitaro said.

"Your payment awaits you on Larix, in our most

secure repository," Celidon said. He sipped, looked at Njangu curiously. "You must have taken up your . . . craft at an early age. I wasn't expecting someone as young as you appear."

"Unfortunately, I'm somewhat older than I look," Yoshitaro replied smoothly.

Celidon waited for details, then realized none would be forthcoming.

"I decided to come along on the pickup," he said, "because I thought you and I should have a chance to talk before Protector Redruth greeted you."

Njangu put on an interested expression, stayed silent.

"I'm sure you're aware that autocrats are, with reason, very suspicious of their secret agents, particularly those who're executives."

"Of course."

"You might be interested in knowing that I not only hold the post of Commander of the Armed Forces but, as of six months gone, head of the Protector's intelligence apparat as well. The latter is a position I despise, and hold only through necessity.

"The man who held that assignment before me fancied himself an expert on Machiavellianism. I've noticed those who loudly pride themselves as intriguers generally end up with a puzzled expression and several inches of steel between their own sixth and seventh ribs, but that's as may be.

"This wight decided he would play politics with Protector Redruth against me. Why, I have no idea, for I'm quite busy and content with my regular duties and had no designs on him or his station.

"At any event, he became a bit of a threat, and it became necessary for me to . . . deal with him. So now his duties are included in mine, and he is ashes in the wind.

"I'll explain how that pertains to you. I rather assume protector Redruth will offer you a post within the government, probably with the rank of *Leiter*.

He'll want you to be his special advisor on the Cumbrian matter, and, if you serve well, you'll be promoted.

"It's not inconceivable you could end up as head of all security services, replacing me. At present, I would neither object nor recommend you for that rank.

"But if it happens, I'd suggest you remember what happened to that other man, who thought himself devious, and restrict any ambitions you might have beyond that."

Celidon smiled coldly. "We'll be arriving off Larix in two more jumps. One of my staff will escort you to more comfortable quarters, and you have the freedom of the ship.

"Welcome to Larix and Kura, Ab Yohns."

Yoshitaro got up, bowed, and followed the woman out of the compartment.

Stupid bastard, he thought. *Telling me those who loudly proclaim their sneakiness always get sneaked on, and then doing the same thing himself. As if I hadn't been around enough fools and their cliques back home that I had to deal with when they got big eyes on me or my people.*

But still, I'd best be careful.

CHAPTER
6

Larix/Larix Prime

A lim with military insignia picked up Njangu and Celidon at the port, and, with many salutes, took off. Yoshitaro, noticing it was escorted by two Zhukov-type gunships, asked what the danger was.

"No danger," Celidon said. "The Protector feels any public appearance by a member of the government should be accompanied with a display of force. It not only gives the workers something to admire, but something to think about if they're considering the slightest dissidence."

Agur was a monolithic city, its chunky buildings high-storied, frequently occupying whole blocks. They appeared to be poured in place, the blank concrete generally dyed brown or light blue, without facing or decoration other than the signs for the businesses within, which were gay and colorful.

The lim flew about ten meters above the street, siren wailing. Njangu could see people afoot, or in small vehicles of uniform design. There weren't many lifters in the air.

"The Protector prefers his people use ground transport, or our extremely efficient undergrounds," Celidon said, sounding like a government brochure. "Lifters are generally reserved for official use or, in larger forms, to take the citizens to the coliseums or to the country recreational areas."

The people wore bright clothing, frequently streaked

with conflicting colors that stood out against the drab buildings. Njangu couldn't tell if they looked happy, sad, angry, or even ground-down.

"As a matter of curiosity," Njangu said, "how do you deal with your criminals and dissidents? Conditioning?"

Celidon gave him a wintry smile.

"We hardly need Condit," he said. "And the term we use is social misfits. The Protector sees no need for them to further fatten on the public by lazing about prisons, devising schemes for illegal enrichment when they're released. Instead, they're put to work, hard physical work in areas of risk. Undersea mines, on our moon stations, things such as that. Those who're given lighter sentences, and survive them, generally are no longer a threat to society.

"As for dissidents . . . *real* ones were a generation ago. As for the others . . . you'll see."

Njangu, once a threat to society himself, and certainly now a dissident in Larix's terms, thoughtfully considered Celidon's words.

A few minutes later, Celidon nudged him. "There's the Protector's palace."

The city encircled the grounds, three or four kilometers in diameter. The great building in the center was as grandiose and rococo as any dictator could dream of, all spires, domes, multicolored bubbles, strangely configured towers.

Yoshitaro decided that, one day, given the chance and enough explosives, he wanted to strike a blow for architects everywhere.

"Do you have any idea what brought about your exposure?" Protector Alena Redruth asked. There were only two people in the huge office, or at any rate only two Yoshitaro could see. He assumed Redruth wasn't foolish enough to meet anyone without gun cover and wondered how many gunmen were hidden behind the walls.

Redruth was under normal height, in his early forties, and balding. He appeared unthreatening, except for his eyes, which held a strange, fixed gleam.

"As a matter of fact, sir, I do," Njangu said. "One of my agents, who was under surveillance, contacted me to report the Confederation element was planning another intrusion. I had relay stations in place for these transmissions, but they succeeded in following the signal to my base.

"I just had time to activate self-destruct mechanisms and flee, with no more than the clothes I was wearing."

Redruth leaned forward.

"Where are they coming, Yohns? Did your agent have time to give you that?"

"I had only a flash," Njangu lied. "The charts they'd requested were for the alternate jump point for the Larix system, since they'd failed on their first try. The agent said nothing about when the intrusion would be mounted."

"What is the Force mission?"

"The agent said one of the men said something to his fellow about 'putting in a wrecking crew,' which I'd guess means they'll be putting in some sort of a sabotage force," Yoshitaro said.

Redruth's mouth worked. "We'll be ready," he said firmly. "We'll stop them offworld as we did the last time, and this time destroy their ship or ships."

"Good," Njangu said. "My theory is the failure of your response to destroy the Cumbrians last time led to my exposure."

"That intercept team has already been punished for its slipshod work," Redruth said. "Forget about what happened."

"Yes, sir."

"You've done extraordinarily good work for me over the years," Redruth said. "You were rewarded for your success, not punished for failure. Now, do you wish further . . . rewards?"

His eyes held on Yoshitaro, evaluating.

Njangu didn't feel he had any choice. "Of course, sir. I assume I'll continue to be compensated as in the past."

"You shall. The first reward will be your immediate promotion to the rank of *Leiter.*

"What I wish you to do is help me evaluate Cumbrian designs on Larix and Kura and, within the next E-year, assist with intelligence missions to Cumbre, preparing for the inevitable invasion."

Njangu nodded.

"When I attack, you'll be part of my staff, and, after victory, I'll find a high place for you in Cumbre's puppet government. You'll have more than enough of a chance to replace whatever you lost when you were driven away. In humiliation as well as material goods."

Njangu let an evil smile come and go.

"In addition, you can help me here, now, since you think like a Cumbrian."

Yoshitaro heard alarm bells.

"I need to know my weaknesses. How could Cumbrian spies, assassins, or saboteurs infiltrate Larix? I want you to tour the worlds of Larix, then, later, Kura, and with your fresh eyes, look for weakness. Maintain as low a profile as possible.

"Anything you discover should be reported directly to me. I shall punish the lazy and unwary, reward the wary and strong."

"Yes, sir," Njangu said. "What about Celidon? He told me he was head of intelligence. I certainly don't want there to be any misunderstandings."

"If there are," Redruth said firmly, "I shall deal with the problem. Celidon will be informed of what he needs to know by me. I am still the master of Larix and Kura."

He stood. Yoshitaro, realizing the audience was over, stood and made an awkward attempt at a salute, like a civilian would attempt.

"In the future," Redruth said, "there'll be great rewards, even greater when, as is inevitable, I expand my empire, first to include Cumbre, then back into what used to be the Confederation. There are millions of worlds trapped in the chains of anarchy, and it's the duty of Larix and Kura to free them.

"Great, great rewards.

"But for those who fail, or think they can serve their own masters, even greater penalties!"

Redruth's majordomo escorted Yoshitaro to a different exit, where another of the military lims waited.

"The driver knows where to take you," he said, and saluted.

Yoshitaro got in the lifter, found Celidon waiting.

"Was your meeting with the Protector . . . interesting, *Leiter?*"

"It was."

"Remembering what I told you aboard ship, is there anything you wish to share with me, say, about what your tasks will be?"

Yoshitaro grinned. "How many rooms in the Protector's palace do you monitor?"

Celidon looked mildly astonished, then laughed hard.

"Good, Yohns. Very good indeed. You are very adept at your analyses. I think that our relationship, assuming neither of us relaxes nor becomes arrogant, might be mutually profitable."

Njangu's city quarters were the three top floors in one of the half-block-long megaliths. He tried counting rooms, got three different figures depending on which elevator he used, and gave up.

He had, already in place, a staff of twenty-four. He asked if this'd been especially prepared for him, was told by his head-of-household, a calm man with shifty eyes named Kerman, the apartments had been previously occupied by . . . "but I must not use his name, sir. He was a member of a Cumbrian spy network our wonderful Protector sniffed out."

Cumbrian spy network?

Of course Kerman, and Yoshitaro assumed everyone else in the household, was reporting to Celidon
and then Redruth. No matter. He didn't talk in his
sleep, nor did he carry anything that'd give his mission
away, except those four com chips he still had hidden.

He was in the middle of investigating the kitchens
and bar areas when Kerman came to him again.

"*Leiter* Yohns, some possible candidates for your
private quarters have arrived, and wish to know if
you'd be interested in interviewing them."

"Private quarters?"

"Yes, sir."

"How're these people different from you, or the
maids, cooks, bakers, and laundry people I've already got?"

"If you'd care to accompany me, sir?"

There were half a dozen women, two blondes, two
brunettes, two redheads. All were most attractive,
seemed intelligent, and very interested in him. Yoshitaro took Kerman aside.

"I think I've got it. These women are applying for
the job of my bed partner?"

"But of course, sir. We use the term companion.
There are also men who serve similar functions, if
you wish."

Yoshitaro said he wasn't interested in boys this week,
then called one woman out of the room, a sultry-eyed
brunette named Brythe.

"You want to become my . . . companion?"

"But of course."

"Why?"

Brythe blinked. "Because that's what I've been
trained for."

"What pressure, sorry, what encouragement did
they put on you to become what you are?"

"Pressure, sir? I worked very hard in my training
to be selected as a potential companion for someone
of high rank, as did the other women in there." She

smiled. "I must say, sir, that I think I've got particular talents they might not have."

"If I choose you, what happens?"

"Whatever you wish, whenever you wish."

"No, I meant, what benefits do *you* get?"

"Well, I'd be permitted to live here, if you wished, which is much nicer than my own place, which is only a couple of rooms. Or I can merely come when you wish whatever services you want from me. Of course I get an increase in my living and clothing allowances. I'll be able to shop in special stores, which are only open for high-ranking members of the government and their immediate staffs, and when I go to the stadiums sit in special sections. My parents also would be raised in status."

"Um." Yoshitaro had an idea. "Brythe, what would happen if I chose more than one of you?"

"Why, you'd be no more than a normal man. And, to be frank," and she licked her lips, "some of the . . . pressure, to use your word, might be taken off me."

Yoshitaro covered his reaction. Redruth's regime programmed the citizens in more than one way.

"Very well. Come with me."

He went back into the room, pointed to two blondes, a redhead.

"You three, and you, Brythe, can stay, if you choose. As for the rest of you, thanks for letting me meet you."

The other two didn't seem disappointed, but twittered about how gracious and noble the *Leiter* was, and perhaps they'd meet at another time, and were gone.

"Is there anyone else that's going to get added to my retinue?" Yoshitaro asked Kerman.

"Only your personal bodyguards, sir."

"Good. I'll let you choose them. Get me big hulks. Male. Quiet ones. They ought to have military experience, and it wouldn't hurt for them to be missing an ear or maybe be scalped."

"Sir?" Kerman sounded shocked.

"I want any social misfit who's thinking of harming me to know I'm well guarded," Yoshitaro said. "Guys with scars are a good advertisement."

"Yes, sir. I understand, sir."

Yoshitaro yawned obviously. "Now, I think I'd like to . . . evaluate . . . my chambers. I assume the four women I chose will have their own bedrooms?"

"They will, sir, although not until I relocate two of the maids. The *Leiters* I've served normally only require one, sometimes two, companions."

"Show them to their quarters, then ask Brythe and . . . what's the redhead's name?"

"Pyder, sir."

"Ask them if they wish to come visiting."

"As you wish, sir."

If he played the part of a sex-besotted fool, Yoshitaro might be taken less seriously by Celidon and Redruth. Njangu hoped he was a clever devil, and not rationalizing being a drooling lech.

The next morning, feeling strangely refreshed, he met his bodyguards, who were just as big, silent, and nasty as he'd ordered, and hopefully as dumb as he wanted. He asked about their training, found out they were both rough-and-tumble experts, no more. Or so they claimed.

One said they'd be more than willing to help Njangu add to his security element. Yoshitaro said he thought he'd already taken care of that.

"Most *Leiters*," the man said, "think it's important to have other men and women . . . generally picked from the military . . . who can take care of the small things we won't have time for. Also, in uniform, they make a better display to the populace."

"What are the little things?" Njangu asked.

"Checking engine drives for bombs, clearing the way for your entrance at social events, generally ensuring that people you encounter are aware of your importance."

"I'll wait to make sure I get the right personnel," Njangu lied, thinking it was going to be hard enough being a spy on this unknown world without carrying a full entourage around. He'd do with what he had.

With his personal requirements taken care of, it was time to get to work, both for himself and for Redruth.

"Your job is?" Njangu asked.

"Door guard, sir."

"Sorry for the dumb question, but the businesses in this block don't seem to need guarding. None of them are government that I can see."

"Nossir, they're not. But I'm to watch for social misfits, keep track of how many people go in and out, report anything suspicious."

"You like your job?"

The thickset man looked around, was reassured by Yoshitaro's smile.

"It's all right, sir."

"You seem to have a little bit of an accent."

"Yessir, I mean, I guess so, sir. I'm from Kura. If you don't mind me being bold, sir, my accent's no worse'n yours."

Yoshitaro's bodyguards frowned, then blanked their faces, seeing Njangu's grin. "Kura, hmm. I haven't been there yet, but I hear it's mostly country. Farms and jungles."

"Yessir."

"Must've been a change, coming to a planet that's got as many cities as Larix does."

"Yessir, it was."

"Ever want to go back?"

The man looked horrified. "To *Kura?* Gods no, sir. Begging your pardon."

"Why? Is life that hard there?"

"Nossir. It's not at all like Larix. Small villages, and not many cities. Big families so everybody knows everybody else, and tries to help if there's any problems. But . . ."

"Go on, man," Yoshitaro said.

"For one thing, Kura's haunted."

"Come on! By what?"

"Sorry, sir," the man said. "Didn't mean to say that, even if it's what . . . what everybody believes. I know it's not really true, the Womblies are long gone, and prob'ly they never were."

Yoshitaro wanted to ask what the hell a Wombly was, but decided it might be better to find out privately.

"The reason I don't want to go back, sir," the man went on, "is Larix is where everything is, and if you can make it here, especially here in Agur, you know you're the best, sir."

"You're a block warden?"

"Yes, sir," the woman said, clearly impressed by being talked to by such a high-ranking *Leiter*. "Been one for six, seven years."

"What happened to the person you replaced?"

"Dunno, sir. Heard he didn't pay close enough attention to what people said."

"But you do."

"Sure do, sir. I don't mean to boast, sir, but I think it's people like me who keep Protector Redruth, bless his name, safe, especially from the Cumbrian infiltrators."

"There's no question about that," Njangu said.

"So these reports come in from the block wardens to you, then?" Njangu asked.

"Yessir," the thin man said. He pointed around his spotless cubicle. "Notice, there's no paperwork left undone here. I read the reports, and report on up to the next level within the day, generally within a few hours.

"Then, if my supervisor tells me somebody needs

talking to or . . . or worse, I go out with the watch and help them pick him up, if that's what's been ordered. I make sure everybody else in the block knows what happens, too, and give the block warden who first reported the misfit to me a reward."

"All these district reports are collated," the brisk man, "then an abstract is made, which goes directly to . . ." He broke off.

"You can use the word," Njangu said.

"To the Protector's intelligence service, and they make estimates from them."

"Suppose there's been twice as many complaints of, I guess you'd call it social misbehavior. Sorry, but I'm still learning your terminology. What happens then?" Njangu asked.

"Then the entire district is punished, by cutting supplemental rations or even refusing permission for them to spend their summer leaves at recreational areas.

"Sometimes we even reduce their sports-viewing or -attendance privileges. This is a particularly important district, as I'm sure you're aware, with our shipyards working at full speed, so we keep a very close watch on trends."

" 'Kay," Yoshitaro said. "Now, suppose a district has less than normal complaints?"

"Possibly minor benefits are increased," the bureaucrat said. "Or, more likely, a congratulatory message from Protector Redruth will be 'cast on their vids. We keep several varieties on record."

Son of a bitch, Yoshitaro thought. *These bastards all seem to like narking each other off, and playing pissant tyrant, level by level. It's like a disease, and every goddamned one of them's running a frigging fever.*

"Several of the people I've interviewed mentioned Cumbrian infiltrators," Njangu asked Celidon. They were in Celidon's apartments, as spare as his ship-board compartment.

Celidon smiled. "What about them?"

"To the best of my knowledge, the Cumbrians didn't start infiltrating Larix until recently," Yoshitaro said. "Where did these spies I never heard of come from?"

"Protector Redruth has an uncanny ability to define and sniff out moles from another system," Celidon said. "He's been discovering Cumbrian spy rings for about two or three years now.

"Before that, we were woefully troubled with anarchists from Confederate worlds spreading their poison. Fortunately, the Protector discovered and wiped them all out."

"I think I see," Yoshitaro said.

"Traitors tend to appear when Protector Redruth is developing an interest in a certain area, so it's only natural that the prospective enemy does inimical things, thus proving the Protector's concerns to be justified."

"And obviously," Njangu said, "you're quite certain the Protector doesn't have these rooms wired."

"I assume nothing," Celidon said. "Being a dedicated servant of the Protector's, I have nothing to fear."

"Oh dear," the blonde whispered. "Not again?"

"You want me to stop, Enide?"

"Oh no. I'm just . . . worn-out keeping up with you. I'm not even twenty and you're, what, almost thirty?"

"A bit older, m'love."

"You don't *ever* seem to get tired."

"It's my clean living, and sanctity."

Enide giggled. "My foot seems to have worked loose. Would you tie it up again?"

Yoshitaro hoped Enide was just being stupid, and not trying pillow talk to get Yoshitaro to slip on his cover story. He'd rather deal with a dumb agent than dumb control. The last thing he wanted was getting his fingernails pulled out from some misunderstanding.

"Should I use the belt again?"

"Yes, please."

"Of course I like sports," Njangu lied to one of his bodyguards, whom he'd dubbed Goon Alpha. "What sort do you play here on Larix?"

"Well," the big man said, "now it's fall, an' so we play Challenge. That's like old-timey army games, with blunted spears, and bows and arrows, and fencing and things like that."

"Which I like," Goon Beta said. "I did real well in the barefist division, back when I was a gosling."

"You want to fight, join the army," the first bodyguard said. "That ain't my sport. It's bigger on Kura, where all those bastards do is chase each other around the hills with clubs. Anyway, after Challenge'll come Rattes."

That was a team game played inside stadiums, with long netted hurlers and a ball with a variable center of gravity.

"Not bad," Goon Beta said. "Considering it's winter. But in spring, we get harnhuns. I like that."

"It's pretty good," the first guard allowed. "Get a man running, bunch of people go after him. They catch him . . . it's all up for his ass."

Harnhuns set district against district, town against town, until a final champion survived.

"Best of all's mobbal, when summer comes," Alpha said, and Beta nodded vigorously. "I was pretty good at that, almost good enough to be a pro. Whole planet stops for the finals."

It took several hours to explain the rules to Njangu, or its lack of them. It was played with a ball, outdoors. At a district or suburb level, it'd be played in a local park, with goals at each end. The number of people on a side could be set by agreement, or played by as many as wanted. The object was to move a ball past a goal, using any means possible short, Njangu learned, of knives or nuclear devices.

At a more organized level, professional teams from cities, then provinces, then worlds, played. There were frequent riots when favorites lost, or umpires made "bad" rulings, riots that sometimes required the army.

Njangu made another mental note: *If people aren't allowed any political say, and the boot's kept firmly against their neck, let them work it out with sports. Make the sports violent, and make the games a good testing ground for potential soldiers.*

He was starting to admire Redruth's cleverness. Redruth or, more likely, his predecessor question mark predecessors.

Njangu tried finding out more about the history of the system. There was almost nothing, other than that the original colonists of the two systems had been fleeing something or someone when they arrived, some hundreds of years ago. How they'd built up Larix so quickly wasn't recorded. And the four or five . . . the records weren't certain . . . men or women who'd preceded Redruth weren't given much in the way of space, either.

One file in the *Planetary Encyclopedia* did give him something:

Womblies: Term given to the original inhabitants of the Kura system, who were instinctively inimical to humans, and opposed our necessary colonization of their disused lands. Little is known about them, since they were wiped out by the cleverness and leadership of the First Protector, and physical descriptions vary so widely there is no point in cluttering a scholarly work with them. Many legendary traits are ascribed to them: invisibility, the ability to sense man's presence and even his intent, and retaliate in horrifyingly unpleasant ways. Folklorists aver there are tales on Kura that the Womblies were not completely destroyed, but linger on in remote areas they held sa-

cred, and attack lone travelers when they can. Such
nonsense should not be allowed to be repeated, and
a conscientious citizen hearing such tales should report
the teller to the authorities.

"Well, humpty, humpty, humpty, and aren't you the
little tattler," he muttered, and probed a little further
into other areas, without a great deal of success.

The next day, Njangu got a call from Celidon's adju-
tant, who said Celidon "suggested he find other areas
of inquiry that'd be more profitable."

So history was decidedly off-limits, even to a *Leiter*.

The ululation of sirens woke Njangu from a happy
dream of visiting one of his bank vaults. He was fully
alert, but had trained himself years ago to appear to
wake blearily, slowly. Karig, the fourth of his companions, was already on her feet, pulling on a robe.

"Come on! We've got to go down to the shelter!"

"F'what?"

"Maybe it's a drill, but maybe the Cumbrians are
attacking! Come on! The block warden takes roll on
things like this."

Njangu slid into a pair of pants, shirt, bathroom
slippers.

Attacking Cumbrians, huh? Let's hope.

Indeed, an officious man was bustling about the
building's basement, checking off names. Yoshitaro sat
in a corner, surrounded by companions, staff, and
bodyguards. Everyone was beginning to relax when,
dimly, came the distant roar of missiles launching, and
then an explosion.

Pyder whimpered. "They're really here."

Another explosion came, then silence for three
hours. Finally the all-clear siren shrilled, and they
were allowed out of the shelter.

Njangu, not sleepy at all, went up to his roof garden
and saw searchlights still sweeping the night. He wondered what the hell had actually happened, and hoped

it was part of the Force's plan. He thought of waking up one or another of his companions, but decided he had paperwork that was more important.

An hour later, Kerman came to his office. "Sir. The Protector requires your attendance at once."

Not good.

Yoshitaro dressed, thought wistfully of taking a weapon, remembered Celidon's warning, and was at the palace within the hour.

Redruth and Celidon were waiting. Celidon wore his usual expression of cold amusement, Redruth's lips were pursed tightly.

"I am not pleased with you, Yohns," he began, without preamble.

"I'm sorry, sir," Njangu said. "Might I ask?"

"You told me a penetration raid was going to be mounted by Cumbre."

"That was what set off the alarms?"

"It was," Redruth said. "However, you said only a single attack would be made."

"There were at least two ships," Celidon said. "One came from N-space in the location you'd told us to watch, but another used the same nav point as their earlier attempt. We're grateful that the Protector, in his wisdom, had all standard nav points within the system monitored."

Njangu kept his face blank. Their sensors were better than the Force had thought, and they were more paranoid as well.

"What happened?" he asked. "I heard missiles being launched."

"Pah," Celidon said. "Pure panic. The capital's defense *Leiter* panicked, shot at shadows, and has been disciplined for his stupidity. What actually happened was the first attacker, the *only* one you'd warned us of, was quickly destroyed, far out in space."

As we hoped would happen, when we set this up back on Cumbre, Njangu thought. He also noted the emphasized "only."

"The second ship evaded us for a time," Redruth broke in, "and made for Prime, much as the last Cumbrian ship had. I don't know whether that first ship was a decoy, and the sabotage team you warned us about was aboard the second ship or not, but that's my assumption.

"We attacked, lost contact, regained it just before the ship went back into hyperspace. We were unable to put a tracer on the ship, but assume it returned to Cumbre."

Njangu relaxed a little.

"This is the second occasion the Cumbrians have bothered me," Redruth said. "They can rest assured that this time there'll be a response they shall not like at all. I do not need to consult your expertise on the system to know *that*.

"The reason I summoned you is to make you aware I allow no error from my servants. You warned us of one attack, not the second. A job partially completed is the same as one not begun.

"Remember that, Yohns, in the future. I'm not pleased with you at the moment. So take this as a lesson, learn to concentrate on the job at hand instead of your own private pastimes, and don't make the mistake again."

Njangu bowed, turned, and left.

He was trebly pleased. *If anything goes awry, no matter whose fault it is, or if it's no one's, there clearly must be someone to blame, and it's never the Protector. Good. That keeps underlings from wanting to report not only failure, but problems as well.*

And all the time, he thought piously, *spent with my companions, hasn't been hem-hem wasted. Redruth clearly thinks I'm sex-happy, and therefore more of a dolt, and it's never bad to be thought stupid by an enemy.*

But his main joy came from what appeared to be the success of the intrusion. The first ship, entering the system far distant from Larix Prime, had been a drone, intended to be discovered, tracked, and destroyed.

Its only purpose was to cover the second ship, which shouldn't have been discovered at all. It had, which wasn't good, but it also appeared that the Larissans had lost track of the ship during the critical moments of its insertion. That ship carried a relay satellite, which should have been, and hopefully was, planted on one of Larix Five's moons.

Now all he had to do was figure out a way to talk to it, assuming it was there.

Ideally, Njangu had hoped Ab Yohns was entitled to a transceiver, which could be modified to his purposes.

Next most likely would be for him simply to buy a nice, powerful com, slide in one of the chips he'd brought, so the set broadcast on an off-frequency, code his transmissions, use a couple of recorders to transform the transmission into a blurt, and send it, keeping one eye open for any direction finders in the neighborhood.

Njangu had figured he was closely watched, and any such purchase would be regarded with lifted eyebrow. He'd planned to resurrect one of his civilian talents and steal such a receiver.

Protector Redruth, however, had matters well in hand. There were *no* transceivers in civilian use. All coms were controlled by the security services, and were sealed units, preset on the state's frequencies. Yoshitaro thought if he could acquire one of those sets, and try to pry it open, either he wouldn't have the skills to do the mod, or the set would self-destruct on him, probably howling on some frequency that a social misfit was messing with it.

Even the transceivers in aircraft were sealed and preset to the needed frequencies.

As for finding a store that sold electronic parts, none such seemed to exist, nor would Njangu have

the slightest idea of what to buy and how to put it
together from scratch.

He considered the omnipresent vids, and wondered
if they might not be more than a box on which to
watch sports, news, or government directives. It would
be very simple to add a small spyeye to each set, and
further tighten Redruth's hold on Larix.

One night Yoshitaro pretended to get drunk, no
doubt depressed by Redruth's chiding, a sad and solitary figure with a bottle, glowering at some sports
show. Reception was very bad, evidently, for he
whacked the set every now and again, without improving the transmission quality.

Finally, after a bottle and a half had vanished, going
unobtrusively down various drains instead of his gul-
let, Yoshitaro could stand no more. He stumbled over,
picked up the set, lifted it overhead and sent it crashing to the floor, to explode in flinders.

That would get him a reputation for being ill-
tempered. He assumed there were other more sophisticated eyes in the room continuing to record.

In fact, a few minutes after he examined the wreckage, his eventual reputation was well deserved.

The set did include a primitive lens and transmitter.
Yoshitaro had hoped he would be able to replace its
chip with one of the ones he'd brought, somehow jack
up the power supply, and use that as his transmitter
to the satellite and then to Cumbre.

The spyeye was a one-piece block, as was the rest
of the television's guts. No doubt an experienced tech
could have figured a way to modify them, but Njangu
Yoshitaro was a thug, not an electronics engineer.

He kicked petulantly at the pieces of television,
woke Pyder, told her to get certain devices and re-
straints, and come with him to Brythe's room.

The next morning, the television had been replaced,
and no one made any reference to Yoshitaro's fit of
rage.

But he still had no way of communicating with that satellite, assuming it was there, and Cumbre.

Which meant that all of his scheming and cleverness, so far, was useless.

And the back of his mind kept wondering just what form Redruth's retaliation against Cumbre would take, and when and how in the hell he could send a warning.

CHAPTER 7

Cumbre/D-Cumbre

"Nothing from Yoshitaro, Jon?" Garvin asked, trying to sound unconcerned.

"Flipping nothing," Hedley said. "An E-month, and zed flipping zed."

"He's probably having trouble finding a pay com that'll take Cumbrian coins."

"Probably," Hedley said. "So did you have any other reason to bother me, other than to see how cheerfully I lie about not being worried?"

"As a matter of fact, I did," Garvin said. "There's no reason we shouldn't be bothering Larix and Kura more than we are. Larix is probably still on alert after our last debacle. So let's send a nice, small team in on Kura, and bash its rural sleepy head a little bit."

"With you, of course, on point."

"Why not?" Garvin said. "I'll let Penwyth, who hasn't been doing squat lately except making sure Angara meets the proper number of Rentiers, take over II Section, and go out with some of Njangu's thugs."

" 'Kay," Hedley said. "I'm listening. Insert shouldn't be too much of a problem, and I don't mind the idea of pulling the tiger's tail a little. What about getting out?"

"If we mess with them just on the ground," Jaansma said confidently, "they shouldn't be looking to space. Plant a relay satellite like we just did for Njangu, and when I holler, come in with three or four *velv*, a couple of the new destroyers, and we scamper, with no casualties except to the goblins.''

Hedley gnawed at his upper lip. "Could work. But I'll run it past the old man.''

"It's a wash," Hedley said. "Angara says way, way too risky without any more data on Kura. Sorry.''

"Goddamit, boss, the only way we're going to lick Redruth is to hit him here, there, and everywhere. Like that old song has it, 'call me the wind or whatever, since I keep blowing down the road.' ''

"Wind," Hedley said. "Try a serious bit of storming. Praise the Buddha without a flipping bellybutton that we're not in the bad old days when you first came aboard, or somebody'd be putting out bulletins calling us Stormforce or some other rabid-ass piece of silliness. Remember, we used to be, what, Swift Lance, or whatever?''

"You're changing the subject and trying to cheer me up," Garvin complained.

"I am that.''

"So what am I supposed to do? Keep waiting on Njangu to call in?''

"Flipping exactly.''

Three days later, Protector Redruth's response to the two pinpricks came.

A ship patrolling off D-Cumbre reported three ships, one an unknown destroyer-class, the other two Nana-class Confederation patrol crafts in-system, not having been reported by any of the outer planets' warning posts. The report had barely been made, and alarms were gonging, when the patrol reported a missile launch from the larger ship. All three intruders fled, using the closest nav point to vanish back into N-space.

The missile was aimed at D-Cumbre, and projections of its orbit suggested it was homing on Dharma Island.

The patrol ship launched countermissiles, and the attacking missile evaded them. A second launch missed as well.

The missile's orbit was further analyzed, and Leggett City, D-Cumbre's capital, was determined to be the target.

Three *aksai,* two piloted by Musth, drove for space. Just out-atmosphere they were in range of the missile, and fired countermissiles.

Two struck home. Nuclear fire in D-Cumbre's skies brought early dawn to the planet.

"Change one," Hedley said. "Angara's approved your run against Kura. PlanGov's in major hysteria with what happened this morning. Nobody wants to grow up and glow in the dark, and nukes are for barbarians anyway."

"Yes, sir. Thank you, sir."

"For what? A chance to get flipping killed?" But Hedley said that under his breath. "Go get your goddamned volunteers."

"There'll be me," Monique Lir said. "Nectan, Irthing, Heckmyer, Jil Mahim for medic, Montagna as sniper, al Sharif, a couple more with electronics cross-training."

"Mostly noncoms, I see," Jaansma said.

"You don't think we're gonna let the pooptitties in the rear ranks have all the fun, do you?"

"Might I ask what you two want?" Garvin said, rubbing his eyes. "It's late, I'm sleepy, I'm only half-through with . . . with whatever I'm doing, and I don't have a lot of time to waste playing."

Ben Dill slid into the chair in front of Garvin's desk, Dr. Danfin Froude remained standing.

"Understand you're going out looking for trouble," Dill said.

"And that you could use a couple of volunteers," Froude added.

"Doesn't this frigging Force have any goddamned security?"

"Not against Ben Dill."

"My answer's a swift, unqualified go away. I'm full up on hee-roes."

"Not a chance," Dill said calmly.

"You're a ship driver," Garvin said. "We're going to be hoofing it. You always snivel when you've got to lug all that poundage around on primary drive."

"I've been known to walk through a jungle or two," Dill said. "Carrying a couple of fagged-out I&R types, come to think about it."

"And you didn't see me falling back when we were stranded on that Musth world," Froude added. "Besides, you'll need someone capable of analysis when you're down on Kura."

"Yeesh," Garvin said. "You, Doctor, I could probably use. But you still ain't convinced me, Ben. Don't you want to stick around here playing zoomie? Think of all the medals and glory and nice clean uniforms, not to mention your fan club. Jungle sluts are definitely not for high-class folks like you."

"There ain't many medals when nothing's going on, and especially since somebody else got all the glory for zotting that A-boomer of Redruth's," Dill said. "Look at it this way, Garvin. I'm bigger than you, faster than you, I used to be your CO, and I'll bust your frigging arm if you don't change your mind, and then *nobody* gets to go play in the bushes."

Garvin snarled in wordless defeat. "Go wake up Lir, and draw the gear she'll tell you to."

"How long will you be gone?" Jasith asked.

"I'm not sure," Garvin said. "A month. Maybe more."

"Was this whole thing your idea?"

Garvin shifted uncomfortably on the soft couch,

looked out across the Heights, across the bay at Camp Mahan. "Uh, yeh. It was."

"You really want to get killed, don't you?"

"I don't believe," Garvin said honestly, "there's anybody mean enough to kill me, yet."

Jasith got up, went to the sideboard, started to pour herself another drink, changed her mind.

"I know what you are," she said slowly. "Probably, I guess, what you always will be. So there's no good in my saying anything.

"Except this, you bastard. You are going to take one day, and one night, off before you go. I'll make sure you eat nothing but your favorite foods, so you have something to remember, out there on whatever horrible world you're going to, eating dried bat shit.

"And I want to make sure I walk bowlegged when you leave, so *I* have something to remember, 'til you get back."

The first ship to lift clear of Camp Mahan was a newly commissioned light destroyer, Garvin's team aboard. Two *velvs* followed, *aksai* hanging from them like remoras.

Off D-Cumbre, they flickered into hyperspace, six jumps from the nearly unknown system of Kura.

CHAPTER
8

Larix/Larix Prime

Njangu Yoshitaro beavered on, scudding back and forth across Larix. He found problems, areas where the system was vulnerable. Small ones were reported to Redruth as he'd been ordered, potential big ones were noted for when—when, not if, Yoshitaro insisted to himself—he was able to find reliable offplanet communications.

He fell into the habit of working out in the same government gym Celidon used. When they sparred, as they did occasionally, Njangu was carefully less quick, less skilled than the other man.

Sometimes they met for dinner at one or another of the restaurants the government's elite favored. Celidon was hardly a gourmet, his standard order underdone beef and raw vegetables. This, Njangu discovered the hard way, wasn't spartanism—Larissan cooking preferred everything either cooked gray, or buried under a highly spiced sauce.

Their conversations were mostly fencing matches, which Njangu quite enjoyed, neither man willing to talk in specifics about his ideas or past or ambitions.

Yoshitaro did learn, however, at least one interesting series of facts:

Redruth had done exactly as Danfin Froude theorized: When the "troubles" started in the Confederation, Redruth had responded instantly, not wanting a "plague of anarchy" to intrude on his domain. As the

situation worsened within the Empire, Redruth had
banned most shipping into the Confederation. The few
ships permitted out-system returned reporting planetary systems pulling out of the Confederation, and
using the chaos to seize neighboring worlds, systems.

"It looked to the Protector," Celidon went on, "as
if civil war, if civil war can have a dozen different
sides, was spreading. When Centrum itself screamed
for support, Redruth refused, saying that war was rag-
ing through his own worlds, and he had no soldiers to
spare. Cleverly, he saw nothing to be gained by losing
his best troops in a distant galaxy, or, worse, having
them come home infected with whatever ideas were
destroying the stability of the Confederation.

"Redruth followed that up with garbled messages
that suggested the situation was worsening."

"Would one of them maybe have been that Cumbre
had fallen out of contact?"

"Something like that," Celidon said, washing down
the last of his meat with ice water. "Ships coming from
your . . . sorry, the worlds you were reporting from
or the Confederation were taken."

Njangu remembered that a ship called the *Malvern*,
which he and Garvin had been aboard as raw recruits,
had been seized by Celidon's men.

"But you knew that," Celidon said. "Weren't you
the bright lad who suborned that official on Centrum
to let us know anytime something interesting in the
way of materials would be passing our way?"

Njangu hid his surprise and smiled blandly.

"Eventually, I suppose, the Confederation assumed
Larix/Kura/Cumbre had fallen into the same shitter as
everyone else," Celidon continued, "and so they
stopped signaling and sending ships.

"Of course," Celidon went on, "this isn't just game-
playing on the part of the Protector. In five or six
years, maybe more, maybe less, when things have had
a chance to get much worse, Redruth wants to start
nibbling at the closer bits of the Confederation. He

wants Cumbre taken so he won't have to worry about his back, plus it's ripe for exploiting, both in men and minerals.

"It's good that you got away from Cumbre in time, Yohns. Although I'll give you a suggestion. When we move against Cumbre, next year or the year after, of course you'll want to accompany the Protector.

"He'll reward you, after the fall, making you possibly the head of his government there. That's well and good, if your ambition is limited.

"But if it were offered to me, I'd find an excuse to refuse. The real prize, Yohns, will be however much of the Confederation the Protector can carve off. Maybe a little . . . maybe a lot. Maybe as far as Centrum itself. Take and hold Centrum, and how many systems will come a-begging for protection?" Celidon smiled. "That's where the real power will lie, power beyond anyone's dreams.

"And there's no reason the Protector won't succeed. He comes from a *very* long-lived line."

Njangu's country estate sat on the edge of a man-made lake, about two hours' flight from Agur. It was quite a compound, with formal gardens, pools, stables, and all the rest that a rich country squire could want.

Njangu hated it.

He was city, through and through, and still had to stop himself from grabbing for a gun when a night bird sang unexpectedly, in spite of his time on jungle patrols with I&R.

Nevertheless, he went to his estate as often as he could, and was seen pacing, dictating into recorders, making notes, preparing reports for the Protector. He made sure he left those notes about, so whichever servants were in Redruth's pay—he assumed all—could read them and testify as to his loyalty and hard work.

Njangu was starting to feel agent paranoia, with every hand against him, and never anyone to relax around. He recognized his twitch, thought he'd gotten soft since he'd been with the Legion, actually having friends he could be honest with for the first time in his life.

To relieve it, he played harnhuns with Goons Alpha and Beta, always as the quarry, which kept him not only in shape, but maintained his cunning as well.

And it was during one harnhuns game that he found a solution to his greatest problem.

Njangu had taken ten minutes lead before his bodyguards came after him, and tried a new escape. He ran to a creek, splashed down it, trying to stay on rocks, until it ended in the lake. He waded out, then swam parallel with the shore, away from the compound, toward the edges of the estate.

He came out of the water, across the gravel beach, and planned to move in a wide circle back toward the compound. If he made it without being caught, he would have won. Currently his record was one in three.

He was moving slowly through brush when he heard the snap of a gun safety. Njangu froze, saw a man wearing a camo suit come from behind a bush, blaster leveled.

"Stay still."

Njangu obeyed. Two other men came out from his flanks, and three from behind him.

"Identify yourself!"

"*Leiter* Ab Yohns," Njangu said. "And what are you doing on my estate?"

"You are not on your grounds, if you are *Leiter* Yohns, but on those belonging to *Leiter* Appledore," the man who'd stopped him said. "Show identification."

"I have none." Njangu wore only one-piece drab overalls, with a small hydration system on his back. He felt hands move over his back, between his legs, around his stomach, kept from reflexively killing the searcher or pitching him overhead into the first man with a gun.

"Nothing," the man said.

The first man frowned.

"STILL!" someone shouted. The first man started to turn, and a blaster bolt slammed into the ground next to him. Clearly a professional, his fingers opened, and his gun dropped. Njangu heard the thud of other weapons falling.

A gun barrel came from behind a tree, and Njangu recognized a bit of Alpha's face.

"Identities?" Alpha snarled.

"*Leiter* Appledore's security element," the man said. "You . . . whoever you are . . . are on his property."

Beta slid out of the brush, a gun in his hand.

Njangu almost started laughing. Beta went to the first man, searched *him,* found ID.

"They're who they say they are," he said. Alpha came out of cover, putting his pistol away.

"I assume this is really *Leiter* Yohns?" the first man asked.

"You assume right," Beta said.

"My apologies, sir," the man said, voice thin. Njangu assumed that meant Yohns outranked Appledore in the hierarchy. "But you set off our perimeter alarms, sir, and we responded as ordered."

Njangu saw barely hidden fear on the faces of Appledore's men, realized he could probably have them sent to the undersea mines or whatever other hellhole he wished.

"Don't apologize for doing your job," he said. "Go ahead and pick up your guns."

"Thank you, sir," and the others chorused their thanks.

"One question, though. You said perimeter security, and I didn't see anything."

All of them, including Alpha and Beta, showed amusement.

"Here, sir," and Appledore's man took Njangu to

what looked like a boulder. Njangu couldn't tell it wasn't real until he examined it closely.

"Ah," he said. "Thanks. You can tell *Leiter* Appledore from me that he has most alert men. I won't have to worry about ever being attacked by social misfits from this side of my estate."

The men thanked him again, and hastily trotted away.

"We have those gimmicks, too?" Njangu said.

"Certainly, sir."

"Show me some of them."

Alpha showed Yoshitaro other rocks, false dead logs, and such.

"Interesting," he said. "I assume they're self-powered, and transmit by radio? Heat- and motion-sensitive?"

"Exactly, sir."

"Active or passive?"

"Completely passive in their base setting, sir, so you could walk past them with a sensor and not get a readout until they begin reporting. The only way they can be spotted is visually, although maybe they put out enough power you could get them with an infrared from close enough. Plus they can be remotely modified by the operator to lie doggo if there's sensors around, just like it can be set to go off for two men, and ignore three or one."

"Sophisticated little sucker," Njangu said. "Are these standard . . . I mean, are you issued a certain number of logs, rocks, stumps per estate?"

"We have several varieties of cases we can put the guard units into. The units themselves are pretty standard, but a technician can modify them for whatever sensing security wants, then make up the exterior depending on what camouflage is required. We keep a dozen or so on hand, since weather's hard on them."

"Interesting indeed."

The perimeter alarms, built for custom modification, yielded easily to exploration. It took no more than two hours for Njangu to finish eyeballing the guts of the one he'd gotten from a storeroom and sketch out what was what. The components were linked by simple universal plugs, so it took little additional time to remove the transmitter chip and slide one of Njangu's specials in, a minimum of cursing and bending required.

The chips had been built by technicians on D-Cumbre, who'd carefully scanned the electronic records of the first intrusion Cumbre had made into Larix's space, examining all frequencies in use. They set their chips to use frequencies close, but not too close, to those common wavelengths. The chips would accept input from any standard recorder via a tiny cord. Njangu kept several recorders handy, using them to dictate his notes into.

The hard part for Yoshitaro was wrangling the power converter from the vid he'd smashed into the circuit as a booster. Now, finished, wanting a drink, he hoped he'd done it right, hoped he'd just built himself a neat little transmitter.

The next day, he went for a stroll, telling his bodyguards he wanted to be alone. He wanted to find as many of the perimeter alarms as he could, see if there were any holes in the perimeter that he could spot.

Careful searching and logical thought located half a dozen, and he found a seventh in a remote spot. It took only a few moments to replace that sensor with his special rock and clip it into the estate's wiring.

Since the alarms were passive, no one should notice his device wouldn't broadcast squat even if a dinosaur wandered past.

The only time the transmitter would be noticeable is when its antenna was strung, and then Yoshitaro would be very close, with a gun ready.

Njangu spent the rest of the day writing a signal with what he felt was the most essential data, including the confirmation of Froude's theory about the Confederation. II Section's cryptanalysts had decided on an

archaic book cipher. They'd given him four, all based
on religious books common throughout the worlds of
man. Njangu had found, in the same library he'd done
his research, a copy of the *Q'Ran,* standard transla-
tion. The agreed code began with sura VI.

Message ready, he shot it back and forth between
his recorders, slow to fast, again and again, until it
was no more than five seconds long.

The next day, he took the tape out to the device,
quickly strung wire from trees into an exotic antenna
as he'd been taught, plugged in the recorder, and
blurted the message into space.

Ab Yohns, *nee* Njangu Yoshitaro, superspy, was
back in business.

All he needed next was to figure a way to receive
messages. But, with his confidence restored, he figured
that would come with time.

That night, to reward himself, he had sparkling wine
with his four companions and let the evening deterio-
rate into a disgustingly sensual, but extremely interesting marathon that didn't end until well after dawn.

Yoshitaro spent the next three days waiting to see
if there were any signs of alarm or detection vehicles
responding to his com. There was nothing, or nothing
he discovered.

He returned to Agur and his duties, again traveling
across Larix, trying to see and evaluate everything.

His second stop was with the Protector's Own, the
elite palace guard. He pretended interest in their moti-
vation, what sort of background they came from,
whether he thought they could be subverted by one
of the infamous social misfits.

They fell, largely, into two categories: dedicated fanatics, whose life would be fulfilled if they had a
chance to take a blaster bolt in the guts for Redruth;
and a scattering of people pretending zealotry with a
cool eye for the main chance and staying close to the
center of power.

Those people he was very interested in, for obvious reasons, and tried to figure out what trigger he could use to make them his, without being betrayed to Celidon, wanting to be sure his eventual spiel wouldn't be something that'd be prize testimony at his trial for treason.

Njangu was heading back to his lims, where his bodyguards waited, when a very striking, redheaded officer, wearing the tabs of a hundred-group-*Leiter,* came up.

"*Leiter* Yohns?" Her smile was knowing.

"Yes?" Njangu smiled politely, admiring her, trying to figure out why the alarm bells in his mind were shrilling so loudly.

"Do you remember me?"

"No, I . . ." Njangu stopped. He suddenly did.

"I'm Maev," the redhead said. "I thought I recognized you, back when you were inspecting the Guard this morning.

"You and I were recruits, and were screwing, back when *Leiter* Celidon seized the ship we were on, the *Malvern,* headed for Cumbre.

"Back then, your name was Njangu Yoshisomething or other, wasn't it? How the hell did you ever get here?"

CHAPTER
9

A port opened in the side of the Cumbrian Kelly-class destroyer, and a small dart, not much bigger than a man, spat out, speeding "down" toward Kura Four.

"Lousy, lousy recon," Dill said, standing behind the *Parnell's* skipper, *Mil* Liskeard.

"Yes," agreed Alikhan. "There should be files from spies, many satellite photos."

"Not to mention a couple of sneaks on the ground checking things out before the combat team gets inserted," Garvin added.

"Would you three morons get the hell off my bridge?" Liskeard growled. "It was almost better when you were second-guessing my piloting on the way in."

"Not me," Garvin said. "I know my limitations."

"Interesting thought," Dill said. "Let me know when you discover any of mine."

"Shall we obey our orders," Alikhan said. "And you can open a file on your faults that I shall happily dictate. A very large file."

"Good idea," the weapons tech at the control station behind Liskeard grunted. "Sirs. And let me fly this goddamned bird in without getting my ass shot off."

The *Parnell*, one of the first four destroyers built on Cumbre, was a compromise between what the force needed, what the Force wanted, and what could be built in a hurry. Essentially, the class used the existing templates of a standard planetary patrol craft, but enlarged the ship in all dimensions. It had a crew of twenty, four Goddard antiship missiles in pods under the ship's "chin," a pair of chaingun turrets, and four Shadow antimissile stations.

The shipyards of Cumbre, newly modernized and expanded after the Musth War, could each roll out one of these destroyers in a month, and the internals could be added in another month. Larger ships weren't possible at the moment: Any building work increases exponentially in cost, complexity, and material, not arithmetically.

No one knew how fast Larix/Kura were building ships, nor how large they were, but everyone assumed the worst, which, in war, is the safest way to think.

"You wish?" Ben Dill said politely to the Musth.

"To inquire as to why you are being stupid."

"Just my normal procedure."

"You are a pilot," Alikhan said. "Yet you have volunteered to play ground-worm. That does not make sense."

"Because," Dill said, "like I told Garvin, back on Cumbre, I'm bored waiting for trouble to come to me."

"I see. That is stupid, indeed," Alikhan said. "But no more stupid than my joining the Force. Why did you not ask me if I wanted to be stupider than I already am?"

"To be real honest," Ben said thoughtfully, "I didn't even think about it. But even if I had, I don't think I would've grabbed you.

"What happens if we get spotted down there on Kura? Don't you think somebody would go completely apeshit if they saw this big brown furry mother trotting through their jungle?"

"Apeshit is not a term I'm familiar with," Alikhan

said. "I can infer its meaning, though. Nor am I of the female gender and capable of giving birth. But would that surprise be any greater than seeing ten humans, dripping weapons, dressed in a strange manner, wandering around looking for things to destroy?"

"Mmmh," Dill said. "Strong point, which I don't wanna consider. I'm sorry, Alikhan, that I didn't give you a chance to get killed. But try this one. You're going to be the insert pilot with the *velv*, right? Since you're not that bad a pilot, second only to me, that'll make sure there'll be somebody with his shit firmed up who'll be around to extract us when we start hollering for help."

"I shall never understand the human fascination with excrement," Alikhan said. "I accept your apology. And I shall be there to pick you and the others up.

"No matter when, where, or what."

Two shifts later, as the I&R raiders tried to convince themselves they were comfortable living on the laps of the *Parnell*'s crew, and that they were nerveless commandos unworried about this near-blind mission, the drone's tech swaggered into the small cargo compartment they'd taken over.

"*Mil* Jaansma," she said. "Admire large head, sir. Admire very large head."

"The drone's back?"

"Not only back, but nobody sniffed nahthing," she said. "Admire large head."

"Okay, crew," Garvin said. "Set up the holo, so we can figure out where we want to start tickling them."

Kura Four had been picked because prewar intelligence suggested that was the most heavily populated of the worlds in the system, although none of the four habitable planets would have to worry about population pressure for a millennium or so.

The drone had initially made eight passes, pole to

pole, out-atmosphere, on a mapping run. The runs were repeated at night, using infrared sensors as well as amplified light.

The team watched the projection of Kura Four, a holograph about a meter in diameter, spin in front of them.

"Eleven main cities," Monique Lir said.

"Twelve," Froude corrected. "There's another light-smear down near the south pole."

"Bring each of those areas up one at a time," Garvin said.

"Yessir," the technician said, and the holo closed in on one area, then another.

"That one's NG," Dill said. "Looks like it's built on the only patch of open ground on the planet."

"Bust that one out, too," Lir said. "Right on that peninsula—no running room there, either, when things start blowing up."

"What about that one?"

"Possible."

Three others areas were considered possibles, and those four studied.

"That one," Garvin decided, blinking tired eyes. "That city's about the biggest on the planet. Maybe, what, a million?"

"Maybe a bit more," Froude said. "In fact, probably. I ran close-up scans on all the possible targets. That one's got a good complement of landing fields, warehousing, what looks to me like military depots, so you can project the population probably a bit higher than a mill."

"Sitting right there where these two rivers run together," Jaansma said. "Then the valley widens, with the sea, what, fifty kilometers below? Mountains back of the city, which'll give us good hiding places."

"What's the plan, boss?" Lir said.

"I think," Garvin said slowly, "if we come in back here, letting that ridgeline mask us, then hump over here . . . we hit this dam. Blow the shit out of it, hope there's enough of a shock to take out this other, bigger dam further downstream.

"With any luck, we put a nice wave down the main valley, maybe fifty meters high, through the middle of that city and wash everybody out to sea."

The medic, Jil Mahim, bit her lip, but didn't say anything. Garvin saw her expression.

"If it bothers you to probably be drowning women and kids," he began.

"No, boss," Mahim said. "It just took me a minute."

" 'Kay," Jaansma said, pretending he didn't notice her embarrassment. "That's the tentative first target. As the op order said, we'll take out the first target, extract, and depending on how battered we are, reinsert on another part of the world and mess with them there.

"That'll give Protector Redruth something to worry about protecting, I hope.

"Now we'll have the tech chance another sweep with the drone over those mountains, see if we can't see where the local soldiery hangs its hat, the size of the dam's garrison, where the local villages are, and like that."

"Second target," Lir said, "if the first dam doesn't take down the big one, we'll get it ourselves."

"That'll make the countryside nice and hostile," *Tweg* Nectan said.

Lir shrugged. "You wanted an easy life, you didn't have to do something dickheaded like volunteer, now did you?"

There was laughter.

"Actually," Froude said, "if we were serious about pursuing war to the hilt with these people, we'd be better advised to abort this commando business, pull back to Cumbre, and then return with the best defoliants science can build. Assuming, as is likely, this and Kura's other three planets are Redruth's rice bowl, as the intelligence indicated."

"Or," Mahim said, "a little radioactive dust here and there."

"That would work as well," Froude said, undisturbed. "If we have no postwar plans for occupying the planet."

"Back to the operation at hand," Garvin said. "For extraction we'll pull back into the mountains, and holler for help. I'd guesstimate operation time at, oh, five to seven E-days. But it could run double that, so don't pack yourselves on the thin side."

Garvin saw Alikhan looking at him, raised a questioning eyebrow.

"A private word, Garvin?"

Garvin started to say there weren't any secrets on something like this, stopped himself, and went out of the compartment with the Musth.

"I am still not that familiar with your fighting rules," Alikhan said. "Was there a reason you did not mention those . . . I do not have a word for it . . . presences we saw in the display from time to time?"

"Presences?"

"They appeared to me like thin, small clouds, but moved in several directions, so they could not be clouds, unless the winds over those mountains are stranger than any I've known."

"I think," Garvin said, "we better go back inside and tell the troops what you think you saw."

Alikhan followed him back. The soldiers were studying the projection, muttering about "steep bastard to be humping," "figure max travel no more'n three klicks a day," "wonder if there's villagers in the jungle we'll have to worry about," and such.

"Crew, listen up," Garvin said. "We might have problems. Would you rerun the sweep over the rivers?"

The tech obeyed.

Alikhan pointed, his head moving back and forth rapidly. "There is one. Another. Two there. That one."

The humans looked perplexed.

"Did anyone see any of what Alikhan was pointing at?"

There was a chorus of "no," nossir," "nah," and such.

"Very interesting," Dr. Froude said. "One of the many things we appear to have overlooked was whether the Musth sense beyond human ranges."

"None of you saw what I did?" Alikhan said, wonderingly.

There was a long silence.

"Technician," Garvin asked, "does your record show anything above/below human perception?"

The technician touched keys on the holo box, read the screen, frowned, hit more keys.

"No, sir. Nothing like *he* says he's seeing . . . and there isn't any way somebody could sight something that the instruments say isn't there."

Alikhan surveyed the woman, ears cocking, eyes reddening in anger. But he said nothing.

"I don't like things to get strange," Deb Irthing said.

"Who does?" Garvin said. "When we send the drone in again, we'll see if Alikhan picks up anything. Maybe," he said hopefully, but not very convincingly, "we've just got some flaws on the recorder."

Another, closer pass over the area gave more details. There were small villages here and there. Just below the first, smaller dam, was a military-looking camp, and there were buildings on either side of the dam's parapet.

Alikhan also saw half a dozen more of the "clouds."

"I do not like this, Garvin," he said. "This time, as they are seen by the drone, they move quickly to one side or another, as if they do not wish to be pictured."

"So now, in addition to everything else," Garvin said, "we've got invisible thingieboppers that can sense drones. Whyinhell doesn't that frigging Yoshi-taro report in with some good skinny to explain all?"

"What's the prog, boss?" Lir said.

"Screw it," Garvin said. "We're going in."

"Bless Ahriman and his putty dildo," Lir said fervently. "I was sure this'd end up another goddamned dry run."

The *Parnell* made a fast swoop, dropping off a relay satellite in a geosynchronous orbit over the target area that would bounce any transmissions from I&R to the pickup ships hovering at the system's edge.

The *velv* came down in a near-vertical dive, Alikhan at the controls. Dill considered the somewhat greenish I&R troops strapped to hastily fitted acceleration pads at the rear of the control room, and chortled.

"Nice to see the guys and gals with the steel ass-holes aren't perfect at *everything*. Be glad a gentle lout like Alikhan's at the controls instead of me, or you'd really be heaving your guts out. Speaking of which, would any of you care for a nice, refreshing vomit before we enter the jungle?"

Lir was the only one healthy enough to manage an obscenity.

Dill laughed even harder. "Hey, Alikhan?" he bellowed. "You need any help up there doing this controlled crash?"

"Negative," Alikhan said. "I could fly this pattern with my tail."

"It feels like you are."

The *velv* flared once about five hundred meters above the tree-covered slope, then lifted into a near stall over the clearing Garvin had picked. Alikhan caught it on antigravs, settled it down.

"Ramp down," he ordered, and two human crew members obeyed. The *velv* hovered two meters above brush.

"Go, go, go!" Lir was shouting, and the team unstrapped and went out the door, dropped into the brush, got a nasty surprise that they were still three meters above the ground, found a more pleasant surprise as they squished down into muddy soil. The soldiers recovered, staggered forward under the mass of their packs for a dozen steps, hit the prone position, weapons ready.

The last solider was down. Garvin looked up at a helmeted face peering out the *velv*'s ramp, gave a thumbs-up, and pointed to the sky. The *velv*'s drive snorted, and the ship lifted for space, very fast.

Nobody moved in the jungle hush, waiting. No shots, no cries of alarm.

Garvin came to his knees, stood, then motioned the team forward, after him. He walked point, with *Tweg* Wy Nectan on slack just behind him. Third was *Dec* Val Heckmyer, then *Dec* Darod Montagna, the team sniper. Behind her was Ben Dill, the biggest and most heavily laden. Garvin, maliciously, had chosen him for prime commo, with *Finf* Baku al Sharif behind him with a backup com. Jil Mahim, the medic followed, then Dr. Danfin Froude. The last two in the initial march order were *Tweg* Deb Irthing, and tail gunner was First *Tweg* Monique Lir.

They were very heavily armed. The basic weapon was the blaster, configured, as common with I&R, as an arm-length carbine. Montagna's blaster was fitted with a variable optic sight and a heavy barrel. Basic load was ten hundred-round drums of caseless ammunition. Garvin, Heckmyer, Dill, and Lir carried cutdown Squad Support Weapons, and fifteen drums of ammo. Each of them had a pistol and the standard-issue double-edged dagger of the Force. Dill also carried a Shrike launcher and four tubed rockets.

From that moment until they were extracted, they'd communicate with the whisper mikes and bone speakers each member of the team carried. But they'd use those as little as possible, even though they were set

on what appeared, from a superficial check, to be unused frequencies. Hand signals were still preferred.

Each soldier carried almost one hundred kilos in his
pack, fighting/survival essentials on his fighting vest, plus
individual weapons. The staggering load was only possible because the pack bases held modified droppers,
antigravity parachutes that cut the load to no more
than four kilos, although the mass remained an un-
wieldy bulk. The problem with the droppers was they
emitted a certain amount of detectable energy. Garvin
was operating on the hopeful assumption nobody
would be scanning that much jungle that carefully.

Most of the load was explosives, one-kilo slabs of
Telex, plus detonating cord, fuses, and timers of various types and nastiness. Their load would lighten as
they found targets, got shot at, and ate.

Garvin had gone about one hundred meters when
Lir's voice whispered in his ear.

"Boss. Lir. Look back. At the clearing."

Garvin obeyed.

"The ship should've gone higher before it put the
drive on," she said. "See the burn?"

Garvin did, a rapidly browning streak in the jungle.

"Maybe we better honk hard out of here," he said,
"and hope nobody wonders what made that happen."

Monique double-clicked her mike in agreement.
Garvin started moving faster, thinking, *Naturally, we
go to full speed just when it's starting to get steep.*

Garvin picked something that wasn't quite a trail,
knowing how suicidal that could be, but an animal
track that appeared to lead to the top of the knife-
edge ridge.

It did, but in its own fashion, winding here and
there, stopping at what Garvin thought might be tasty
herbs or merely a quiet place in which to defecate.

He remembered the two hardest parts of I&R. The
first was obvious—never to fall out, to keep marching
until you were chewing on what tasted like dry heart—

your own—and trying to remember your body was a damned liar when it wheezed about how there weren't any reserves left to call on. Listening to that voice was what washed out volunteers for I&R.

The second was the worst—not only to keep moving, but to stay alert, in spite of your exhaustion. Never let yourself fall into the agonizing one step then another way of moving, eyes fixed on the trail ahead, not looking up, not seeing what was around you.

The first lesson, unlearned, kept you from getting into Intelligence and Recon. The second killed you as you staggered into a booby trap or ambush.

Garvin pushed on, relearning the hard lessons about ignoring the body's sniveling, eyes always moving, weapon ready, alert for anything touching off an inner alarm.

Or for a sudden silence that could signify danger.

Here, on this strange world, his ears and brain began memorizing what appeared to be the normal sounds of this jungle, and what could be new and lethal surprises. All he, and the others, could do, was file noises, try to keep their gasping as quiet as possible, and not lose their footing as they inched up the near-vertical slope.

They stopped below the crest, let their lungs agonize back toward normal and looked around for anything threatening.

There was nothing, there was everything. They moved on, topping the knife edge, saw higher ridges around them, jungle all around, no sign of the lake.

Shit, Garvin thought. *I thought we were just one slope this side of the dam. Guess again.*

He motioned Heckmyer to take point, Montagna to move up to slack, let them continue the march. Nobody could walk point for very long without losing the edge. Garvin fell into the column in front of Dill, who, though sweating like a saline factory, appeared unbothered by the climb.

They went down the ridge, slipping every now and

then, catching themselves on saplings or each other, and reached the bottom, which was a rocky ravine with a creek splashing down it.

It would've been easy to lose discipline and dive into one of the pools and suck down all that wonderful cool water. Instead, Mahim tested the water, nodded approval. Two troops went across, maintained far-side security up and downstream. Two remained on the near side, and six got to dunk their heads and bodies as they went across, trying to submerge into the meter-deep pools. Then it was the turn of the other four.

They were wet, but cool now, their backpack-mounted canteens refilled before moving on.

Suddenly the sun was gone, and it was late afternoon. Garvin realized they'd most likely not make the next crest before night, and they'd have to camp wherever they found themselves.

Wonderful, he thought. *All we need now is a good serious rain.*

A few minutes later, Kura Four quite cooperatively drenched them.

An hour later, they found the best of several bad lots for a campsite—where the hill leveled for about ten meters to only forty degrees. They moved past the designated site for another hundred meters, stopped in ambush formation. Nothing was moving around them.

They went back downhill into the chosen bivouac site. Paired up, they ate from their ration paks, then put the debris into heat pouches also used for body waste. Just before dark, the pouches were gathered, and tabs pressed. The pouches seared into self-consuming life, without smoke or odor. None, at least, that humans could detect.

Garvin sent a four-symbol burst to the satellite: *Bivvied. All right. Moving toward target.*

Then they lay in a starburst formation, each soldier's heel touching the next. Less-skilled soldiers would've kept full alert, lazy ones would've gone to one-in-four. That would be the procedure once they were farther away from the Landing Zone, but not tonight. Half of the I&R soldiers stayed alert.

But nothing happened, other than al Sharif emitted, in his sleep, an enormous fart that not only woke three soldiers on either side of him, but forced them to move away until the odor dissipated. Revenge was silently vowed.

Their wrist chronometers had already been set for Kura Four's twenty-seven-E-hour day. An hour before dawn should appear, Garvin, who always took first and last watch, woke his troops. Again they ate, splashed water on their faces, a great luxury permitted by the creek crossing, defecated, and went on, up and up.

This time was lucky: The land opened into a wide valley, with V'd walls. In its center was a lake, and, across its end, the damn that had created it.

Nectan grinned at Garvin, signaled with his fingers: man walking downhill; man putting heavy charge in place; twisted a demolition box; and then signed waves roaring over everything. Then he clasped hands in victory.

Garvin crossed fingers, held them out to him.

Then the team started downhill toward their target.

The watch officer woke Liskeard in his tiny cabin aboard the *Parnell.*

"Blurt transmission from Cumbre, sir. Marked EYES ONLY, in the R-Code. The com officer decoded it."

The R-Code was the most carefully kept code, except for diplomatic ciphers, of the Force, with personalized access limited to involved unit commanders and their communications officers.

Liskeard grunted, took the sheaf of paper, dismissed the officer, then sat up and unsealed the folder with his thumbprint.

"Quite a package," he muttered, then, reading the first lines, came fully awake. He'd been told, on initial briefing, that there was a "source" somewhere within the Larix/Kura system, who so far hadn't been able to report.

Now, Njangu's first com had come through. Liskeard scanned it, looking for any reference to Kura, but found nothing.

Still, he felt heartened. The Force was no longer operating in complete darkness.

Garvin's team had been moving no more than an hour when Lir, on point, stopped, held out one hand, palm to the rear.

Stop.

Her hand pushed down.

Down and freeze.

The signal went down the line and the ten men and women crouched, weapons sweeping their assigned sectors, looking for movement.

Nothing.

Lir used binocs to scan the area immediately below, the valley and lake, the skies.

Garvin was in mid-column, waiting. Lir turned, touched her shoulder with two fingers.

Commander up.

Garvin wondered why she didn't use her com, what she'd seen. He slid carefully forward, inscribed a question mark in the air.

Lir leaned close, whispered:

"I feel like we're watched. No indicators."

Garvin thought for a moment. He didn't believe in mumbo jumbo at all, but a scout's honed senses might come up with something she couldn't readily identify—a momentary silence in the jungle, a flash of equipment, anything.

He used his own binocs to sweep their front.

Nothing.

He moved his finger in an arc, up, down, around, then a question mark.

Where do you feel it?

Lir looked disgusted, pointed up and out, to somewhere over the lake.

Garvin saw nothing in the air, but he remembered Alikhan's invisibles. He put his lips next to Monique.

"Remember what our hairy alien couldn't see, either. Signal when it's gone."

Lir nodded. A few moments later, she stood, swept her hand forward at the waist.

Continue the march.

The team moved on. Garvin slid back into his position, and they went down toward the lake.

The ground grew more level, and again Lir brought the team to a halt. Ahead, in neat rows, were carefully tended, low trees, bearing purple-green fruit.

Beyond that was a small village, a dozen long, rectangular wooden houses, roofed with an insulated, dull metal.

Without command, the team was down, frozen.

Lir keyed her mike.

"Boss?"

"I saw," Garvin subvocalized. He checked his compass. "Skirt the village. Move south, trying to stay within eyeball contact of the lake."

Lir double-clicked, motioned, and the team followed her, back into the jungle a dozen meters, then along the edge of the grove. She'd gone no more than a dozen steps when she heard noise, and again became a statue.

The noise grew louder, and a young girl wearing baggy pants and a multicolored top appeared from behind a tree. She was intent on her work, cutting jungle vine runners back with a wide-bladed and very sharp hoe.

Lir signaled again, a hand held out, thumb down.

Enemy.

She waited, hoping the girl would move past. But her shoulders hunched, and she involuntarily looked in Lir's direction, then carefully returned to her task.

Lir touched her mike, reported.

Before Garvin could respond, Irthing, behind Lir on slack, touched her hand. Lir glanced down, saw a metal tube with a rudimentary trigger. It was an old-fashioned suppressed weapon, firing a solid subsonic round. Old-fashioned, but still the most silent killing tool other than a knife.

The girl was moving backward, slowly, trying to keep from looking up, trying to appear innocent.

Lir lifted the weapon, then caught herself.

No. We don't kill children.

She handed the weapon back to Irthing, just as Garvin's voice breathed in her ear.

"Wait until she's out of sight, then move on. Don't kill her."

The girl suddenly spun and ran hard. Lir came to her feet, and moved her clenched fist up and down.

Move quickly.

The team went on, and the village was lost behind them.

Lir reported, and Garvin responded: "Let's hope there's no com set to report strangers in that village."

Probably Monique should have shot the girl.

But they didn't kill children, at least not face-to-face. Not unless there weren't any other options.

Now the hiking was easier. The ground was more level, there were frequent streams flowing into the lake, a cool breeze refreshed them, and the thick jungle had been burned clear, leaving only light secondary growth to push through. But they moved far more slowly. There were villages every few kilometers, and fields. They saw more of the locals, but only one man was armed, and he looked to be no more than a village policeman.

There were no signs of alarm, either on the ground or air, and Garvin began to hope the little girl hadn't been believed with her tale of green/black-faced monsters laden with guns.

Every now and again they came to clear ground, enough to see the looming mass of the dam ahead.

They came to a larger village, and Garvin ordered them back into the jungle to high ground. He motioned for defensive positions, then he, Lir, and Froude slid through the brush to a promontory, where they could examine their target.

After a while, they came back and gathered the team for a face-to-face.

"Here's my idea, folks," he whispered. "I don't know if we were reported, but I've got to assume we were. That means we're going to hit them tonight, before they've got time to come up with a major reaction to our asses being around."

There were mutters of approval.

"It's still a hike to the dam base," Lir pointed out. "We'd better cut this short and get back in the saddle."

"First good news," Garvin said. "No more foot-pounding for a while. We'll strike from here."

"Long swim, boss," Mahim said.

"No swim," Garvin said. "See those double-hulled fishing boats moored out there? Or is everybody but me blind?"

"I saw 'em," Dill said.

"As did I," Froude said. "I was wondering if they couldn't be put to use. Unlike you fiends, I don't love hiking as my primary pastime."

"So the drill is," Garvin said, "we make up the demo packs now. Set them on remote timers, which'll give us all the options.

"At full dark, we'll drop down and snag two boats. Three men per boat. Two stay-behinds here with the packs.

"There'll be a moon, so we'll row along the shore-line to the far side of the dam. Then we drop two twenty-kilo packs close together, by the penstock. Two lucky lads get to climb up the pipe and stick two more packs as close to that structure . . . I guess it's the control room for some kind of hydropower . . . as they can get.

"Once the charges are in place, everybody except, uh, Monique, me and—"

"And me," Dill said.

"And you, Ben. You can carry me when I get tired. The rest of the rowing party heads back here after the charges are planted and waits until we rendezvous. We reassemble, with luck, and go for the hills and wait for the smoke to clear. The Rendezvous Point will be where we slept last night. Simple, straightforward, in and out."

"No it isn't," Nectan said. "You haven't given deployment orders for two of us."

"You are correct," Garvin said. "Monique and I are going to slither off right now and eyeball the joint from up close. We'll signal if there's any nasty surprises, like sentries, tracks, aircraft, IR/available light alarms, like that, and deal with them as seems appropriate. If there's a real cluster, we'll com from the dam to abort and rethink things."

"Another thing," Irthing said.

"Go, Deb."

"Are we going to paddle with our bare hands? Or did anybody think to see if either of those catamarans have oars."

"Crudoo!" Garvin muttered. "I *am* blind."

"There are oars," two voices said, in near unison, and Lir and Froude grinned at each other.

"That's," Garvin said ruefully, "why we have First *Twegs*. And scientists."

"Another question," Dill said. "Who is going with me to scale the heights with the big boom?"

"As junior man on this thing," al Sharif said, "I'll volunteer."

"That's it," Garvin said. "Monique and I'll be waiting on top of the dam for you folks. Al Sharif, after the charges are set, get your butt back down into the boat. Dill, you'll stay with us, like I said.

"See how easy a briefing is," Garvin beamed, "when you don't have good maps, don't know the size of the enemy, his plans, deployment, SOI, or anything else?

" 'Kay. Nectan, you're Senior *Tweg*. Take charge of things. You think you'll have any trouble stealing the boats?"

"If he does, I'll give him advice," Montagna said. "I was a swim instructor when I was a kid."

She grinned at Garvin, who smiled back. Time back, when he'd run the patrol set up as a graduating exercise for I&R trainees that ended in a nightmare of blood, and began the Musth War, Garvin had admired, in a very casual way, her clean athleticism and quick manners. She reminded him, vaguely, of a girl he'd known, far back in school, who the other students had been in awe of—a bit too pretty, a bit too bright, and more than a bit too mature for the others. But, of course, he'd said and done nothing about that to Montagna, since she was enlisted, and he was an officer. Besides, at the time, he was mourning the seeming loss of Jasith, and his observations about the trainee weren't much more than academic.

"Honk us up when you're in motion, Wy." Garvin got up. "Everybody who can't find work, get your head down."

There were murmurs of amusement. No one would have time to sleep, even if they had the inclination, after the explosive packs were readied, weapons cleaned, magazines checked, knives sharpened, and other forms of death readied.

"C'mon, Lir," Garvin said. "We've got klicks to go before we sleep."

"I've seen better formations," Monique Lir said, lowering her binocs, "from shithouse flies around a bucket."

"Not too military," Garvin agreed. "Thank Saint John of the Apukalypse."

There appeared to be about a hundred or so guards assigned to the dam, quartered in a small compound about half a kilometer away from it.

"You also notice how nice and sloppy roll call was?" Lir continued. "Half of 'em were still straggling out of the mess hall when whatever his rank is was shouting names."

"I love 'em just the way they are," Garvin said. "You also notice the troopies live downstream of the dam. With any luck, our bang'll wipe 'em out, and we won't have to worry about pursuit."

"With any luck," Lir agreed, returned to her survey. "I count one, two pickups on this side of the ramparts, which oughta be easy to Rat-Fiddle."

"Looks like a third, or some kind of pressure detector, just beyond that fence gate," Garvin said.

"I got it."

They watched on, as the sun sank behind a mountain, and shadows grew across the dam. Men came out of one building and formed up.

"I guess that'll be the sentry-go," Garvin said. "Sixteen men, plus a noncom. Yeah. There they go. Eight posted on this side, eight on t'other, two walking."

"I guess whatever invisible thing me and Alikhan got bothered by isn't reporting on schedule," Lir said.

"Keep your fingers crossed when you say that."

"What, give it another couple of hours, and slide down then?"

"Don't be so ambitious. We'll move out when Nectan says he's amphibious. 'Til then, sweet dreams."

Garvin rolled over on his pack, closed his eyes, and gave every pretense of being asleep.

Monique looked at him skeptically, did the same.

After two minutes, she began snoring in a very soft, catlike style.

Darod Montagna swam silently to a fishing boat, arms and legs moving underwater as she'd learned as a girl. Only one of Kura Four's moons was out. Montagna waited until a cloud scudded over its face, climbed over the side of a boat, untied the painter to the anchor buoy, and shipped the rudder. Keeping low, she slowly and awkwardly rowed the boat, about six meters long, away from the village, toward the distant bulk of the dam. Seconds later, another boat followed her.

She was sweating heavily by the time she rounded the nearby point and zigged the boat toward shore. In the shallows, six men and women came out of the brush, lifted heavy packs into the boats, and climbed in.

"Moving," Nectan muttered into his throat mike.

A double-click from Garvin answered him.

Garvin and Monique slid through brush past the guard shack, then made their way through a few strands of rusting barbed wire up toward the dam's parapet. The two standards with an intrusion sensor and pickup were just where a road crossed the dam's rampart. Garvin slipped across the road to one pole, clipped a tiny rubberized box to its power line, and turned it on. Clamps dug into the line, probed deep. Lir planted a second device on the other line. The signal from the pickup was recorded. Any change or break in the real transmission would be blocked, and the normal transmission sent out form the device's internal power supply.

The pressure sensor, if that was what it was, had been carelessly laid, and it was easy to tiptoe past it.

Lir positioned a small pack against the parapet, facing inward.

Then they crouched along the rampart, about four hundred meters of curving concrete with low walls to the far shore, the rampart fifteen meters across. Close to the other side was the square concrete control room.

Somewhere before that would be the roving guards.

*　　*　　*

Baku al Sharif looked up at the dam walls, towering darkly above him, and shivered. Nectan, beside him in the bow of the boat, felt the movement, gripped his arm reassuringly. The other boat was about two meters to the side.

The guard stared out and down at the water pouring out of the power station far below into the rocky canyon and down the valley, calculating exactly how many more times he'd have to look at these goddamned backwoods until his enlistment was up. He thought about saying something to his fellow, but that'd only get a mock about how much longer he had to go, and how eagerly his friend was looking forward to his transfer out of here in only a month and some-odd days.

Something bulked out of the darkness. The guard had no time to unsling his blaster before a knife drove up and into his guts, driving his breath out. He was trying desperately to pull in air, then his head flopped back and he was dead.

Garvin pulled the knife out, resheathed it, as Lir's victim gurgled the last of his life out of his slashed throat.

"Come in. It's clear," he said into his mike.

Montagna and Irthing in one boat, Mahim and Dill in the other, activated detonators on their packs, sliding them into the water against the dam's rear. The explosives sank quickly, down to the deep, muddy bottom, close to the concrete.

The boats bumped against the dam, next to the penstock piping, huge ribbed tubes over a meter in diameter. Al Sharif braced on one pipe and clambered out of his boat, while Dill tossed his pack atop another pipe, pulled himself onto the dam, braced against the ribbing.

The moon came from behind a cloud, and al Sharif saw Dill motion upward with his chin. They shouldered their packs, and started upward. The grade was about 80 percent, but the ribbing on the pipes every half meter or so made it fairly easy to pull themselves upward.

Nectan, below, motioned the other boat to pull back, away from the dam's face. He should've headed for the shore, but waited, in case one of the climbers fell.

Al Sharif went up and up, climbing easily, getting his second wind. Dill paused, feeling the strain in his arms, adjusting his pack strap, and let the *Finf* go past him.

They were twenty meters above the water, thirty, forty, and the parapet was above them, and to the right the control house.

Al Sharif reached the top, slid out of his pack straps, and rolled the heavy pack over, onto the rampart. He reached back, grinning, to give Dill a hand he really didn't need when a man came out of the control room, lifting a blaster.

Al Sharif heard the scuffle of his boots, turned, saw the leveled gun, put his hand up to push away the bolt just as the man shot him in the face. Al Sharif was instantly dead, falling.

Ben Dill had him by the back of his collar, knee all that was holding him on the dam face, his other hand grabbing the monstrous handgun he always carried. It went off with a crack, as the blaster above was swinging toward him, and the man spun, fell.

Dill felt his center of gravity overbalance, was about to fall. He let his knees sag, regained his balance. He stuffed the pistol inside his shirt, scrabbled for a hold, concrete tearing at his hand. He had a grip then, and, dragging al Sharif's body, he went up the pipe and over the parapet.

There were two darknesses coming toward him, and he reached for the pistol.

"Sibyl," one of them said, and he recognized Garvin's voice. Dill took one look at al Sharif's head, most of which was missing, and let the body drop.

"No," Garvin said. "Over the far side with him. We don't want anyone to know if we took hurt."

Dill hurled al Sharif's body over the parapet, down into the rocky valley.

They heard shouts, saw lights coming toward them along the rampart beyond the control room.

"Ben," Garvin said, "take care of the charges. We'll sort these people out."

Dill grabbed al Sharif's pack and went, a crouching bulk in the night, into the open door.

Garvin and Lir flattened, slid the safeties off their SSWs, and opened fire. Bolts spat down the rampart, ricocheted off concrete, exploded into bodies, and the screaming began.

"Back of us," Monique said, turning, seeing the rest of the guards running toward them, idiotically illuminating themselves with portable lights.

Garvin thumbed a grenade, lofted it toward the first eight at the control room, sent another behind it. After the double explosion, even his ringing ears couldn't hear any sounds of life.

Then Monique sent most of a drum across the bridge, into the second guard element.

Dill trotted out of the control room. "Anytime you want to depart's just fine with me."

On the other side of the dam, lights were going on in the guards' compound.

" 'Kay," Garvin said, changing drums. "I guess we'll take our chances on whatever's on this side, and figure out some way to cross back over when we're clear." He touched his mike. "This is Garvin. One Keld Ind Alf. Where are you?"

"Look down," Nectan's voice came, bone-inducted against Garvin's breastbone.

He did, saw the two boats waiting.

"Goddamned insubordinate bastards," he growled

happily, pulling rope from his pack, double-looping it around a finial on the parapet.

"Monique. You go."

"Your ass."

"That's an order!"

She gave him a foul look, but slid quickly down the rope, and a boat came to meet her. Dill followed.

Garvin let about a hundred rounds chatter down the parapet, just as, in the boat, Monique Lir triggered the small charge of explosive she'd left just on the far side of the pressure sensor.

Jaansma slung his SSW and rappelled down the dam's rear. He let himself go too fast, burned his hands, splashed into water to his knees, and hands were grabbing at him, pulling him into the boat.

"Row like hell," he said. "I want to get this thing over with."

The Kuran soldiers might have been sloppy, but no one could slight their bravery. The ranking noncom, all officers down in the brief firefights, crept forward, some of his men behind him, the others across the rampart.

No one shot at him, and he saw no movement ahead.

He rolled the igniter on an illumination grenade, threw it far ahead. It went off, and he saw nothing but sprawled bodies.

The two boats had reached the shore away from the control room, on the same side of the lake as the guards' compound, when Garvin saw the flare of the illums.

"Mister Dill? Mister Nectan?"

Dill, grim-faced, thumbed the two det switches as Nectan did the same.

The four charges blew at the same time. Dill had planted his against the penstock gates, and the blast sent them pinwheeling up, and the control room splitting apart.

The other two, deep underwater, blasted at the same time, and silver boiled up as the blast crashed against the concrete wall.

Perhaps the dam had been improperly surveyed and laid on a fault, perhaps the contractor had fiddled the concrete mix, perhaps over the years the dam was naturally breaking up.

The blast should have cracked the dam wall enough for water pressure to slowly tear it away. Instead, a good third of the dam folded forward, dropping into the valley, and water avalanched, taking control room, turbines, and the power station below with it.

The soldiers on the wall had no time to run, swept over the wall with the current.

A great wall of water, seventy-five meters high, rushed down the canyon, obliterating the guards' compound.

There were small villages perched amid the rocks farther down. The water swept them away as if they'd never been.

Five kilometers downstream, the canyon widened into a valley. The water rushed through it, killing herding animals, sleeping villagers, even a scattering of Redruth's soldiers, and roared on.

Another twelve kilometers away, the water boiled into a second, larger reservoir, and another wave rose, smashed across the lake against the greater dam. One powerhouse was shattered, the other's controls were ruined.

But the dam held, and the city below wasn't destroyed.

" 'Kay," Garvin said, as the booming echoes of the wave died against the valley walls. "Now let's get on back to the RP. Tomorrow we'll wander downstream, take a look at whatever damage we did, decide whether we'll have to blow that second dam."

He turned to Dill.

"Ready?"

"I wonder," the big man said slowly, "if I'd been in front, I would've had time to drop that asshole."

"Come on, Ben. What's past is past, who's dead is dead."

"Yeh. Yeh. Now I'll never get a chance to do paybacks for that goddamned fart of his."

The seven soldiers picked up their weapons, packs, moved away into darkness.

A half day later, after they'd maneuvered past the ruined dam, the lake draining, its blue waters now muddy, the lake villages far distant from the water, they reached a hillcrest, and Garvin was able to see the second dam and its reservoir.

" 'Kay, gang. Bad news. We didn't take out the second dam. We're going to do a reprise, but this time louder and funnier."

But two E-hours later, a shot came from behind them, was echoed by two more ahead.

They were being tracked.

CHAPTER
10

Larix/Larix Prime

"You notice," Maev went on, "we're in a nice, isolated corridor, where there aren't any big or small ears. I swept it myself before I ambushed you."

"Young woman," Njangu said, flailing, trying to sound paternal, someone far too old to have been a recruit within this person's lifetime, "I have no idea at all what you're talking about."

"I'm not wired."

"Only the fact that I have the greatest respect for Protector Redruth and his Protector's Own is keeping me from calling for a guard and having you taken away for mental examination. Perhaps, Commander, you've been working too hard lately."

Maev's smile slipped a bit, then came back as Njangu took a notebook from his pocket and scribbled an address on one side, a note on the other:

> *Pass the bearer into my quarters.*
> *Ab Yohns*

He flashed ten fingers once, nine fingers again.

"Very careful, Njangu," Maev said. "Nothing incriminating at all. And remember, I don't know if you're wearing a wire, either.

"But I'll take the chance. I'm desperate to get the hell out of this trap I'm in, and I figure if you found a way in, you'll have set up a way out."

She snapped a salute, pivoted, and hurried away. Njangu watched her go, hoping his face didn't show how worried he was.

By the evening, Njangu had recovered and even made a plan, assuming Maev wasn't Redruth's, Celidon's, or some unknown enemy's, agent. A plan of sorts, anyway, that involved what one of his goons had told him on the day he'd gone to work for Njangu.

Yoshitaro thoroughly swept his office, both with instruments and visually, then told his bodyguards and his staff he was having an important meeting this night and didn't want to be disturbed for *any* reason. The only reaction was from one of his companions, Brythe: "My, my. A *fifth* one to join us? Have we started taking vitamin supplements?"

"Why couldn't it be a secret meeting with Protector Redruth? Or Fleet Commander Celidon?"

"You wouldn't look guilty if you were meeting either of those *Leiters*."

Yoshitaro made a noncommittal noise, wondering if he was really cut out for being a spy.

Maev showed up exactly on time, befitting an army officer. But she wore an outfit more in keeping with a streetwalker, black net pants and a matching shirt that stopped below her breasts. Her black hair was cut as short as Njangu's.

Njangu blinked in surprise, but said nothing until they were in the safe room.

"You came prepared for a body search? Although, wearing that, there's surely no need."

"Don't be an asshole," Maev said. "Don't you think I'm watched, too?"

Njangu shook his head, pretending he didn't understand.

"I'm assuming somebody saw the two of us talking today," Maev went on, "and might wonder what a Commander and a top *Leiter* might have in common. I'm giving them the obvious answer. All the butt-

breath men who run Larix/Kura think that every
woman would give her firstborn to bed them."

"Oh. Sorry. Would you like a drink? Or something
to eat? My kitchen staff is still on duty," Njangu said.

"I ate at the officers' mess," Maev said. "As for
drinking, I don't drink much, and never when
there's business."

"Well forgive me all to hell for being an alcoholic,"
Njangu said, going to the bar. However, he contented
himself with a beer.

"Here's where we stand," Maev said briskly, sitting
in a plush chair, but not relaxing. "If you're really Ab
Yohns, the Protector's own spy against Cumbre, you
have me on toast, since you could have a dozen bugs
around the room.

"But I don't think you are, as I said. Your inviting
me here makes me even more sure."

"I could," Njangu said, "be subtly sucking you in, to
find out what other Cumbrian confederates you have."

"That would fit with the Protector's thinking,"
Maev agreed, "and probably get me pumped full of
talkee-talkee drugs, which means, with a good interrogator, I'd blab that I think you're Njangu Yoshitaro . . . I remembered your real last name about an
hour ago . . . which wouldn't do your career any good
at all. Would it?"

"No," Njangu agreed. " 'Kay. No games. I'm . . .
who you think I am." He wondered why he was so
reluctant to speak his name. "And by the way, back
on the *Malvern,* I don't remember taking the time to
look at your name tag."

"Maev Stiofan." She relaxed a little. "Yeh. We
were . . . busy, weren't we?" A tiny smile appeared.

"So give me the hot word on what happened to
you," Njangu asked, "after Celidon took the ship and
I made my exit."

Maev was very brief. The recruits had been taken
to Larix, scattered through various formation, and put
through Redruth's harsh training. "I'd enlisted in the

Confederation military for communications training, thinking that'd be a skill I could use anywhere once I got out, since I wasn't exactly thrilled by the idea of spending the rest of my life on the farm world I grew up on. I realized, a little late, just after signing the contract, I didn't want to spend all my time sitting with a com in my ear. I didn't have much interest in hiking through the mud, either.

"So when I got to Redruth's personnel office, I applied for, and was trained, in long-distance communications with a Zhukov squadron . . . that was the Confederation designation. We call them Ayeshas. They're—"

"I know what they are," Njangu said. "We use them on Cumbre, too."

Redruth required all able-bodied men and women to serve three years, one training, one in branch training, one in active service.

"A surprisingly large chunk of those troops with anything going for them end up in the fleet," she said. "Redruth evidently thinks starships are his primary protection. The army, in spite of its size, is mostly a super police force. Not that there's any Resistance. He and his father and grandfather ground everybody down so well nobody even thinks about the possibility of change."

"That's what I've seen, too," Njangu agreed. "A hard goddamned regime to overthrow."

"Which is why I assume you're on Larix Prime," Maev said. "Redruth's been making noises about Cumbre being rightfully his since I was a ranker."

She looked desperate. "Njangu, is Cumbre in touch with the Confederation? What the hell is going on, anyway? We don't ever find out anything, and I'm not dumb enough to believe Redruth's propaganda machine."

Njangu told her what they knew of the Confederation's evident collapse.

"So our media wasn't lying. What happened? Does anybody know?"

"We know just what I told you, no more. Maybe things out there aren't as bad as they're presented, and there hasn't been a complete collapse. I hope. Go back to your story."

Maev survived the somewhat brutish barracks by being very quick with an equalizer, whether a kick in the crotch or a roll of coins hidden in her fist, and even quicker with a scheme. "Nice military Redruth's got. Nobody seems to give a shit if a warrant takes it in his . . . or her . . . mind to order a lower ranker into bed, or to give up a meal here or there, or shine boots or become a goddamned servant. A one-striper gets screwed by a two-striper, a two-striper . . . you get it.

"Plus there's legalized dueling for warrants and officers. You can only challenge an equal or inferior, although generally someone who outranks you and wants you out of the picture just arranges for you to be transferred to some asteroid space suit. And somehow there's a lot of people who just 'happened' to take over their superior's slot after a duel for which the superior was dumb enough to issue a challenge.

"I'm amazed there's any military at all. But I have to admit it's passing efficient," Maev grudged, "even if it seems to kill as many of its own as anybody else."

"So why'd you stay in? It's been almost five years, and you said the enlistment was for three."

"The military sucks fungi, but it's better than being at the bottom rung as a goddamned peasant," Maev said. "If you've got any intelligence, don't mind work, and volunteer every now and then, that automatically sets you apart from three-quarters of the poor buggers they drag kicking and screaming into uniform. So you get noticed and get promoted.

"After a while I realized the Ayeshas weren't the answer, did what seemed necessary with some people who paid their debts and ended up being recommended for officer training, which was a bigger pile of shit then enlisted training, then got myself assigned to the Protector's Own.

"I figured, close to Redruth, here in the palace, here in Agur, maybe I could find some way to get the hell out. But nothing came up until I saw your smiling face.

"So what happened to *you,* and what're you doing here?"

Njangu gave her an abbreviated version of his travels, and how he'd come to replace the late Ab Yohns.

"A mole, eh?" Maev mused. "Get in, report . . . can I ask how you report?"

"No. Sorry."

"I wouldn't tell anybody either. Anyway, so you report and then get out when the getting's good. I assume you've got a back door and can make it fit two people, which is why I'm here."

"Actually, I don't."

Maev blinked. "Are you suicidal?"

"Just dumb. The theory was I'd hold in place, doing what I could, until war started, then talk about extraction."

"Which won't be long," Maev said. "I've heard rumors we sent a mission against Cumbre."

"You did. Nuclear-type," Njangu said. "Everything's very classified, but Celidon's claiming significant damage on D-Cumbre, that's our capital world. I don't know if it's true or not."

"Will Cumbre declare war?"

"I'm sort of surprised we haven't already."

Maev looked at him closely. "I get the idea that you're not exactly in touch with your high command. Or are you just being very, very careful?"

"You *are* clever," Njangu said, deciding to take a chance and tell the truth. "I've got a way of sending data, but no way of receiving. The powers that be don't like anyone, not even a Leiter, having access to an interstellar com setup, and I haven't figured a way around it yet."

"But *I've* got one," Maev said smugly. "I assume that you know a frequency that might be transmitting to you?"

"I do."

"Given the numb-nuts I'm in charge of, and all the com gear that's lying around, I could have a dozen coms listening to any damned frequency I want. I'll throw that into the deal."

"I'll take you up on that," Njangu said. "However, I've got a better proposition . . . or, anyway, one you might be interested in. When you're a muckety like me, you get to pretty much requisition any people you think you want."

"No kidding," Maev said. "I've had three *Leiters* who thought I'd be just perfect guarding their mattress perimeter."

"Make that four. Hang on a second before you beat me bloody," Njangu said. When I was looking at the Protector's Own, I noticed there's a certain number of your troops that're just a little bit on the overly dedicated side."

"Yeh," Maev said. "We call them the Death-or-Glory Kids. Not very loudly, though. Any one of those idiots'd cheerfully nark us off as traitors if it got them an autographed pic of Redruth."

"Are these people dumb enough to, say, take over a spaceship if they were told it was part of an exercise?"

"They'd insert it in their butts if I ordered them to," Maev said, her voice excited. "So that'll be your way off?"

"Maybe. Or maybe I'm just looking at setting up an exit. I'm not ready to scarper yet," Njangu said.

"Good," Maev said. "I become your bedwarmer, plus you've now got a private army of a couple dozen D or G idiots."

"That was sort of what I was thinking."

"So I guess I'm spending the night, you incredibly

masculine *Leiter,* you, and I'll stumble out in the morning, eyes dazed with your passion and potency."

"You get the bed," Njangu said. "I'll stack some cushions on the floor."

Maev looked at him in astonishment.

"Don't be stupid. Or do you think your maids, your laundry people, your servants don't see everything and talk about it later, or not see anything, like marks of wild passion on the sheets?

"Besides, I've thought back, on what we were doing back on the *Malvern* more than once, especially since I blew in your ear, not the other way around. Remembering that's kept me from throwing up sometimes when I was with other people who weren't nearly that much fun."

The next day, after Njangu digested and tried to analyze a surprising com from Redruth, Goons Alpha and Beta were introduced to Commander Stiofan and told of the planned increase in the security detachment. They seemed to approve of having others who could take care of the scutwork that went with security, so they could specialize in looking lean and mean in public places.

Njangu ordered Kerman, his head of household, to see to the housing of Maev and her detachment.

"I assume, sir, you'll want her bedroom next to the other four?"

"Uh . . . for the moment, anyway."

Strangely, Njangu felt a little uncomfortable about his companions. He pushed that aside.

"I'll be away on an inspection tour with the Protector."

Kerman looked impressed.

"The Protector Himself, sir? What an honor, sir. For how long, sir?"

"I have no idea. I just got invited. I don't even know what I'm going to be inspecting."

*   *   *

Protector Redruth beamed down proudly, his face ruddy in the reflection of the blast furnace. Below the catwalk the hull of a ship was moved surely, quickly, by robot handlers through the stages of assembly.

"This plant," Redruth shouted in Yoshitaro's ear, "can produce a destroyer, almost as big as my *Corfe*, in six weeks. And there's three others like them on Prime, another two building on Secundus. Not bad, considering I ordered their construction just over two years ago, when the Musth problems were building, and I was prescient enough to realize Larix and Kura needed greater protection.

"They'll be the start of my battle fleet, that one day might reach as far as the heart of what was once the Confederation!"

Yoshitaro wondered why Redruth was showing him all this. The answer came quickly:

"When we make a real assault on Cumbre, not the mosquito raid that went so well before, there'll be ships like this swarming the system.

"Ships like this . . . and others. So you'll have no fears about our total victory."

Redruth smiled mysteriously.

"Once this ship is complete, the factory will go off-line, retooling for greater things."

He didn't elaborate, but turned to Celidon and his flanking staff and patted the sweating, fat plant manager on the shoulder.

"This man has done well. Very well indeed. He shall be raised to the *Leiter* class, and given great rewards, to inspire his fellows."

Njangu thought the fat man was going to kiss Redruth.

Celidon enlightened Yoshitaro on the flight back to Agur.

"The Protector has great ideas," he said, and there was no sign of appreciation in his voice.

"I am aware of that."

"Not in the instance shown today, you weren't."

Njangu showed interest.

"That factory, as the Protector told you, has been designated to begin production of a new class of ship. Are you familiar with any of the Confederation battle cruisers?"

Yoshitaro wasn't, other than from action holos he'd snored through as a boy. But Ab Yohns, having spent much time on Centrum, undoubtedly would know something.

"A bit," Yoshitaro said carefully.

"Perhaps you recall the *Naarohn*-class?"

"Not at the moment. I'm sorry, I was always more interested in finding out specific economic plans for the Protector when I was within the Confederation."

"Mmmh. Well, you might look the *Naarohns* up when you get back to your office. Protector Redruth plans for his new ships to be at least fifty meters longer, and far more heavily armed, than any of those ships were.

"Other, even greater creations wait in the wings for his approval."

Yoshitaro put a pleased expression on his face, then a questioning look.

"You seen to disapprove, Fleet Commander. I don't understand."

"Because," Celidon said, speaking as if to a child, "the Confederation is . . . was . . . a great empire. It takes such an empire to support a great fleet. And a fleet is more than copies of obsolescent ships like the *Corfe,* and a scattering of dreadnoughts. Big ships need big support and big escort.

"I expect I'm wrong," Celidon said, and Yoshitaro realized he was speaking to any possible monitors, "and Protector Redruth is more than capable of leading such a great fleet, and I shall do all I can to aid him.

"In fact, I'm sure there shall be no problems."

But Celidon's face suggested quite the opposite.

* * *

Njangu read the entry on the screen, lips pursed. The *Naarohns* had flush turrets here, there, everywhere, tubes launching antiship and bombardment missiles twice the size of the Goddards. Huge, almost two kilometers long. Antimissile batteries everywhere. No chainguns, but who needed them with such firepower?

Then he noted the entry at the bottom:

Class abandoned because of in-atmosphere lack of maneuverability, plus large crew requirements.

Still, he thought, one of those, loose in Cumbre's system, could do an enormous amount of damage, just standing off D-Cumbre and lofting missiles in-atmosphere.

There was a tap at the door.

"Enter," he said in the lofty manner of a *Leiter,* and Maev came in, wearing lounging pajamas.

"And how did your day with his never to be sufficiently praised majesty go?"

"Very interesting. And yours?"

"Nicely. I'm now officially transferred to your command, resident within this complex, drawing separate rations, and with an allowance for, get this, appropriate clothing to be determined by my new commander, which is you.

"Twenty-four of the most dedicated, most eager, most drooling of the Protector's Own will arrive within a day or so. *And* I had time to make the acquaintance of your companions."

Njangu hoped he wasn't blushing, wondered why he would be.

"*Leiter* Yohns, I must say, you are a pervert. Sir."

Njangu *knew* his face was flushed.

"The devices and ways you cavort, sir, is shameful," Maev went on. "If I'd known that, before I agreed to accept your . . . offer, well, Shiva with a slingball knows what my response would've been."

Njangu had just an instant to notice she was smiling when the com buzzed a series of bleating EMER-GENCIES.

He touched a sensor, and a harried officer came on-screen.

"*Leiter* Yohns, sir. This is Protector Redruth's headquarters. This com is directly from the Protector. He advises you to be ready to accompany him aboard ship within the hour."

"Of course," Njangu said, feeling slight alarm. "I'll be ready in ten minutes. Might I ask the problem?"

"The Protector has advised us that Cumbrian raiders have landed on Kura Four and committed atrocities. They have been located, though, and are being tracked.

"The Protector is leaving to supervise their capture or killing at once, and requires your immediate presence and assistance."

CHAPTER
11

Kura/Kura Four

The team acted smoothly, as they'd been trained. Half kept moving, the rest slid into brush, spread out, waited. About an hour later, three uniformed men came up the trail, moving cautiously.

Garvin waited until they were very close, then hammered a burst from his SSW into them. One had time to shriek, then fell with the others.

Jaansma wasted a few seconds searching the corpses, then the team moved on, joining up with the others in half an hour.

Garvin waited until they hit a stream, pointed downhill. He didn't want to use radios unless they had to—whoever was after them might've stumbled on the frequency and was direction finding any coms.

The team slid down the rocky, muddy incline for three hundred meters.

Garvin snapped his fingers, pointed to Irthing and Heckmyer, motioned for them to keep moving . . . a finger held up, then thumb and first finger touching twice . . . one hundred meters.

They nodded.

The rest crept up the stream bank, flattened, waiting.

Less than an hour later, they heard movement above them. A rock tumbled past Lir's head, and, through the brush, they saw two men coming down the stream.

Garvin pointed to Lir, and Montagna. Motioned twice—a thumb across the throat.

Kill them.

A finger to his lips.

Silently.

The two women put their blasters aside, drew their combat knives. Garvin motioned to Dill to be ready for any backup.

They waited until the men were just past them, then leapt out. The second man grunted as Montagna's knife went into his kidneys, and Lir's target dropped silently, her knife driving down into his neck.

They rolled the bodies out of the rivulet, to keep blood out of the stream. Garvin pointed to Mahim, then down stream. His fingers twiddled, like a man walking, toward him. Mahim, moving as silently as she knew how, brought Irthing and Heckmyer back.

Garvin pointed along the slope. It'd be hellish walking, but they'd be less likely to be discovered than if they went back uphill, or down to whatever might be below.

His fingers formed two letters . . . *C* and *M*. Climax Mass.

Continue the mission. The large dam was still their target.

At dark, they went back to the bivvy site Garvin had picked an hour earlier. They ate, then half stayed ready, the other half pretended sleep.

The night passed very, very slowly. Twice something moved in the brush near them. Grenades were readied, then the something moved on, making animal noises.

Before dawn, they saddled up. At first light, they started off. They'd gone only a dozen meters when Lir, on slack, signaled for a freeze. She tapped her shoulders, and Garvin moved up beside her.

"I got that feeling again," she whispered.

Garvin made a face, waited.

"Now it's gone," she said, after a while. "Sorry, boss. Prob'ly just a chill."

"You keep telling us when you chill," he ordered.

Lir nodded reluctantly.

They crept on for the rest of that morning, stopped for noon rations. Garvin went to Froude, leaned close.

"Opinion, Doctor. Monique's too good for me not to take her shivers seriously. What's she reacting to?"

"Science doesn't allow for ooee-ooee," Froude said. "And I don't believe in things that only one person can see on a screen, like Alikhan claimed, especially when there's no hard data in the input."

"So I should ignore her?"

"You're the boss," Froude said. "But if I were running things, I sure as hell wouldn't."

"You're a mountain of help."

Garvin put his ration pak on the ground with the others, triggered the destruct charge. A tiny flame spurted, went out. Garvin wrinkled his nose, smelling shit. Someone had used his empty ration pak to defecate in, and destroyed it with the rest. The smell was gone in seconds.

Garvin changed point, slack, tail gunner, signaled to move on.

Perhaps a kilometer later, they heard the whine of aircraft overhead, orbiting them. Not long afterward came another gunshot from behind.

Garvin considered the options, held up a finger for the team to assemble.

"This is *not* goddamned working," he announced.

No one needed to say anything. Their scared, angry, worn faces said everything.

"We'll abort going after the other dam, go straight up and deep into the hills, breaking contact, then get extraction in to pick us up.

"Dill, gimme the handset."

Ben passed the microphone across.

"You're live, boss."

Garvin checked his map, assumed where they

should be, where he thought they could go that might be safe, touched the mike's RECORD sensor.

"Sibyl Six," he said, and the recorder automatically scrambled the transmission. "First target destroyed. In contact, no shooting yet. Aborting. Moving Nan Nan Wef toward point Climax Keld. ETA approx two days. Will try to break contact, then need immediate extract. Out." The com compressed the transmission, shot it out toward the positioned satellite.

Garvin waited. Just as he was about to touch the button for a retransmit, Dill nodded painfully as a double-squelch squealed into his headphone.

" 'Kay, troops. They heard us. Let's hike."

They went back up the mountain, muscles tearing, lungs pulling for air. Just before the crest, there was a break in the cover. Garvin heard aircraft noise again, chanced looking up with binocs, saw two ships, looking like Zhukovs, cruise past. After a moment, two more came in sight.

The team moved around the fringes of the break, crested the hill. Once more, they heard the sound of a gunshot, from immediately below them.

Two other shots came from either side, as if other trackers were coming up the slope, flanking them.

Are they following us, or driving us? Garvin wondered. Not that it mattered much.

He had Nectan and Montagna ready a booby trap while he watched downslope. He saw movement near the break, focused his binocs on it.

Garvin saw men in uniform, with two people in native garb at their head.

Native trackers for guides. Guess the locals don't mind Redruth's government that much. Or they're pissed at us breaking up their fishing hole. If my people set the bang right, they're gonna get madder in a bit.

He slid the binocs back into their case, moved backward to the team, nodding, thumb down on one hand, then pointing downhill.

They're there.

They waited until the aerial searchers had passed on, went over the crest and down once more, moving quickly. Lir found a trail, made a question mark.

Garvin nodded. Take it. We've got to put some distance on.

The trail wound down and down, through a deserted village. They were almost at the bottom of the slope when the booby trap went off, a dull thud above them. Thin screams filtered through the jungle.

I hope we got the guides.

Alikhan's *Velv* sped toward Kura Four, two *aksai* escorting him. He'd planned to take a polar orbit, then, when the team on the ground signaled, swoop in after them.

The control room was silent, except for necessary commands. The com officer had patched the signal from Garvin's com into the main speakers, and everyone listened to the silence, hoped for another 'cast.

An alarm shrilled. Alikhan's human XO looked at a screen.

"We have two large ships, two smaller ships, four escorts on-screen, in close orbit off Kura Four. They have detected us. I've slaved the pickup to the escorts."

"Can we evade?"

"Negative, sir. They've got us in three . . . four detector beams."

Alikhan suggested jumping to the far side of Kura Four, trying a different approach.

"You can try, sir," the other officer said. "But I don't think that's enough of a distance for them not to pick us up again."

Alikhan thought.

"I promised," he said.

"Pardon, sir?"

"Nothing. We'll—"

"I have a launch . . . two launches from the smallest

ships. Both have us targeted," the weapons officer said.

Alikhan's eyes reddened, his ears cocked.

"Take us out of here."

"Yes, sir. All Confederation units . . . stand by to jump . . . NOW."

The *velv* and *aksai* vanished into N-Space, seconds before the pair of shipkillers flashed through the space they'd occupied.

Garvin scanned the ridges ahead. He saw no sign of settlements, roads, or anything else except jungle.

He motioned the team forward, and they lurched, exhausted, across the crest and down a few meters. They crouched, hidden by the scrub brush.

Garvin heard turbine whine and swore at being this much in the open—if the oncoming ships had infrared monitors on, the team would stand out like they were carrying searchlights.

The roar got louder, louder than any aerial combat vehicle could produce. Half a dozen Larissan freighters—starships, probably troop transports—flew overhead, escorted by patrol craft. One landed atop a nearby ridge. Through his binocs, Garvin saw ramps drop, and the ship spilled troops out. Another one landed on a second crest, did the same.

"Double-time out of here," he said aloud, and the team went downhill, hoping to hide in the thickest jungle.

They came to a clearing where a village had been—they saw spiky remnants of lodge poles, where fields had once been cleared, now almost completely overgrown by jungle.

Garvin held up his hand, and the team sagged against anything, wanting to collapse, knowing better. The farther you went down, the harder it was to get up.

" 'Kay," he said, in a normal voice, involuntarily flinching at the volume. "We'll dump the droppers here. Maybe they're tracking us by their power paks.

I don't know if that's possible, but they *are* emitting power. Stack them neatly, side by side, like we'd just taken them off for a breather and were gonna come back this way. Monique, put timers on the explosives for . . . two hours."

"Better idea, boss," she suggested. "Howzabout antihandling devices and, just in case they're that careful, timers for tomorrow about dawn?"

"You're right, That's better," Garvin said. "We'll lug patrol packs. The only thing to take is iron rats, as much ammo and grenades as you can carry, and water. Dump everything except your personal weapons. Keep your radios, but leave 'em off, in case they're tracking us that way.

"We'll smoke on deeper into the hills, hope we can lie low long enough for them to give up, then we'll try for an extract.

"Deb, give Monique a hand with the charges.

"Five minutes. We're going to run these bastards into the ground, then stomp 'em while they're wheezing for air.

"Oh yeh. Keep your Search and Rescue beacons handy."

Which fairly ruined his nice little bit of dishonest optimism. Not that it mattered. Nobody, including Garvin, had believed it anyway.

Five minutes later, they were ready to march. Garvin saw Ben Dill still had his Shrike and launcher on his shoulders, was about to say something, then saw Dill's stubborn face and saved himself the effort.

One ridgeline later, Froude pointed back.

"Garvin. Look. Here they come."

Jaansma could see a long column of troops, but Froude hadn't needed keen vision. Hovering over the column was one of the transports, following closely.

"Prob'ly got their li'l nappie-poo binkies aboard, so they don't have to suffer," Nectan said.

"It ain't polite to 'cast jealousy that loudly," Montagna suggested.

Nectan grinned, turned back to the march.

If they're that dumb to broadcast their presence, maybe they'll be dumber, once they get down into the valley, Garvin thought. A more disquieting thought came: *Maybe they're not dumb at all. Maybe there's so goddamned many of them they just don't give a rat's earlobe who sees them coming.*

An hour later, the ground rumbled, shook, and a blast wave washed over the trees above them.

"Look!" Heckmyer pointed. High overhead spun one of the transports, gouting flame from both ends like a play rocket.

"Must've been right overhead when all that Telex with the paks blew. Think that'll discourage 'em, boss?"

"Not a chance, Val," Garvin said. "More likely piss them off a lot larger."

Just before they found a bivouac site, Lir felt that shiver, once, then again. No one wanted to move, but they did, forcing another kilometer before they stopped. Just after they let their packs slide off, explosions thudded through the jungle. Garvin sent Dill up a tree with binocs. He slid back down.

"Looks like somebody's lobbing artillery or maybe mortar rounds back where we used to be."

Garvin, and some others, considered Monique Lir thoughtfully.

Near midnight, Montagna pulled Garvin's leg. He was a bit surprised that he came awake instantly, weapon ready. Montagna pointed up, through the thick cover.

Lights moved slowly past, far overhead. A starship. A big starship. To one side flew another, then a third ship, smaller, then another big craft.

I guess, Garvin thought, *we can kiss off any immediate extraction. Not even Alikhan could get around all those bastards. So what we'll have to do is lose our tails, eat bushes for a couple of weeks, and then try again. Hoping our pickup hasn't been chased all the way out of the system.*

He thought wistfully of Jasith, wondered if he'd ever see her again, decided it didn't seem likely, put his head back down, and was instantly asleep.

They kept moving for two days. No one wanted to look at anyone else, not needing a reminder of how haggard, exhausted, filthy, and scared they were. At least there was enough water in the frequent pools and streams they crossed. Twice they saw fish in pools, chanced dropping poison from their survival packs, and scooped up fish to eat raw later.

They only stopped at night. The Zhukov-like ACVs, spaceships, other craft constantly orbited overhead. When the team hit high ground, they could see, from time to time, columns of soldiers pushing after them. Garvin thought there were four columns, Lir opted for five.

Monique's strange feelings came regularly. Froude wondered, since it appeared there were some sort of invisible beings helping their pursuers, how the hell Redruth's men were able to get them to cooperate.

"This could be an interesting field for an anthropology team to investigate," he said.

Garvin couldn't believe the man, who had to be twice Garvin's age, could still sound enthusiastic, when all he wanted to do was curl up in a soft bed of leaves and sleep for a week.

"Well Mother Mary with a hangover," Dill said, staring at the ruins that spread before them.

"What the hell kind of city is this?" Darod Montagna asked in a whisper.

"One people didn't build," Dill said.

That deduction didn't require much logic. Those buildings that still sort of stood, or tilted crazily with trees growing over, through, between them, would have been three or more stories tall. The only entrances that could be made out would have been ten meters above the ground.

"Maybe they used ladders," Nectan whispered. For some reason, having nothing to do with the Kurans behind them, it seemed right to whisper.

"Maybe this leads to something, somewhere we can duck for cover," Garvin said hopefully. "I'll take point. Monique slack."

Weapons ready, they started forward, down what had been a very wide avenue.

Dill wondered how old the ruins were, guessed, since the jungle had completely overgrown the city, old. Very, very old. Behind him, Froude was trying to figure first what sort of beings built this city, and what the purpose of the various buildings, some nearly whole, others fallen rubble, had been.

There were wall carvings, but they gave no clue about the builders, being entirely abstract to the human eye.

Maybe those invisible suckers built this place, Garvin thought. *Maybe they weren't that invisible, a long, long time ago, or maybe they couldn't fly, and when they learned, they walked off from their cities.*

Too wild, too wild, troop. Keep your eyes moving, looking for trouble.

"Look," Monique said, pointing down a cross street. Far away, almost a kilometer, Garvin saw the glint of water. He turned the team down the street.

The closer they got, the bigger the river got, maybe seventy-five meters across, the trees on its banks almost meeting in the center.

We can build a boat, or some kind of raft, Garvin thought, and then he saw the grounded ACV, just as a chaingun chattered, blowing a stone column in half and sending the building it barely supported crashing.

They hadn't quite walked into the ambush, but almost. They tumbled, rolled, ran for cover, weapons spraying.

Nectan saw a cluster of heads around a mortar tube,

stayed in the open, and blew half a drum through them. He started to roll away, wasn't quick enough, and the cannon caught him, chewed at his body, and spat it away.

Lir, flat, had the Zhukov's turret in her sights. She held firm and fired at the open hatch. Rounds slammed against metal, ricocheted down into the body of the ACV. They heard a muffled explosion, screams, and a burning woman crawled out of the hatch, waving her arms.

Montagna sniped the woman in the heart, was almost shot down before she could find better cover.

Garvin fired, killed her attacker, and the three behind him.

Now the team had cover. Fire lulled for a moment. The Kurans, emboldened, started to move forward, and every man . . . or woman . . . who was in the open died.

A loudspeaker boomed: "Cumbrian soldiers! You are trapped! Surrender now, and our Protector will let you live! Surrender or die!"

The team held one end of a multisided square, the Kurans the far end, close to the water. Garvin saw another Zhukov nosing forward, behind the flaming ruin of the first, fired at it, saw his rounds spang off armor.

Over the battle sound came a louder roaring. Garvin looked up, saw one of the transports hovering forward.

"Eat me," Ben Dill screamed, stood, his Shrike launcher aimed. He triggered the missile, and it shot off. A Kuran thought he had a target, just as Danfin Froude blocked Dill at the knees, dropping him as rounds rang off the stones around him.

The Shrike couldn't miss a target that big, that close. The transport shuddered with the impact as the missile took it just behind the crew space. Nothing happened for an instant, then the transport rolled sideways, and its midsection gouted fire. The ship exploded, spraying fire and metal down across the ruins, over the water.

Garvin had a moment to hope the transport would give them a chance to break away, then two Zhukovs appeared on either side of the square, and a patrol craft dived down, missile tubes afire.

The ground roiled around them, and Garvin heard somebody scream.

"Break contact," he found himself shouting. "In pairs! E&E! E&E!"

Other voices took up the command, and Garvin, guts clenching as he realized he'd utterly lost this battle and most likely his life, grabbed Montagna by the back of her combat harness.

"Come on! We're gone!"

Montagna came to her knees, hurled a grenade, then was on her feet.

"After you," and the two zigged away, into the ruins.

The Kurans fired on for a time, then realized they weren't taking any return fire.

Now they'd have to hunt their prey down, two at a time.

Monique Lir and Jil Mahim moved stealthily down a narrow passageway, ducking under columns that leaned across the space, almost blocking it.

Lir darted across an open space, turned to cover the medic. Mahim came after her, and a pack strap caught on something. She was pulling at it when a grenade came from nowhere, and blew up. Mahim sagged.

Lir saw the man who'd thrown it, shot him just as two more grenades exploded. She had an instant to realize they were shock, not frag grenades, then the double blast sent her down, spinning into darkness.

The column of soldiers moved slowly down the street. A patrol ship orbited overhead.

Val Heckmyer was bandaging Deb Irthing's side, where she'd caught some shrapnel. Irthing was barely conscious, biting her lip, trying to hold back a moan.

Someone shouted, and Heckmyer dropped the bandage, grabbed his SSW.

The enemy column—maybe forty men—had turned, and saw him. They started forward, assault firing.

You can't kill them all if you don't kill one, Heckmyer reminded himself, and methodically started at the left, double-tapping the trigger of his SSW. Soldiers screamed, fell silently, grabbed at themselves, stumbled.

Something burned through Heckmyer's chest, and he saw blood, then another bullet hit him, lower, and that was tearing agony. He dropped the gun, clutched at the pain, and three more bullets tore into him.

Deb Irthing grabbed the SSW as Heckmyer dropped, brought it up, and two bullets struck her in the head. She flipped back, spasmed, and died.

"Come on," Garvin said. "We'll make the river, then swim downstream, go ashore in a while."

"Sounds good, boss," Montagna said, trying to smile, trying to appear as brave as she thought Jaansma was.

They came to the end of the street, moved up an alley, saw water in front of them.

"'Kay," Garvin said, trying to sound calm, wishing he was as unworried as Montagna, strangely thought she was as beautiful a woman, here, now, as he'd ever seen. "I hope you enjoy swimming."

"I'm an eel, boss."

They slung their weapons, moved into the open, to what might've been a dock. Garvin looked at the water, thought it looked deep, dark, fast-flowing, sucked deep breaths, packing his lungs with oxygen.

The Zhukov lifted out of the brush to their side. Its command cupola hatch was open, and two chainguns were aimed at them.

A speaker crackled.

"Do not move. Do not even breathe unless you want to be very dead."

CHAPTER
12

Kura/Off Kura Four

Protector Redruth's smile was terrible.

"We have the raiders. All of them. Dead or captured, and those that're still alive won't be for long. Cumbre's learned a hard lesson this day."

"What form of execution have you decided on?" Celidon asked as calmly as if they were discussing the weather on the planet below.

"I'm not sure," Redruth said. He looked around the ship's bridge, thinking. Then he turned to Njangu.

"I suppose you're not pleased you weren't able to be in at the kill, Yohns. Give you a bit of revenge for your own chase from pillar to post."

"I'm not a soldier," Njangu said. "I get just as much pleasure from seeing another do what's necessary as doing it myself."

Celidon curled a lip. "Who was it who said a spy's nothing more than a bureaucrat with ambitions?"

"No doubt some bureaucrat. Or admiral," Njangu said.

"Enough of that, both of you," Redruth said. "I have two questions, Yohns. What is the worst Cumbrian form of execution?"

"They have only one, no, two," Njangu said. "Public hanging for civilians, a firing squad for soldiers."

"Neither especially spectacular," Redruth mused. "Unless it happens there are terrible shots or the drunken hangman miscalculates the drop and either pulls his victim's head off or lets him strangle slowly. Not enough for my tastes. Does either of you . . . or any of you other staffers . . . have any ideas?"

Njangu, wondering if Garvin was one of the raiders and, if so, whether he was still alive, considered how to make a suggestion without bringing suspicion.

Celidon saved him.

"I don't know about how to kill them, nor especially care," he said. "I'm sure *someone* can come up with *something* to meet your desires, Protector. But I think simply executing them isn't gaining full use of these bandits."

"Continue, *Leiter* Efficiency," said Redruth, evidently a little angry at the implication he was a sadist.

"I think a show trial would be of interest to our citizenry," Celidon went on. "It would give us a chance to expose completely the villainy of the Cumbrians, to verify what our propaganda experts have been accusing them of for so long."

"It would also," Redruth interrupted, "give us a chance to discover what allies they have, both down there on Four, and elsewhere in the Kura system.

"And," he said, becoming more excited, "also to implicate the allies they must have in the Larix system. For no sensible being can doubt there must've been others on the capital worlds waiting for the chance to begin their own terrorist campaigns."

"That seems very logical to me," an aide said. "Again, you've cut to the heart of the matter, Protector."

No one paid the claque the slightest attention.

"Yes," Redruth said. "A nice proper interrogation, and they'll certainly be ready to make full confessions that confirm my worst fears about traitors in our midst."

"Not to mention," Celidon said dryly, "that certainly gives us reason enough to declare war, in the event we ever have to justify ourselves to . . . outsiders."

"You mean if the Confederation ever returns?" Redruth snickered. "I doubt if that'll happen in your lifetime, nor in that of any of your descendants. But it *is* well always to have a spare arrow in your quiver, isn't it?

"Yohns, I'm going to detach you from the duties I assigned and make you part of the interrogation team. You'll be able to word questions in familiar ways to these terrorists, keep them from lying, and when they begin talking, to make sure the wording of their free confessions is appropriate, both for our citizens and for dissemination back to Cumbre."

"You honor me, Protector," Njangu said, half-bowing.

The room stank. It was nothing more than a windowless concrete cube, with a sealed air conditioner and two monitors on the ceiling, one barred double door at the end, and four mattresses on the floor. The four prisoners had been stripped, thoroughly searched, and every hideout device found. They were then given gray coveralls with a black cross on the back that looked suspiciously like an aiming point.

Twice a day, the door opened, and ration paks and water were tossed in by empty-faced guards, and every now and then some hardly sterile dressings for the wounded. No other medical supplies had been given out, and requests for a doctor and proper treatment for Lir and Mahim were ignored.

Mahim tossed, feverish, barely conscious. Monique, ignoring her own superficial wounds, carefully unwrapped the dressings on Mahim's leg. Garvin knelt beside her, looked at the puffy, swollen limb.

Lir wrinkled her nose, and Garvin smelled the sweetness as well. Gangrene was developing. Either Jil Mahim got treatment quickly, or she would lose her leg. Or else die.

Mahim opened her eyes.

"Hot," she said with difficulty.

"They don't seem to have any controls on the environment settings around here," Garvin said.

"How am I?"

"Doing about as well as expected," Lir said. "Recovering nicely."

"*Giptel* shit," Mahim said. "Remember, I've got the medical training." She winced as pain hit her. "And I've still got a nose."

"We're still trying to get a doctor in," Garvin said.

Montagna got up, went to the cell door, shouted.

A muffled voice beyond the doors told her to shut up.

"Nice folks," Mahim said. "If we had them in our claws, we'd at least let them die healthy, wouldn't we?"

Garvin tried a reassuring smile, found it didn't fit well.

"Away from the doors," someone shouted. Obediently Montagna moved back. Jaansma got to his feet, wondering if finally somebody was going to tell them what was going on. Since capture, none of their warders had said anything other than to get away from the door, and shut up.

The outer door banged open, and a key buzzed in the second's lock. It opened, and Njangu Yoshitaro walked in.

Garvin and Lir recovered most quickly. They knew where Njangu had disappeared to. But the other soldiers hadn't a need to know, so were told nothing. Montagna gaped, and Mahim came up to a sitting position.

"Boss," she managed, before Lir jabbed her swollen leg, and she half screamed in agony, fell back, just as she realized Yoshitaro was wearing a dark brown uniform, hardly that of the Confederation.

Behind him were three gun guards, one a rather striking woman, and a small, balding man who looked like a university don.

"I am Ab Yohns," Njangu said. "*Leiter* Ab Yohns.

Protector Redruth has appointed me to oversee your interrogation and the preparation for your trial as war criminals as well."

"We committed no crimes," Garvin said. "And we were in proper uniform before your goons stripped and looted us."

"No crimes?" the scholarly man said in some astonishment. "Murder, mass murder, attempted murder, destruction of state property, attacking government personnel, attempting to bring about revolution, conspiracy against a legal government, theft, possession of illegal devices, and . . . the list goes on and on.

"Remember, no state of war exists between Cumbre and Larix/Kura. You are no more than the commonest of criminals. You shall be questioned until you decide it is wiser to give up the names of your accomplices here in the Kura system, and the conspirators in the Larix system as well.

"Then you, and the others, shall be brought to trial and convicted. This trial shall be 'cast throughout Larix and Kura, for the education of those who aren't fully convinced of the evils of Cumbre, and probable eventual dissemination to your homeworlds as well, to discourage other banditry."

"This gentleman," Yoshitaro said, "is your chief interrogator, Dr. Petteu Miuss. He has degrees in medicine, surgery, pharmacology, and psychology. You *will* confess, needless to say. We are prepared to use any means necessary, physical and chemical, to reach this end.

"My role is simple: I spent many years on D-Cumbre, and am most familiar with your military and society. So you needn't bother lying to me, Dr. Miuss, or his underlings. Such antisocial behavior will be severely punished."

"What made you turn traitor, Yohns?" Garvin snarled, trying to sound outraged.

"I am hardly a traitor," Njangu said. "In the Cumbre System, I remained a citizen of the Confederation, then renounced it and was granted citizenship on Larix/Kura.

"I would suggest that your time might be better spent not accusing me of falsehoods, but considering your own crimes. The greater your cooperation, the better you will be treated."

"Like this?" Garvin waved around the bare room.

"This is merely a holding cell," Njangu said. "You are to be transferred immediately to Protector Redruth's flagship. You will be given complete medical examinations and whatever treatment is necessary, and issued standard military rations—unless your behavior warrants otherwise."

Njangu glared at the four.

"By the time of the trial, we don't want any of our citizens to make the mistake of thinking you deserve pity because of your physical appearance.

"That is all I have to say. Dr. Miuss?"

The scholar considered each soldier carefully. He bent over Mahim, looked at her leg, tsked in seeming sympathy. Mahim stared coldly back.

"This shall be an interesting period," he said. "Four disturbed ones who've participated in the same aberrational crimes. My examination shall be interesting, very interesting.

"I truly look forward to knowing each of you better." He smiled pleasantly, went back to Njangu's side.

Njangu turned to the woman. "Commander Stiofan, if you'll have a detail of our security troops reinforce the normal guards during the transfer?"

"Yes, *Leiter*."

"You two," Njangu told Alpha and Beta, "make sure there are no mistakes in the transfer."

"Yessir," one said.

Njangu eyed the prisoners.

"Rogues," he said softly. "Definitely rogues, perverts, and psychopaths, all of you."

Garvin almost started laughing, and noticed Njangu had to turn away quickly.

*   *   *

Njangu stopped washing Maev's back, let the 'fresher's water roar down on them.

"Why'd you stop?"

"Because I wanted to talk, and this is the safest place on this goddamned ship I could think of. I can't see any bugs, and the water noise should drown out that one in the 'fresher light."

"*Now* you tell me, after you get my hopes up."

"I didn't say I was going to stop for good. Now, here's the plan."

"Nj . . . I mean, Ab, don't think I'm a complete clotpole," Maev interrupted. "I caught what that poor woman with the rotten leg almost let go. Not that I think Miuss, that bloodless corpse understood, if he even heard, since I know your secret and he doesn't. You're pissed off, because you're going to blow your carefully contrived cover and do a manly rescue of your friends.

"On the other hand, I'm happy as a maniac with a new ax, because I can finally quit walking on eggs and get the hell out of this nightmare. See how confident I am in your capabilities?"

"You're too bright for me," Njangu allowed.

"Of course," Maev said comfortably. "Now, do you want to tell me how we're going to pull off this great prison break from the heart of Larix Prime?"

"Uh . . . I haven't quite figured out all the details," Njangu confessed. "But I think it's gonna involve a lot of explosions and bodies. As many as I can manage."

"But no details."

"Not quite yet."

"I wouldn't dare suggest that all you've got is an idea, and zed-squelch in the way of an actual plan."

"I'm glad you're so respectful of my innate capabilities," Njangu said.

"Especially at back washing. You can go back to that anytime you want."

*   *   *

The next morning he woke Maev by moving his tongue in and around her ear. She yawned, reached for him.

"Last night you inspired me," he whispered.

"I should hope so," Maev said, conscious of the bug Njangu'd found in a particularly revolting piece of military art above the bed.

He mouthed: I have a plan.

"Mmmh. That sounds good," she said. "Nice, subtle, and orgasmic?"

He came very close to her ear, whispered: "No. Stupid, obvious, and bloody. But I think it'll work. And the first thing we need is a good gossip."

CHAPTER
13

Kura/Kura Four

The *aksai* came in-atmosphere very fast, over the southern pole. It plummeted toward the middle of one of Kura Four's oceans as if on a suicide dive, pulled out less than a thousand meters above the water.

At full drive it flew toward the nearest land, looped around a pair of coastal villages and over the jungle beyond. The *aksai* slowed as a brown expanse of mud surrounding a small lake appeared.

In the cockpit, Alikhan looked at a time signal that suddenly flashed up on his canopy. A holo of mountainous terrain hung to one side of his controls, a dot of red light flashing in its center. He waved a paw, and a microphone swung down.

"ETA two-point-three minutes. Stand by."

A double-click sounded in his headphone.

Alikhan was the only being aboard the *aksai,* which was configured with three other fighting pods.

Below him a nearly sheer buttress with a tiny plateau rose out of the jungle. Alikhan wondered how they'd managed to climb it, then dived directly for the plateau, speed brakes open. The *aksai* shuddered in near stall as he flared it ten meters above the plateau, cut the drive, and went to antigravity. The *aksai*'s wings rocked as Alikhan slid the antigrav control back, and the ship landed, grounding hard on its skids.

Alikhan popped the canopy, slid out, taking a blaster with him.

He found a bush, crouched, waited.

A dozen seconds later, two men stumbled out of the brush. Their clothes were ragged, their bodies filthy, scratched, and Alikhan smelled them three meters away.

But both the older man and the younger, a giant, held their weapons very ready, and their eyes darting back and forth.

"You said you'd come," Ben Dill managed. "You did."

"I am sorry I could not arrive earlier," Alikhan said. "But there were too many ships for us to chance. We returned to Cumbre. When the satellite received signals from one Search and Rescue transmitter, we returned. The *velv* this *aksai* belongs to will return to real space every two E-hours to make pickup."

"I am very damned glad to see you," Danfin Froude managed. "It's been a long, hungry week . . . I think it was a week."

"Get on board," Alikhan said. "I do not think I was picked up by any sensor, but who can know? I would like to leave as quickly as possible."

He went back to the main pod, touched controls, and two other pod canopies swung open.

"I just hope I can stand my smell 'til we get to civilization," Froude said. "Then I'm going to bathe for a week, eat rare steak, never again vegetables or raw fish. Six steaks sound about right. Then I'll sleep for a month or two." He clambered into the *aksai*.

Ben Dill was looking at Alikhan. "You did come back," he said once again.

"I gave my oath," Alikhan said. "You saved me once, so now it was my turn."

Ben Dill started to say something, then shook his head.

"Did anybody else break away? Did you get SAR signals from anybody else?"

"No," Alikhan said. "We still don't know what happened to them. But the Force will continue to monitor the satellite."

CHAPTER
14

Cumbre/D-Cumbre

Events Editor Ted Vollmer didn't like the expression on his boss's face.

"We are going to make a very loud noise," Loy Kouro gloated. "And when award time rolls around, we're up there!"

"Prest'n came up with something?"

"Something with a big brass band," Kouro said. "The Force is going to get egg not just on its face, we're going to bury them in the world's biggest omelet. This is big, big, big, Vollmer, involving the potential safety of Cumbre itself!"

"You want to tell me about it, sir?" Vollmer said. "All I know is Prest'n got some call from some relative of some soldier, went to you, and then has been haring around in all directions.

"It'd be nice if I knew the story, so I could figure on how to play it. I'm only Prest'n's boss."

"Don't worry about it," Kouro said. "When we've got all the pins in a row, you'll be told everything. Right now, I think it's better to keep things under wraps.

"Besides, I still remember how to be a journoh," Kouro said, smiling. He started back toward his office, and the smile became a laugh.

"A journoh?" Vollmer's assistant. "Since when is a publisher—"

"Leave it," Vollmer said wearily. "The son of a

bitch is a purple pirate if he says he is, as long as it's his name on the paychit."

"This," *Caud* Angara said, "could be a very expensive rescue." He reread the printout.

"At least we've got confirmation there are survivors of Jaansma's raid. I assume notification's been made to the next of kin?"

"Yessir," Erik Penwyth, acting head of Force II Section said. "I thought I'd best handle that myself, and tell them their principal is a prisoner of war, rather than allow it to go through normal channels or leave them as Missing in Action, so we can keep some sort of security hold on matters." He grimaced.

"A problem?" Hedley asked.

"Yessir," Penwyth said, "but not an expected one. Of the four who're reported as POWs, only two, *Tweg* Mahim and *Dec* Montagna, have relatives of record. But that's not the problem. I also notified relatives of the still-missing . . . There were only two in our records, for *Tweg* Irthing and *Dec* Heckmyer . . . and told them their people were still considered Missing in Action, but their status had been changed to MIA—Presumed Dead.

"*Tweg* Irthing's sister's response was to ask how quickly the Force's insurance would pay off, and couldn't Irthing's status be moved to Killed in Action to speed up payment, since obviously she's dead, wherever we sent her?"

"Ouch," Hedley said softly.

"You always forget that some people, a fair number of them, join up to get away from their families," Angara said.

"That's still not it, sir," Penwyth said. "She said, if we kept playing games, and not taking care of things the way we're supposed to, she'd go to the holos."

"Double ouch."

"Worse still," Penwyth said. "I think she already has, because one of Kouro's reporters has been digging around. Trying to reach the CO of I&R, getting told Njangu's in the field, trying to reach the CO of II Section, getting told Garvin's unavailable, grinding me as temp honcho about any covert operations the Force has mounted against Larix and Kura. I suspect the son of a bitch is adding one and one and might just get lucky."

"Let's consider worst case," Angara said. "*Matin* comes out with a story saying there's been a covert operation mounted against Larix and Kura, that there has been at least one casualty. Does that hurt that much?"

"It's not flipping good," Hedley said. "We can't assume that the late Ab Yohns was the only agent Redruth has in-system, although I think he was. What happens if *Matin* decides to run pics? We won't cooperate, but I assume they have file shots of at least Jaansma and Yoshitaro. A nice holo of Yoshitaro in uniform that gets to Larix isn't exactly going to improve our agent's cover."

"Perhaps we should ask *Matin*'s publisher, that Loy Kouro, to sit on his story until we clear it, even though he's no particular friend of the Force."

"I don't think I'd do that, sir," Penwyth said. "Perhaps you've forgotten, but Garvin . . . sorry, *Mil* Jaansma's, well, romantically involved with Jasith Mellusin, who just happens to be Kouro's ex-wife."

"Mohammad's camel in a bright pink dress! What the hell is this?" Angara snarled. "I'm running a goddamned romance, not an army."

Neither Hedley nor Penwyth answered.

"Eeesh," Angara muttered, rubbing a hand through the gray stubble he called a haircut. "And of course, what'll make it worse, if Kouro spreads this, there'll be questions asked by the Council.

"We've got authorization right now to do anything we want with Larix and Kura, short of open war. But there are waverers. It's a bit of a pity Redruth's nuke didn't hit on solid ground. That would probably keep the politicos' feet nailed to the floor about this for a while longer."

"Yessir," Hedley said. "Which means we'd better talk about Njangu's message, and about getting everybody out of Redruth's clutches on roller skates."

"You're right, Jon," Angara said, and for a third time read the message. "Nice that Njangu's able to com on a regular basis. I notice, Erik, that somebody in II Section noted that the receiving freq he's finally using is close to one of Larix's military lengths. Wonder how he managed that? Don't bother answering; I'm talking while I'm trying to think. Let's go back to this expensive rescue. First, we've got to do an explosive drop, without being blown."

"Not flipping impossible, sir," Hedley said. "We'll use two *aksai,* with a *velv* to mother them. Put pods under the *aksai,* so all they have to do is hover over the site, dump the load, and flipping begone."

" 'Kay. Stage One's possible," Angara said. "I already assumed that was feasible. What concerns me is Stage Two. Yoshitaro wants a heavy hit squad on Prime's capital, Agura, at a specific time, to be named after the ships are in-system.

"Then we have *another* team a few kilometers away. Two *more velv* . . . he'd be better off with our new destroyers . . . plus two fast transports. All to rescue four people, sorry, five."

"Six, sir," Penwyth said. "One Larissan's been added to Njangu's list. I dunno who he is. And the extra transport's for redundancy, in case we lose one."

"Six people," Angara said. "And I could lose seven ships, not to mention the what, three hundred crew members, on this part alone? For which, in return, I no longer have my very valuable agent in place, our only source inside Redruth's government. I gain . . . under best circumstances . . . two junior officers known for their independent ways, to put it as politely as possible, three other ranks, and one Larissan traitor.

"Is it worth it?"

"Do you want the book answer, sir?" Hedley asked.

"Of course I don't," Angara said. "I already know what we have to do. And we're in agreement we have to do it quickly, before that frigging Kouro becomes the spanner in the works.

"I wish," he said, "that we could actually be the goons he keeps calling us—when he doesn't want something, and then we're his goddamned Defenders of Freedom—and arrange a convenient accident."

"A bomb in Kouro's flipping shorts would be heaven," Hedley said dreamily. "And we've more than enough thugs on the payroll to handle that. If only it weren't for that goddamned oath we all took."

"And our own honor," Angara said.

"Pardon, sir?" Hedley asked.

"Never mind," Angara said.

"Sir," Penwyth said, "remember, I'm part of his social circle."

"You think *you* should approach him?"

"Hell no," Penwyth said. "Sir. I'm not much more a friend of his than Garvin. But I know Jasith Mellusin fairly well. Maybe she knows some way to gag him."

"Be very careful," Hedley said. "We don't want to make matters worse."

"Have confidence, sir," Penwyth said airily. "Have I failed you yet?"

Jasith met Erik at the gates to Hillcrest, the family mansion in the Heights above Leggett. She was pale.

"You said it couldn't be talked about over the com. Is he—"

"No change in Garvin's status," Penwyth said hastily. "He's still a prisoner of Redruth's, still alive as far as we know. Sorry. I should've said that when I commed you."

"Come inside. Please. A drink or something?"

"As much as I'd love one, duty calls and all that. Jasith, the Force needs a favor."

"Anything. You know that."

Erik explained the problem with Loy Kouro and *Matin*.

Jasith went to the bar, automatically poured two snifters of brandy, handed one to Penwyth.

"Oh, I'm sorry, I wasn't—"

"Never mind," Erik said, sipping. "You've twisted my arm."

"I said anything I could do to help, I would," Jasith said. "But there are some things I can't deliver. Loy Kouro's one of them. I might've been married to the pig, but that doesn't mean I know, understand, anything about him.

"If I did," she said, bitterly, "or about myself, I never would have done what I did in the first place and married the bastard. Instead, I went and—"

She broke off, drank her brandy. "If I called Loy," she went on, "that'd make the situation worse, not better. He hates me more now, I think, than he does Garvin. And if he could take it out on both of us, he wouldn't hesitate for a second."

"Mmh," Erik said. "I knew that, actually. What I was looking for from you was, to put it delicately, some way of putting pressure on Loy."

"You mean like blackmail?"

"Just that. Any of his nasty little secrets you'd like to share, or hint at that we could do some scummy digging on . . ."

Jasith thought, then shook her head. "I can't think of anything. He's a bachelor now, so whoever he beds is his own business. Not that any Rentier's ever dropped anyone for adultery, unless it's his wife that's getting screwed, and generally not even then. As far as drink, everybody drinks. Drugs . . . I don't think so."

"We *are* sort of decadent bastards, aren't we?" Penwyth said, draining the brandy. "Well, I must be off, so blithe farewells and like that. If you think of something, com me. Oh. One other thing. What are you doing socially these days?"

Jasith smiled ruefully. "Damned little. Working as

many hours as I can to keep from thinking. Sitting and worrying about Garvin, mostly. Trying to go to bed early. Probably not eating right."

"Whyn't I have Karo ring you? Maybe you two could go out drinking or dancing. Don't think I'm being an altruist. With you as a chaperone, that'd be one way to keep Karo from going home with the first well-hung sort who asks her to dance, when I'm stuck out on the island playing soldier boy."

Jasith managed a smile. Redheaded Karo Lonrod had been one of the staples of the Rentiers' hard-partying set until she found herself with Penwyth, first as a casual bed partner, then as a sometime cover for him, during the Musth occupation, since then, something else that neither of them wanted to talk about. To everyone's surprise, she appeared to have completely lost her wandering eye.

"That might be fun," Jasith said. "And I promise I'll com you if anything comes up."

She watched his lifter take off, went back inside, poured herself another brandy, and sat down in a couch, staring down at Leggett City.

An hour later, the drink was still untouched. Jasith's eyes suddenly widened. She went to the com, started to touch sensors. Then she stopped, thought for a few moments, and dialed another number.

"Scrambling," she said when she heard a voice at the other end, then read the code from her display. "R-Three-six-seven."

The voice blurred, then came back clearly as the scramble code was entered on the other com.

"Scrambled on code R-three-six-seven. What's the problem, Jasith?"

The man at the other end was Hon Felps, personnel executive for Mellusin Mining and her late father's former personal assistant.

Jasith said, "I want to access the GT-Nine-Seven-Three team."

There was a long silence. The code, which Jasith

was given after her father's death, had been set up
by her father years earlier. Every senior executive at
Mellusin Mining was told that if GT973 was invoked
by any member of the Mellusin family or their repre-
sentative, they were to provide any, repeat any, service, without questions, comment, or records. In
addition, Felps had told Jasith there were certain people on the Mellusin payroll, in innocuous functions,
who had unusual training and background, and would
carry out any, repeat any, service she needed.

Jasith had passed the code along to Garvin during
the Musth War, but he hadn't occasion to use it.
But now . . .

"Are you sure . . . sorry, Jasith. Stand by. You'll be
contacted at your number shortly." The connection
went dead.

Jasith waited, thinking about her idea. A smile
touched her lips. It wasn't terribly pleasant. Then the
situation became funny, and she laughed aloud, just
as the com buzzed.

"Jasith Mellusin," she said.

"T-One-Two-One," an absolutely neutral voice
came, most likely synthed. Jasith entered the code,
then explained her plan.

The alarm chimed pleasantly, once, again.

Loy Kouro rolled over, reached for the cutoff switch,
felt paper instead of plas. He opened an eye, and saw
an envelope leaning against the clock.

Kouro sat up, and the blond head pillowed on his
arm snorted in sleepy surprise.

*How the hell did that get in here? I didn't have any-
thing to drink before bed—is Bet trying to surprise me
or something?*

He tore the envelope open. Inside was a card that
looked handwritten, but was a script face:

*Here's wishing you the best of days, now, and hope-
fully forever.*

There wasn't any signature.

Quite suddenly, the card burst into flames. Kouro yelped in surprise, dropped the card on the carpet as it burned into ashes.

Bet sat up. "What's the matter, honey-bun?"

"Nothing. Go back to sleep."

He'd never quite realized how irritating her nasal voice could be.

Kouro grabbed for the com, thought he should at least rinse his face off before tearing his security people apart. Growling in anger, he went into the 'fresher, reached for the tap, saw more blackened ashes around it.

Another note. But it could've been a bomb. Like the other one might've been. And anybody who broke in could've had a gun or a knife instead of paper envelopes.

He opened the medicine chest, saw more ashes inside one of his headache remedy bottles.

The medicine could've been replaced with poison, and I never would've known.

Kouro's hand started shaking. He held it on the washstand, pressing down hard, until it stilled. He grabbed his robe from its hook, pulled it on, heard crinkling. He dug into the pocket, found more ashes.

A poisonous reptile.

Almost blind in his rage, he grabbed the com, pressed the EMERGENCY sensor.

Alarms began shrilling. A voice came on.

"Response team on the way, sir. What's gone wrong, if you can talk?"

"Somebody . . . somebody broke in," Kouro gobbled, then the door slammed open. Two men in combat harness, blasters ready, burst in, flattened to either side of the doorway. One of his security officers crouched around the side of the door, weapon leveled.

"What is it, sir?"

"There's been an intruder, goddammit! And he got right past you!"

"Get down and out of the way!"

"He's gone, you stupid frigging idiot!"

The watch leader came to his feet, pushed past Kouro, saw nothing but the wide-eyed young woman in bed.

"What happened, sir? How did you know there was a break-in?"

Kouro gaped, then stammered, too livid to speak coherently.

Those goddamned Forcemen. Had to have been them. None of my other enemies has that capability. The bastards came right through the best guards I could hire, and they could do it again, and there's nothing I can do to keep myself from being murdered, and I can't press charges on some goddamned ashes and a weird story that nobody, not even Bet, will believe.

Goddamn them, goddamn them!

Prest'n picked up the com.

"*Matin.* This is Prest'n."

"Loy Kouro here."

"Yes, sir?"

"We're killing the Larix/Kura story."

"Whaaat?"

The only answer he got was the click as Kouro disconnected.

CHAPTER
15

"I'm not pleased," Celidon snapped. "Nor is the Protector."

"I hope it's not me," Njangu said, the quaver in his voice quite unforced.

"No, Yohns. You're one of the few people the Protector and I are thinking favorably of at this moment.

"Have you heard the tales of the Gray Avengers?"

"The who?"

"Neither has the head of state security, not the commander of the Protector's Own," Celidon said. "It seems there are a certain number of soldiers—how many and their duty assignments is still unclear—within the Protector's Own, who think Protestor's Justice will not suffice to deal with the bandits we rounded up on Kura Four."

"That's absurd," Njangu said. "Dr. Miuss is ready to start the treatment in a day, now that the prisoners are healthy enough not to die from the side effects of the drugs he's going to use. The trial after that will be swift, sure, and deadly."

"I know that, the Protector knows that, but these half-wits seem intent on taking matters into their own hands," Celidon snarled.

Njangu looked appropriately shocked.

"The Gray Avengers' intent," Celidon continued, "so the initial reports say, is to seize the prisoners after the trial begins and peremptorily execute them in front of all the holos. Thus, supposedly, proving the Avengers' loyalty to the Protector.

"Of course, if they think that, they're truly foolish. The results of an action such as they plan can have a very different effect. Should, say, there be problems or setbacks in the forthcoming war against Cumbre, it would be very easy for the populace, properly instructed, to consider the gray Avengers the real spirit of our worlds.

"Assuming they're ambitious, they might consider a coup, of course in the name of the Protector, intended to take care of those lacklusters and ninnyhammers who don't support him to the hilt.

"No doubt certain people, such as Protector Redruth and myself, would be unfortunately killed during such a rising, which would mean the cabal of Gray Avengers would be forced to take charge of the government until the emergency's over.

"It's an interesting way to plot revolution. From within, not without, in the name of greater security for the people and their greatest hero."

"They can't be that clever," Njangu said, "if you've gotten word of their plot."

"Just rumors, gossip so far," Celidon said. "But my agents are hard at work, within the palace itself. Since the bandits committed their depredations on Kura Four, we're interrogating any of the palace staff or the Protector's Own who came from that system."

"Why are you trusting me with this information?"

"Because, since you've more or less taken over the matter of these bandits, you might wish to check your security even more thoroughly than you have."

Njangu walked to the window, looked out at the gray monotony of Larix Prime, appearing to think.

"Actually," he said, turning, "I *would* rather steal the march on these conspirators, rather than patch the leaking dike here, there." Yoshitaro thought, with a bit of pride, that his mixed metaphors were worthy of the Protector himself.

"You suggest?"

"The prisoners are currently housed in the palace prison."

"It's the most secure facility on the planet."

"Not if there are conspirators inside the palace, as the rumor has it."

"True. So you want to move them? Where?"

"Dr. Miuss's sanitarium is very well guarded, and most secure," Njangu said, "since a great number of the enemies of the Protector have been given to him for interrogation and treatment."

"And the sanitarium's not far from the Palace of Justice," Celidon mused. "But the passage between Dr. Miuss's enclave and the Palace of Justice would be open for attack."

"Not necessarily. We move the prisoners to the sanitarium," Njangu explained. "We tell the Protector's Own they'll be responsible for the security between the court and the sanitarium, allow them to prepare their positions and so forth.

"Then, when the prisoners have been softened up enough for the trial, we bring in conventional troops for route security, and return the Protector's Own to their barracks. The Gray Avengers, assuming they exist, will no doubt be plotting to make their strike against the Protector's Own, and their plans will be shattered."

"Mmmh," Celidon said, considering. "Not bad. Not bad at all. I suspect the Protector will be interested in your suggestions."

"I hope so, sir."

"It appears we did well, bringing you away from Cumbre, Yohns."

"Thank you, sir." Njangu made an awkward salute, and left Celidon's office.

Very good, he thought. *Very, very goddamned good. That gossip Maev picked must've cornered every fool with an eardrum to drop the tale about the ever-so-patriotic, never-to-be-found conspirators.* Just as Njangu had hoped.

Now we've got the prisoners out in the open, where it'll be easier to lift them, away from that goddamned unbustable jail they're in now.

"Commander Celidon says that you had some interesting thoughts on matters that shouldn't be discussed," Protector Redruth said.

"I'd hoped you'd find them such, sir," Njangu said.

"I did, indeed, and your suggestions will be implemented. Also, my current head of security has proven himself unqualified by his ignorance of this matter, and must be replaced. I propose you for the post."

"Why . . . why, thank you, sir," Njangu managed. "But may I ask a favor?"

Redruth frowned.

"Could my appointment wait until after these raiders have been dealt with? I think I have the situation well in hand with them, and Dr. Miuss and I are working well together. It would take a bit of time to familiarize a new official with the way you want the matter handled."

Redruth thought, then nodded.

"Good thinking, Yohns. Finish one task before you start a second, as I always say. With you on top of matters, the bandits will soon become the public example I've promised."

"You almost got too canny for your own good," Maev snickered, turning off the sweep and tucking it in the dresser drawer. Both she and Njangu had become very adept at constantly checking for bugs, changing sweeps regularly, and never talking openly in a room with any sort of electronic device. Their bedroom bugs were fed taped harmless conversations, sex scenes, or snoring when matters of real importance had to be discussed.

"No shiteedah," Njangu agreed, collapsing on the bed. "Teach me to be that efficient and almost get transferred. Such high-level conniving takes it out of a man. I am for a fast shower, a faster meal, and total unconsciousness."

"Not for a while yet," Maev said. "There's another problem you're going to have to deal with."

"Not tonight. And it better not be you. I'm too tired to raise a smile."

"Not me, oh stud of the greater universe," Maev said. "It's your companions."

"Uk," Njangu said.

"Brythe came to me today, and, rather hurt, wanted to know what my special bed talents are."

Njangu groaned, rolled onto his stomach. For some reason he refused to analyze, since a short time after Maev had joined him, he'd found himself feeling . . . not guilty, of course, since there was no reason for guilt . . . reluctant, yes, that was the word, no doubt because of the complexity of what was going on, to visit his companions.

"You know," Maev said, "you shouldn't be deviating from normal practice, you deviant. That's one of the first things a good counterintelligence agent looks for."

"God give me true strength," Njangu said, muffledly, head buried in the coverlet.

"She might," Maev said. "I assume you're going to rectify matters, you raving stallion you, and go hopping from bed to bed to bed tonight. I've heard tales about your proficiency. Perhaps you could leave a com on, and I could watch."

Njangu sat up.

"You'd like that?"

"Don't sound so shocked, my little libertine," she said. "But no, I wouldn't."

Njangu wondered why he felt relief, why, in fact, he'd let this nonsense go on as long as it had.

"Tell them . . . tell them I got a social disease on Kura, and that you and I aren't doing it either, but you know about this loathsomeness, and so I'm having you sleep in this room so nasty rumors don't start."

Maev came over on the bed, looked down.

"You mean you aren't going to take my invitation to go screwing your little lights out?"

Njangu shook his head.

"Why not?"

"I don't want to talk about it," he said.

"And aren't you just the most romantic of unromantics," Maev said, lowering herself down on him. "Kiss me, you scoundrel."

"Awright," Njangu said. "But no more than a kiss. Like I said, I ain't got no energy, and I'm telling major truth here."

"We'll see about that."

The red-faced man in the black coveralls leaned close to Garvin. He tried to smile in a friendly manner, showed yellowing teeth and foul breath.

"Now, listen, son, you know your parents want you to tell me the truth about all those machines behind the midway."

Garvin's stomach was twisting, and he was fighting back tears. He looked down the long bench at his father and mother, expecting them to smile encouragingly, for him to keep his mouth shut. A Jaansma never talked to a diddly flatty, let alone a damned rozzer.

But instead, his father nodded, said, in a booming voice, "Tell the nice policeman what he wants to know."

Garvin firmed his lips, then said, and wondered what his words meant, "Mil Garvin Jaansma, Service Number J-Six-Nine-Three-Seven-Zero-Four-A-Seven-Two-Five."

The cop backhanded him, but the pain went through his entire body. Garvin jerked.

"Come on, son," the policeman said. "You can do better than that. What was the name of the ship you landed on? What is your call sign? What were your targets on Kura Four."

"Mil Garvin Jaansma, Service number—"

He was no longer in the police station, but in a world

*of flame, canvas tearing around him, animals screaming
as they burned. His parents danced in the fire before
him, blackening, dying.*

His mother's ghastly skull face loomed:

*"What was your ship's name? How many raiders did
you land? What is your call sign? What were your targets on Kura Four?"*

"Mil Garvin Jaansma. Service—"

*The diddly flatties had cornered him in an alley, and
none of the circus people was within shouting distance.
Rocks and bricks thudded against his teenage body, a
thug with a board smashed his fingers, and pain roiled
through him.*

The citizens were shouting questions:

*"What was the name of your ship? How many men
did you land? What was your call sign? What were—"*

"My name is Garvin Janus Six," *Garvin said.* "The
ship I landed on Kura Four had no name, but—"

Garvin woke suddenly, as nausea swept him. He
barely had time to roll off the gurney and reach the
sink before he began vomiting.

None of the three—Njangu Yoshitaro, a hulking
guard who called himself a nurse, Dr. Petteu Miuss—
moved to help him. Garvin turned the faucet on,
drenched his head, washed his mouth before the nurse
slammed him back against his cell wall.

"You see, Garvin," Miuss crooned. "You *will* tell
us everything, sooner or later, and tell it in the manner
we want to hear. This is only your second treatment,
and already we know your call sign. Soon you'll tell
us about your men, about your mission, and exactly
how you reached Kura Four."

Garvin started to say something, vomited once
more.

"The drugs I'm giving you are quite powerful,"
Miuss said sympathetically. "And have pronounced
side effects, both short-term, such as you're experienc-
ing now, and long-term. I can tell you, with prolonged
dosage, the effects increase.

"You *could* ease your burden, and cooperate. Also, remember that the other members of your team, now that they've recovered their health, will also be undergoing treatment.

"You could spare them that discomfort."

"Screw you," Garvin managed. The nurse growled, came forward. Garvin ducked under his reaching arms, came up with a knee in the guard's groin. The man yelped. Miuss, eyes wide in fear, hit a pocket alarm. But Njangu moved faster. He brushed the guard aside, somehow driving an elbow into the man's ribs, hearing them crack. He hit Garvin on the side of the head, and Jaansma rocked sideways. A hard knife strike came in, and Garvin sagged. Njangu was about to strike to the back of his neck when Miuss yelped.

"No! No! We mustn't harm him! Stop, *Leiter* Yohns."

Njangu obeyed, and Garvin sagged down to his knees. After a minute, he picked himself up, reminding his body where he was supposed to be in agony from Njangu's pulled punches, besides the overwhelming urge to vomit.

The cell door burst open, and more guards in hospital whites burst in.

"The situation's in hand, boys," Njangu said. "Next time, we'll keep at least two guards on this man. Or at least one a little more competent than this idiot. You can take him out, by the way. Tell his superior I don't want to see the man ever again."

"Yessir. Sorry, sir." And the wheezing guard was dragged away.

"You see what violence gets you, Jaansma?" Njangu cooed. "Now, sit back on that gurney and let me tell you about an offer Protector Redruth has made."

Miuss showed surprise for an instant, then his face blanked.

"Doctor, if you'd mind stepping outside for a few moments?"

"Of course. Of course. But I should know of whatever you're discussing with the patient."

"As soon as I get his response," Njangu said, "you'll be the first to know."

He winked broadly at Miuss, who got the message, and went out, locking the door behind him. He'd scurry to the next room, where the monitors and technicians watched everything that happened in Jaansma's cell, just as other techs kept track of the other prisoners.

Njangu's hands moved quickly . . . a thumb point at the door, a sweep of a thumb across the throat.

I'm going to kill that bastard.

Garvin's head moved sideways once, and his curled fingers tapped his own chest.

You'll have to stand in line.

"Here's the situation, *Mil* Jaansma," Njangu said. "As Dr. Miuss said, the treatments will get worse until we get the information we need before the trial. Also, your subordinates will be given the same drugs."

"Torturing sons of bitches," Garvin spat, hoping he didn't sound too much like a romance.

"Possibly," Njangu said. "And you're a mass-murdering psychopath. Now that we've shared compliments, let me tell you what the Protector is offering, in his infinite grace.

"If you cooperate, if you order your entire team to cooperate, which means full and complete confessions of your sins, as well as an acknowledgment that you've now become aware of your evil ways, courtesy of the Protector's education, there'll be no torture. No drugs, no thumbscrews."

"Why should I believe you?" Garvin growled.

"Why shouldn't you?" Njangu asked reasonably. "If you give us what we want . . . and remember, you're not exactly bringing any of your fellow soldiers on Cumbre into any jeopardy . . . why should we bother with the rack and such? We aren't sadists, you know."

Garvin snorted.

"Oh yes," Njangu said. "We'll also need information on the traitors here on Larix and back on Kura who were willing to help you."

"There weren't any, goddammit!"

"Come now, Jaansma. No one is stupid enough to mount an operation like yours on a completely alien world without *any* intelligence." Real amusement came and went on Njangu's face.

Garvin promised himself, if they lived, he'd get revenge for that cheap shot.

"If your memory's a little fuzzy about the traitors," Njangu said, "our skilled counterintelligence teams will guide you through the preparation of your confession.

"Oh yes," he went on. "The ultimate thing you'll gain from this full, willing cooperation is your life. Instead of a nasty, protracted execution, you and the other members of your team will be given prison sentences.

"Long sentences, of course, and you'll be in isolation to avoid the righteous wrath of even our Larissan criminals. But life is life, isn't it?"

"You promised him *what*?" Protector Redruth snarled.

"I dangled an offer," Njangu said. "Jaansma seemed most interested in it, especially since it would avoid pain to his fellow soldiers."

Redruth's face was flushed with anger.

"Of course," Njangu went on, "after the trial, after the guilty verdict, there will hardly be any record of any of your satraps making such a stupid offer. And we all know how murderers lie and lie again to save their worthless necks, sir."

Redruth's face returned to its normal color.

"Very good, Yohns. Very good indeed. You have a rare ability to understand the realities of governing."

"Not really, sir. I just thought of what you would do in such a circumstance."

Redruth actually laughed aloud.

"I must say," Dr. Miuss mourned, "I'm most disappointed in the course of events. I would have had a whole new field of endeavor, determining if those conditioned by a different social system have another response to pain than Larrisans or Kurans. I was hoping that Garvin Jaansma would be a little less logical and reject Protector Redruth's generous offer."

"Well," Njangu said, "into each life some rain must fall. Besides, we've got more than enough work to do, making sure the confessions are properly worded and the bandits won't present any surprises once they appear on the stand.

"You're not forgetting their trial will be commed throughout the Protector's worlds, so the bandits' performance must be as skilled and convincing as any actor's."

"Oh, no, of course not," Miuss said hastily. "And of course I don't want you to think I'm being critical of the Protector in any way.

"Yes, yes, you're right. We have work enough ahead."

Not forgetting, Njangu thought, *my working hard to get you between a nice, steep stairwell and my boot.*

"So it was through seeing the deaths of those innocent children at play, who seconds before had been miming the rise of the Protector, that first made me aware of my own corruption and, worse, the evils of the Cumbrian regime." Lir turned the page. "Aw for fugh's sake, how much more of this shit do I have to parrot?"

"Now, now," Darod Montagna said smoothly. "Remember what we've learned, and consider how much nicer our quarters are, now that we've agreed to cooperate."

"Yeh, nice," Lir snorted. "We actually have a steel cot, and a hole to crap in instead of a bucket. Damn, but that Protector's just the salt of the goddamned earth."

"Our various targets had been given us by members of the Kuran Liberation Force," Garvin said. "I remember, when I was briefed, being told the names of some of the traitors on Kura who'd managed to communicate with Cumbre and offer their assistance in overthrowing Protector Redruth, and then, in the ensuing anarchy, to seize power for themselves. These traitors were, umm . . ."

The technician handed him a printout.

"Hafel Wyet, Mann Sefgin, Twy Morn, Ede Aganat . . .

Larix Prime was blanketed with observation satellites, pointing down, pointing out. The two *aksai* 'cast ECM long enough to block a transmission, using the satellites as a screen to close on the planet, then zigging at speed when their sensors reported a satellite was reporting their presence.

Evidently Larissan techs weren't confident about their electronics, because no patrol ships rose to the attack, when none of the ships' detection alarms went off a second time.

Ben Dill, still recuperating from the time in the jungle, flew in the second *aksai*. He'd asked Alikhan, in the first ship, to make the drop, and the Musth had refrained from harassing him about weakness.

Alikhan took his *aksai* in-atmosphere, dived for a mountained area behind Agur, then, hidden in its radar shadow, flew nap of the earth toward the beacon.

The beacon was broadcasting on an unused frequency, and the minute the *aksai* closed on the ground and was picked up by a motion detector in the beacon, it shut down to ensure no Larissan monitor caught the transmission.

Pods had been mounted under the *aksai*'s wings, and hydraulics lowered them to just above the ground, gently opened and turned them on their sides. Small blocks, each labeled AGRICULTURAL WASTE, dumped into neat piles.

There was a kiloton of the blocks, actually Telex explosive and resin casting.

The pods turned, lifted back to seat under the *aksai,* and the ship went softly upward, and vanished.

One of *Leiter* Appledore's guards thought he'd seen something over the neighboring estate, but no alarm came, nor did any of the other sentries report. The guard decided he was just tired, and said nothing.

Similarly, the next day, the workers on Njangu's estate saw the piles, which appeared to have come from nowhere, but showed no interest, assuming that someone else, anyone else delivered them. One learns, very quickly, in an authoritarian state, to see only what you're ordered to, and sometimes not then.

"This is important, troops, so I want your full attention," Commander Stiofan said. "We're going to build weapons pits along the road we're to guard when the prisoners are taken each day to the Palace of Justice, to keep anything unfortunate from being done by social misfits. Luckily these ag/waste blocks from *Leiter* Yohns's estate will keep us from having to fill sandbags, so we'll get our pits dug and bagged within a day or two.

"Now, men, set to! The Protector has other work ahead for us!"

There was a cheer. The Telex was quickly loaded into the lifters and, within hours, was being stacked in front of three weapons pits near a crossroads not far from the sanitarium.

"Sir, I think the bandits are sufficiently prepared for the trial," Njangu told Redruth.

"Good. Excellent! We'll . . . um . . . schedule it for Five-Day, two weeks from now. I've already named *Leiter* Vishinsk as prosecutor, so you can coordinate with him.

"Congratulations, Yohns, to you and to your staff, and of course to Dr. Miuss."

"The doctor is a little upset that he wasn't allowed to complete his experiment, sir," Njangu said. "Perhaps, after the verdict, it might be interesting to permit it to continue."

"Mmmh. Mmmh. No, Yohns. I do not want any of the doctor's skills shown in public. I want my enemies to cower at the mere mention of his name, never knowing exactly his talents until they've been arrested and turned over to him."

"Very good, sir. I'll inform him of your decision. Speaking of enemies," Njangu asked, "have there been any arrests of the supposed conspirators within the army, the Gray Avengers?"

"No," Redruth said, mood turning sour. "As if I don't have enough things to take care of, none of my investigators has been successful.

"I don't like that at all."

"Nossir," Njangu said. "Nor do I. I've also had my ears open every time I've been around any of the Protector's Own. Fortunately, none of the twenty-four men detached from the unit to me is anything other than fanatically loyal to you, sir."

"You're sure?"

"I'm sure. But I have agents within the group who'll report the slightest hint of dissidence."

"Good. I'll be depending on your bodyguards for any emergency security during the trial, and afterward there'll be a purge of the Protector's Own. They must always be without the slightest stain on their escutcheon."

"I agree, sir," Njangu said fervently, wondering what the hell an escutcheon was.

The long transmission squeaked offplanet, was received, retransmitted. It would be the next to last Njangu planned to 'cast, unless there were problems.

He waited for a return by the receiver Maev had set up in one of the com rooms of the palace, getting nothing more than a single code group that translated as:

READY.

Sixteen days until the operation would be mounted.

"*Mil* Jaansma," the guard lieutenant said, "this man will be yours, and the other bandits', defender."

The lean man with a sloppy shave and bad breath bobbed his head up and down.

"*Judicate* Blayer is my name and rank, and I want you to know I was assigned this task. It was hardly of my own wishes, naturally."

"Naturally," Garvin said. "I assume you normally work in a rope factory?"

"No. No. I'm a *Judicate*, as I just said," Blayer said in an annoyed manner. "What makes you think I have anything to do with rope?"

"Nothing at all, Judicate," Garvin said dryly. "I was thinking of some other hangman. Let me introduce you to my fellow brigands."

Twelve days.

The Protector's Own were well deployed in positions from the sanitarium to the Palace of Justice. They'd spent days practicing moving from their Aerial Combat Vehicles into the fighting stations they'd built along the road, securing the approaches to the Palace of Justice.

Their officers therefore went into shock when the unit was suddenly withdrawn and confined to barracks. No explanation was given, nor did Protector Redruth or Commander Celidon agree to meet with any of the unit's officers.

The only exceptions were a scatter of the soldiers on diplomatic guard in distant cities, and the twenty-five assigned to *Leiter* Ab Yohns.

Six days.

"You may stand at ease," Maev shouted.

"Stand at! EASE!" the warrant bellowed, and the

boots of the twenty-three soldiers slammed against the concrete outside their hasty-barracks on Yoshitaro's estate.

"You've been assigned a special duty," Maev shouted. "This comes directly from the Protector himself, through *Leiter* Yohns."

In spite of their discipline, an awed intake of breath ran through the ranks.

"SILENCE IN RANKS!" the noncom shouted, and there was silence.

"Your task is very important, and is a test of the security of the Palace of Justice itself, during the trial of the Cumbrian outlaws. There will be no chance of a full-scale rehearsal before this exercise is mounted, other than computer gaming and mapboard exercises, so you must be sure you miss no opportunities to comment and criticize as you learn.

"You will tell no one about your new assignment task, on pain of the most severe punishment, and are forbidden to discuss it among yourselves except when senior officers are present," Maev ordered.

Five days.

"I love Telex, yes I do, and my whole goddamned family loves it, too," Njangu crooned as he fitted the detonator into the pliable block of explosive, flattened the block, and slid it into a padded envelope that was labeled DRUG SAMPLES. HANDLE WITH CARE.

"Now, we just add this little bitty antihandling device, in case the good doctor decides to go through his mail ahead of time, and walla! We are ready to come down dancing!"

"That'll be enough to vaporize a whole room," Maev said.

"Well, he might not have it on his lap when I start fondling the switch, and I don't want to make any mistakes and leave the puke alive," Njangu said.

"You're sure he's going to hold still for that envelope getting stuck in his briefcase?"

"Sure. It'll happen when he goes through standard security check that morning. I'll be dancing and brilliant and telling him all about new triumphs the Protector is interested in that'll leave him up to his shoulder blades in blood, and the sadistic prick'll never be watching my hands."

Four days.

Njangu landed the lifter and went into the rural mail delivery post, coming back a few moments later.

"And what was that?" Maev asked.

"A letter, signed by my four patriotic companions, Brythe, Pyder, Enida, and Karig, to Protector Redruth, saying how they suspect I'm in league with social misfit elements, and that they hope they're wrong, but they feel they must report this, as their patriotic duty. Also, they suspect Kerman is in on the plot, which is why they feared to report their suspicions to him.

"Maybe that'll get the narking bastard of a household head strung up. Always lurking around with an ear cocked. Never *could* stand a snitch."

"And now your girlfriends . . . sorry, former girlfriends," Maev said, "maybe won't end up in front of a firing squad or in one of Dr. Miuss's experiments when the smoke clears and you and I are gone goslings."

Njangu's smile vanished. "Yeh. That's what I hope. I couldn't come up with any better idea.

"Come on. We've got to pick up Alpha and Beta. They get worried if I don't have a gun guard hanging over my shoulder for longer than a minute and a half."

"Speaking of which, what're you going to do about *them*?"

"You know, if I didn't keep reminding myself they'd drop me in a Kuran instant if they knew who I really was, I might get slightly fond of those oxen. But the matter'll be taken care of. Let's leave it at that."

Three days.

*   *   *

The convoy was very impressive to guard three
women and a man:

A column of soldiers, now conventional infantry instead of the Protector's Own, lined the steps out of
the sanitarium. Garvin, Lir, Montagna, and Mahim,
who still limped a little, went down the steps into the
windowless troop transport, an unarmed lifter that re-
sembled the Force's Griersons. Two Ayesha, the Larissan Zhukov, sat in front and back of the transport. A
Nana-class patrol boat hovered overhead.

The gunships and transport lifted, turned through
180 degrees, staying over the road in case the shoulders had been mined, and went down the winding
road, through the city suburbs to the Palace of Justice.

All crews were well briefed, their orders overseen
by Njangu: If they were attacked, the escorting ships
were instantly to move against the threat. The prisoner
vehicle was to ground immediately, button up, and
wait for support elements to arrive.

Two days.

"The people of Larix and Kura call for Justice,"
Judicate and *Leiter* Vishinsk snarled, "and their valiant
cries will be, must be, heard.

"These beings—I can hardly bring myself to call
them women and men—at the bar show their horrible
guilt in their bearing, their furtive expressions, and I
doubt that the State will require more than a few moments to find them most guilty of all the charges
they're accused of.

"The four accused are Garvin Jaansma . . ."

Garvin tried to look unfurtive as Vishinsk shouted
on. The courtroom was huge, with stainless-steel pan-
eling instead of wood. There were few spectators, but
many vids, covering the four from every angle. Paired
guards with blasters at port arms stood at the two
main doors, another pair at the door to the judge's
chambers.

Vishinsk sat at a high podium, with two flags—Garvin assumed Larix and Kura—and a more-than-life-size holo of Protector Redruth, dressed in the same red-and-black robes the judge wore, behind him.

Garvin noted in Redruth's society the judge and prosecutor were combined in a single man, which certainly made matters convenient.

There also didn't seem to be any jury present, so Garvin guessed Vishinsk would present the charges, listen to whatever defense was presented, and reach an equitable verdict.

Garvin was very glad he wasn't Larissan or Kuran, especially a guilty Larissan or Kuran. Or an innocent one, for that matter. He supposed, from what little Yoshitaro had told him about his past, Njangu might find this sort of "justice" familiar.

It was tempting just to let everything wash over him, and worry about what, exactly, Njangu had planned. He hadn't told any of the prisoners anything. Garvin wondered why, then realized Yoshitaro was afraid Miuss would try again, covertly, with his drugs.

That was quite sensible, and part of standard procedure for anyone without a need to know knowing nothing.

But Garvin Jaansma liked it damned little.

"I'm most impressed with your performance," Maev told the assembled noncoms of her special unit. "I think, if your security test goes, in practice, as smoothly as our mapboard trials have, there will be not only medals, but promotions.

"I think I shall be able to increase that probability, since I've been chosen by Protector Redruth to monitor your performance from his private headquarters.

"I'm disappointed, of course, that I won't be able to lead you in person. But I have great faith in your ability to make the day of execution one that no one will ever forget."

You, not to mention Njangu, and hopefully a whole gaggle of his friends, she thought.

The first day of the trial had been confined to reading the long list of charges, and hearing *Judicate* Blayer squeaking "Innocent" or "Not to be Proven" to each of them.

On the second day, Vishinsk ran through the witnesses he would offer, and how he would take the people, step by step, through the nefarious deeds the raiders had committed before they were finally brought down.

Njangu's final com consisted of one coded word: "Go."

He shut the transmitter down and sprayed the inside of the phony rock with solvent that'd melt the components into a nice unanalyzable blob.

Judicate and *Leiter* Vishinsk had just presented the first holo of Kura Four, with skillful animation showing how the raiders had been inserted, when two *velv* popped out of hyperspace. The single Nana-boat guarding the nav point didn't have time for a challenge or alarm before missiles blew it apart.

Seconds later, two transports, four Kelly-class destroyers and seven more *velv,* with mounted *aksai,* came out of N-space and drove for Larix.

The testimony droned on, and court was finally adjourned.

The four Cumbrians were escorted back to their ACV, booted in, and leg shackles fastened. One of the guards growled something threatening, was backhanded for overstepping his bounds by his warrant.

The lifter took off, and the three ACVs started back for the sanitarium.

Njangu grounded the lim on a hilltop that gave him line of sight to the sanitarium, less than a kilometer away.

"What's wrong, sir?" Goon Alpha asked, weapon coming into his hand, as he scanned the ground around them.

"Nothing," Njangu said. "I want to watch the prisoners come in from up here, make sure there aren't any gaps in our security."

He lifted the lim's canopy, got out, stretched. His bodyguards came out, moved ahead of him, eyes scanning the brush for any threats.

A gun was in Njangu's hand, and he aimed carefully, shooting Alpha in the back. As he went down, Beta turned, a stunned expression on his face. Yoshitaro shot him in the neck, corrected his aim and put another bolt through his chest as he fell. He checked the bodies. Both were dead.

"Take over and carry out the simulated attack," Maev ordered, and the noncom saluted, spun to the waiting Protector's Own.

"Weapons ready . . . all right, like we've been ordered, we're pretending we're trying to take the Palace of Justice. Come on now, move out! At the double!"

The twenty-four men, in open formation, trotted down a passageway toward the Palace of Justice.

Maev jumped back in the lifter and went at full speed toward the sanitarium.

On the palace grounds, alarms screamed as the running, armed men were spotted.

An infantry officer of one of the units guarding the road between the palace and the sanitarium heard his com shrill, had the receiver in his hand.

"Sixty Squad, Nair."

"The Palace of Justice is under attack!" the com squawked. There was no ID, but Nair recognized his superior's voice. "Pull back to your transports and proceed immediately to the palace for further orders!"

"What about the road security?"

"Diddle the goddamned road! Protector Redruth could be in danger!"

Nair was shouting orders as he shut off the com, and bewildered men piled out of their weapons pits, ran toward their ACVs as equally perplexed pilots and gunners started the drives.

Security officers were momentarily stunned, then reacted with grim competence. There *had* been a plot, the goddamned Gray Avengers existed, and they were after the Cumbrians. Thank Redruth the criminals weren't still in the courtroom. The officers wondered, as they gave orders for full alert and shoot on sight, what had gone wrong with the plotters' timing.

Seconds later, high overhead, patrol ships reported unknown ships in-atmosphere. The Cumbrians struck hard, driving through the unready defense.

Below lay their target, Larix's Palace of Justice.

Aboard the lead Kelly, *Mil* Liskeard watched the ground close, wished the target was that damned Redruth, wished whoever'd given them their targets, who must have some good ground intel, had also been able to find out where the Protector was skulking. Hell, maybe Redruth was right in the center of the target area. Liskeard hoped so.

"Target . . . acquired," his weapons officer said.

"Fire one through three," Liskeard said, and three Goddards slashed down toward the Palace of Justice.

The three ACVs in the prisoner convoy were in view. Njangu counted, watched as the lead Ayesha closed on the crossroads guarded with three now-empty weapons positions.

"And two, and one, and go," he said, touched the detonator switch.

The three charges concealed in the sandbags exploded as one, catching the Ayesha as it flew overhead. The ACV's gyros tumbled, and the ship skidded sideways, rolled onto its back, smashed into the ground and exploded.

The rear Ayesha banked, gun and missile crews coming to full alert, looking for a target.

The ACV carrying the prisoners dropped, hit hard on the road, skidding into cover behind a stone building just beyond the crossroads.

The Ayesha sent a rocket into the boiling smoke from the blast, accomplishing nothing, as a pair of *aksai* came out of the setting sun. Two rockets from each ship hit the Ayesha, and fire balled where it had been.

Dr. Miuss was examining a holo of a human body, its skin stripped away, stimulating certain nerves to see, in slow motion, which nerve centers received the pain impulse first, when the briefcase on the desk across from him exploded.

The blast tumbled him back through a table laden with glass labware, then into a fume cabinet.

Nurses were in the lab almost instantly. They thought they were well used to horror, but the man hanging upside down, impaled on a shard of supposedly blast-resistant clear plas, spurting blood as if he'd been razor-slashed a thousand times, sickened them.

By the time they found a way to get Miuss down, he'd bled to death.

The Goddards smashed into the center of the Palace of Justice. *Judicates* Vishinsk and Blayer were in Vishinsk's chambers, going over their notes for the next day's testimony, when the first missile went off. They had a moment to look up, to feel terror, and an explosion ripped away the roof, and turned them into a red-gray-white mosaic on one of the steel walls.

"None of you shitheads move," the guard said, turned in his seat, weapon held ready on the four Cumbrians. "If anybody's trying to break you out, I'll have to—"

"Knock it off," the pilot said. "There's that *Leiter* . . . what's his name, Yohns, waving at us." Automatically his voice went mechanical: "Watch yourselves. Ramp coming open."

Both ramps dropped, and Njangu ducked into the ship.

"We're being hit by social misfits," he said. "Stand by to take off."

"Yessir," the pilot said. "But—"

"I'm countermanding my own orders. Come on, man, move! I'll watch theses bastards."

The guard turned to the front, and Njangu shot him in the back of his helmet. The blaster noise deafened Yoshitaro as the blood, plas, and gray matter sprayed across the controls. He shot the pilot, and he slumped forward, onto his instruments.

The four, even Garvin, gaped.

Njangu pulled compound bolt cutters from a pouch, quickly cut the four's leg irons.

"Anytime, people," Njangu said. "It's time to go home."

The prisoners were on their feet, pushing toward the ramp. Garvin grabbed Njangu by the arm.

"Thanks for thinking of us," he said.

"See what happens when you try to do something solo?" Njangu responded. "Hope you learned your lesson."

Garvin had enough strength to growl, then pushed past, into sunlight, just as a lighter grounded in front of them, and Maev Stiofan jumped out, pistol in hand. The prisoners flinched, then realized the woman must be on their side, since she wasn't shooting them.

"We're going home in that lifter?" Lir managed, then two Kellys were overhead, the armed transports behind them. They lowered, crushing the buildings on either side of the road, and ports slid open. The prisoners didn't wait for orders, but ran, stiffly, awkwardly, toward the transports.

"Come on, Maev," Njangu said. "I want to introduce you to some friends of mine."

*   *   *

Aksai, velv, and Kellys swept across the government compound, firing with missiles at anything bigger than a man, chainguns at anything on two legs.

Sometime in the swirling chaos, the last of Maev's fanatics died, either killed by the Cumbrians or by Larissan security troops.

A rocket coming from above missed an *aksai* by a few meters, exploded against a tower and the tower lifted as if it wanted to become a rocket, collapsed.

"Gotcha, gotcha, gotcha," Ben Dill said, as he rolled over the top, acquired the Nana-boat that had tried to shoot down the other *aksai,* blew it apart.

A voice came in his headphone:

"All recovery elements, disengage. I say again, disengage and withdraw."

"Aw," Dill whined, "and Ben was just starting to have fun."

Mil Angara stood on the field at Camp Mahan, watched the formation of ships settle toward him.

"*How* long did you say the raid took?"

"Less than ten E-minutes," Hedley said. "In, down up, and gone. Just like that."

"I heard the report," Angara said. "And I know all the goddamned tac manuals talk about the virtue of surprise. But I still don't believe *no* goddamned casualties."

"Actually, there was one. Some crewman on one of the destroyers broke his leg on a missile loader. But, yessir, no real casualties. Probably a bad thing, sir," Hedley said. "Probably make them flipping overconfident, won't it?"

Angara started to snarl, saw Hedley's grin.

"Oh yeh," Hedley went on. "Revision on that casualty list. A certain *Cent* Ben Dill reports a torn hangnail, getting out of his *aksai,* and wants another wound stripe."

CHAPTER
16

Larix/Larix Prime

"Larix and Kura have taken enough from the brigands of Cumbre," Protector Redruth ranted into the coms. "This last offense is intolerable.

"Cumbre has repeatedly refused any peaceful settlements of our differences, and has responded with outrageous force, proving that Cumbre has no intention of respecting our worlds and, in fact, clearly intends to take them over.

"Not only have we been attacked by these barbarians, but there have been certain traitors who've sold out their birthright to the Cumbrians for gold.

"Now is the day our enemies, both within and without, are to be extirpated!

"It is with deep regret, but remembering my duty to the men and women of Larix and Kura, I must announce that a state of war now exists between Cumbre and Larix/Kura.

"From this moment forward, force will be met with force, until our soldiers grasp ultimate victory, and the spoils of Cumbre are ours!"

CHAPTER
17

Cumbre/D-Cumbre

Garvin Jaansma was awarded the Order of Merit, the Force's third-highest medal, which he hadn't wanted to accept, since the raid had been a failure. Njangu told him not to make waves. He himself was damned well going to take his Star of Gallantry, the second-highest decoration, and wear it on his goddamned kepi or maybe tape it on his nose, and Jaansma had best not screw up the ceremony. Garvin backed down, after a bit of consideration, took the medal, and thanked *Caud* Angara in a very humble manner.

The other military survivors got Silver Crosses, and the casualties posthumous Bronze Crosses. The enlisted also got promoted a grade. Monique Lir was now *Adj-Prem*, the highest enlisted rank the Force had, even though her job slot didn't call for the rank.

Grig Angara, Jon Hedley, and Angara's staff had finished a quiet meal in a private dining room of the Shelburne Hotel. The room had been swept for bugs, and three security techs lurked unobtrusively outside against electronic intruders.

"A question about work, sir?" Angara's III Section, Operations, *Mil* Ken Fong, asked.

"As if we've been talking about anything else," Angara said. "Go ahead."

"Going to basics, just how are we going to fight Larix/Kura? Have you developed a strategy yet?"

Angara drank tea and considered his answer.

"Ideally, we'd be able to mount the old Confederation special: Send a fleet, punt some missiles in to get their attention, tell them they're going to be good boys from now on, and if the slightest objection came, invade."

"All we lack for that to be a flipping option," Hedley said, "is a fleet. Assorted steel and alloys in shipyards still a-welding don't generally fight that well."

"Not to mention," the Personnel officer said, "the Force is undermanned for any major campaign. Assuming the old rule holds true, that you need at least ten to one odds to win an opposed invasion."

"Ah, but our morale soars and our hearts are pure, which gives us a mighty edge," Erik Penwyth said cynically, and there was a ripple of amusement.

"There is a bit of truth to that," Hedley said. "Yoshitaro's reports suggest there's some conscript sullenness in Redruth's army. Which doesn't mean they won't die well under certain circumstances, or that certain elite elements in the army aren't brave. Still."

"And why aren't our noble heroes present?" someone asked.

"This is just one of my unofficial-idea dinners," Angara said. "I don't pull people back from leave unless there's an emergency."

"It seems before there's any kind of invasion, they'll have to be whittled down somewhat," Hedley said.

"I suppose, since I'm not one of those fools who believes strategic air does anything but make big holes in the ground, sir," Fong asked, "there's no way we could bash them somewhat, then ignore them?"

"I don't think," Angara said, "that Protector Redruth would accept a bashing, shut up, and mind his own business. He appears to be one of those sea monsters who's got to keep swimming, or, in his case, looking for enemies, or he drowns."

"I agree," Hedley said. "Let's face it. Sooner or later,

unless they suddenly show up with wrapped presents, and saying they lost our com number and they're ever so sorry, we're going to have to go find out what happened to the Confederation. Which means prepared to deal with whatever enemies done 'em in.

"And the last thing I want, when we do that, is a flipping open wound like Larix on my flanks."

Maev had to lean close to Njangu and almost shout above the music:

"I love it!"

"Love what?"

"All this." She waved her arm around the crowded, dimly lit club. "I can get roaring drunk, and there won't be any goddamned monitors making sure I'm not thinking anything disloyal; there aren't any assholes wondering if there's some way they could backshoot me and call it a duel; and nobody's looking to hop in bed with anybody else because it'd help his or her career." She sighed happily.

Njangu sipped his wine and stretched like a contented cat. Noise, people, music, good wine . . . why in the hell did he keep insisting on going into places without any of the basic necessities, especially when the people in those places kept trying to kill him?

He took the bottle out of the bucket when a large and drunk man stumbled up to the table.

"Hey cutie . . . wanna dance, dansh, oops."

He pivoted through 180 degrees and fell on the table, which was insufficient for his bulk. The table collapsed, and the ice bucket and chairs smashed.

Maev still held her glass, and Njangu deftly emptied the bottle in the glass, dropped the bottle on the now-snoring drunk's chest, and shouted for a cleanup crew and another bottle.

"Y'see," he said. "I know how to take you to all the right places. Wanna dance some more?"

"I called this minisymposium," Dr. Ann Heiser said,

"not only to let our esteemed colleague have a chance to tell his tales of slaughter, but to pose a very serious question:

"Do any of us have any suggestions we might offer to the Force on how this war might be fought?"

There were two dozen men and women in the room, all civilians except for *Alt* Ho Kang. She'd been recently commissioned for her scientific research during the Musth War, and transferred to Force II Section as an analyst. She still didn't quite believe her new rank, the pay that went with it, and that she wasn't still driving a Grierson around the landscape.

"I'll be more specific about what we're looking for," Froude said. He was still badly underweight from his time in the jungle, but the pallor and the fatigue had mostly gone. "Only because Ann and I discussed this before you were all kind enough to show up here and listen to my war story.

"Let me open with something you may find fairly surprising:

"No one knows very much about hyperspace, about the nature of the beast itself. Stardrive has been around for several millennia, but no one seems to have done intensive research in the area of what, exactly, we're moving through.

"We know, or rather deduce, that N-space is quote real endquote, because it fits into our equations neatly, not to mention the empirical evidence that we actually get somewhere. We generally use certain predetermined navigational points, more for convenience than anything else, to travel from one place to another.

"We have machinery that can guide us from point to point. That machinery, should we make a blind jump, that is, a transition from a known to an unknown point, or unknown to unknown points, can tell us where, in normal space, we emerged.

"Generally, at least.

"In war, if our ships detect an enemy in normal space at a close enough distance, we can follow the enemy into N-space, launch a missile, and destroy that ship or track it as it jumps from place to place. If we are quick enough, we can even launch a special missile from normal into hyperspace, and the enemy can be destroyed. Or so it's presumed, for those circumstances have happened often enough, without that enemy returning to bother us, to make such a generalization. It's very interesting to note, by the way, that very seldom has a ship, to my knowledge, been hit once it enters hyperspace, then later return to normal space with damages. Does that suggest hyperspace acts as a conductor of shock, as water can? Or are the normal alloys used in ship construction weakened, during the time the ship is in hyperspace, so that it is extraordinarily vulnerable to shock?

"All these are most basic questions, and I've not been able to find an answer, nor can I find, anywhere in the literature, any research that's significant, even in those two minor areas.

"There's a great dearth of hard data. We know hyperspace is a finite entity, but—"

"Pardon me, Doctor," Ho Kang asked. "And forgive my ignorance. But *how* do we know it?"

"At least two reasons," Froude said. "First is that we can consistently go from one point to another using the same amount of power and navigational settings. Secondly, it takes the same amount of internal, perceived and recorded, time to make that transition.

"But that's no more, in my opinion, than a blind man who has learned to move around his house by rote, remembering the chair is here, the table there, and so forth. Move the furniture, and the man will become confused and possibly bark his shins.

"I wonder if the Confederation never commissioned a thorough investigation because its wars generally covered a huge area, with ships and fleets going from one place to another before battle commenced, just as ancient warship leaders didn't much care about the oceans they crossed, other than that they were mapped for dangerous reefs to avoid."

A woman stood. "Even though practical physics isn't my area of interest, I agree we know little, damned little about this convenient dimension called N-space. But I don't see how that pertains to your opening statement about fighting this conflict with Larix/Kura. Other, of course, than basic research has historically been well fueled by a good solid war."

There was laughter as the woman sat down.

"I'm not sure, either," Froude said. "All I know is that when two men are going to have a flight, and neither one knows anything about the field of conflict, the one who finds a map, or better yet visits the potential battleground, has an infinite advantage.

"I'll simply—I hope—clarify what I'm stumbling around with this illustration."

He went to the old-fashioned greenboard, picked up a marker.

Froude put a large K on one side of the board, an L about half a meter away.

"Here we have Kura, over here, Larix. Kura is the food basket for Protector Redruth's empire. Larix is the industrial complex. Eliminate Kura, and the Larissans starve. Eliminate Larix, and the Kurans go back to harvesting their crops with hand tools."

Froude drew a circle around one letter, then a tube to the other, and a circle around it. His sketch looked like a weightlifter's dumbbell.

He drew an X on the tube.

"Here, then, might be the vulnerable area. Strike here, in the hyperspace between the two systems, or at the nav points where a ship emerges from hyperspace to reset its navigational apparatus before jumping again, in a manner I haven't the foggiest about, and the results might be most impressive."

"I think," Ben Dill said, speaking precisely as he picked up the pitcher of beer and drank directly from

it, "the next stage oughta be going over and ham-
mering those goddamned Kurries and Larries."

"Ah, but where, specifically?" Alikhan asked. He
wasn't in much better shape than his friend, having
eaten a container of the spoiled, spiced meat the
Musth used for a narcotic.

There were about twenty soldiers in a corner of the
comfortable, old-fashioned noncommissioned officers'
mess. Almost all were I&R people. Alikhan and Dill
were the only officers, present by invitation for a quiet
wake for the three I&R soldiers lost on Kura. The
only other raider there was medic Jil Mahim, who
claimed the best vacation imaginable was to lie in bed,
listen to the shouted orders, old-fashioned bugle calls,
and loudspeakered commands, then roll over and go
back to sleep because none of them was for her. Dill
had already accused her of Strange Thinking, and
been punished with a pitcher dumped in his lap.

"Why," *Tweg* Lav Huran, Oct Team Leader, Second Troop, I&R, "where they are, of course."

"Who in hell promoted *that* man to warrant?"
someone said. "Outstanding frigging talent for the
obvious."

"That," Alikhan said, "will be determined in the
course of events, I suspect. I have a better question:
What do you humans plan to do with these people
after you win the war?"

"You see why I love this guy?" Dill bellowed. "He
always assumes on the sunny side of the street."

"I'd guess," said *Tweg* Rad Dref, a Grierson aircraft
commander with I&R, "we'll hang that Redruth and
the rest of his war-criminal ossifers by the balls, and
let the other people go on about their business, leaving
us alone."

"Or maybe we oughta sorta scoop 'em up," another
noncom said. "Import 'em to Cumbre to do our
scutwork.

"Especially the cute ones," she added. "Leaving
their balls intact."

"I asked the question," Alikhan went on, "because of what I've heard about these people. Unless all of you are exaggerating, the people on Larix and Kura seem to have little free spirit or independence."

" 'Ats what the intel has," *Senior Tweg* Als Severine, II Section Senior analyst, said. "We've gone out and talked to a lot of the Rentiers an' such, who used to go over to Larix for shopping and getting in trouble they didn't want to get back here, back before the Confederation went and vanished on us.

"They all talk about how the Larissans would be terrified of anybody who had more clout than they did, and, if they couldn't get out of the way of those anybodies, they couldn't be enough of a slave for 'em."

"I wouldn't believe a Rentier about anything," Mahim said. "But didn't these Larissans have that evil little side glance you get when you're on the bottom that says someday your back's going to be turned, and I'll have a big long knife, and then you're for it?"

"Believe it or not, Jil, I know what you're talking about, and that was one of the questions we asked," Severine said. "Nobody claimed to have seen anything like it."

"Hmmph," Mahim said skeptically. "Hard to believe the trampled class doesn't want to do paybacks."

"We also checked any old holos from Larix or Kura," Severine said, "when we were building our profile of your average, mythical kind of Larissan. We knew goddamned good and well those holos didn't report nahthing but sweetness and light, but still looked for stories about, oh, some servant wiping out all of the children he was put in charge of, or some chauff . . . shoof . . . sorry, a little too much alk . . . some pilot doing a headfirst into the ground with his employers in the backseat.

"Nothing."

"So far, this bears out my question," Alikhan said. "If these people appear to have been beaten down by this Protector, and I guess he was the third generation to do this, what happens after the war?"

"Howzabout," Dill said, emptying the pitcher into his glass, tossing it back over his head to thud down somewhere, "we just blow 'em out of the skies and move on?"

"That will not work," Alikhan said. "They will do nothing but fret for a time, then find themselves another dictator, and try once more."

"So that means," Huran said, "we'll have to first beat their butts flat, then go in on the ground and play nursemaid for a generation? Shit, I don't like that at all, at all."

"Who knows?" Mahim said. "But I feel sorriest for the poor bastards around this table, who are going to make that landing, and get dead flattening butts."

"That's what we get paid damned little for," Dref said.

"Shuddup, everybody," Dill said, standing. From somewhere, he'd found another full pitcher. He clambered on top of the table, and started singing the age-old song:

> *Did you ever think when a hearse went by*
> *That you might be the next to die?*

Then, changing tempo:
> *The worms crawl in*
> *The worms crawl out*
> *The worms dance tangos*
> *All over your snout.*

He went back to speech:
"A hymn to the next of us to go south:
"Hymn . . . hymn . . . screw him . . ."
None of the other drinkers in the cavernous club, nor the barkeeps, thought of intervening. I&R mourned their dead in their way, and would retaliate terribly against any interruptions.

When the singing started, Jil Mahim put her head down on the table and began snoring gently. A considerate warrant moved her head out of the pool of beer it was lying in.

Monique Lir clambered the last few meters to the top of the sea mount just before dawn. A thousand and more meters below her, waves crashed sullenly on the rocks around the pillar and rocked the small boat she'd rented.

Lir had driven in a skyhook at midnight and hung a hammock from it, a little angry at herself that she'd take a third day to finish the ascent.

The top of the sea mount was about thirty meters to a side and had collected enough dirt for a few small, twisted trees to grow.

Lir slid out of her pack and her climbing harness, stretched, allowed herself two sips of water as a reward for this first ascent.

She sat, cross-legged, on the stone as the sun slowly came up, emptying her mind. As far as she could see, in any direction, was nothing but water. No boats, no people, no aircraft, no loudspeakers, no officers, no noncoms, no crunchies.

A perfect leave.

Lir knew there were horrendous stories about how she spent her leaves, from running a whorehouse specializing in sadomasochism to being a millionaire recluse on some far-off island where no one knew her real name. She didn't bother to deny them.

All that mattered was this stillness, this peace atop a mountain, preferably one that had never been climbed, even more preferably one that was unknown or considered unclimbable.

She would eat, sleep until midday, then rope back to her boat and navigate for that second sea-pillar no one seemed to have gone up.

Monique Lir was having a wonderful leave.

CHAPTER
18

"Here I thought you went and learned your lesson about doing anything without my kind fatherly hand," Njangu Yoshitaro said briskly, swiveling in his chair to face Garvin. "But you didn't. Which got you in a goddamned dungeon, rotting your toenails off.

"After that, you shoulda figured out you're supposed to be the Perfect Leader, out there all nit and tiddy in your goddamned white uniform waving the saber, and I'm the guy that tells you when to charge and in what direction.

"Now, let's talk about this flight-school shit," Yoshitaro went on. "You're gonna leave that frigging Penwyth in charge of me and I&R while you go farting around for what, six months?"

"What's the matter with Erik?" Garvin asked.

"Not that much, actually," Njangu admitted. "Rich people just make me nervous. Forget him. Go back to that six months you're at Zoomie school."

"A lot less than that," Garvin said. "They're doing a lot of hypnopacking, like they did with basic drill."

"I thought hypnosis only conditions you to do things reflexively, like right face and to the rear harch and shit like that."

"They think, with enough repetitions, they can give us more than that."

"Us. Who's us?"

"The old man's ordered a big push on pilots. Anybody that's ever wanted to fly is going to get a chance. No bullshit, no drill, just intensive hands-on stuff,"

Garvin said. "Hypno can give you instant response to say, spin recovery, at least the book response, just like it can teach you how to do hup-ho inspection arms."

He grinned sheepishly. "And don't I sound like I know what the hell I'm talking about. We'll find out whether that works in a week or so."

Njangu stared at Garvin for a very long moment.

"One more time: We?"

"Oh yeh. I went and volunteered you, too."

"You don't screw around, do you?"

"Can't," Garvin said briskly. "We got a war to win. The first raid goes out against Kura tomorrow morning. Besides, weren't you ragging me a couple of minutes ago about daring to do things without you being two steps to my right and two to my rear, butting in and telling me what I'm doing wrong?"

Njangu considered. "Well, shut my moneymakin' mouth. I think I went and argued myself into an untenable position, like the educated sorts say.

"So I guess I'm gonna go learn how to crash into things. Maybe that'll get me a couple extra credits a month, knowing how to swoop around the heavens."

Njangu frowned, turned serious. "Actually, Garvin, m'friend, that does bring up an interesting thought."

"What, you crashing into things?"

"No. Look. We're gonna go beat up Larix/Kura, right?"

"Gad, no wonder I follow you in wonderment. You reach such amazing conclusions without needing any hard evidence like us commoners."

"You got that right," Njangu said. "The first stage is going to be farting around in outer space, right? That doesn't give a lot of opening for I&R, does it?

"Second stage will have to be a ground invasion. So we'll go in front, like always, and get killed."

"That sounds like SOP for Idiots and Runners," Garvin said.

"Uh-huh. Then, after we beat Redruth to a bloody pulp, then what? Then we go looking for the Confederation to try to figure out what happened, right? Which will probably involve some folks of Evil Intent and, again, will be, at least in the first stages, fought or at least investigated in space."

"Mmmh," Garvin said. "I'm starting to track."

"Yeh," Njangu agreed. "It doesn't sound like I&R's gonna be a real astounding place to get medals, which translates to more money and loot, now does it?"

"You're thinking it's time to move on?"

"No way," Njangu said. "What, go into one of the regiments and specialize in shining boots, spaceship corridors, and saying yessir in chorus? That idea blows *giptels*.

"I think what we'd better start thinking about is how we transition I&R, in toto, into the future."

"I'm listening."

"I'm not ready to tell you Steps Alpha through Omega," Njangu said. "But I'll give you a clue. If we go hootin' after the Confederation, we're gonna need a bigger army, right?"

"You don't think the ten thou of us in the Legion aren't going to conquer all, what with our clean livers and pure thoughts?" Garvin said. "Sorry. Didn't mean to get silly. You're right."

"Damned straight I'm right. The Force gets big, I&R gets big, too."

"What, like a Recon Regiment if the Force goes up to a Division in strength? That'd make you a *Caud* and me, what? *Super-Caud*?"

"Think armies, bwana," Njangu whispered. "Think beeeg armies. Think of all those Larries and Kurries we're going to be drafting when this war is over. Think of that Star Marshal rank you're always trying to bullshit me into believing you're the illegitimate son of. By the way, does that rank really exist?"

"Hell if I know," Garvin said. "Daddy might've been lying to Momma. I'm just a simple circus boy." He looked out the window of the I&R office as a squad of new trainees doubled past.

"Beeeg armies, huh?

"Maybe we *better* do some serious plotting. And also see about making some under-the-counter investments in ship factories."

The six Kuran ships lifted from scattered airfields, each heavy-laden with processed or fresh foodstuffs for Larix, and joined up out-atmosphere. There was an elderly patrol craft as group commander, more a formality than anything else.

They were about to enter hyperspace when the Parnell, the newly named *Nectan,* a third Kelly-class, and two *velv* spat from behind one of Kura's moons. The patrol ship CO challenged them, realizing they were enemy ships only as the four Force craft launched missiles.

Suddenly there were four fire-streaked gasballs in space. The fifth Cumbrian missile detonated early, and the merchant ship that had been its target had an instant to yelp a mayday before a second launch blew it apart. The sixth ship turned back toward Kura and was in the ionosphere when a missile from one *velv* took it, and Kura's night sky became a fireworks display.

The patrol ship scuttled for hyperspace, but a *velv* had a lock on it and launched. The modified Goddard went into N-space after the patrol ship, which was never seen again.

The Cumbrian ships jumped back into invisibility. War was now joined.

"This," Ben Dill said into the microphone, "is going to be the most goddamned weird flying school any of us has ever attended.

"Look around."

The sixty trainees, from recruits to warrants to officers, Garvin and Njangu among them, obeyed. They also considered the line of officers and enlisted men on the stage with two aliens, their future instructors.

"The standard thing," Dill continued, "is say good-bye to the one on your right, the two on your left, or whatever the number the school figures it's gonna bust out.

"That's bullshit. We—the Force—want every swingin' Richard of you to graduate, to get your ickle-pretty pilot's wings. So help the woman or man next to you if you can. We'll make a First in Class award, no more, so you don't have to worry about backbiting for minor points. Everybody else is just Pass or Fail.

"We're in a war, and we don't have time for batshit. That means us instructors aren't gonna worry about whether you shined your boots last night or if you're even wearing boots. For those of you who're fresh enlistees, you'll get all that stuff hypnotically, like the more experienced sorts did.

"We want you to learn. Every one of you's said she or he was interested in flying, and you've all got the brains. I've looked at your test scores.

"So you're capable. Maybe you're going to find out you really didn't want to fly, don't like space, aren't that quick with your math or spatial relationships or have the common sense to not want to leave nice, safe dirt.

" 'Kay. You gave it a try, and you can go back to your home formation not feeling bad. Nobody's going to be screaming at you, making you run up and down hills or do push-ups or any of the rest of the crap.

"The OIC of the school is Force Commander Angara. Everybody else works for him, no matter what the rank. That means I'll be teaching, Alikhan here'll be teaching, this little shit here named Gorecki'll be teaching. We want to help, not hurt you. Sometimes one person'll be instructing you, sometimes another. Don't worry about changes in your instructors. Like I said, we've got a war to fight, so your instructor on one day might be out there beatin' up Larries the next. This whole mess is gonna be catch-as-catch-can.

"Another thing. Don't be afraid of asking questions

or even pulling something semidumb. If it's too dumb, and it doesn't kill you, but it damned near kills me, then you're gone. Otherwise, you get another chance at an instructor.

"This whole deal is going to be hard and fast, down and dirty.

"Make me . . . and the Force . . . proud of you. Now, let's go to work."

"Sorry to lift you from going round about in the middle of the air, Njangu," Hedley said. "But you're our current expert on what Redruth and his number two, that Celidon, might be thinking.

"You were copied the report on the first raid, which was a total success. What do you think the response from Larix/Kura will be to that?"

"I can't say precisely, sir," Njangu said. "But I'd think Redruth's first reaction would be to beef up the patrols around Kura. Celidon might think we're going back and forth to confuse them, so he might want heavy patrols around Larix, figuring that'll be our next target."

"Mmmh," Angara said. "That's exactly our plan for the next raid."

"Then, what I'd suggest, maybe, is hit them as hard as you can. Celidon will probably be expecting another light raid as we escalate . . . and not have as heavy a response element as he should have. Maybe. Sir."

"Not a bad idea at all," Hedley said. "Assuming that we eventually are going to have to invade them, wouldn't it be a good idea to take out as many of their warships as possible, right now?

"Thank God we've got the Musth nice and happy and mining half of flipping C-Cumbre for metal to sell back to us as *aksai* and *velv*, so maybe we're actually able to build more ships than Redruth can shoot down.

"A slight veer, Njangu. I've read your report on these Naarohn-class cruisers Redruth supposedly wants to build. We've seen none in action or on the ground yet, although the heaviest intel I've been willing to commit to is a zoom-by pass on Larix Prime and Secundus. You said that Celidon was opposed to building these cruisers. Is there any possibility he convinced Redruth and we won't have to worry about those pigs coming out of the woodwork?"

"No, sir," Njangu said flatly. "If Redruth changes his mind, all on his own, then no Naarohns. But from what I saw, nobody's got much of a chance to change anything with Redruth, once he's set."

"Like most dictators," Angara said.

Njangu saw Penwyth look at the ceiling, could read his thoughts: *And Commanding Officers.* He buried a grin.

"If I may make a suggestion, sir?" he said.

"Go ahead."

"If I were you, rather than screw around waiting for these cruisers to show up, I'd jump the gun and go after them in the shipyards, sir."

"We don't really have the ships ready for that heavy a raid," Angara said. "Or, we do. But I'd have to assume we'd take significant casualties going after the yards with any kind of precision attack.

"Not to mention we'd have to find all of them . . . you only gave us three or four locations."

"That's why I'd go nuke, sir," Njangu said. "Redruth's already opened the option. If their damned shipyards are glowing in the dark, it'll take time for them to rebuild."

"No," Angara said flatly. "The Confederation policy is to use nuclear weaponry only against a purely military target, and then only as a last resort."

His voice didn't encourage further discussion. Njangu caught Penwyth's eye, and he nodded once.

"Yessir," was all Yoshitaro said.

"I guess that's all," Angara said. "Jon, do you have anything more?"

"Nope."

Njangu stood, saluted, and went out. Penwyth was right behind him.

"You see, you atrocity-committin' radioactive snake, the way we upholders of truth and justice think?" the slender man drawled.

"Yeh. Damned glad we're fighting such a *moral* damned war. And I think I can weasel out of the rest of the day's training, since it's only got an hour to go. You, you truthie justicer, can buy the first round."

The next raid lasted longer and was a great deal bloodier. For both sides.

Two Cumbrian Kellys, *Caud* Angara on the bridge of the lead ship, dropped from hyperspace and took out the nearest patrol ship. It should've been a give-away that they let the ship report before they blew it apart, then hung around, waiting.

Half a dozen of the new Larissan destroyers responded. They got the two Kellys on-screen, just as other Cumbrians arrived—two more Kellys, plus ten *velv* and supporting *aksai*.

The Larissans called for more backup and, outnumbered, attacked. No one had ever accused the Larries of lacking courage.

Another formation of destroyers, flanked with patrol ships, took off from Larix Prime. Celidon himself was on the bridge of the command ship.

Again, the Cumbrians stayed in Larissan space, and the battle was fully joined as other Kelly-class ships appeared. Ships swirled, darted in and out of N-space, took hits, and some died.

It was less a battle than a swarming melee, and no one, starting with the fleet commanders, had any idea of what was going on beyond his own short-range screens and bridge.

Caud Angara had figured on the confusion, so each of the Cumbrian ships had a synchronized time tick. At the ordered time, the Cumbrian ships broke contact as best they could and jumped to a prearranged sector of "dead" space. The one Larissan destroyer and two patrol boats able to put tracers on the Cumbrians emerged from N-space into a hail of missiles, and died.

The toll at "day's" end was two Kellys destroyed, with the survivors of one crew recovered against orders, two *velv* destroyed and one *aksai* lost, three *Kellys* damaged.

Larissan casualties were five destroyers and seven patrol boats killed, and an unknown number of ships damaged.

It was a Cumbrian victory, but Angara thought it was far too expensive, a judgment he shared with the other field-grade officers of the Force, and not his men or the exultant holos.

Jon Hedley noted, with cynical amusement, that Loy Kouro's *Matin* was now the loudest to sing praises for the heroic women and men of the Legion.

Hedley kept the detailed assessment of the engagement close, but it was no surprise: The smaller Kellys were more maneuverable and had better electronics suites than the Larissan destroyers, which intelligence arbitrarily dubbed the Lan-class until they'd learn the Larissan designation. The Lan-class, on the other hand, were faster in secondary drive, more heavily armed, and had bigger crews.

Velv were quicker, more maneuverable than both the Lans and the Nana-class patrol ships, and could be more heavily armed than any patrol class. But they were far more fragile than either of the Larissan class, as, of course, were the *aksai*.

The Force's biggest advantage was that the Cumbrian pilots had more combat experience. But that, Hedley and everyone else knew, would change as the war went on.

There were three scales to be considered: which side could outbuild the other; which side could train pilots more quickly; and, of course, which side fought more skillfully.

* * *

To Garvin, Njangu, and the other students, this first battle between the ships of war was no more than noted in passing. They were too busy with their own affairs. Dill might have honestly articulated the school's philosophy, but that didn't mean the instructors, both field and classroom, weren't working their pupils to the bone and beyond.

The *aksai* pod was double-canopied. In one lay Alikhan, in the other Garvin.

"Are you comfortable with the situation?" Alikhan asked.

Garvin wanted to say no, not really, that there was no frigging way he'd been trained enough to even push an out-atmosphere Grierson around, let alone the quirky Musth attack ships.

"Yes, sir," was all he said.

He heard a hiss, looked over at the other bubble, saw Alikhan's mouth open wide, fangs showing, in amusement, obviously knowing Garvin's thoughts.

The *aksai* hung a planetary diameter off D-Cumbre, with nothing but a single chase ship behind it.

"You will note that we are surrounded by nothing but vacuum," Alikhan said. "So if you do go out of control, there is nothing to hit except that other *aksai*, and its pilot is very skilled at evading out-of-control students.

"You have completed both the hypnotism and the computer simulation of the controls and how this ship behaves, so you should not be unfamiliar with what it shall do under your control.

"Are you ready, Garvin?"

Garvin inhaled deeply.

"One question, Alikhan?"

"Ask."

"How many hours did you have in an *aksai* before you were allowed to fly it?"

"That is a hard computation . . . let me think . . .

perhaps two hundred of your hours in various other craft."

Garvin, with a bit over fifty hours, took the controls.

"For our first exercise," Alikhan ordered, "we will accelerate at half drive, and make a complete orbit around the moon Fowey, staying well clear of the surface, and return to this point as closely as you can."

Garvin applied power, felt the increased hum. The *aksai* shot ahead. Fowey grew visibly larger. *Damned thing kicks out,* he thought.

"Very good, Garvin," Alikhan said after a while. "I notice you have been anticipating the behavior of this ship. That is the only way to successfully pilot it. You must stay ahead of the *aksai,* or . . ."

"Or it kills you," Garvin said grimly. They'd lost two students already. War thinking had come fast—the loss of the ships was mourned more than that of the prospective pilots. Besides, the disasters had to have been pilot error, everyone in the class *knew,* since there has never been a flyer who believes in things like luck, fate, or unflyable craft.

"That is true," Alikhan said. "Prepare for the orbital change as you approach the satellite. And do not forget your charting, to reach your desired point of return."

As if I'm not busy enough.

"This is most relaxing," Alikhan said. "After we do two, perhaps three of these simple exercises, it shall be time to learn evasive and quick-response piloting.

"We shall not, initially, practice these tactics against another pilot, for obvious reasons. Instead, you will transition out to the asteroids off G-Cumbre.

"They make perfectly acceptable enemies for the beginner to attack."

Garvin, who'd begun to relax a trifle, found himself as tense as when he'd stuffed himself into this cockpit.

*　　*　　*

"Boss," *Adj-Prem* Monique Lir told Erik Penwyth, "even though you're just acting II Section honcho, I'd like to request a favor."

"Big or small, Monique?" Erik, being an ex–I&R enlisted man, still wasn't used to the woman who'd trained him and then controlled his entire universe sirring him.

"Pretty big."

"Then I think you'd best wait until Garvin and Njangu get their wings or bust out, and the chain of command goes back to normal."

"I already talked to both of them and, well, what I'm asking for is actually sort of their idea. Although the other noncoms and I agree."

Monique didn't explain that it'd taken Garvin and Njangu most of a night they desperately needed for study and sleep to hammer the always-traditional warrants in I&R into seeing beyond the present.

"If both those two have signed off, and want you to push it through, this is goin' to get tricky," Erik said. "Not to mention possibly putting my ass in a crack."

"Not a chance, boss. The Old Man'll probably give you a medal for creativity." Lir wondered where she was suddenly coming up with this sneaky approach, decided she'd been around Yoshitaro too long.

"I&R's up to full strength again," she went on. "Matter of fact, I'm hiding five warm bodies off the roster. And we're not doing anything these days except running up and down hills and trying to keep from being a paintbrush brigade for headquarters."

"I've been tryin' to keep them off your back as much as I can," Penwyth apologized. "But sometimes they get around me, and you folks end up clipping the damnation grass."

"Forget about it, boss. Anyway, the idea we've got is to bust up I&R into the basic two-man fighting pairs, and then put us to work learning how to fight in ships."

"There's no way Angara's going to let I&R be dissolved," Penwyth said. "And I'm a little shocked you can even think about something like that."

"Not permanently," Lir said. "Just for additional training, hopefully going out with the raiders. But the way the war's going to go, I think the Force could use some extra missile crewmen and gunners. Once somebody's learned how to fight from a ship, we can add the specialty to their records."

Penwyth tapped fingers on his desk, realizing that he wasn't the perfect Rentier anymore, since he badly needed a manicure.

"Interestin'," he said. "And not that bad an idea. Not to mention that as the Force gets bigger, which it's going to have to do, I suspect, those I&R people with the extra skills'd be in line for instant promotion."

"A little money never hurts," Lir said.

"The only problem, Monique," Erik said, "is if things get too hectic, everybody who needs a shooter'll be lookin' at I&R as a replacement pool. You could lose some of your best crunchies like that."

"Not to worry," Monique said, expressing a confidence she didn't feel. "The real sneaks'll manage to stay with me, and the rest can go on to glory."

"I'll talk to the Old Man," Penwyth said. "And I don't see any reason he wouldn't let I&R go on temporary duty hither and yon away from home and justify all those rations you clowns suck up.

"Go ahead and start drawin' up the orders and settin' up the pairs."

"Already in the works, boss. I started punching computer buttons this morning."

"Hmph. You presume a lot, *Adj-Prem*."

Redruth tried another surprise attack, sending half a dozen destroyers into the Cumbre system from a nav point "below" the system ecliptic, trying for another strike on D-Cumbre. But Cumbrian detection systems found them, and patrols went after the six. The Larissans were slashed apart far off D-Cumbre, although two Cumbrian ships were destroyed, and three damaged. The war was escalating.

CHAPTER
19

A surprising number of the students made it through flight school: forty-seven total. As promised, the cadre had done everything they could to help. Also I Section—Personnel—had done a good job of trying to put square pegs in square holes.

Of the forty-seven, only a handful were chosen for *aksai* specialty training, which demanded the highest ability—and a fairly unimaginative character, since fighting ships were not high on any insurance actuary's list.

Neither Garvin nor Njangu made the cut, especially since they already had important slots. Nor did they much want to fly *aksai,* even though that was the prestige assignment for pilots.

More students were picked for second seat on a *velv* or a destroyer for seasoning and quick promotion if they fulfilled their promise.

The lower third of the class was assigned to either Griersons or Zhukovs. Angara had decided the Force could take their chances with a lesser pilot at the controls of an ACV, but not of a spaceship. Highly rated aircraft ACV commanders, in spite of their frequent protests, had been scheduled for the next flight class, starting immediately.

After Angara had made a speech, Dill had stumbled through congratulations and gotten teary, wings had been pinned on by friends or family, the graduates stood around the parade ground, wondering what to do next. Somebody said they should start a tradition and throw their kepis in the air, an idea quickly vetoed when somebody mentioned what a new one cost.

"There's always simply getting drunk," Garvin said. "Highly regarded in some circles."

"I could do that," Jasith said, an arm around Garvin.

"If you've got the energy," Njangu said, "have one on me. Maev and I are going to haul to the Shelburne, where she can watch me sleep around the clock. The other two days the Force so magnanimously gave us will be spent finding the loudest hard-nuts bar in Leggett City with a good band."

"Oh come on," Maev said. "We can have a drink before you crap out on me. You're not *that* old yet."

"You're right," Njangu said. "I hope. Garvin, whyn't you grab a noncom and have them invite everybody to their club? Us elite ossifers aren't permitted to invite lower ranks to our club, for fear the enlisted swine'll realize what dull bastards we are, socially.

"What a bunch of yoinks we are, indeed," Garvin said. "Hey! *Tweg* Renolds! C'mere a second! We're gonna impinge on you!"

It wasn't much of a party. The training had ground the students down pretty well, and after a drink or two, they filtered away, yawning, toward transport to Leggett City and on, or to their barracks.

Garvin ordered a final round for the half dozen people at his table, felt nature's call, and went for the bathroom. He saw Darod Montagna sitting by herself at a table with a beer, stopped.

"Hey, Darod," he said, and wondered why he felt a little awkward. "Congrats again on your promotion."

"Thanks, boss," she said.

"Are you sulking or just shy?"

"Neither," Montagna said. "Waiting for a friend to get off, then he and I are having the pure joy of checking our teams' Class IV equipment."

"A noncom's work is never done," Garvin said in his best, most obviously sanctimonious tone. "Uh . . . I'll see you later."

He stopped at the bar, dropped a bill, and told the barkeep that was for Montagna's tab, went to the 'fresher, came back to his table.

"Who's that?" Jasith asked, curiously.

"One of the people who was on Kura with me."

"Why didn't you ask her over to join us?"

"I dunno," Garvin said. "We're on our last shout, aren't we? Didn't think of it."

"Mmmh," Jasith said. "Pretty, isn't she?"

"I hadn't really noticed."

"He isn't permitted to notice," Njangu explained "The life of a serving soldier is an unhappy one. We can't lust after anybody with more rank than we've got, or less, and the odds are anybody with the same rank's uglier'n death on a holiday."

"Ah," Jasith said, looked at Garvin a bit strangely, but she said no more.

The two *aksai* ungrappled from the *velv,* went to full drive toward the five dots on-screen. They were about three AUs off Larix.

"This is One," Alikhan said. "Suggest we split, and hit the outer ships first."

"Two," Dill said. "It's a plan. On your move."

Seconds later, the two ships orbited away from each other, closed on the Larissan ships "below."

Dill armed his launchers, swung his sight to one dot, touched the ENGAGE sensor.

"Closing . . . closing . . . closing . . . son of a bitch!"

An alarm blatted in his ear, and a red bull's-eye appeared on his canopy. He'd been targeted by something. He touched countermeasure sensors, changed orbit, and the bull's-eye flashed again.

"That mother's no goddamned merchantman," he muttered, keyed his com.

"One, there's enemy in that enemy."

"Understood," Alikhan's voice came. "I, also, am the target of a hostile ship, and have fired a countermissile."

Info flashed on Dill's canopy.

"It's one of their destroyers," he reported.

"And another after me, also."

"Shitaroo," Dill complained, toggling launch buttons. "I've got three destroyers on-screen . . . guarding two lousy merchantmen!"

"Suggest a double-launch, self-targeting, and we flee."

"Agree all the way," Dill said. "We're outgunned, outmanned and maybe out-thunk."

He fired two Goddards in the general direction of the Larissans, dumped three Shadow antimissile missiles to guard his rear, went back as quickly as he'd come.

"This is Two," he reported to the *velv*. "The bastards have discovered the convoy system. We gotta do some rethinking."

The next encounter was between four *aksai,* mothered by a single *velv,* and a ten-ship group of Larissan ships. It was a disaster. Six of the ten Larissans were destroyers. Three *aksai* were destroyed and the last limped back to the *velv,* which barely escaped into hyperspace as the destroyers attacked.

The Larissan convoy system was becoming very efficient.

There were five in the command center on Chance Island, Dr. Danfin Froude, *Alt* Ho Kang, Garvin, Njangu, and Erik Penwyth. All were intent on their computers, except Penwyth, who appeared half-asleep.

Njangu muttered as his screen scrolled data.

"Goddammit, but this is elderly shit! Some of these files are reporting battles on water!"

"Anything interestin' that the spear-and-arrow set did back then?" Penwyth drawled.

"Uh . . . not yet," Njangu said.

"I got something," Garvin said from the other computer terminal. "No I don't."

"Garvin," Froude said gently, "why don't you share it with us, and see if there isn't something hidden in the dross?"

" 'Kay. But this just plain doesn't pertain. The idea was to take a convoy apart with capital ships, like those cruisers we all hope Redruth isn't building which we don't have any of."

"What about using a different kind of hammer?" Ho Kang said. "Just overpowering the convoy escorts with massive strength?"

"We still don't have those kinds of numbers," Froude said. "We can't afford to put a dozen destroyers or even *velv* out at every wide place in the road, hoping we find a convoy here and there."

"You're right," Kang said. "Bad thinking."

"Whyn't you, *Cent* Penwyth, quit sitting there looking aristocratic and help us?" Garvin said. "Angara wants a solution to this convoy idea yesterday. And I've gotta go out someday yesterday and make sure C-Cumbre and the Musth are all happy and feeling secure, again at our fearless leader's request."

"Yes, sir, *Mil* Jaansma. Sir," Penwyth said. "Actually, I do have a suggestion. Whyn't you, when you're out playing footsie with our furry alien friends suggest that, just for excitement, they might want to provide us a war fleet or six? Even the odds a bit, give them a chance to murder some more humans, and so on and so forth."

"Alikhan tried that one," Froude said. "They said they would take the matter under advisement. I suspect the Musth are more than happy to see humans killing humans, and see no particular reason any of their ichor needs be shed.

"If Redruth or his admiral had any strategic brains, which I doubt, they'd try to blow up the mines on C-

Cumbre, kill a bunch of Musth, and get them to sever relations with us."'

Garvin produced a mock shudder.

"Don't even think things like that, Doctor. Remember when the 'Raum did just that, and all of a sudden we were in a whole new war?"

"Hang on," Njangu said. "I think I just might have a way to go. Transferring data."

The room was very quiet as Njangu's discovery was considered.

"Mmmh," Froude said thoughtfully. "Of course. The only problem is modifying the ships and training the operators, which takes time."

"Unless somebody comes up with something better," Garvin said, "I'm going to take this to the Old Man and suggest we try it."

Angara did approve, and ordered three Kellys currently on the ways to be modified, losing half their armament for massive electronics suites.

Then the search began for the operators.

"Which should be most simple," Penwyth said. "All we need is someone capable of juggling four rather sharp objects at the same time, while duckin' a feller throwin' knives at them."

"Do you know something," Maev Stiofan said. "I'm of a majority, I'm free, thanks to you, I'll be able to vote in another year, once I get Cumbrian citizenship, if I don't want to remain a Confederation citizen, and I don't have the foggiest idea on what the hell I want to do next.

"Oh yeh," she added. "And I'm broke."

They were lying on the beach on the far side of the Shelburne. Njangu'd managed a few hours off, because *Caud* Angara was having a dinner conference at the hotel, didn't need him to be anywhere but nearby, and they had seized the moment to go anywhere that wasn't military-looking.

Njangu was grateful Maev had brought the subject up. There *were* problems. He'd had enough in savings to rent a small apartment in Leggett City under her name, but even with flight pay, combat pay, and proficiency pay, he was barely breaking even at the end of each pay period.

He supposed there wouldn't be any problem tapping Garvin, since he had access to the Mellusin billions, but didn't want to do that. That'd make him dependent on Jaansma . . . or Jasith. Not to mention the fact that Maev was currently dependent on *him*. He hadn't had time, back on Larix Prime, to think about what would happen after he and Maev got out alive, since that option didn't seem likely at the time.

"You could always go back to school," he suggested.

"I could," Maev said. "Once I decided what's worth studying."

She dug toes in the sand.

"What a goddamned trap," she said. "I'm born on that stupid hydroponics world and grow up going out of my mind with boredom. So I enlist. I get highjacked, end up in some goon's army, where I'm either scared shitless or angry for almost five years.

"Then . . . free like a goddamned bird. At least birds have some idea on what they want to do next.

"The way things are going," she said morosely, "I might as well join the goddamned Force."

"You could do that," Njangu said. "Apply for a commissioned entry, so we could still screw. Assuming you still wanted to."

"Why wouldn't I?"

"I dunno," Njangu said uncomfortably. "It's just that you didn't seem to have much choice in the matter, back when I was playing *Leiter*."

"Njangu, if I hadn't wanted to stay on with you," Maev said, "you wouldn't have seen anything except dust trails.

"Maybe," she said thoughtfully, "the real question

is, do you still want to see *me* when you wake up in the morning?"

"Well . . . I . . ." Njangu's voice trailed off. The realization came. "Yeh. Hell, yeh. I do."

" 'Kay," Maev said, trying to keep relief out of her voice, "that's one part of the puzzle solved."

"Let's go back to this idea you've got of enlisting," Njangu said. "I sure wouldn't like it if anything happened to you."

"Staying a civilian's likely to keep me out of harm's way?" Maev snorted. "Redruth's still out there, and I haven't heard of him distinguishing a whole lot between soldiers and civvies. Especially after that one nuclear try.

"And let's not forget I'd be worrying about *you*, wouldn't I? Things are getting hotter, and I don't want to be just sitting when you go out, worrying my ears off."

"Enlisting," Njangu said thoughtfully. "Now, if we got you some nice, safe job out of the line of fire, but where you could be part of things, and not in my chain of command . . . hmm."

"Safe?" Maev said. "I thought you said one of the virtues of the Force is everybody fights."

"Well, yeh," Njangu said. "But there's degrees of getting shot at."

"Mmmph. All right. Here's my résumé. I'm good at what? Ordering people around. Spit and polish, which the Force doesn't have a lot of. Fine shot. Quick on weapons assimilation. Fair with a knife. Good at hand-to-hand. Field maneuvers. Small-unit leadership."

"Hey, that's an idea," Maev said. "I could go I&R."

"Like hell you could," Njangu said, outraged. "That'd be ruination city, and thoroughly screw—"

He broke off, seeing that Maev was laughing at him.

"We better think about this one," he muttered.

"Congratulations, sir," Hedley said. "It flew like a flipping bird through PlanGov on the second vote, and

I swear neither Penwyth nor I did any real blackmailing. Two percent emergency tax—some of the Council members gargled at that one—to pay for the manpower increase. Just like that.

"Sameo-sameo with your second proposition. The draft'll be set up as soon as possible, but volunteers are preferred, and you're now in charge of 20K flipping crunchies-to-be. Two brigades instead of just one.

"I forget, sir. What's a Regimental commander called?"

"I shall be dipped and then drowned," *Caud* Angara said slowly. "I never thought the pols would go for it without Redruth personally invading the planet and raping and maiming their next of kin. Maybe these bastards aren't as self-centered as I thought."

"Sir," Hedley said, "please don't get maudlin. I'd worry. They're just piss-scared. In a couple of weeks, they'll be whining like a turbine and wondering what strange hypnotics you used on them."

"Twenty thousand goddamned men," Angara said again. "Now, if I could only figure a way to double that again on them . . ."

"That's what I like about you, sir," Hedley said. "You never take yes for enough of a flipping answer."

"Don't be insubordinate," Angara said. "And shouldn't you be figuring out who's going to cadre for Second Brigade?"

"Well, me for *Caud,* and I'd love to take either Fitzgerald or Rees with me. You can bring up Ken Fong as your new XO. I'd suggest Jaansma, since he's quicker than Fong, but still needs some seasoning. I've got a little list here of some other people."

"You did some fast planning on the way over here."

"Sir," Hedley said. "I've been organizing my own brigade since the day I got commissioned, all the way back on Centrum."

"I should have known. Beware the skinny bastards, for they have a lean and hungry look, or however that goes."

"Congratulations again, sir," Hedley said, becoming serious.

'It's a start," Angara said. "A definite start."

"Hey, Garvin," Njangu said. "I've got a question for you."

"Go ahead," he said. "You're not pregnant, are you?"

"Ha. I laugh," Njangu said, and Garvin finally noticed his friend's slightly worried look.

"Sorry. Listening."

"How do you know what love is?"

"Uh-oh," Garvin said. "Two uh-ohs, in fact."

"I mean, I wasn't ever shy about things with women or anything," Njangu said. "My clique wasn't celibate, and there were girls I liked beyond going to bed with. And I guess Jo Poynton and I got along fine. But it didn't matter that much when we split up, either time, other'n being maybe a little lonely for a while.

"Not that there's anything wrong with being lonely," Njangu said. Suddenly introspective, he said, softly, "Hell, maybe I been lonely all my goddamned life, and not known it."

Garvin shifted, a bit uncomfortably. Their friendship was firmly founded on not talking seriously about the important things.

"Sorry," Njangu said, seeing Garvin's expression.

"So you think you're in love with Maev?"

"Shit, I dunno *what* I'm feeling about her," Njangu said. "I like seeing her, being around her, and she's always got good ideas.

"But love? I don't know what love is, I think I realized. Which is why I thought I'd ask you."

"Of course I'm a grand expert," Garvin said. "And just so you don't take anything I come up with seriously, I was thinking about asking you the same question."

Njangu stared at Garvin.

"Uh-oh," he said.

"That's what I said, a couple seconds ago."

"So what's the matter with you and Jasith?"

"I . . . I dunno," Garvin said. "Maybe nothing."

"So why are you asking?"

"Well . . . the whole thing with me and Jasith has been so goddamned strange. I see her at a party, and whambo, high-illum flares go off, and we're running here, there, falling in bed every chance we get.

"Then the 'Raum thing explodes, and a whole bunch of people get killed, and Jasith doesn't want to see me.

"I hang around like a stomped *giptel,* and then she goes and marries Kouro, which she now says she doesn't know why the hell she did it.

"Neither do I. So they're married, and I'm stumbling around here behaving like a shit under glass, and then the Musth come roaring in.

"Now it's Kouro's turn to be a prize prick . . . except that he does it on everybody, sucking the Musth off. So here comes Jasith back, and we're kazoingo again, and then the war's over, and Kouro's history."

"That was a very quick sitrep, *Mil* Jaansma," Njangu said. "What's the problem now? Can't you handle being the toy of somebody who's maybe the richest . . . and sure as hell the prettiest . . . Rentier in the whole frigging system?"

"I don't *know* what the problem is," Garvin said.

"Has Jasith gotten unhappy with things?"

"No," Garvin said. "Whatever problem there is . . . if there's even a problem . . . is me."

"Awright, let's try it with simple questions," Njangu said. "Have you started jumping the bones of anybody else?"

"No."

"Are you *thinking* about wanting to jump somebody's bones?"

"I don't know."

"Could I ask who . . . never mind. None of my goddamned business, and not part of the question, anyway," Njangu said. "Let's stick to Jasith. Since I know zip-squat about love, which has been established, what's wrong? Don't the ol' bells and whistles go off?"

"I think so."

"What do you mean, you think so? Put it vulgarly . . . do you two still screw like rabbits?"

"Well, yeh."

"All right," Njangu said with finality. "Let's call the matter settled. You still get hard, she still gets soft, so there's no problem there. Beyond that, if either of us believed in any kind of a god, I'd say you should talk to the chaplain, which, come to think, I just realize the Force hasn't replaced since whatsisface got blown away in the war.

"So let's leave it at this . . . you're still in love, you're just having a moment of self-doubt. Which no big-time *Mil* can afford, especially one who's expected to be a symbol to his men. Right?"

Garvin smiled a little tentatively, then his grin firmed up.

"Right. Sorry. Maybe I'm just tired. Or it's the weather."

"Probably," Njangu agreed. But, when Garvin went back to his spreadsheet, Yoshitaro considered him carefully, a slightly worried look on his face.

Ho Kang, four other officers, and two dozen other trainees stared up at the ship. It appeared to be a shining-new Kelly-class destroyer, but was another fifty meters longer, and was referred to as a kane-class attach controller.

Kang wondered what she was doing here, having found a nice, safe slot as a thinker. But she'd discovered she was more of a soldier than she'd thought and couldn't stand that her friends in the Force were going into jeopardy without her. Plus she had a nice, healthy streak of bloodthirstiness, and so she'd volunteered for this new section.

The job she was being trained for was nearly as ancient as the convoy system the Larissans had adopted—to attack organization with organization. The system, back in the Very Dark Ages, had been called the wolfpack, and had worked very well, especially when an attack commander was able to keep himself just away from the actual battleground to coordinate the attackers, but close enough to be able instantly to react to any change from the enemy.

Kang had taken the quick tests Force doctors had devised, done very well, not surprising since she was already a qualified pilot, good at instinctive targeting, had a liking for probability analysis, and found herself once again in school.

It was tough. Ho hadn't realized how rusty her advanced math had gotten, how much of her prob-analysis came from experience and instinct rather than a systematic use of the Neumann-Haller equations. Not to mention having to learn other areas, from the logistics of how many bullets and beans the ships she'd be controlling had aboard, when their crews were scheduled for leave, resupply capabilities at various Legion bases. Not to mention strategic intelligence understanding of what Redruth and company might have in mind for their next plot.

One thing that helped her was her earlier background as a warrior. She was in good physical shape, stayed there, so when the school problems were dumped on the trainees, hour after hour, she was one of the few capable of still blearing through to a solution.

An emaciated-looking technician who was cultivating a drooping moustache in the faint hope it might make him look slightly more military stood in front of the class.

"This never happens in the romances," said the technician, who had the equally uninspiring name of Spelvin. "A warrior's sword or helmet is always ready for him to clap on and go out and smite away. The *Kane* should've been ready two weeks ago.

"However, one of the suppliers decided to lower his pay scale, and the electronics guild has struck. The government's intervening, but that'll take another week or so to resolve.

"We brought you here so you can rest assured your training isn't in vain, that there actually is at least one craft being set up as a control ship, and hence we shall have a place for you.

"We just aren't sure when."

Adj-Prem Monique Lir and *Tweg* Darod Montagna sat in the wardroom of the Merchant Ship *Brns,* cups full of a murky substance imaginatively called caff, talking away another dull watch.

All around them, working in their bones, was the hum of a spaceship under drive. The *Brns,* on secondary drive, was making a quick transit from D-Cumbre out to the research station/warning post on K-Cumbre, with a small patrol ship as escort. The two I&R soldiers were aboard the transport because *Caud* Angara had decided all ships traveling beyond the orbit of G-Cumbre must not only be escorted, but be armed as well.

Plas blisters were hastily cast and mounted to merchant ships' hulls. Two Goddard shipkillers were mounted inside the blisters, and small Shadow countermissiles added in smaller blisters to either side. A control station was located somewhere within the ship that didn't get in the crew's way too badly, and four Forcemen assigned as auxiliary military gunners. The ship's captain was their nominal commander, unless special circumstances, clearly defined, required them to follow general orders issued by the Force.

Two of the Forcemen on the *Brns* were assigned to the freighter on permanent duty—one a Forceman who was getting a bit old for hill-running, the other a new recruit. The other two, Lir and Montagna, were floaters, dividing duty time between their normal station and a starship. The I&R people didn't wear rank tabs or uniforms aboard ship, but civilian clothes or ship's coveralls, trying to fit into the civilian world as cleanly as possible.

Other Cumbrian ships received the same weaponry, the same assignment of gunners.

There'd been some trouble at first. The soldiers resented the merchantmen's vastly higher pay and living conditions during wartime, and the civilian crew members scorned the military for being not much better than armed sheep.

Three things ended the potential feud—*Caud* Angara's orders that gun crew would work as hard as any crewmen on any task the captain chose to ask them to perform, whether or not it had to do with their missiles; the slow realization that, if Larissan raiders hit the Cumbre system, these four women and men would be a ship's only chance; and the willingness most Forcemen had to escalate, with Angara's tacit approval, any forecastle brawl.

At first, many of the soldiers swore they'd never get any sleep offplanet, that the hum of the ship drive would turn them into babbling idiots long before the ship ported. But after two days in space, they didn't notice the noise any more than the crew.

"And here I went and thought riding shotgun on these transports would make life a little more interesting than sitting around the barracks spit-shining a blaster." Montagna sighed.

"Careful, young *Tweg*," Lir warned. "Every war I've been in starts slow, with everybody pissing and moaning about no action, and they're never going to get forward in time for the shooting, shitting and shouting. A year later, people are stumbling around, shell-shocked, thousand-meter stare, wondering why they were so damned foolish.

"Stand warned, Darod."

"Mmmh," Montagna said.

"Another thing about wars," Lir continued. "You always seem to remember the beginnings best. After things get serious, it's just a dull, bloody blur. Also, the people that get dead at the beginning of a war generally are the best remembered. So if you want barracks or a landing field named after you, now's the best time to die heroically."

"I'll pass on that idea," Montagna said. "Question. How many wars have you been in, *Adj-Prem*?"

I&R troops might have been informal in combat or in their own company, but not around outsiders, and the soldiers assigned to escort duty kept things especially formal, just as they kept themselves as immaculate as possible, even in the rather oily working spaces of a merchant ship, with the whispered slogan, "Anybody can be piggy enough to be a sailor."

Monique considered. "The 'Raum . . . then the Musth . . . then this bit . . . before that two minor campaigns before the Force got sent to Cumbre. That was back when we were called Swift Lance, for shit's sake, under *Caud* Melk, and then *Caud* Williams, who got killed in the 'Raum rising. Plus, on Cumbre, chasing what they called bandits in the hills, which never rates a campaign ribbon." She paused, tallied.

"Enough, I guess."

Darod thought better than saying Lir was obviously a little older than she looked, found another question: "What was it like, being under the Confederation?"

"About the same as now, to be truthful. Independent Strike Forces like this one always were assigned to the edge of nowhere. I never had the chance to operate with a full-scale Confederation army, just like I never saw a full-tilt war." Lir sounded envious. "But there were differences. We had better supplies, faster, naturally. 'Though when I think back, toward the end, when we were on . . . what was it, Qwet VII, that was it, before we got shipped to Cumbre, we were operating pretty thin. Promotions were a lot slower, since there were tests and stuff, and after you got temp rank, the promotion had to be vetted all the way back to Army Headquarters on Centrum."

"What do *you* think happened to the Confederation?" Montagna asked.

"Hell if I know," Lir answered. "Most likely they got soft, got lazy, let other people do their thinking and fighting for them. But I guess that's probably what any soldier'd say about any empire, back to Roma or whatever, a long, long time ago."

"Okay, old soldier," Montagna said. "What comes next?"

"For who?"

"For us."

"First, we whip up on these Larissans, teach them not to be messing with their betters. Then we rebuild, and, most likely, go looking for the next bastard."

"Which'll be?"

"Hell if I know," Lir said again. "I'm no pol or General Staffer. I go where they point me, kill people and break things 'til they tell to stop."

"Did you ever want to be anything but a soldier?"

Lir was quiet for a time.

"When I was a kid, I wanted to be some kind of professional jocker . . . an athlete." She shrugged. "But I wasn't going to the right schools, my parents didn't have any money for special training, and the teams I played on didn't have any talent in depth. Teams with only one star don't win tourneys or get noticed, generally, 'cause everybody's got to have backup to win.

"The best I could do was, real young, join an opera company."

"What's that?"

"Doing stories live, on a stage, instead of a holo. Everybody sings, instead of talks. I didn't sing much, but I was a decent dancer. And an acrobat. Which meant I got to do the fight sequences. There were a couple of older dancers who knew a bunch of martial arts, and didn't mind passing time between bookings teaching.

"We were good enough to tour a couple of star systems," Lir went on. "Then we got stuck in the middle of a war with the government collapsed around us, and the best way to stay alive was to learn how to use a blaster.

"I did . . . and, hell, I guess I fit right in. When the war was over I didn't want to go out on the street again, worrying about my next meal and doss, and so I ended up joining up with the Confederation.

"Simple story. What made you join up?"

"I'm from near Launceston," Montagna said. "And my folks had some credits, so I could play any sport I wanted. Mostly swimming. I thought everything was real well planned, and then there was the 'Raum thing, and my father's business got wrecked, so we weren't doing as well as we could've.

"Then there was a big tournament. You're not supposed to say anything like this because it makes you look like a pissy loser, but the tournament was rigged, and somebody else . . . two somebody elses . . . got the medals and the chance to go on. Plus there was a boy, and that didn't work out at all, and all of a sudden I wanted to be someplace else."

"The Force," Lir said.

"Yeh," Montagna agreed. "Why not?"

"A lot of people with that kind of story end up here," Monique said. "You fixing on staying in?"

Montagna shook her head slowly.

"I don't know. I really don't know." She got up. "More caff?"

Darod refilled both cups. Without turning from the machine, she asked, voice deliberately casual:

"Can I ask a question that's none of my business? Not about you, *Adj-Prem*."

"You can always ask," Lir said.

"It's about *Mil* Jaansma. Is he married?"

"Nope. Not yet."

"Who's that lady he's always with? The rich one."

Monique gave Montagna a thumbnail sketch of Jasith.

"What do you think of her?" Darod returned to the table, sat down.

"This isn't anything more than my opinion," Monique said. "And I don't know the woman well enough to be sure. But I don't have a whole helluva lot of use for her."

"Why not?"

"First, she dumped *Mil* Jaansma after the 'Raum rising, for no reason I ever heard. Then, when things got shitty again, with the Musth, and her husband turned traitor, which is what he was, even if he managed to buy himself out of a war-crimes trial afterward, she's back putting a liplock on Garvin.

"I'm not real large on people who don't stick by what they decide. I just wonder, if the stick gets shitty again, if she'll still be there.

"But then, I'm one of those people who aren't sure if a soldier ought to have *anybody* on the outside. Your friends are enough, and when it itches, go somewhere and scratch it with somebody you don't have to see again, or worry about what kind of person they really are."

"Kind of a lonely life," Darod Montagna said.

Lir shrugged. "So? You come in this world by yourself, go out by yourself, don't you?" She eyed Darod. "Jaansma's good-looking enough, and smart enough, although, if you ask me, the smartest thing he's ever done is let the boss do his heavy thinking for him."

Darod shivered. "*Cent* Yoshitaro's a good officer. But he's cold. He looks at you with those hard eyes of his, and it's like you're nothing more than a figure in an equation."

"So?" Lir asked, a bit of scorn in her voice. "You want humanity and concern, you've got Garvin. Or, rather, lemme put it another way. *You* don't got Jaansma. At least not right now. And you could end up feeling like a *stobor* on a treadmill if you try to change that and get personal with him.

"A rule I've got, which has done me good as a soldier and on the outside, is don't go after what isn't intended. If you do—"

Alarms roared, and a synth voice came:

"All hands, all hands, Condition Red! Forcemen, please report immediately to your weapons station!"

The two scooped up their weapons vests, always nearby, ran down a passageway, up a ladder to the bridge deck.

The captain was waiting. "We've a report from System Control that unidentified ships have been detected."

"Where?"

"Fortunately for us, they appeared well in-system. They were reported by a station on one of F-Cumbre's moons, and there was a mayday from a transport off E-Cumbre. I'd guess they're headed for D-Cumbre, although the plotting shows the sun's between them and D. Closest settled world to them is C-Cumbre.

"I plan to maintain our current orbit to K-Cumbre unless advised otherwise or the situation changes. If the ships are Larissan, and change their orbit, we'll run back and hide in the asteroids."

"Right, sir," Lir said. "Our station'll be manned and ready until further notice."

"Now, isn't this a better way to fight a war?" Jasith Mellusin said.

"I suppose so," Garvin admitted. "But I've got this niggle that says I should be on a canvas cot instead of where I am."

"Where does it say soldiers all have to be poor and miserable?"

"I dunno," Jaansma said. "But it's got to, somewhere. Just like it says we've got to be scared and dirty."

"Pfoo," Jasith said. She was lolling on a bed only slightly too small to land an *aksai* on, in the owner's stateroom of her yacht, the *Godrevy*. If it wasn't for the slightest vibration through the carpeting and the two screens showing ship position within the system, and relative position within the convoy instead of windows, they could be in a luxury suite onplanet. If maybe Garvin thought the stateroom was a little overstated, with its antigrav-controlled waterfall near the entrance, and if he wasn't fond of baby blue as a color theme, he said nothing. It was, after all, her yacht.

"So why do you want to be over in one of those *velv*?" she went on. "That isn't your job, is it? They've got nice half-trained pilots, with barely trained people in the second seat, learning how to zoom around, right?"

"Yeh."

"You're the noble Intelligence Chief, directly sent out by *Caud* Angara to make the Musth feel all comfy and secure."

"Right," Garvin grudged.

"So work on a nice, comfy, and secure speech. Or else come over here and help me feel comfy and secure, since, after all, I'm Mellusin Mining and a lot more important than a lot of very tall fuzzies."

"I just did that."

"Then get to work on that speech. Put some clothes on, first."

She rolled lithely off the bed, went to her own desk, pulling on a robe.

"I didn't say anything about *you* needing clothes," Garvin said.

"Shut up and concentrate."

The *Godrevy* was one of six ships making a medium-track transit from D-Cumbre to the mining world of C-Cumbre. Two new *velv* were in forward position, then a merchantman with mining supplies, then the *Godrevy*, a second supply ship, and a third *velv* at the rear.

Then an alarm blatted as the report of enemy ships in-system reached the convoy.

Garvin told the bridge he was on his way, pulled on boots and his coverall.

"What should I do?" Jasith said.

"Nothing. No. Get into your flameproofs, just to be safe. Wherever these ships are, assuming they're Larissan, they've got to be only light-seconds from us. Oh yeh—if you want to see everything, you better come up to the bridge now. The skipper's liable to seal the ship. Also, there's better places to strap down to than that bed, if we're going to be bouncing around."

"Bouncing around?" Jasith waggled her eyebrows suggestively, but went to a closet, opened it and went inside. She came out with a sealed package, opened it, and put on coveralls like Garvin's as he hurried out of the hatch.

All three watch officers were on the small bridge of the *Godrevy*. Two looked worried, but the captain, Lar Porcen, a bluff man who would've been at home on the deck of a water ship, appeared quite calm.

"*Mil* Jaansma," Porcen said. "You're the soldier, and you heard the com. Any suggestions?"

Garvin had tried half a dozen times to get Porcen to call him by his first name, without any more success than convincing Jasith's household staff.

"Since it's really unlikely that anything is going to happen," Garvin said. "I think—"

The com crackled as two blips appeared from hyperspace on a screen, figures scrolling underneath them.

"Unknown ships closing on convoy, assumed hostile. Tracking data being transferred. All ships stand by to take appropriate action."

Jasith was on the bridge, somewhat excited.

"What's happening?"

"I think," Garvin said, "I'm a rotten prophet, and we're about to get hit."

Porcen touched a mike.

"Engine room, stand by for maneuvering. And you

better suit up down there." He clicked off. "That goes for everybody here, too."

Light space suits hung in a nearby emergency air-lock. The two officers helped each other into them, and Jasith, having more experience in space than Garvin, gave him a hand, then slid into another, just a bit large for her small frame.

Garvin strapped Jasith into an acceleration couch, then looked over Porcen's shoulder, reading the screen data.

"Larissan," he said positively. "Those are their new destroyers. Lan-class, we're calling them."

The Larissans were driving toward the convoy center. Commands chattered from the com, and the three escorts set interception orbits.

A flash came from the nose of the lead *velv* on-screen, a sim-indicator of a missile launch.

"That's a long shot," Garvin said, from his recently gained trained.

Flashes came from the two Larissan ships, and another flash in empty space.

"Countermissile . . . and a hit on that launch of ours," Garvin said, not aware he was speaking aloud. "Now they're launching against the convoy."

"Your orders, sir?" Porcen's normally calm voice had become a controlled croak.

Garvin blinked, then slipped easily into a familiar role.

"Since we're not armed," he said, "I'd wait for orders from the escort commander."

The first *velv,* with the convoy commander, suddenly flashed, and ceased to exist.

"Son of a bitch," Garvin muttered. "Captain, I think we're going to have to think about getting out of here."

A calm voice on the com agreed:

"All ships, all ships, this is Holburt Two. Break away and maneuver independently. We are engaging the enemy."

That was the second *velv*.

Outgunned by the two Larissan destroyers, the Cumbrian ships still held to their interception track. All four ships launched missiles.

Alarms blared through the yacht.

"Collision alarm," an officer muttered as hatches slid shut. "A missile's targeting us."

"Captain, go for N-space," Garvin snapped.

"What setting, sir?"

"Anything, anywhere," Garvin said, trying to keep his voice flat. "Blind jump."

Another officer was at the hyperspace controls.

"Engaged, sir, time to jump four, three . . ."

On-screen, one of the supply ships blew up, and seconds later, another *velv* spun wildly, taking on an orbit no human could have set.

There was an explosion, and the ship tumbled. A second later, everything went black, Garvin's stomach churned, the antigravity went out, and the *Godrevy* jumped into N-space for an instant, then flashed back to normal space.

"We're hit!" somebody shouted. Garvin was floating somewhere between the deck and overhead in zero gravity. His faceplate snapped shut, and he realized the bridge deck, at least, had been holed.

There was no one at the secondary-drive controls. He saw Porcen sprawled across an acceleration couch, neck at an impossible angle. If he was still alive, he wouldn't be for long, and no one had any time for him.

Garvin was in the main control couch, very grateful that he'd spent as much time on the bridge as he had, and the controls weren't completely unfamiliar.

"Hyperdrive will not function," a flat voice said in his ear. Garvin saw one officer at those controls, the other staring at the system screen.

They hadn't jumped very far—the ongoing battle wasn't that far from the center of the screen, which always reflected the *Godrevy*'s position. The second supply ship showed two flashes, then there was only empty space.

One of the Larissan ships took hits.

"Hit one," the officer at the hyperdrive controls exulted.

But then another *velv* vanished.

"Now they'll destroy that last escort, and come after us," the first officer moaned.

"Shut up," Garvin snapped. "What's going on in the engine room?"

"Sorry, sir." The officer recovered, touched a sensor.

"Engines," a somewhat shaken voice came.

"What's your status?"

"Goddamned stardrive's out . . . secondary drive's in fine shape. I think."

"Do you still have compartment integrity?"

"That's affirm," the engine room said.

"Good," the officer said. "We're breathing vacuum up here."

"Screw that," Garvin said. "Set us a nice, irregular orbit, generally out of here, generally toward C-Cumbre."

"And quickly," Jasith added from the acceleration couch.

"Yes, Ms. Mellusin," the man said.

Garvin checked the screen, was amazed to see only one blip, ID'ed as the last surviving *velv*.

"Well kiss my moneymaking ass," he said. "The Larissans took off on us. Wonder if somebody hit them."

"I'll cheer," Jasith's voice said in his ear, "after we actually get somewhere solid. I'm not as fond of space-ships as I used to be."

She appeared utterly unruffled.

Darod Montagna was yawning heavily, trying to keep her eyes from blurring as she stared at the screen. It was cycling from system view to local. They were closing on K-Cumbre, maybe two, three ship-days out.

Lir'd ordered three on duty, one off, which didn't give much time for sleep, after eating and 'freshing. Montagna had two shifts to go, and didn't think she was going to make it.

There was something on-screen for an instant, then it vanished.

Reflexively, she triggered an alarm, and then the object appeared again.

Hell, it's almost in my lap.

She triggered the ID sensor, and it flashed twice, then said UNKNOWN SHIP.

She damned the freighter's less-than-current *Jane's,* decided that the unknown ship had to be Larissan. One of the raiders. But what the hell was it doing?

Again the ship ceased to exist, then came back, and she realized it was flashing in and out of hyperspace, for some unknown reason.

The bridge behind her was suddenly full of people. The com to the patrol ship came alive.

"We have contact . . . ship positively identified as Larissan . . . Lan-class."

Their fiche was up-to-date.

The com came back.

"*Brns,* full drive toward destination." Then a pause. "I shall take position on your stern."

Montagna supposed it wasn't entirely logical to expect the patrol ship, about a quarter the size of the Larissan, to do something stupid like attack, even though that would have been the ship captain's orders.

"Oughta just jump," somebody said behind her, and Lir was there.

She read the screen.

"Sorry bastard in that spit-kit," she said. "It'll haul past us, leave us in the rear, and that goddamned Larissan's got legs on both of us."

"What about," Montagna said, "we dump a God-dard out after it?"

"The damned thing's way out of range—what the hell's the matter with it, jumping back and forth like that?"

"Maybe somebody hit it with something?" Montagna offered.

"Yeh," Lir said. "Yeh. Of course. I'm not awake yet. Hit, and trying to limp back home, jumping as far and as quick as it can."

"If I put a Goddard out now," Montagna persisted, "say with a Shadow beside it, let it lie doggo until the Goddard says it's in striking distance . . ."

"I'm not half-asleep," Lir said disgustedly. "I'm half–goddamned dead. Sure, Darod. Put it out there. And if that frigging destroyer jumps right on out of our area, that's just fine, too."

The missile was launched, drive at minimum.

As predicted, the patrol ship quickly moved past the *Brns,* showed no sign of reversing thrust.

"If that frigging Larissan doesn't nail us," Lir said, "I'll have the whole goddamned crew of that runner hung by the balls they don't have."

A light flashed on Montagna's panel.

"The Larissan's in range," she reported. "Standing by to drive . . . Target Acquired . . . Full drive . . ."

The other Forceman at his controls nodded. "Shadow under drive . . ."

The two missiles drove toward the Larissan.

"Now, don't go and jump on me, baby," Montagna whispered. "Come on, come on, come on . . ."

The Larissan ship vanished in a flash of light.

"Hit!" Montagna shouted. "I *got* the pigola!"

"Indeed you did," Lir said. "Congrats and all that. Four more and you're an ace."

"But what am I gonna do with that Shadow that's hanging out there?," the other soldier said. "It's too far out to bring back, and those bastards cost money!"

"I'll sign the chit," Lir snarled. "Blow it in place! And when we get on the ground, you're buying for being a cheap sourpuss."

Montagna was paying no attention, but smiling contentedly at the screen where a Larissan ship had been.

That, she thought, *was a lot better than killing them one at a time with a blaster.*

The *Godrevy* wobbled toward the field, the field controller talking it down.

"*Godrevy* . . . you're doing fine . . . pick that nose up . . . you're a little low, can you pick it up . . . not that much . . ."

"The drive's sloppy, like I said," the pilot said.

"That's all right, all right," the controller soothed. "You're doing fine. Skids down if you've got all three . . . I see them, looking good, looking good, 'kay, you're over the fence now, you've got a nice big bunch of nothing to set it down . . . nothing expensive to hit . . . nose up, nose up . . . the emergency lifters are on their way . . . anytime you want to put it down . . . anywhere . . ."

The *Godrevy* hit hard on its bow skid, crumpling it, bounced back into the air, then slammed down and skidded, turning, almost rolling, the screech of metal against concrete loud even in the distant tower.

Dust boiled around it, and the fire and ambulance lifters sped toward the careening starship.

The *Godrevy* spun twice more, rocked back and forth, then slowly came to rest.

Down on the field, an airlock opened, and people in space suits dropped out, staggered away from the ship, then stopped. One knelt and kissed the field's tarmac.

"I didn't think they'd make it," the controller said, forgetting he had an open mike.

"Neither did we," Garvin's tired voice came back. "Neither did we."

CHAPTER
20

N-Space

The Larissan convoy was big—twenty merchant ships, escorted by ten patrol ships and eight destroyers. They'd made their first jump from Kura to Larix and emerged in normal space, when the Cumbrians hit them.

High "above" the convoy, two *velv* came out of hyperspace, then two of the Kane attack controllers, then five more *velv* and half a dozen Kellys.

Five Larissans broke away from the convoy on interception orbits, expecting the usual head-on combat.

Ho Kang, aboard the first Kane, the *al Maouna,* issued orders through a scrambler:

"Vann Four, Vann Five, this is Vann Control One. N-space, one-point-five seconds, R-five-seven-eight-six-slash-N-three-five-three-three, jump and immediate attack, on command, Go!"

The leading two *velv* went back into hyperspace, jumping back out between the five destroyers and the Larissan convoy.

"Vann One . . . launch on destroyers . . . Vann Two . . . try for the convoy rear elements."

Three *aksai* spun off each *velv*. Nana-patrol boats broke away from the convoy to intercept the second element, while a Larissan destroyer's stern blew off as an *aksai* missile took it.

"Vann Six, Seven," *Tweg* Jenks Farrel said from the other Kane. "This is Vann Control Two. Attack N-space point nine, R-five-seven-eight-zero-slash-N-three-five-three-two, frontal attack on merchantmen, Go!"

Two Kellys vanished, came out in front of the convoy, and drove in, missiles firing.

The convoy commander was shouting orders, but his com was blanketed by interference, as were commands from the escort commander.

The added midsection of each Kane, a large single compartment, was a swirl of motion, as technicians reported, checked sim screens, fed data into the ships' computers. Kang sat in a boom-controlled seat overhead, trying to watch only the main screen showing present ship positions, and the secondary screen that showed ships' orbits, assuming they continued at their present trajectory/drive. She made herself ignore the bustle below, her chair dipping to an individual station only when she wasn't sure of something, then lifting away.

A Cumbrian ship would attack a Larissan, and seconds later, hit or miss, another target would be given to the Cumbrian, often on the other "side" of the convoy, along with precise navigational data, generally including a momentary jump in and out of hyperspace.

The Larissans fought hard, but they were confused, not knowing when or where to guard as the raiders appeared in mid-convoy, launched, killed merchant ships, and were gone.

This deepest space became a tapestry of light, as if so many stars were being born, as missiles struck or blew up automatically at the end of their runs.

In half an E-hour, the Larissan escorts were destroyed or crippled.

"All Vann elements," Ho ordered. "This is Vann Control One. Reassemble in fighting formations on Control Ships."

The *velv* and destroyers obeyed, and the eight surviving Larissan merchantmen had an instant to hope.

"All Vann elements," Kang sent. "Targets of opportunity . . . attack when ready."

Again, tiny suns blossomed as the raiders smashed at the merchantmen, then there was nothing left to shoot at.

"All Vann elements," Ho ordered. "Assemble on me, and return to base."

The entire Larissan convoy, and its escorts, had been obliterated.

Loss to Cumbre: two *aksai* and one *velv* destroyed, one Kelly damaged.

Cumbre/D-Cumbre

"Maev Stiofan, put your hands on the flag," *Caud* Angara ordered. Maev touched the Force guidon.

"Repeat after me, using your own name. I, *Caud* Grig Angara, do swear by all that I hold sacred, whether God or gods or my own honor, I will obey the lawful commands given me by my superiors and swear to defend the Confederation, its life-forms and its way until death, or until I am released from this vow.

"I also swear I shall conduct myself as befits a Confederation officer, to issue no laws violating the standards of the Confederation nor common humanitarian standards, and to uphold the laws of the Confederation Parliament?"

"I so swear," Maev Stiofan said, surprised her voice was a little hoarse.

"I now commission you, Maev Stiofan, as *Aspirant* in the Armed Forces of the Confederation."

Stiofan, like Angara, Yoshitaro, Jaansma, and Hedley, wore the dark blue dress uniform of the Force. Angara handed her a leather box, which held the Force. Angara handed her a leather box, which held the Force emblems, the single silver crown of her rank, and a very lethal combat knife.

Stiofan saluted smartly, and Angara returned it.

"If we still had a band," he said, far less formally, "it should be playing. And this ceremony should be done on the parade ground, with the entire Force as witness. But these are parlous times. Perhaps later . . ." His voice trailed away.

"Thank you, sir," Maev said.

Angara studied her carefully, then nodded.

"Dismissed."

He and Hedley about-faced, and left the briefing room.

"You may kiss the *Aspirant*," Jaansma said.

Njangu obeyed.

Maev pulled back after a minute or so.

"I'm not committing any breach of etiquette or regulations, am I, by kissing this officer? I mean, nobody told me just what I'm going to be doing, where I'll fall in the Table of Organization, and I'm not sure—"

"You're not in any sort of violation," Njangu said, grinning. "And I've saved your new job for last. You're going to be one of *Caud* Angara's personal bodyguards."

"Allah's claws," Maev said, astonished. "No wonder he gave me that weird look, me being one of the Protector's Own, once. How's he know I'm not under some kind of deep conditioning to rip his throat out the first chance I got?"

"He knows," Garvin said. "Where do you think the last Second-Day went?"

Maev thought, blinked, realized she really was missing a day.

"You were colder than a flash-frozen fish," Garvin went on. "Every security tech in II Section was up to his elbows in your soul, making sure you weren't anything other than what you say you are."

"Oh," Stiofan said in a small voice. "I'm not sure I like that."

"I don't either," Njangu said. "I remember when . . . never mind."

"At least," Garvin said, "it'll never happen again.

And whatever the techs came up with was destroyed,
after they analyzed it."

"Did you scan it?" Maev asked Njangu.

"Only the dirty parts."

"You'd better be lying," she said, just a touch
grimly. "Or there won't be any more dirty parts for
you, buster, not ever."

Njangu looked at Garvin.

"You see why I love her?"

Maev looked very surprised, as did Garvin. He was
the only one who'd caught the momentary hesitation
before Yoshitaro said "love."

The wolfpacks went out again, and again, savaging
the convoys from Kura. Then pickings grew leaner,
as the Larissan convoys assembled just out of Kura's
atmosphere, then jumped to new, unknown nav points.

Sometimes, but not often, the packs could follow
them and attack. Once again, the Larissans learned
from loss. The question now was which side would
come up with a new tactic?

"The problem, Doctor," Ho Kang said earnestly,
"isn't with the wolfpacks themselves. We seem to have
that system working very well, and improving it with
every mission.

"It's finding the convoys, once they make that first
jump. We can't track them too closely or with too big
a starship on initial takeoff, because if we're detected,
they abort and return to Kura.

"When we use a smaller ship, an *aksai*, it gets ambushed a lot of the time."

"Let me show you," Danfin Froude said smugly,
"Stage Two of the wolfpack/convoy situation, to solve
your problem, which I was already well aware of. That
is why I asked you to drop by."

He slid open the door. Two identical globes, each
about two meters in diameter, were on stands in the
otherwise bare conference room.

"Call this one . . . oh, Ohnce, and this other one Bohnce," he said. "Those were, by the way, two stuffed animals I had when I was a boy. I suppose I wasn't very imaginative.

"Ohnce and Bohnce both have small hyperdrives. Essentially, they're small, fairly sophisticated robot trackers. They can be planted in either normal or hyperspace. Initially, we'll most likely use normal space deployments. When an unfamiliar—i.e., Kuran—convoy is detected, the drives on both robots are activated. When those Kurans enter hyperspace, the first will jump with them. After a moment, the second sphere does the same. The first sphere exits hyperspace when the convoy does, signaling to the second. Thus, we have established the second nav point the Kurans are using. Hopefully they use no more than two or three, for these have just enough power to do their little tricks twice.

"If the Kurans are being very clever, and making several jumps, it should be a simple matter to plant another set of these—call them spy-spheres if you wish—in normal space at the second nav point. Then that set will follow the Larissans to the third, and so forth.

"Of course, each satellite can be keyed to report to you, as well as to its brother."

"That is clever," Ho Kang said.

"I rather thought so," Froude said. "We'll have the first production units ready for issue in the next few weeks. And there are further nasties yet to come."

"So we have reason to celebrate," Ho said. "At least for the moment."

"Uh," and the scientist looked slightly nervous, "yes. We do. Uh, would you care to help me celebrate our cleverness over dinner?"

Kang took off her old-fashioned glasses, looked at Froude in surprise, then smiled.

"Why . . . yes. I think I would."

Kura/Off Kura Three

The convoy was only five merchant ships, with three destroyers as escort. The wolfpack had been waiting in real space, waiting, its control officer having studied the situation and realized the Larissans used the old nav points one convoy in three.

There were one Kane, four *velv,* two Kellys in the pack.

"Charner One, Two, Six, point three, Y-two-three-four-eight-nine-eight, Three, Four, Five, remain in normal space, attack inward flank."

The ships attacked, and the controller watched as first one, then a second Larissan destroyer was destroyed. She was about to give the order to savage the merchant ships when a technician below her hit an emergency sensor, and the controller saw a new blip on-screen.

She cut to the tech's frequency.

"Unknown ship, no details, no *Jane's,* entered real space three-point-nine-nine seconds ago," the tech droned. "Dopplering . . . estimate speed and dimensions to you. Two escorts accompanying unknown ship."

The controller's eyes widened as she saw the size of the new ship as it arced toward the battle. It was unbelievably huge, twice the size of any Larissan ship her *Jane's* held, almost the size of some of the old Confederation warships she'd read about.

"We have five missile launches from this unknown ship," an electronics officer said. "All aimed at this ship. Five spoofers launched, no effect. Making counterlaunch."

The Kane's antimissile battery tracked the incoming missiles, blew up four of them. The fifth exploded close in, and circuits in the war room flashed into black, then secondaries recovered.

"All Charner elements," the controller began, realizing the battle was lost, then a pulse swept all frequencies, and she lost contact with her ships.

The ECM was enough to alert the attacking Cumbrians, though, and they broke contact with the Larissans and went for hyperspace, even as missiles from the great ship exploded around them.

The two Kellys and one *velv*, against all orders, stayed in normal space, and counterlaunched. Their first strike was destroyed, and a second made as the lighter ships attacked the huge Larissan vessel.

One missile blew up close to the monstrous new ship, and very suddenly it, and its two escorts, disappeared.

"Son of a bitch," a Kelly's CO marveled into his com, realizing he was still alive. "He ran out on us."

"Must've been a mistake, Charner Five," the CO of the *velv* said. "His, not ours. You want to give me a hand with these freighters and that other destroyer? It's just lying there, leaking."

"Backing you, Two. I guess we're living right."

The three Cumbrian ships went after the scattering Larissans.

The first of the kilometer-long Naarohn-class battle cruisers that Redruth had dreamed of was a reality.

But no one with the Force could understand why the cruiser had retreated, with victory clear in its sights.

Cumbre/D-Cumbre

"Thank you for dinner," Ho Kang said. She and Danfin Froude were outside her quarters, a small apartment in a BOQ block.

"Certainly my pleasure," Froude said. "It was nice to not have to talk just about science, which is what usually happens when I dine with my colleagues. An old widower like myself loses his social graces fairly easily."

"You could have talked more," Ho said. "Better

that thân the usual barracks chat. I just realized I
haven't said anything obscene since we went out."

"Yes, well . . ." Danfin Froude looked around. "It's
a very nice night, isn't it?"

"Yes."

"If I weren't three times your age," he said wistfully, "I'd feel like kissing you."

"You're only two-point-seven-four times that," Ho
said. "And I wouldn't mind at all."

She slid her glasses into her uniform pocket, then
leaned forward. After a time, her arms went around
his, and the kiss went on.

When it finished, Kang found herself breathing a
little hard.

"Would you," and her voice was a little throaty,
"like to come in?"

Danfin Froude smiled. "I would, Ho. I would very
much."

The huge cruiser appeared again as Cumbre attacked another convoy. This time, it appeared bolder,
and drove the raiders off, with a loss of one Kelly,
one *velv*.

A week later, another convoy attack was broken,
and this time there were two of the great ships.

Perhaps there was something in the air.

Haut Jon Hedley sat, nursing a drink in the Shelburne's main lounge, watching the dancers in a not
unpleasant melancholy and tapping a foot to the band.

A woman approached him. He admired her, grace-
ful in a sleek, simple gown that iridesced slightly from
purple to black at irregular intervals, with an occa-
sional star-flash here and there. *A Rentier's wife . . .
no, not old enough, not hard-looking enough, more
likely his daughter. Or mistress. Now why don't I ever
get lucky and . . .*

The woman stopped at his table, and he recognized
her, stood hastily.

"Dr. Heiser!"

"*Haut* Hedley," the physicist, cohead of the Force's Scientific Analysis Section, said. "May I join you?"

"Of course, of course. What are you drinking?"

"I'm not," she said. "I came here to dance."

"Oh," Hedley said.

"Which is why I came over. It's difficult when you're as tall as I am, finding someone the proper height to trip the light whatever with."

"Actually," Hedley said, "I suppose being tall . . . at an early age . . . is why I never learned to dance. My coordination took a few years to catch up to my body."

"You don't know how to dance . . . Jon?"

Hedley shook his head.

"Then," Heiser said firmly, "it's time you learned."

Hedley blinked, then a slow smile came as he stood and held out a hand.

"Maybe it is, Ann. Maybe it is."

"When I was a wee tot," Njangu said thoughtfully, "my mother gave me a present. That didn't happen very much. Like never. Very expensive it was, and now I don't want to think about where she got the credits to pay for it."

Garvin listened carefully. It was very seldom Yoshitaro said anything about his family.

"It was a little spaceship, and when you touched little sensors, it would make a drive whine, and landing lights would go on, and a little voice would say 'preparing for takeoff,' or landing, or whatever.

"I loved it a lot," he said. "Which is why I was afraid to take it outside and let the other kids play with it, or even show it to them, for fear somebody bigger'd take it away from me."

He stared out the window, across the parade ground on Chance Island at Leggett.

"So?"

"Protector Redruth's got a brand-new couple of toys, doesn't he?" Yoshitaro said.

"Oh. That's why he's so damned cautious with those cruisers. Afraid to use them, for fear they'll get blown apart."

"Maybe"

"That's worth developing a scenario, isn't it, to maybe confirm our buddy Redruth in his caution?"

"Maybe."

"By the way," Garvin said. "Whatever happened to your little spaceship?"

"My father came home drunk and stepped on it." Njangu's voice was flat, as if it didn't matter.

Larix/Off Larix Prime

Now this is real remote control, Ben Dill thought. He hung, in an *aksai* anodized and given special fittings and ECM capabilities not to reflect much of anything, from normal light to radar to any other detection device—or so the Force scientists thought—about one AU off Larix Prime.

Farther off the planet was his controlling *velv,* which hopefully wouldn't be found out by Larissan detectors.

Puppet strings from Cumbre to the velv, *from the* velv *to me, from me to* . . .

Dill's normal control helmet was in a niche beside him. He wore a larger, fatter headpiece that completely covered his eyes, and held a small box, with a single control stick with a small wheel atop it. And he wasn't seeing the space around him, but rather the surface of Larix Prime, rushing toward him.

Far below, a tiny reconnaissance drone dived into the planet's atmosphere, over one of its small seas.

Dill flew the drone through the control box, and saw what it saw, through a realtime camera in the drone's nose.

Alarm lights bloomed, faded on either side of his vision as the drone closed on land.

Dill was muttering mightily: "No, you don't see me, right, keep on sweeping, you moron goddamned early-warning point, prob'ly thinking about somebody you want to boff, right, maybe there's something up there in the sky way over the next continent, go look for it, and forget about me . . . awright, now we're closing, bring this puppy back level, come on you, don't tumble on me, there we go, now down, down, don't eat a tree, Dill, they aren't good for you . . . over the beach now . . ."

The drone shot inland, on a semiprogrammed course. Ahead was a large military complex which might have interesting things to tell the Force. If the drone succeeded in transmitting data, unlike the last five that'd been tried on other parts of Larix Prime.

The Force still lacked an enormous amount of intel on Larix Prime, but Larissan antiaircraft crews were entirely too proficient and alert.

Dill swore the problem was that the drones were piloted by technicians sitting comfortably on a *velv,* and a real pilot ought to be given a chance, from as close as he dared get, to make sure he had the proper feel.

He was given that chance, as were Alikhan and Jacqueline Boursier. The three were attempting simultaneous penetrations, on the theory if one was spotted, the ensuing hue and cry might make life easier for the other two. *Or,* Dill thought cynically, a *great deal harder if all the goddamned skywatchers quit daydreaming and started paying attention to business.*

He slowed the drone to just above stall speed, saw treetops reel past just below him, saw a housing district and banked to avoid it, as other alarm lights flashed.

"So far, so good . . . and Mama's favorite Benjamin is under their goddamned screen . . . ho-ho, and here we come up on that thingie what we hope's a base, and punt it up a few meters so we get good coverage and start the recorders and make Big Daddy happy . . ."

The drone went to full power, and images flashed . . . open land . . . perimeter fence . . . a swept, bare death zone . . . another fence . . . guard tower . . . rows of barracks . . . a landing field over there . . . maybe a parade ground . . . *goddamned construction equipment, almost bagged that crane* . . . high-stacked steel plate . . . industrial building . . . a rolling mill? . . . *hell if I know* . . . high, closed hangars.

"Now we have it, now we have it . . . look at that, hangar door wide-open, and look at that goddamned prime mover with a frigging cruiser on its back, how many frigging rows of tracks . . . biggest goddamned thing I've ever seen on ground . . . whup, almost ate that hangar, two, four other building ways, no ships on them, camo cover, easy to see from down here, and holy kee-ripes!"

Smoke blossomed close to the drone, and Dill banked hard, went even lower.

"Shoot at me now, you silly bastards, bet your goddamned launchers don't depress that far, and we're coming on to another shipyard, or maybe finishing yard and . . ."

And the screen flashed to black. Ben had only a millisecond to see something very big loom as the drone smashed into something . . . another crane, a ship, *who the hell knew, hope it was expensive.*

"Aw crap," Dill moaned. "Everybody's gonna break my balls because Ben went and rammed something instead of paying attention like he should've been doing."

But no one did. Alikhan's drone had been shot out of the sky on entry. Boursier's had returned, but the industrial area she'd investigated had nothing at all happening of interest.

"Think we could get away with that again?" Dill wondered.

"Why not?" Boursier said. She was a very thin, very intense brunette who, as far as anyone knew, had no life beyond the cockpit.

"We certainly should try again," Alikhan agreed. "There are another six drones in the hold of this *velv*."

The watch officer came in, holding a com printout.

"You glory hounds can sack out if you want. We've been recalled."

"Why?"

The officer shrugged.

"You three are required for some sort of special mission. They don't tell us common flyboys anything, you know that."

Cumbre/D-Cumbre

Garvin finished briefing the I&R troops who'd volunteered to beef up the crews on the half dozen destroyers in his plan's forward element. There'd been some debate as to how much anyone beyond command staff should be told. Hedley'd argued that, if things went wrong, as they could quite easily, everyone should know "everything about our flipping cleverness while they're turning into vacuum-packed corpses."

Garvin finished, wished he could find something inspiring to send them into battle with, then turned the detachment over to Njangu, who told them to report to their ships and dismissed them.

Jaansma noticed, as the troops moved away, under the harsh midnight glare of the dock's floodlights, Darod Montagna. She saw his gaze, and smiled. Then she was gone.

He got into his lifter, told the pilot to take him to his own ship. Garvin wanted to know what destroyer she was crewing on, knew better than to ask. He wished he'd not seen her, for he didn't need to be thinking of those six ships as anything other than bait.

"You be careful now," Froude told Ho Kang.

She grinned. "I'm always careful, Danfin. Generally it's the other fellow who isn't."

"I just want to make sure you come back," he said.

"Oh, I'll be back," Kang promised, then told him, rather explicitly, what she wanted to do with him on her return.

He blew a kiss, cut the connection, turned and saw Ann Heiser looking at him slyly.

"Private coms on Force time, Doctor?"

Froude colored, then realized Heiser was grinning at him.

The com buzzed, and the technician on the board said, "Dr. Heiser . . . it's *Haut* Hedley, from Force Headquarters. He wants to say good-bye."

It was Heiser's turn to flush. Froude wasn't too much of a gentleman not to deliberately arch his eyebrows before going back to his sketch panel.

Kura/Off Kura Four

Drones were sent to just out-atmosphere, and Kuran planetary patrols reported two of them.

An E-day later, seven ships that might've been freighters, but could also have been armed Larissan fleet auxiliaries, lifted and formed a convoy off the planet. Five destroyers were escorting them.

The convoy was clumsily shadowed by two small Cumbrian patrol ships to the standard nav point, and went into hyperspace.

The two patrol ships jumped after it using full power, came out of N-space at the nav point they hoped the slower convoy would use.

A few seconds later, the convoy appeared in the same space, as if everything was quite normal, and the shadowers hadn't been detected.

The six waiting Cumbrian destroyers moved in for the attack. The Larissans took a standard defense formation. Intent on the attackers, the Larissans paid little mind to the distant Kane control ship, whose presence they'd grown used to.

In its battle room, Hedley and Garvin watched Ho

Kang's chair as it boomed back and forth in the compartment, Ho calmly giving orders into a headset.

Hedley caught Garvin's expression, grinned.

"Ain't it a bitch when you've got to sit there and watch other people get their balls in the flipping wringer on your orders?"

"Damned uncomfortable, sir."

"Get used to it," Hedley advised. "I had to, the farther away I got from being up to my flipping belly button in the mud and blood."

Ho's chair dropped down over one technician, who was reading a screen. Suddenly her voice came through speakers next to the two officers.

"Your trap's sprung. Two of the *Naarohns,* plus escorts, have entered this space."

Garvin looked at the big screen, reading it well enough to see the two blips that suddenly simmed into tiny holograms of the Larissan battle cruisers.

Kang was giving more orders, and other, tinier, holograms appeared not far away from the two cruisers and their four escorts.

"Vann First Elements, this is Vann Control," Ho said. "The biggies have shown up . . . you haven't seen them . . . let 'em close on you . . . all right. You've spotted them. Now general panic as practiced."

The six destroyers, almost ready to engage the Larissan convoy escorts, broke into new courses. Two fired countermissiles behind them as they fled.

"All right," Kang said. "You're not jumping back into hyperspace yet . . . you think you've got speed on those Larissans . . . right . . . there's a chance you'll be able to come back on the convoy . . ."

She switched channels.

"This is Vann Control. You weren't spotted. Go after them on independent control."

Half a light-second away, in empty space, seven *aksai* lay doggo. They'd been released by mother *velv,* who went back to N-space in seconds.

"I want him, I want him, I want him," Ben Dill chanted as his fingers danced across sensors.

His canopy was full of ships—the convoy to his left, their escorts just right of them, down and in the front the "fleeing" Cumbrian destroyers, far to his right and up was the Kane. Dead "ahead" were the two cruisers and their escorts.

"Proctologically speaking," Ben said, "Dr. Dill is delivering a surprise. Launch one . . . launch two . . . launch three."

More missiles spat from underwing mounts of the other fighter ships at the cruisers.

On the Kane, Kang keyed a sensor.

"Vann First Elements, this is Vann Control . . . on the count of five, jump for hyperspace . . . four . . . three . . . cancel that, jump now!"

She'd seen the flash from one of the cruiser's escorts, realized the *aksai* or their missiles had been detected and the Larissan was firing.

Countermissiles were hastily launched by the Larissans, to mixed effect.

One missile, later to be hotly argued as to whose, closed on the rearmost cruiser, and exploded. Another blew up right behind it, and oxygen-fed flames from the cruiser jetted into space for an instant, were cut off. A secondary explosion shook the cruiser, and it canted forward, pinwheeling in its trajectory.

A missile almost got one of the *aksai,* blew up nearby.

Dill's canopy showed a bull's-eye. He was targeted by somebody's Target-Acquisition devices.

"Nah, nah, you've not got me," he said, fingers touching the ECM panel.

The missile from the cruiser, almost as big as Dill's attack ship, swung in confusion, then, in obedience to basic programming, exploded harmlessly.

"All Vann Elements," Ho ordered. "Break contact and withdraw."

"Aw," Dill muttered. "Just one more shot and that

cruiser's Ben Dill Sandwich Spread, dammit!" But he obeyed.

Alikhan ripple-launched his remaining missiles as he made rapid course changes toward the *velv,* which had come back from hyperspace for the pickup. He thought he saw one explode seconds later, which meant a hit on something. He considered reporting it, then told himself he was thinking entirely too much like a human. Glory should be self-evident, not advertised.

The Larissan destroyers started after the *aksai,* but were recalled to guard the crippled cruiser and its mate.

"Now, with any flipping luck," Hedley said, "your little mousetrap should give Redruth even more reason to pause."

Cumbre/D-Cumbre

"Very good," Angara told the assembled officers. "Very subtle. Especially you, Jaansma. Your performance was in the best traditions of the Force."

"Thank you, sir."

"I think you'll be a little less grateful when you realize the next thing to come is a circus."

Garvin brightened visibly, then realized what Angara meant.

"*Haut* Hedley," Angara went on. "Here's the list of our performing bears, and the medals they'll be getting.

"I think this is a good occasion to announce the cadre for the new Brigade. Initially, we'll name you as CO of Second Brigade. Which means you've just been promoted to *Caud. Mil* Fitzgerald will take over this Brigade with the same rank. There'll be other changes, of course.

"Just to keep matters from getting confused, I'm giving myself the brevet rank of *Dant.* This will be confirmed or rejected when we return to Confederation Command by higher command.

"That's all."

It was a circus indeed. A media circus that swarmed over Garvin as impossibly good-looking, Jon Hedley as the very picture of a young Force Brigade commander, if a bit too thin and intense, Ho Kang as a scholar-warrior, the *aksai* pilots as daredevils of the skies, Alikhan as proof the Musth-Human alliance was very firm, and Ben Dill as, well, Ben Dill.

Medals cascaded in all directions, and after it was all over, everyone was given leave.

"Wold you let me turn over, you lummox?" Jasith complained. "There you are on the holo again. I want to see."

Garvin obeyed, rolling over on his back.

Jasith stared at the projection. "Let me turn the sound up . . . oh, this is a clip I haven't seen. You know, I'll bet Loy is just grinding his teeth into powder, having to see you all over *Matin*.

"Garvin, aren't you interested?"

"I know what I look like," he said. "But as far as interested . . ."

"Oh. Don't bite me there. Mmmh. That feels good. When you bite my neck, you send chills all the way down my. toes. Garvin! Don't you ever want to do anything else?" She stopped talking, moaned sharply. "Don't stop! Don't ever stop!"

Garvin did wonder about himself. All he did want was to eat, sleep, and be alone with Jasith, preferably naked.

It was a momentary, necessary curtain between him and the ugliness of war.

Two months passed.

Raiders went out against Kura, bold enough to strike the fringes of Larix. Now their prime targets weren't the escorts, but the merchant ships they were escorting.

The cruisers only made careful, token appearances, when they were sure no ambushes had been laid.

The deployment of the robot trackers made it easier to make contact with the convoys, but the Larissan escort commanders had gotten more skilled, so casualties on both sides mounted.

The Force had destroyed about 20 percent more Larissan ships, about the same number of Larissan soldiers. But given the population of Larix and Kura, and the data Njangu had learned about Larissan production rates, these cold numbers said the war was slowly but inexorably being lost.

The first reports tumbled in from the distant alert stations, a report from M-Cumbre, then its signal went dead. Shortly thereafter, automatic stations on the planet broke off, then communication was lost with K-Cumbre.

The Larissans were attacking, systematically taking out any manned or unmanned tracking stations they could find, then sending missiles after them.

Half an E-day later, a research ship off the ice giant I-Cumbre reported ships, many Larissan, then it also went silent.

Patrol ships from the bases on G-Cumbre went out. A scattering survived to report an entire Larissan fleet was in the Cumbre System. Four of the gigantic Naarohns, forty or more destroyers, and a swarm of lighter support ships, patrol craft and auxiliaries.

The Force responded instantly. Kellys, *velv, aksai,* even a few *wynt,* the barely space-capable Musth armed transports, and Zhukovs came up from C-, D-, E-Cumbre, moons, and asteroid-monitoring stations. All six of the Kane-class controllers lifted with the motley formations.

Dant Angara was in the battle room of the command ship, the *al Maouna*. Ho sat in her chair, depressed to eye level with Angara.

"Damned if I can see why I didn't find the time to learn how to run a battle from here," Angara growled to Hedley.

"There'll be no problem," Kang said. "You tell me who you want and where you want them. We've set a small screen here that'll give you just the inner planets, stationary to keep things simple, our ships in white, the Larissans in red. Projected orbits are those little green arrows."

"All right," Angara said. "Then let's run these shitheels back to where they came from."

The Larissans closed on D-Cumbre, cutting inside its orbit, almost to C-Cumbre's, then came back on the capital world.

They were in two inverted V's, their support ships to the rear of the formation. Three Naarohns were in the lead V, the other with the second wing. That element had ten more destroyers.

"We go for the biggies," Angara said, and the orders were commed.

Space in-sun from D-Cumbre became a swirling mass of fighting ships, trying for the cruisers. But the destroyer screen was too strong to break through. The cruisers fought from long-distance, their missiles longer-ranged and heavier.

A *velv* got close, hit one cruiser, not hard enough to take it out of battle, then was destroyed. The first V opened, trying to envelop the Cumbrian ships.

Angara ordered a pullback and regroup, flanked one wing of the V, and began shattering it in detail.

Ships fought, killed, and died, then the emergency com came—the rear V had broken away from the main formation, was not being held in reserve, but was going for D-Cumbre.

Angara's reserves were out of position, but he ordered them in, better late than not at all, broke off his attack, and went after the second V, swearing at himself helplessly, knowing the Larissans would get in-atmosphere with their damned nukes and there'd be hell to pay.

But a formation of seven Kellys came from behind Bodwin, D-Cumbre's moon, where they shouldn't have been. They smashed into the Larissans, earning the formation commander a medal instead of a court-martial. The single cruiser took three missiles in as many seconds. Its bow blew off, and the cruiser spun off toward Cumbre's sun.

Some of the Larissans broke to fight the Kellys as other Cumbrians hit the V. But four held course, and there was nothing between them and D-Cumbre.

People in D-Cumbre's cities puzzled at the unfamiliar howl of sirens, realized what they meant, and scurried for the hastily designated shelters, mostly basements or even first stories of large buildings.

The Larissans crashed in-atmosphere, sonic booms whiplashing the sea and islands, and in finger-four formation came in on Dharma Island from the south. Bays opened just short of the city, and bombs dropped, black rows walking down the sky, sending fingers of fire across Mount Najim, over the Highlands, and rich Rentiers died as their mansions shattered. The last of the bombs dropped just on Leggett City's waterfront, exploding glass in the Shelburne Hotel.

Redruth had changed his mind, realized radioactive real estate wasn't worth conquering, and the bombs held conventional explosives.

The destroyers rolled, came back for another run, and *aksai* swarmed them, missiles filling the sky with smoke, fire. Two ships blew up, the third went for space, directly into the flight pattern of the fourth ship, and there was, very suddenly, nothing left to shoot at.

Angara had only a moment to feel relief before he ordered the Force to reassemble and go after the remaining Larissans. But they were in full retreat, and as soon as they cleared world limits, blipped, one by one, back into N-space to their homeworlds.

"I guess we won this one," Hedley said, wincing as the casualty list of ships scrolled across a screen. "Flipping expensive."

"Not as expensive as it'll be next time," Angara said. "Next time they come it'll be an invasion."

CHAPTER
21

The Force casualties were fairly grim—over a thousand dead, about the same number injured, sixteen ships lost, twenty crippled badly enough to be scrapped.

Civilian casualties were worse, all from Leggett City: eighteen hundred killed, three times that injured, billions of credits in damage. It was noted, though, that this battle had something unique in human history, as far as known: Most of the casualties were rich.

There were three good things to come of the Larissan bombing:

The half-ruined Eckmuhl, formerly the 'Raum ghetto in the center of Leggett City and never seriously rebuilt after the rising, was nearly leveled. Architects privately licked their lips at being able, once this nonsense called war was over, at being able to completely redesign and build a city center from scratch;

The Planetary Council became a rubber stamp for any and every suggested emergency military appropriation;

Most importantly, recruiting for the Force skyrocketed, as the media showed endless hours of the bombing, mixed with "heart" coverage of the victims. The already-passed Conscription Measure, which had been lackadaisically creaking through the bureaucracy, was immediately implemented, and able-bodied sorts who weren't particularly patriotic or warlike suddenly realized they were quite likely to be grabbed. That, in turn, sparked more enlistments, as the Force made it loudly clear the choice assignments went to volunteers,

and a draftee would have to be very well qualified in
something to avoid becoming a greaser on a spaceship,
an airfield sweeper, or a common duty soldier.

But Cumbre just didn't have that many people. Angara thought enviously of the thundering herds on
Kura and Larix, and wondered if, after the war, some
genius like Froude would figure a way to educate the
Larissans into something better than what the ancients
had called *Kadavergehorsamkeit*—obeying orders with
the mindlessness of a corpse.

But first there was the small problem of Redruth
and his regime . . .

Angara hadn't been being pessimistic when he predicted an invasion. It had to be coming, for Redruth
had no other options. His family had gotten and kept
power by constantly reminding the people of their enemies, including the now-not-considered-mythical
Womblies. Now Cumbre was the new horror, and he
had to destroy it, or the populace would eventually
realize how downtrodden they were and rise against
him. Whether that was the only probability, Angara
didn't know. But he *did* know that Redruth, like most
autocrats, would believe there could be no other
choices than violence.

So Angara pushed, shouted, ordered, and reasoned
for more ships, more training, more men. He ran endless map exercises, field exercises, computer games,
exploring every option his staff could arrive at. D-
Cumbre would not be the only target. C-, D- and E-
Cumbre were slated for landings. Redruth would first
take and hold a foothold on one of the other worlds
before moving in-system. And so on and so forth.

To further complicate his task, Angara also was preparing something that none of his own people nor
Redruth would be expecting.

Caud Ceil Fitzgerald wore her just-graying hair
close-cropped, matching her all-business manner and
ex-athlete's build.

Garvin and Njangu stood at attention in front of her.

"I'll make this brief," she said. "There were suggestions as to who should be the Executive Officer. You were among them, *Mil* Jaansma. Even though you're the youngest of the ones *Dant* Angara offered, I'm picking you.

"I like the way you've come up with unorthodox ideas, even though they haven't worked out quite as expected, always. I think I'll have no problem riding herd on what we'll call your youthful exuberance."

"Uh . . . thank you, ma'am," Garvin managed.

"Naturally, you're promoted *Haut.*"

She turned her attention to Njangu.

"I have very mixed feelings about you, Yoshitaro."

Njangu kept his face blank, wondering which of his tricks Fitzgerald hated. Like most paranoiacs, he misunderstood her meaning.

"On the one hand, I think your devious mind is exactly what's needed running Infantry and Reconnaissance Company. On the other, we're not in a position to cozy up in slots where we're not extending ourselves.

"And craftiness has other homes. Effective immediately, you're promoted to *Mil,* and will replace Jaansma as head of II Section. I understand you, *Dant* Angara, *Caud* Hedley, and Jaansma had an irregular relationship, in that the four of you felt comfortable scheming without going through any chain of command.

"I want to maintain that same irregularity. We are badly outnumbered, possibly outgunned, and none of us has really recovered from the last few years of unrelenting combat.

"That is unfortunate. But there'll be no relief until Redruth is beaten and, I suspect, his worlds taken by force. We've got to keep pressing him until he breaks.

"It's the last fighter who can ignore his exhaustion

and pain, stagger in, and deliver the last blow who triumphs.

"I've taken the opportunity to read your files, Yoshitaro, on Larix, and I've had a few conversations with *Aspirant* Stiofan. I do not wish either myself or my children to live under a tyranny like Redruth's.

"So we mustn't slacken now.

"That's all. You two can select the new commander of I&R from within its ranks. I want the officer to hold the rank of *Cent,* so I've gotten authorization from *Dant* Angara to jump whatever ranks are necessary. I trust your judgment.

"You're dismissed."

Both men saluted, about-faced.

"Oh," Fitzgerald said. "I almost forgot. I seem to have the reputation of being a harsh taskmaster. I prefer to think I merely am more focused than some others.

"Both of you can take the rest of the afternoon off, to celebrate your promotions. However, there'll be a staff meeting tomorrow morning, an hour after general reveille. I expect both of you to be present and capable.

"Thank you."

Outside, the two looked at each other wryly.

"Looks like it's going to be a young man's war," Garvin said. "The book says you can expect to make *Mil* if you're a good little rank filler about forty or fifty, and *Haut*'s a good rank to retire with after twenty more. Congrats."

"You too," Njangu said. "You're on your way to Star Foozle."

"Yeh," Garvin said. "That's me. Youngest fleet honcho in the history of the Universe. Wonder if I should start looking for a tailor to make up my uniforms now? Or for a fleet to command?"

Njangu started laughing.

"Nope," Njangu said, "ol' Fitz isn't a slave driver.

Not at all, no way in heaven. A whole, what, three hours off? My heart melts."

"Guess we aren't going to get too drunk, are we?"

"Guess not," Njangu said. "Maybe we better com the ladies, tell them the news, and see if they've got any nice, sedate ways to celebrate. Maybe a brisk walk, eh? Or a refreshing cup of herb tea?"

Garvin grinned, then caught himself.

"Aw crud! Jasith's off looking at some kind of new ore transporter the Musth came up with over on C-Cumbre. Guess it *will* be a quiet evening."

"If you want, you can tag along with me and Maev. Maybe have a drink or two or dinner over at the Shelburne, then come on back so we're bushy-eyed and bright-tailed for tomorrow's staff bullshit?"

"A plan," Garvin said. "Not that I especially like the idea of watching you two suck each other's tongues while I stew in solitary splendor. But it's better than having to buy every goddamned *Alt* in the Force a drink 'cause we got promoted. Go ring your lady up, and tell her to get cracking."

"After we get the pleasure of talking to the new I&R Commander," Njangu said. "Heh. Heh."

The reaction was predictable.

Monique Lir's head swiveled, like a poisonous snake about to strike, between Yoshitaro and Jaansma.

"You pair of bastards," she hissed. "I can see you standing there just eating this shit up!"

"Now, Monique, is that any way to talk to your superiors?"

"Goddammit, you two knew I don't want to be an officer! Not ever!"

"Adj-Prem," Njangu said, trying to keep from laughing, "as *Caud* Fitzgerald has informed us, and as you should know full well, into each life some piss must tinkle."

"Look at it this way, Monique," Garvin said reasonably. "You're not an *Aspirant,* not even an *Alt.* You've leapt into the heights of the not-quite-field-grade, in one swell foop."

"Think of the money," Njangu said.

"Yeah," Lir growled. "About a hundred credits a month less than I make as *Adj-Prem.* Whoopie"

"I know what the problem is," Njangu said. "You're worried about not having the social graces to handle the Ossifers' Club, right?"

"Screw you, boss," Monique said. "You know god-damned well what it is. Warrants run this Force. This army. Any army. Always have, always will. Now I'm one of you snots, and now I'll have to start worrying about what my noncoms are trying to put over on *me*! That isn't right!" she almost wailed.

"Tsk. Tsk," Garvin said. "Uh, *Mil* Yoshitaro, isn't it customary to throw a promoted I&R person in a pond or something? I don't think the Musth left us any pools, so I guess we should throw *Cent* Lir in the bay. Right?"

"Uh . . ." Njangu began cautiously.

"Try it," Lir gritted. "Please. One of you try it."

"I think," Garvin said hastily, "we'll pass on that local custom, eh? Congratulations, *Cent.* I'm sure you'll serve in the highest traditions of the Force."

"And, by the way," Njangu added, "Just so you don't think we're harsh taskmasters, you can have the rest of the afternoon off to celebrate your promotion.

"But we'll want I&R on a dawn run tomorrow. Say, out to Tiger Maneuver Area and back. Can't have the children getting stale, now can we?

"That's all, *Cent.* You're dismissed."

Again, Lir gave them the deadly stare. "Some-time . . . I don't know when . . . somewhere, I don't know that either . . . there'll be a chance for me to get revenge."

Her salute could have illustrated a textbook.

An Ohnce in an orbit over Kura Prime, hidden near an ancient piece of space junk, counted, in its moronic

way, the number of ships exiting atmosphere. Too
many, too quickly. It coded the count and the size of
them, blipped the transmission to its sister in hyperspace, who passed the word down the chain.

"Well hmmph and horseshit," Njangu said, discon-
necting. "Guess who's off guarding the good *Dant* in
Taman City. Helluva way to celebrate a promotion."
"Yeh," Garvin said. "Look. I've been thinking. The
Shelburne's 'kay, I guess. But shouldn't we have at
least one uncivilized drink first?"
"What, you want to go impose on the noncoms, like
we usually do?"
"Why not? Everybody's busting ass, so it shouldn't
be that rowdy. One drink, then cross the bay for some
serious rare roast, a bottle of wine, and then we toddle
off to bed like good little boys and girls."

Njangu either forgot, or chose to forget, that the
NCO Club would be drinking Monique Lir to perdi-
tion, on her final night as a noncom.
It looked like all rank barriers were off. Garvin and
Njangu weren't the only officers in the roaring melee,
and Yoshitaro thought he saw every member of I&R
in the huge club, except for those unfortunates off in
space or on duty.
And it wasn't one drink they had. Each of them
had to buy the other a round, then someone spotted
them who'd heard about their promotions, sent over
a round, and then another. Plus well-wishers dropped
by with a drink or two to talk.
"Howmanyzat?" Garvin inquired after a while.
"Eightyleven for me, sixtyfourburp for you rump-
kins," Njangu said.
"Only one solitary rumpkin, like only me, at this
table."
Njangu owled at him.
"Looks like more."

"Maybe I better cancel dinner reversations . . . sorry, reservations, huh?"

"Maybe," Njangu agreed. "And have 'em send over another round when the bar slows down enough for you to talk to it. Thirsty out."

" 'Kay," Garvin said, and got to his feet carefully. He took a sight on the bar and set his course, pleased that he wasn't weaving at all, but still careful on where he put his feet.

He stopped, watched *Adj-Prem* . . . correction, *Cent* Monique Lir, dancing on a tabletop. She appeared quite sober. Garvin wondered where she'd found the saber that was her partner, went on.

He found a com, dug through his pouch, peering at each card until he found the right one, swiped it through the payslot, and, when the Shelburne answered, very carefully gave his name and announced that he and his fellow officer would be unable to keep their reservations . . . last-minute call of duty, y'know.

He was quite proud of his clarity of tone, spoiled the effect with an enormous belch, muttered an apology, and disconnected.

Now what? Oh yeh. Order a drink for Njangu. Better get one for myself to keep the guy company. Get two for each of us, since the bar looks busy, and I'm a firm believer in economy of effort.

Coming down the hallway from the com and the freshers was Darod Montagna. She didn't look in much better shape than he was, keeping one hand lightly on a wall for guidance.

" 'Lo," Garvin said.

Darod looked up, recognized him.

"*Haut* Jaansma! Congratulations on your promotion, sir. Everyone's real pleased for you."

Garvin nodded, tried to think of a snappy reply, failed.

Darod took a step forward, stumbled a little, and Garvin caught her. She looked up at him, smiled happily.

It seemed a good idea for him to kiss her, so he did. She moved against him, both her arms went around his neck—she wasn't that much smaller than he was, he realized—and kissed him back, tongue running in and out of his mouth. Garvin's hand came up reflexively, cupped her breast, and she moved against him, pressing herself close.

Someone coughed, and Garvin came back to military reality, and pulled back.

"Uh, the *Tweg* had something in her eye," he started, then realized it was Njangu.

"Sorry, sir," Montagna said. "I, uh, just—"

"I saw shit," Yoshitaro announced. "I just came to remind *Haut* Jaansma we're running late. So if you'll excuse us, *Tweg* Montagna . . ." putting emphasis on the rank.

He had Garvin by an elbow, a smile fixed on his face, leading him back into the bar.

"And I think it's time we're going," he hissed.

"You aren't kidding," Garvin said fervently. "We should've been gone before I went to make that com. Thank you, thank you, thank you."

"Yeh," Njangu said. "You're bound and determined to stay in trouble, aren't you? I assume that's the person you were being so frigging vague about. Good goddamned thing I'm around to rescue you."

The next morning, Njangu malevolently watched Garvin, suffering the torments of the damned, try to answer *Caud* Fitzgerald's questions about Larissan intentions.

Before the staff meeting, while he sucked caff and chewed antacids in the Officers' Mess, Garvin had plaintively queried him about hangover remedies. Njangu had thought about suggesting raw *giptel* eggs in hot sauce, or some of the other disgusting folk remedies he'd heard of, then said lots of ice water and mild analgesics were the only thing that'd help. Beyond going back to bed for the rest of the day.

Actually, Njangu knew a couple of real hangover cures. But they were high on the illegal-drug market and, besides, Yoshitaro had no idea where to score something like that these days.

He sighed for lost youth and concentrated on Garvin's miseries. It kept him from remembering he didn't feel all that much better, himself.

Neither of their conditions was improved when, an hour after the staff meeting ended, sirens screamed full alert.

The Larissans were on the move.

Dant Angara had no intention of being caught at the bottom of any gravity well. As soon as the satellite had reported Larissan ships mobilizing off Prime, the Force went to combat positions.

The Cumbrian ships were already armed and fueled, and half of the troops assigned to the ships on board. The rest of the Legion drew arms and went to their duty stations at a dead run.

Landing fields on the human-occupied planets and moons of Cumbre trembled, and dust clouds swirled as ships lifted for space.

The first to take off were the *Kanes,* now nine strong. They moved into parking orbits just off their assigned planets, their controllers reeling streams of orders to the incoming ships while the rest of the fleet assembled.

There were more than just the *Kellys* and *aksai*-carrying *velv* in the formations. After the Larissan attack, every Force vessel a weapon could be lashed to became a warship, from tiny patrol boats to merchantmen to Force supply craft.

Against the rules of warfare, which Angara somehow thought Redruth didn't have memorized anyway, civilian ships were armed, and the women and men who volunteered to serve on them given hasty instructions. The tough mining cargo ships of Mellusin Mining were particularly suited for this modification.

Space-rigged Zhukovs and even Griersons hung in
space, their mission the close-in defense of the
homeworlds.

Here and there were a scattering of yachts. Somehow, word had spread through the Rentiers across D-
Cumbre that it'd be "awf'ly appropriate, old boy, if
you actually stood up for something in this life, and
anyway, wouldn't it be kickers to see if that racer of
yours'd be able to fight, say, one of those damned
Larissans? Or make a stab at it, anyway."

Word was that Erik Penwyth had been the one who
came up with that idea, but he piously pleaded innocent. Another, more personal reason some of the play-
boys found their elaborate yachts floating in close
orbit with drab merchantmen and the odd, shep-
herding *wynt* was that almost everyone in the close-
knit Rentier community had lost someone in the
bombing, or knew someone who had.

One of those yachts, unknown to Garvin, was the
repaired *Godrevy*.

Angara's staff had decided on the four most likely
nav points the Larissans might use. Angara had rejected one as being too far away from Cumbre's heart,
another because it lay close to the asteroids, and might
be considered a navigational risk to the newly expanded Larissan fleet with its less-experienced officers.

The two remaining were between C- and D-Cumbre, and just inside the orbit of H-Cumbre. Angara
thought the first not the most likely. Redruth, or
rather Celidon, who most certainly would actually be
commanding the invasion fleet, would need some time
and space to assemble his forces before attacking.
Nevertheless, Angara had a full twelve destroyers
guarding that point.

The bulk of his fleet he ordered positioned just beyond the H-Cumbre point, in the orbital plane of the
ice giant.

There they waited, for almost two E-days.

An *aksai* was the first to report the Larissan fleet

as they burst out of hyperspace at the predicted H-Cumbre nav point.

They blinked into being in concave arcs. The horns of each arc were secured by patrol ships and destroyers. The cruisers were mostly in the forward elements, two at the rear. In the center of the rows were the troop transports, some design-built assault ships, vastly more hastily converted merchantmen, each packed with even-more-hastily trained soldiers.

All their search apparati must have been aimed at the occupied worlds, for long minutes passed without any sign they'd noticed the Cumbrians waiting "behind" and "below" them.

That was long enough for Ho Kang and the other controllers to determine the exact Larissan orbit—directly toward D-Cumbre, in the least-subtle strategy—and run programs sending orders to each of the Cumbrian ships.

Kellys, *velv,* went into hyperspace for an instant, coming out just on the fringes of the Larissan mass. Others appeared in front of the Larissans, a long gauntlet to D-Cumbre.

Alikhan, without realizing it, was making a low humming sound in the back of his throat as his sights swept down the nose of the Larissan destroyer, back up, centering on the bridge. His paw rested over the launch sensor, touched it.

One of his three Goddards hissed out of the tube, targeted the destroyer and sped off.

As ordered, Alikhan returned to N-space, jumped to his second destination. He never saw the Goddard rip the Larissan's bow open, leaving the rest of the crew to die behind automatic airlocks in a slowly rotating tomb.

Mil Liskeard got lucky, or so he thought at first. His jump coordinates put him in the middle of the Larissan transports. His collision alarm blatted, and his hyperdrive kicked him back in, out of N-space, barely avoiding a collision. He was close, too close, to the enemy ships.

His screen showed him at the rear of a fairly coherent wave of ships, quickly ID'ed as assault transports. He ordered his weapons officers to seek targets and fire at will, and for his navigator to put him across the rear of the formation.

The *Parnell* arced down the row, missiles volleying. A patrol ship tried to intercept, and was destroyed. Liskeard was close enough to the Larissans to use visual screens as the transports bucked and exploded. One ship, still boiling fire, was close enough to be seen through a porthole, and Liskeard put a zoom on one screen.

A moment later, he almost vomited over his control panel. The screen showed the freighter, wrack and ruin consuming it as it sprayed tiny white objects into space, white objects that had been men, soldiers who would never survive to land on any planet, hostile or friendly.

Liskeard ignored his churning stomach, ordering his Kelly back the way it came, all available hands helping the weapons crewmen reload the ship's tubes. The *Parnell* struck again. Liskeard called his control ship, and the controller put three more destroyers and a dozen *velv* in on his signal. They savaged the transports, men spewing out of the ruined ships like the guts of depth-exploded fish.

Finally, the Larissan ships' screams were heard, and two cruisers flashed into being. A *velv* was hit, but the other Cumbrians went back into N-space, calling to their controllers for more targets.

Except for the two *aksai*—Ben Dill and Boursier—who'd been vectored in on the holocaust. The cruisers and their escorts were looking for big ships to take revenge on, not one-man mites. Dill and his wingmate, masked by pinwheeling wreckage, cut through the carnage on luck and very fast reflexes. A destroyer loomed "close"—no more than a thousand kilometers, and Boursier gutted it with a missile.

"Ben Dill's boy is after bigger, bigger game," Dill snarled. "And this time no goddamned 'claimed as damaged' will be allowed . . . and there you are, dead center, you big fat pig." He launched two Goddards, changed his point of aim to the cruiser's stern, fired his last missile.

All three struck almost at once, and the cruiser vaporized.

"Ho-ho," Dill said into his open mike. "Ben Dill wants another medal and a pay raise."

"If you have anything left," the com said, in accented Basic, "sssome help could be provided for me." It was Tvem, another of the Musth mercenaries. Dill touched sensors, saw two Larissan destroyers closing on Tvem's *aksai,* and went to full power.

Boursier, not needing any orders, was not more than a thousand meters to his side. A third *aksai* came from nowhere, and Alikhan's voice came over the com:

"We are on our way."

Tvem barely avoided a double launch, fired back at one destroyer. His missile was destroyed by a countermissile, and then the three *aksai* were in range.

Dill, in front, fired one of his four remaining Shadow countermissiles at the lead destroyer and was astounded to see it strike home. Two Goddards hit just behind it, and the destroyer was debris. The other destroyer fired a missile at Tvem, and the *aksai* was a plume of fire, then as if it'd never been.

Dill heard a hiss of rage from Alikhan, then the destroyer exploded. Alikhan's *aksai* slashed low, near the ruined ship, came back and fired once more. Then there was nothing left to take revenge on.

"Let us return for more rockets," Alikhan said, and his voice held hissing rage. "I desire to kill more of these Larissans."

*   *   *

First Brigade's fighting troops were either standing by in loading bays or airborne in Griersons and Zhukovs, flying in the high stratosphere, waiting.

Garvin sat in the rear of a command Grierson, listening to the battle in deep space, grinding his teeth.

He looked at another screen, showing the interior of Fitzgerald's Grierson. She didn't look any happier to be out of action than he was. She was also unhappy because Angara had borrowed her heads-of-section until he could build a staff of his own, so Njangu and the other section heads were off with Angara, while Garvin had to fart around in circles in D-Cumbre's atmosphere.

He was not at all sure he liked being a field-grade officer, even if it'd most likely keep him alive a lot longer.

In spite of heavy casualties, the Larissans pushed on, closing on D-Cumbre.

Two more cruisers were hit and destroyed.

An electronics officer hurried to *Dant* Angara, aboard the *al Maouna*.

"Sir, we have a message intercept, and a tentative decipher. It's from someone who calls himself White Leader . . . ELINT suggests it's most likely their admiral, Celidon."

The signal read:

> All fleet assault ships. Continue your (mission?) . . .
> Attack given targets on planet. This is the greatest
> day in Larissan history.

"And what does *that* change?" Angara muttered to himself.

Njangu was watching one of the main screens. He thought he saw something, grabbed a mike, keyed it to Ho Kang in her chair, and asked a question. She changed frequencies to one of the control technicians below and suddenly, on the big screen, a scattering of red lights flared. A loudspeaker went on.

"All stations," Ho said. "We appear to have an interesting development. Observe the highlighted ships. These are some of the Larissan battle cruisers we have been monitoring as the most important threat, about half of their known contingent."

Green arrows came on-screen, and Njangu heard another staff officer gasp.

"You'll notice," Ho said calmly, "all of the observed capital ships have changed orbit, and appear to be withdrawing, repeat withdrawing from the system."

"Son of a bitch," someone said slowly. Njangu realized it was his voice.

"Redruth's leaving his soldiers to cover the capital ships' retreat. I'll bet good credits he's not with the transports," Angara said grimly. "Now it'll get bloody. Patch me through to the troops onplanet."

Not only the cruisers, but the destroyers as well were retreating, going at full drive for the nav point they'd dropped out of.

Haut Johnny Chaka, once a hot-rod Zhukov flight commander, now a hot-rod *velv* group captain, with four ships under his command, swarmed their rear.

"One missile per ship," he told his weapons officers. "All we have to do is cripple them, then we can come back and finish them off later."

One of his ships took a hit, broke formation, reported the damage was repairable, but she was out of the battle.

Chaka's lips pursed for an instant, but he showed no other sign of emotion as he harried the stragglers, hoping he'd kill enough of them to get a chance at one of the cruisers.

The transports arced in past D-Cumbre's largest moon, Fowey. A handful of destroyers had disobeyed

Redruth's orders to abandon the transports, and defended their charges, dying in the attempt.

Cumbrians from the fleet, from the moons, smashed at the formation, and the Larissan officers went for the only chance of survival they had—D-Cumbre.

Lights flared in the planet's skies, the greatest meteor display in history as the Larissans slammed down toward the ground.

Rising to meet them were the Force's Griersons and Zhukovs, too small to show up on the weapons stations on the armed transports, but more than big enough to kill a spaceship.

Larissan soldiers, half-trained, many sick after the jolting trajectory their antigravity systems had failed to compensate for, felt the shudder as the ships entered atmosphere, some even hearing the dim scream as the transports plunged toward the ground, braking down from Mach numbers, ship skins white-hot.

For some, that was all they'd ever hear or feel, as Goddards struck home.

"All First Brigade elements," Fitzgerald said calmly. "Find a target, and if you can't destroy it in the air, pinpoint it when it reaches ground, and relay that to your commanders. If they're dispersing troops, land and go after them. Let them surrender if they will, but take no chances."

"Well?" Jasith Mellusin asked. Her yacht hung on the tail of a Larissan troop transport as it dived through the atmosphere.

Her new captain, Halfin, was not only a fellow Rentier, if one of the bankrupt sort, but formerly one of the ranking contenders in the rich people's sport of point-to-point, now played with spaceships. But he'd never killed a man, let alone a thousand or so men before. He licked his lips, hesitated.

The transport filled a new screen that had been mounted to one side of his position, hooked to the

chin-mounted bank of unguided Fury rockets that ug-
lied up the smooth lines of the *Godrevy.*

"Shoot him, goddammit!" Jasith ordered, and the
man convulsively hit the firing sensor.

Furies rippled out, crashed into the Larissan's drive
tubes, exploded. The transport banked to the side, and
smoke poured out a hole in its side, then it went completely out of control.

The ship spun down through two thousand meters,
hit water as hard as steel at speed, and was ripped
apart.

Jasith looked down at the swirling water, and something moved inside her as she thought of the murder
of her father by the 'Raum, the friends she'd lost from
the Musth, and again from the bombing raid, and a
rather terrible smile came.

Halfin looked at her, then quickly away.

"Now," Jasith said. "Let's look for another of the
bastards."

She thought she was starting to understand why
Garvin was a soldier.

"Set it down, next to those Griersons," Garvin ordered, closing the clip on his fighting harness.

"Sir," his pilot said, bringing the command ACV
toward the ground.

There were a pair of fat Larissan merchant ships
that'd tried for a beach landing on Mullion Island. The
first had hit the water's edge and dug a furrow into
the jungle that grew right up to the black sand. The
second had tried for a landing parallel with the beach,
hit a rock outcropping, and split in two.

Half a dozen Griersons from I&R Company were
grounded nearby, and a pair of Zhukovs orbited
overhead.

Garvin saw jubilant soldiers herding Larissan troops
toward an improvised holding area, others, in small
patrols, sweeping into the jungle.

He hoped all of the Larissans surrendered, having

heard tales from Ben Dill about the monsters living in those jungles and, worse, in the water close to them.

His Grierson grounded, and the ramp dropped. Garvin put on his combat helmet, checked his blaster, and ran out onto the sand. Behind him, two soldiers detailed as his bodyguards swore and followed him.

Jaansma knew he had as much business being on the ground with a gun as he would have swimming naked across the straits to Dharma Island, but didn't give a damn. It had been too long since he'd had a chance to do anything other than look at maps and studies, and besides, he wanted revenge for what'd happened to him and the other I&R troops on Kura Four.

Garvin heard the smash of blasters from the jungle, grinned tightly, and looked for a patrol to join up within.

"Sir!"

Jaansma stopped, turned, saw Lir.

"Can I ask what you're doing here, sir?"

"Thought I could help."

Lir's smile was utterly malevolent.

"I'm *very* sorry, *Haut* Jaansma, but I simply can't permit such a valuable staff officer as yourself to risk yourself in this minor mopping up."

"Goddammit, Monique, I'm serious!"

"So am I, *sir*. And I have to ask you to return to your ACV, to avoid any possibility of your being harmed, *sir*."

Garvin started to snarl something, realized it would do no good, especially as she leaned close, and her lips formed the words:

"I told you I'd get my revenge."

There were two grinning I&R men behind her, and there wasn't any doubt in Garvin's mind they'd cheerfully relieve him of his blaster and tuck him forcibly back in his Grierson if Lir ordered.

"*Thank* you, *Cent* Lir," Jaansma said, teeth on edge.

"I'll always remember that you have my best interests at heart."

Rapid blaster fire came from behind him, and he half ducked, caught himself. He realized neither of the three I&R soldiers had bothered moving. Maybe he *had* gotten a little rusty.

"Now if you'll forgive me, sir," Lir said. "I've got Larissans to round up."

Garvin went back to his ACV, was airborne, trying to decide if he should fume or laugh.

The invasion by Larix/Kura ended in a long, drawn-out whimper. Larissan soldiers, ragged, starving, were still being winkled out of the jungle two E-years later.

One more step, Dant Angara thought. *A fast one. And then it'll be our turn.*

CHAPTER
22

The undamaged Cumbrian warships and their crews weren't allowed much time to rest and recuperate. Angara had kept certain factories out of primary war production, building some very classified, fairly small devices. Now the Force starships went back to the space and N-space around Larix and Kura, sowing these devices around every known nav point.

There wasn't much risk—the Larissans were shocky by their unexpected and harsh defeat, and weren't eager to seek and destroy the enemy until they recovered and rebuilt.

So the planting went on, trip after trip after trip.

Then the Cumbrian ships vanished, and Larissan scouts reported the starways were open.

Ohnce of the Second Generation hung somewhere in N-space, "close" to one of the nav points off Kura Four. Time passed, was counted by its recorders, was meaningless.

Then a sensor responded to input, and the Ohnce came alive. Its circuits found a disturbance in hyperspace, and the Ohnce II, now a globe sitting atop a cylinder, came alive. Its small hyperdrive sent it toward that disturbance, closed on it.

Another circuit came on, a proximity detector.

The Ohnce closed on the disturbance, a ship full of agricultural products bound for Larix Prime. A tidy sort, it sent a signal to a Bohnce, somewhere "nearby" in hyperspace, that another Ohnce would be needed.

A second—if real time existed in hyperspace—later, it exploded as directed, close enough for the blast to remove that disturbance.

Some time thereafter, a *velv* set another Ohnce in place, waiting for the next Kuran ship. Its crew said it was very spooky, as their detectors reported an Ohnce approaching, then tracking away as it "recognized" the friendly ship. "Sniffing like a damned *giptel*," one technician said with a shudder.

Other Ohnces hung off Larix, and backtracked ships from Kura that used other nav points to travel to the capital system, or laboriously navigated from projected point to projected point to reach Larix, establishing new fixed nav points, after which the Ohnces remorselessly destroyed them.

The destruction of one merchant ship didn't bother Protector Redruth at all, Celidon only slightly. But then ten, thirty, eighty-six transports from Kura were missing, without ever a distress signal or explanation.

Celidon was the first to note that ships going from Larix to Kura remained untouched.

Insurance firms on Larix refused to write coverage for any ship bound between Kura and the capital system.

By then, it was obvious to Celidon, and shortly afterward to the Protector, what was going on:

Cumbre was starving Larix to death, using some completely unknown weapon.

Then ships outbound from Larix to Kura started disappearing as more Ohnces were built and set in place, these "close" to Larix's nav points.

The two systems were cut off from each other.

Celidon couldn't figure out what could be done, even after Larissan scientists discovered the destruction wasn't being done by raiders, but by unglamorous, unmanned, very deadly mines.

The Larissans never discovered the whimsical names

of Ohnce and Bohnce that Dr. Danfin Froude had
given the devices, nor, in the short time before the
war escalated once more, any countermeasures.

The mines were very unglamorous, and no dashing
young officers wearing scarves piloted them, but they
were far more effective than the most highly trained
aksai drivers.

Ben Dill fumed very loudly at the way romance was
being taken out of war.

Cumbre/D-Cumbre

Two E-months had passed since the Larissan catastro-
phe. Angara's staff had been very, very busy.

Dant Angara summoned his commanders to Camp
Mahan. "Within one E-month," he announced with-
out preamble, "the Force will land and conquer
Larix Prime.

"It is time for this war to be ended."

CHAPTER
23

Cumbre/D-Cumbre

"I think," Jasith Mellusin told *Dant* Angara, "I want to throw a ball."

"A victory celebration would be excellent," Angara said. "And thank you for your faith in the Legion."

"No, *Dant*," Jasith said. "Everyone and anyone will be having a party then. I want mine to be now . . . or as soon as I can arrange things, given your approval."

"Since you're evidently asking my approval," Angara said, "might I ask who your guests will be? Remembering that anyone from the Force will be unavailable in a very short time."

"I want the entire Force," Mellusin said.

Angara blinked. "The whole Force? *All* of us? That's . . . well, my strength report is classified, but let's say that would be well over fifteen thousand men and women, given the new recruits."

"That sounds about right from my people's estimates."

"Lord God in a bucket, Miss Mellusin. That'll be the biggest party in Cumbre's history."

"Not quite," Jasith said. "My father, when he reached his majority, invited all his employees and anyone else in the system to a two-day bash. It shocked the hell out of the other Rentiers, since he made the 'Raum welcome, too.

"But that's the dim past. And by the way, it's Jasith, please."

"What an impossible idea," Angara said. Then a thought came. "You know . . . if our propaganda folk could arrange for this to be transmitted to Larix and Kura, that would certainly be a shock to Redruth, thinking that we had time to play . . . hmm. Interesting. Possibly not at all a bad idea—even if it is impossible.

"Let me think on this," he said. "I'll be back to you within the day. Now, if you'll forgive me, duty calls."

He smiled, and blanked the screen.

Jasith turned to Garvin, who'd wangled a few hours away from *Caud* Fitzgerald.

"We're going to have a party."

"How can you tell? Angara didn't say 'kay."

"I just know. Women know these things."

"Why do you want to do this before Larix?" Garvin said.

"Sometimes," Jasith said, a touch of asperity in her voice, "you're somewhat thicker than a brick, Gavin Jaansma. Did it ever occur to you that some people are going off to fight who won't be able to come back to any victory ball?"

Garvin jerked, then slowly nodded.

"And maybe people would like something to think about when they're out there in a ditch getting shot at," Jasith said. "I'm going to invite every loose-moraled woman . . . and man . . . and some people even I'm not quite sure of . . . which, come to think about it, is just about the only kind of person I know. And I'll make sure they know I'll be very unhappy if they go home alone.

"How much would you like to bet *Dant* Angara figured out exactly what I'm intending?"

Garvin shook his head. "Jasith Mellusin, you're amazing."

"I know that, too."

"Here," Monique Lir grunted, tossing a small box

across her desk to Darod Montagna. Montagna opened the box and her eyes saucered.

"Uh . . ."

They were the rank tabs of an *Alt*.

"What're *they* for?"

"So I can have somebody to drink with," Lir growled. "*Cents* can't be hanging out in the NCO club every night."

"But I'm only—"

"Twenty?" Lir said. "No shiteedah. Wars get fought by young women, in case you hadn't noticed, or seen all of the idiots who've gotten themselves promoted lately.

"By rights, you ought to leave I&R, so the rankers don't get familiar. But there ain't nobody left to get familiar with from the old days," Lir said.

"Thank you, boss."

"Don't bother with gratitude. I'll work your butt to the bone before we transship, and you're a lot more likely to get blown off in the invasion."

The Force *was* changing, very, very rapidly. A soldier returning from hospital or leave might not recognize her old formation. Some changes were from casualties, but more were caused by the Force's doubling in strength. Experienced officers and noncoms were promoted and transferred, some requiring a direct order from *Dant* Angara before they sullenly packed their traps and changed barracks to become cadre for new formations.

Even I&R, in spite of Lir's futile rage, had been gutted: Ton Milot and Stef Bassas, promoted Senior *Twegs*, moved to new line units in Second Brigade; Medic Jil Mahim, commissioned *Alt*, to First Brigade Medical, with a promise of civilian medical school after the war; Rad Dref, no longer just a Grierson pilot, now commissioned and an *Alt* in charge of a Zhukov flight.

Some I&R people were still around: Lav Huran, Senior *Tweg*, now First *Tweg*, which meant all three command slots of I&R were women; Calafo, a Tweg and a Second Troop senior noncom; Felder, now a *Tweg* and given a whole section of her beloved "Rumbles" recon robots, yet another change to the I&R's Table of Equipment; and finally *Striker* Fleam, who refused all promotions and, when forcibly given stripes, made sure he'd gotten in enough trouble by dawn to lose them.

No one in I&R, consequently, had time for any private life whatsoever. Lir refused to lower I&R standards, which meant the old guard spent two-thirds of their time getting ready for the invasion, and the other two-thirds training or testing the new volunteers.

Montagna told Lir she was looking forward to the invasion, so she could get some rest.

"Haven't you figured out the army yet?" Lir asked. "We do this shit deliberately, bustin' everybody's balls, so combat actually comes as a relief. And what the hell, young *Alt*, are you doing wasting time jaw-jackin' with me? Come on, Darod. There's work to be done!"

Other formations were equally shredded as new recruits streamed in, and the Force grew toward its newly authorized twenty thousand strength.

Erik Penwyth saluted smartly.

"You sent for me, sir?"

"I did," Angara said. "I'm assigning you to a very special mission."

"Thank you, sir. Might I ask what?"

"You're going to help put on a party."

Njangu Yoshitaro was headed for Angara's office, carrying a fiche with the latest intelligence appreciation of Redruth's ship positioning, when one of Angara's aides, Ushant, stopped him.

"Maybe you don't want to go in for an hour or so, N'jang. The Old Man's looking to tear some ass, and I don't think he's particular about whose."

"Why?" Njangu asked the woman. "What happened?"

"*Mil* Liskeard just went in, dropped his wings on Angara's desk, said he was quitting. Angara could put him anywhere he wanted, court-martial him if he wanted, as long as he didn't have to kill anybody."

Njangu blinked. "Liskeard? Shit, he's a tiger on skates."

"He *was* a tiger on skates," Ushant said. "*Dant* talked to him for an hour, tried to get him to change his mind, finally blew up and told him to get his ass out of sight and to Maintenance Section until further notice. He said he'd decide whether he was going to court-martial Liskeard or not after the invasion, and he didn't have time to waste now."

"I wonder what the hell happened?" Njangu said.

"My, uh, monitoring of the situation wasn't that good . . . I had to take another com . . . but when I came back Liskeard was saying something about 'bodies, nothing but bodies.' I dunno. I guess he just cracked.

"Interesting thing," Ushant said thoughtfully. "I never heard Angara call him a coward or anything."

"Yeh," Njangu said. "Interesting. I'll go grab midmeal, try again later."

He went back down the corridor, wondering what had broken Liskeard, wondering if everybody had a breaking point, thought of the people he'd seen after a firefight, shaking, crying, some just staring. For some of them, something terrible had happened, the bloody death of a teammate, a close call, for others, nothing. Or nothing that anybody could understand. Some came back after a few minutes or some time in a ward, some never returned to the Force.

Njangu hoped it'd never happen to him. He rather be dead. Or so he thought he thought.

"*All* of you are members of Tvem's clan?" Jon Hedley asked. There were eighteen Musth in the room, all wearing fighting harnesses, standing in the inverted-V formation Musth soldiers used. The alien in the center had told Jaansma his name was Rlet, and he was the most skilled flier of all of them. His accent was perfectly atrocious, but he spoke better Basic, or so he said, than the others.

"Mossst of usss were of Tvem'sss clan," Rlet said. "But sssome of usss from other clansss heard of the losssss of Tvem, decccided we wissshed revenge. Or, perhapsss, what isss your word for an action that makesss the ichor flow fassster and everything more alive isss what we sssseek?"

"Excitement." Hedley almost added a few extra hisses to the 'c.'

"Jussst ssso. There are few sssuch eventsss happening within our sssectors. Ssso we wisssh to enlissst."

"And you're also *aksai*-trained?"

"All of usss. We are rated Expert or Sssenior Flier-quantified."

"I may kiss every flipping one of you," Hedley said. "Hang on. Let me get ahold of somebody named Alikhan. He's been pretty lonely lately.

"And welcome to the Force. We'll swear you in as soon as I can get the old man free."

"Sssswear?"

"It's a custom, before we go handing our *aksai* promiscuous-like."

"Force Headquarters," Garvin said briskly, touching the ACCEPT sensor. "This is *Haut* Jaansma."

Then he recognized Darod Montagna.

"Good morning, sir," she said. "This is sort of an irregular call, sir."

"Uh, right, *Alt*. By the way, congratulations on your commission. I saw it in the General Orders, never got around to calling you. Sorry, but it's been chaos up here. You've got an open chit on me, anytime you want it at the O Club bar, since I don't seem to be able to break free these days." Garvin thought he was babbling slightly. "But how may I help you?"

"That's why I commed you, sir. You already have. Ever since we went to Kura, a lot of things . . . good things, I think . . . have been happening to me. And I just wanted to thank you for giving me the chance."

"I didn't do anything," Garvin said.

"Except maybe keep me from getting killed," she said.

"Or maybe you kept *me* from being iced," Garvin said, finding a grin. "Teaming works both ways, you know."

Darod smiled back.

"You know, it sounds a little strange, calling you 'sir,' instead of Garvin or boss, since you're out of I&R now."

Garvin wanted to say she could call him anything she wanted, fortunately stopped himself.

"Things change," he said.

"They do, don't they? Now, and maybe in the future. Sorry to have taken up your time, sir. But thanks again for what you've done."

"Anytime . . . Darod."

She smiled again. "One other thing . . . Garvin. I wasn't *that* drunk."

And the screen blanked.

Very irregular, Garvin thought. *I probably ought to have Lir tear her off an enormous strip. And it's probably complicating my life. So why don't I mind at all?*

"Jasith's Party" went down in Cumbrian and Force history. Jasith never told anyone how much it cost, and estimates ran between a million and three million credits.

"Only" about forty-seven hundred of the Force showed up. Others were in space, on other planets of Cumbre, or part of the Angara-mandated minimum one-quarter on duty at all times. Others were basically misanthropic or had other ideas about proper recreation. Of course, as the years passed and the tales grew bigger, almost no ex-Force person would admit to not having attended.

Jasith emptied one of Mellusin Mining's fields, a kilometer square. On each corner a *Kelly*-class destroyer sat on its rear fins. Hung between the ships' noses, covering the field, supported by small antigrav lifters, was what appeared to be a single piece of gossamer. Actually, it was fiber filter sheets from the mines, each roll held to the next with clips.

In the center of the field sat an *aksai,* a *velv,* and a *wynt,* a Grierson, and a Zhukov. Smiling soldiers offered tours of the ships to civilians. Some of their fellows sympathized with their having to work, until one striker waved a list. "Work my left nipple," she chortled. "I've gotten enough boys' numbers to get me laid until the millennium."

The widely respected Seya Symphony played, its music bounced to monstrous speakers ringing the area. Transports shuttled soldiers back and forth from Camp Mahan or other onplanet posts, and they streamed onto the field in full-dress uniform. Invited civilians—and sometimes it seemed Jasith, like her father, had invited the whole planet—parked their lifters and lims and, resplendent in formal dress or simply the best they owned, arrived, and were swept into the throng.

Even Loy Kouro had been sent an invitation. He'd thought of ignoring it, realizing that would make him appear even more of an ass, and so appeared for a teeth-clenched half hour before leaving. *Matin* reported the event . . . but not on its main menu.

There were tables filed with various foods, light drinks scattered around. No one left hungry, or quite sober.

Njangu Yoshitaro handed Maev Stiofan out of one door of a lift as Jon Hedley shut the drive down, hurried to open the other for Ann Heiser.

The four stood a moment, considering the panoply.

" *'There was a sound of revelry by night,' "* Njangu suddenly quoted. *" 'And Belgium's Capital had gather'd then/Her Beauty and her Chivalry and bright/The lamps shone o'er fair women and brave men.' "*

The other three looked at him in surprise.

"Didn't know you liked Byron," Hedley said. "Hell, I didn't know anybody on D-Cumbre even flipping knew who the guy was."

"Something I read when I was a kid, about the night before some battle," Njangu said, a bit embarrassed.

"You have depths," Maev said, impressed.

"That's me," Njangu said cheerily. "Up to my heinie in deep things."

Dant Angara danced quietly with his wife, a small, very friendly, very cheerful woman. Some people tried to approach him, were steered off by an aide, who told them, as politely but firmly as he could, the *Dant* was off duty that evening, and wanted to spend time with the person he got to spend the least with.

Maev Stiofan and Njangu danced, not far from Angara.

"Aren't you being a little too conscientious?" Njangu complained. "I doubt if any Larissan assassins got invited to this bash."

"I've got the shift," Maev said. "Did you forget you're sleeping with a soldier?"

Njangu growled, then laughed, and she grinned back at him.

"Besides, T'Laan's over there for backup," she said. "So we can go for drinks or food anytime we want."

"Maybe in a while," Njangu said. "I'm quite happy here."

"Then shut up and dance."

"Yes ma'am," Njangu said. Maev put her head on his shoulder.

After a while, Njangu asked, "Happy?"

"Surely," Maev said. "You know what I've been thinking, Njangu? About after the war?"

Njangu flinched a little. "I'm superstitious about things like that."

"Don't be," Maev said. "You're too much of an evil bastard to get killed doing something legitimate like a war with uniforms and things like that."

"Thanks. 'Kay. What've you got in mind for . . . for later?"

"I've never been able to figure out what makes me tick," Maev said. "Let alone anybody else."

"Welcome to the crowd."

"I was thinking, maybe, if . . . sorry, *that* afterward I could go back to school. Study psychology or maybe sociology."

"Dunno if I like that," Njangu said. "You go and get educated, you might be able to stay one step ahead of me."

Maev laughed, a lovely silver tinkle.

"Darling, you are slow. I've *always* done that."

"What do you think of children?" Hedley asked Ann Heiser as they put their plates down on a table and sat. A white-uniformed waiter asked what they wanted to drink, went away with the order.

"Be more specific, Jon," Heiser said. "As a side dish, as students, as conversational companions, as physicists?"

"I meant, well, like having them."

"Oh. Now *that's* an original question," she said. "Is there any particular reason you're wondering?"

"Well, I . . . not flipping really, I just was, sort of flipping curious," Hedley floundered.

"I don't consider the idea inconceivable," Ann said.

"That was a pretty bad joke."

"It was, wasn't it?" Heiser agreed. "Since you seem to be having trouble enunciating, let me narrow the field of inquiry. You mean, having *your* children?"

"Well, sort of."

"Sort of? Are you accepting the premise of Immaculate Conception?"

"Ann, would you flipping stop, already? I never thought I'd be asking something like this, but, well . . ."

"Yes, Jon Hedley," Ann Heiser said, quite seriously. "I've been waiting for you to ask. The answer is yes."

"And what does that signify?" Jasith asked Garvin as she examined the bracelet with a single charm on it.

"That is as close as the jeweler could come to making up a little model of a Larissan spaceship," Garvin said. "Like the one you shot down. You'll notice there's space for more of them."

"Hmm," Jasith said. "Jasith Mellusin, Ace of the Legion. It sounds like a romance."

"It does," Garvin said.

"Why?"

"Well, I wanted you to know how impressed I was with what you did . . . and, well, what you are."

"You may kiss me, Garvin Jaansma. I'm also impressed with you."

Garvin did. After quite a long time, they broke apart, in time for Garvin to see Darod Montagna dance past with a rather tall and handsome *Cent* he vaguely knew.

He looked away, kissed Jasith again.

"And aren't you passionate," she murmured.

"I hope so."

"Well, maybe you want to dance with me, at least until the bulge in your pants goes down," Jasith giggled.

"That's not likely to happen, especially the way you dance."

"Then we better start looking for a dark corner."

"That's quite something," Danfin Froude said, after

congratulating Heiser and Hedley. "You won't have to change the monograms of your sheets, Ann."

The physicist laughed. "Men are so romantic, aren't they, Ho?"

"Actually," Ho Kang said, "sometimes they are. But what's the matter with being practical?"

"Danfin," Heiser said, "you better propose to her on the spot. I don't think you'll ever find someone better suited."

Kang turned a little red.

"Actually," Froude said, "I did have something like that in mind. But I never thought of having witnesses."

"Then let us get the flipping hell out of here," Hedley said. "This appears to be contagious. Besides, I'm lusting to show off my newfound talent at tripping the fantastic light."

He grabbed Heiser's hand, and they went for the dance floor.

"Were you serious?" Ho Kang said.

"Never more," Froude said. He took a small box from a pocket, opened it, and a rather large diamond caught the swirling spotlights.

"Oh," Ho said. "Oh. You *were* serious." She touched her lank black hair, looked down at her thin frame. "I never thought anybody would ever—"

"Shut up," Danfin Froude said, taking her in his arms and kissing her.

"I guess," Ho said thoughtfully after a while, "I'm not exactly left with many options, am I? Not that I want any other than the obvious."

Others made less legitimate, more temporary liaisons, and left with newfound partners.

Angara saw them trailing off, figured next morning's morning report would be either the least honest in the Force's history as far as the number of troops present for duty, or, if honest, he'd be forced to take notice of the shattered ranks.

"What *will* you do, dear?" his wife asked.

Angara thought he'd spoken aloud, then realized he hadn't.

"It's frightening when you've been with someone so long you don't even have to speak," he said. "I guess the Force is going to have the cleanest toilets ever."

"You can't just ignore things?"

"Of course not," Angara said.

"Of course not," his wife echoed.

Darod Montagna danced until the last number with assorted people, went back to her BOQ alone, not unhappy.

A week after Jasith's party, the Force, in various elements, slipped into space for the final confrontation with Larix/Kura.

CHAPTER
24

Larix

The first wave went after the Larissan ships in space. The Cumbrians took no chances, made no heroic moves. A Larissan destroyer would be attacked by three of the smaller Cumbrian units, more vectored in for the kill by the *Kanes*.

The *velv* simply swarmed the patrol craft that were their assigned prey, and the *aksai* were used, always in flights of four or more, to take care of auxiliaries and merchantmen.

Lone wolves like Dill and Alikhan fumed, but the casualties stayed low.

Larissan ships were driven back to their home planets, now as isolated from each other as the system of Larix was from Kura.

Other ships moved into Larissan space: the transports and their escorts. Aboard the ships, infantrymen and -women cleaned weapons, sharpened knives, and, as always, fed the rumor mill:

The Larissans were about to surrender, and invasion wouldn't be necessary;

The Larissans had a secret weapon, which is why they pulled back to their homeworlds. The fleet would be hit at any minute.

There'd be an invasion, and it'd be bloody, for all the husbanded Larissan ships would come out of their hiding places and rip the Cumbrians before they reached the ground.

One favorite was that the invasion would be a walk-over. That had some evidence on its side, since the Larissan soldiers hadn't exactly fought like lions when they hit Cumbre.

A quick war, a lot of the officers agreed, sudden promotions, and everybody goes home would be the agenda.

Garvin, Njangu, and Maev flatly said this was fool-ishness. The Larissans fought badly on D-Cumbre be-cause they were on an alien planet, and couldn't understand attacking someone who shouldn't be their enemy. Fighting on their own worlds, for their homes, things would be quite different.

They weren't seriously listened to by most. It didn't matter that the three were among the few who'd actu-ally faced Larissans on the ground. Informed sources, as always, knew better, particularly when they didn't have to be that specific about their sources.

Garvin was dismayed to find that *Caud* Fitzgerald agreed with the others. "We've seen how badly trained the Larissans are, how badly led," she said. "All that'll be necessary is a few sharp blows, and the white flags will start coming out."

Dant Angara and Hedley kept their own skeptical council.

Stage Three was begun. Small squadrons hit the three secondary Larix planets in-atmosphere, taking out whatever they could find in the air or on landing grounds.

But the main thrust was against Larix Prime. Pha-lanxes of warships swept over the land. Any ship that lifted or could be spotted on the ground was hit and destroyed, along with their fields, control towers, maintenance facilities, aerospace factories. The Cum-brian casualties mounted. Larix Prime's antiaircraft crews were well trained, and their weapons first-rate, which included a rank of missiles, like the Furies ex-cept guided; radar-aimed 100mm autocannon; and syn-

chronized chainguns for low-level attackers, capable
of passing a target from gun to gun.

When aerospace targets grew few, the ships went
after the Larissan government buildings, troop instal-
lations, public transport, waterborne ships, and the
power grid. All too often the airstrikes went a little
wide, and civilian buildings were hit, and more Larissans died.

One pilot bragged that the troops, once they were
finally landed, would have a cakewalk. There wouldn't
be anything for them to shoot at, and all they'd have
to do would be round up demoralized soldiers.

Dill, Boursier, and Alikhan remembered how ulti-
mately ineffective Musth tactical air had been against
the dispersed Cumbrian troops, kept their mouths
shut.

They'd also noted how cleverly the Larissans dispersed their remaining ships. A warehouse, a park, a
clearly marked hospital might conceal one of Redruth's warships. And no one could find the surviving
cruisers.

Larix Prime was a cratered moonscape, its road system pockmarked, its cities with gaping wounds here
and there, but the landscape wasn't quiet—the pilots
never could quite suppress the antiaircraft gunners,
and so Cumbrians kept dying.

Griersons and Zhukovs were committed to action,
and they strafed, rocketed relentlessly. But the Larissans still shot back.

The command staff ran numbers, studied aerial ho-
lographs, ELINT and SIGINT. Angara transferred his
flag to the *Bastogne,* a modified assault transport. He
knew he should command from space and keep the
clearest overview of the battle. But he was an old
infantryman, and refused to send his troops where it
might look like he was unwilling to go himself.

In the next day's ALLFLEET com, he announced
the hour and time for the first wave to land on
Larix Prime.

CHAPTER
25

Celidon was passed through a dozen guard stations, winding ever deeper into the Protector's command post. Redruth had, a bit cleverly, not located it under the palace proper, but about half a kilometer away.

Clever, but not that clever, Celidon thought sourly. While it probably protected him from a burrowing nuke, it didn't make instantly responding to his summons any easier. Celidon traveled in an Ayesha ACV these days, with four others as decoys/support, and only when necessary. They'd barely evaded a pair of patrolling *velv* as they left Celidon's own bunker near the largest spacefield, and an *aksai* had made a strafing run after Celidon's ACV had set down outside the palace, and he was hurrying toward one of the tunnels to the command center, then down and down, past computer rooms, staff offices, even dormitories and cafeterias.

Two armed aides, Protector's Own, ushered Celidon into Redruth's Office, but didn't leave the room. They remained, at attention, hands on their pistol holsters.

The room was huge, steel-walled, wood-floored, with huge screens and maps. Holograms came and went over a large table. The room was dark, illuminated only by a few hidden lamps here and there, and the screens. Celidon happened to notice, next to the aides, a dark stain on the floor.

Redruth was at a desk, examining a screen. Celidon

approached, saluted him. The white-haired mercenary was very proud of his command face, utterly expressionless no matter what was going on around him.

Celidon was grateful for that, because Redruth looked terrible. His face had wrinkled, aged, although it had only been an E-month since Celidon had last had a face-to-face with the dictator.

Then he caught a flashed reflection of his own face in a screen, and realized he didn't look that much better himself.

"Welcome, *Leiter,*" Redruth said, without returning the salute. "I've summoned you because I've finally developed a master stroke to shock the Cumbrians out of their foolishness and drive them back to their own system."

His eyelid ticked once, twice.

"Here," Redruth said. "The plan is on this screen. Examine it carefully, for I desire you to be the one to lead my dauntless soldiers into action."

Celidon noticed that, for the first time since he'd served him, Redruth was wearing a sidearm in this, the safest place in what remained of his kingdom.

Celidon scanned the screen, again grateful for his stone face.

"Well?"

Celidon temporized. "The latest intelligence reports say that both the *Heifet* and *Qaaf* have been damaged by bombings, and are incapable of flight, so they wouldn't be able to participate in your plan." He didn't add that the swarm of destroyers specified in the operations order simply didn't exist anymore.

Redruth acted as if Celidon hadn't spoken.

"Well?" His voice was sharper.

Celidon looked at Redruth, saw his dilated pupils, the glaring eyes.

"Do you want me to speak honestly, sir?"

"So I've always ordered you!"

"This is . . ." Celidon was about to choose one word, found another. ". . . not what I consider the wisest of maneuvers. Our cruisers lack the support ships necessary for such a bold stroke . . . which I assure you it is, and I admire your acumen in developing it.

"But I doubt if this would be anything other than, forgive me, Protector, suicidal, at this point in the war. I think—"

"Enough!" Redruth said, voice rising to a near shriek.

"You're like the others, without vision, without that final courage that divides great men from their followers, always thinking, thinking, thinking! I have been considering this move since the Cumbrians arrived in the system.

"I do not wish to be questioned. That is not your place or duty, Celidon! Your place is to follow orders, my orders, no more, and to carry them out as efficiently and precisely as I demand.

"I thought better of you, Celidon. You've always been the first to support me, to acknowledge my genius. Yet now you hang back, you quibble, like the rest of them.

"Very well. Very well. Perhaps I expected too much of you.

"Therefore, I give you the following orders: You are to immediately execute this plan of mine, which I have named Guiding Star, for its results will be like a beacon to my army, my people.

"Single strokes, if mounted by men of sufficient vision and genius, win battles and wars. Guiding Star shall be one of them!"

Again, Redruth's voice rose.

"Now, I order you to take charge of Guiding Star, and lead it to total victory! Is that understood, *Leiter* Celidon?"

"Of course it is, Protector," Celidon said, making his voice calm, certain, confident.

"Good," Redruth said. "Good. I was afraid, for a

moment, Celidon, that you would fail me too, like . . . like some others.

"My plan is quite precisely worked out. Go and carry it out within the day, then report back to me when you've decimated the Cumbrians!"

Celidon took the fiche with the plan on it, saluted as crisply as he ever had, about-faced, and marched to the door. The sentries saluted, hurled the doors open for him.

Celidon glanced down as he left.

He was now quite sure he knew what the stain on the floor was.

The word he'd started to use to Redruth, then rejected, was "insanity."

CHAPTER
26

Eight monstrous Larissan battle cruisers came out of their coverts. Analysts had been looking for their hiding places since the Force arrived in-system. But Redruth and his camouflage experts had been most devious. Ships had been hidden in tunnels under monuments, schools, or worship places, underwater in lakes, in natural caverns. The analysts, not finding the big ships, had then looked for their crew quarters, and the necessary maintenance buildings.

But Redruth had quartered the crews on the populace or even outside, under canvas in the open. The ships had been given full maintenance before being concealed, but no work was performed on them other than first-echelon, minor repairs while they were in hiding.

The cruisers rose out of the ground like ancient monsters, and alarms screamed.

Two never made it out of the atmosphere, one getting hit from below by two destroyers and blown apart, the second by a Musth *aksai* pilot, who saw what he thought was his duty, and crashed at full speed into the cruiser, just below the bridge. A fully trained crew might have saved the ship, but the men and women on this cruiser—partially trained and mostly without combat experience—were anything but completely proficient. The cruiser, out of control, spun, slammed through a city slum, then exploded.

Six made it into space. Protector Redruth's orders had been for them to destroy the invaders' transports, paying no mind to the Cumbrian warships until the most dangerous target, the invading army, was taken care of.

The troopships were assembled in their assault formations, vertical stacks, in geosynchronous orbits within ideal range of their targets.

Since the Larissans had lost control of space and their atmospheres, the Cumbrian warships were mostly either in-atmosphere or just above it, waiting for the go-ahead to support the landings, rather than in deep space. Some had even pulled back to Larix's outer planets, for servicing by fleet support vessels.

There was only a scattering of destroyers between the cruisers and the transports. Most knew what they must do, and attacked. One more cruiser was crippled, another wounded. The destroyers were smashed aside, and the five surviving cruisers drove toward the troopships, already picking their targets.

All that remained were the seven Cumbrian destroyers screening the troopships. And one control ship.

Alt Ho Kang stared at the big screen, at the onrushing Larissan warships. She'd reported to the combat elements so far distant, been told help was on its way, and there was nothing else that could be done. Except one thing.

She lifted her mike, touched the sensor. She tried to speak, found a knot in her throat, swallowed convulsively.

"All Watchdog ships," she said, pleased her voice was toneless. "This is Vann Control. You have enemy ships on-screen. Attack, repeat attack."

Without waiting for acknowledgment, she keyed the bridge of the *al Maouna.*

"Set course for the Larissan ships. Full drive."

The watch officer hesitated, looked at the ship's captain. Set-faced, he nodded. The officer snapped the orders.

Eight small ships, the *al Maouna* in the lead, attacked the five huge battle cruisers.

"All Watchdog elements," Ho said. "You may fire when you have the range. Maintain position on this ship." Again, she switched frequencies, back to the bridge of her own ship. "Give me the captain . . . Sir, this is Ho Kang. I'd suggest our best chances would be to set the following orbit . . . Yad-three-four-five, toward Melm-four-four-one."

"That's put us just above the cruisers?"

"That's affirmative," Ho said. "We might get away with arcing 'over' them. Suggest you begin firing . . . in volleys . . . as soon as possible. Anything to confuse them."

The captain smiled, twistedly. "At least we'll give them a scare, eh?"

Kang smiled, didn't answer, cut the connection. She looked at her large screen, saw formations of destroyers swarming from a distant orbit toward the troopships.

Too far, too late, she thought.

The *Leiter* on the bridge of the forward cruiser looked at his screen.

Absurd. Those tinies, against us? Brave fools. Then alarm came. *Perhaps there's a trick. Perhaps there's something we can't detect, like those damned hyperspace weapons they've got.*

"We're within range, sir," his weapons commander said. The *Leiter* hesitated for long seconds.

Ho Kang saw sparkles from the noses of the two leading destroyers as they launched, then the others fired at the cruisers as well.

"We have launches," an officer on the bridge of the Larissan cruiser said.

"Begin countermeasures," the watch officer ordered, and countermissiles hurled out against the on-coming Goddards.

"Sir?" the weapons commander asked.

"Launch," the *Leiter* ordered.

One, two, then three of the cruisers fired missiles.

"We have four . . . no, six missiles targeting us," a technician aboard the *al Maouna* reported. "Count-ermissiles launched . . . tracking . . . tracking . . ."

A million years passed.

"Two . . . three of their missiles destroyed," the technician said. "A second pattern of countermissiles launched. Tracking."

Ho looked at the screen, didn't need to read the reel of numbers as the Larissan missiles closed. She felt a moment of overwhelming sorrow, for a marriage that would never be, children that would never be born, science that would never be studied and ex-plored, a life that would never be lived.

Two missiles hit the *al Maouna* at the same time, and the lightly armored Kane ceased to exist.

Another Cumbrian ship was hit, destroyed. But the other five kept coming.

There is something very, very wrong, the *Leiter* on the first cruiser thought. *No one is this stupid.*

Now, if there is something deadly behind this non-sense, they are no doubt expecting us to continue our attack as it was begun, racing into their ambush.

"Captain," he ordered. "I wish to change the bat-tle plan."

"Yes, sir," the officer said, who also had been nurs-ing doubts.

"Reset the course to put us 'above' those troop-ships," the *Leiter* said. "They'll be between us and Prime, which shall be the anvil, and we'll be the ham-mer. Issue orders to the other ships to follow our lead."

"Yessir," the captain said, and the navigator's fingers flew across his computer. A talker began speaking, in careful but urgent tones, to the other Larissan ships.

The cruisers had time to make the first jackleg, and then a formation of Cumbrian destroyers hit them from "above" and their "left."

Countermissiles spat, and the Larissans seemed to forget the five watchdog escorts. Two of them launched against the flank of the cruisers. A Goddard got through the missile screen, holed a cruiser in its drive spaces. The cruiser lofted on in its orbit, into a swarm of other destroyers, was obliterated.

Another had its countermissile suite overwhelmed by the number of incoming missiles, since there were no destroyers screening, and was smashed out of action. Its crew was lucky—there was time, later, before the air ran out, for patrol ships to rescue them.

The four remaining, as Cumbrian ships flashed at them from nowhere, realized they stood no chance at all of reaching the transports. They were terrified of Redruth's rage, but Redruth was a maybe, and a Cumbrian missile was for sure.

One was caught just in Larix Prime's ionosphere, took four missiles, and burned, a twisting, smoking torch falling, falling to explode against the side of a mountain. Another suddenly blew up, although no one ever claimed credit for hitting it with a missile.

A third must have been hit, for it made a hard landing in a desolated mining area. *Aksai* went out to ensure it was destroyed, seeing Larissans run, panicked, in all directions from the wreck before they volleyed missiles in.

The last made it to a hard landing on Agur's main field, and was hastily camouflaged. The crew was arrested, taken to prison, where all of the officers were shot for cowardice, and the crew was decimated.

Before the last man fell, writhing in his blood, *aksai*

discovered the cruiser under its nets and bombed it into a fiery ruin.

Protector Alena Redruth watched the executions, one eye ticking uncontrollably.

Celidon paced back and forth in the main command center in his own bunker. His staff watched, was afraid to ask what had happened, what had gone wrong at the meeting with Protector Redruth.

Celidon was considering his options, finding them few, especially since he'd been intelligent enough not to board the commanding cruiser as he'd been ordered.

At this point, there appeared to be only one choice. He didn't like it greatly. But at least it was logical, and almost certainly guaranteed his survival.

Survival and, he brightened, a decent possibility of advantage.

CHAPTER
27

Second Brigade, still not built up to full strength, was assigned the task of attacking Larix Prime's minor cities. Jon Hedley didn't like it, but had to recognize the logic, just as the other worlds in the Larix system were being bypassed and temporarily ignored. When Prime was taken, then there'd be time to worry about lesser problems—if they hadn't taken care of themselves and surrendered.

First Brigade's mission was to take Agur. *Dant* Angara hoped that if the capital fell, they could capture or kill enough of Redruth's top leaders, hopefully including the Protector himself, to make whatever ranking *Leiters* Larix/Kura had sue for peace.

The transports went in. There were eight main traffic arteries into the capital, and landings were made around each of them.

A scattering of ships was hit coming in, but casualties were surprisingly low. Since the Force hadn't picked the obvious landing grounds—sports arenas, open land, airfields, parks—but found others, flattening warehouses, setting down in wide avenues and office complexes that had enough open areas for two or three ships, the Legion was able to debark and assemble in combat formations without being hit hard.

More troops were convincing themselves this would be an easy campaign as the columns started into the city. None of them made it more than a kilometer before they learned otherwise.

Larissans came out of nowhere, hitting hard, recklessly. Cumbrians died, others found cover, fought back.

Sometimes the Larissans kept coming. Sometimes they surrendered. Sometimes they fell back into hasty positions, fought to the death. Sometimes they milled about and were killed or gave up.

The Force took only a few hundred meters that first night.

At dark, shots went back and forth. Sometimes there was someone shooting back, more often it was just a nervous new soldier killing shadows. Noncoms raged, even battered a head or two. But the near panic didn't subside until almost dawn.

Rat paks were issued to all but the most forward elements, and the Force continued on, into the city.

A Larissan patrol was hit by an infantry company. They broke and ran. The company went after them, into a town square.

Fire roared at the Cumbrians from three sides, and when they tried to fall back, were pinned in the buildings on one side of the square.

They squealed for help, and seconds later, three Zhukovs smashed in at low level. Their 150mm autocannon churned buildings into rubble, and the chainguns shredded smaller, moving targets.

A rocket came out of the swirling dust, hit the lead Zhukov in the nose, and exploded in its cockpit. The ACV lifted, took another rocket in the belly, rolled, bounced, came back upright, flames licking from the hole in its nose.

The rear ramp dropped, and a Cumbrian staggered out, was cut down.

A dozen whooping Larissans dodged toward the ACV, grenades ready.

The commander's cupola grated sideways, and its machine cannon chattered, ripping men and women's bodies. Then the Cumbrians attacked through the haze, driving the Larissans out of the square.

One woman approached the smoking Zhukov, peered into the crew compartment.

"Hell's nostrils," she shouted. "There's somebody alive in here!"

A dozen Larissans came out of a gun bunker, whitish flags tied to sticks. An *Alt* and the two men went forward to accept the surrender. The Larissans dropped, and blasters behind them opened up. The officer and her two men went down, hit hard.

The men of her platoon growled, swept forward, surrounding the bunker, firing. When the return fire sputtered out, there were real attempts to surrender.

The Cumbrians shot them down as they staggered out, and that particular platoon didn't take prisoners for the rest of the battle.

Monique Lir, pushing a small recon team forward, saw an *aksai*, crashed into the side of a building. She had the team cover her, zigged forward. The canopy was open, and the corpse of a Musth dangled out.

He hadn't died in the crash—his body was almost blown apart from close-range blaster fire and knife wounds.

Lir looked at the other I&R soldiers, but said nothing. There wasn't any need.

Jil Mahim was bloody to the elbows, and her operating gown looked like she'd been swimming in gore.

"No go," she said, pulling a sheet over a man's face. "He's gone."

The gurney was hastily trundled away. Mahim had time to stretch, wish she could have a drink, wish she was a lowly enlisted swine back with I&R, when the casualties only came one or two at a time, and another gurney was pushed in front of her. Male, some kind of flier, flameproofs already cut open.

Bad, she thought. *Chest wound . . . sucking, somebody*

put a compress over that, good. Some intestinal damage.
Heavy bleeding. Probably not going to make it.

She looked, impersonally, up at the casualty's face,
recognized him as the man's eyes opened.

"Jill," *Alt* Rad Dref, onetime I&R Grierson pilot,
said. "Or am I dead?"

"You're not dead," Mahim said.

"Good. I saw those Larries coming . . . didn't want
them to get me . . . got to the cupola gun . . . guess
somebody dragged me out . . . not a bad way to go,
now, here, out of the dirt. Not much pain. Not much
at all, unless I breathe." Dref smiled beatifically. "Letter in my pouch . . . see my people get it, 'kay?"

Mahim was bending over him.

"Goddammit, you coward son of a bitch, you aren't
gonna die!"

Dref just smiled on.

"Breathe, you gutless bastard," Mahim snarled.
"Anybody can give up and die! Breathe, I'm telling
you, or I'll dig my thumb in your guts!"

Dref's smile vanished. He sucked in air, grimaced.

"Hurts."

"Damned right it hurts," Mahim said. "It means
you're still frigging alive! Breathe again!"

Dref obeyed.

"Respirator," Mahim called. "Now, goddammit!
Over here! Breathe again, you sorry sack of shit!"

Again air came in painfully, went out.

The respirator was there, and Mahim's fingers
moved over Dref's body quickly, connecting sensors,
pumps, stabbing a hollow probe through his rib cage
into a lung.

"Keep breathing," she ordered. "This box is just
gonna help a little. Breathe, or as the life spirit's my
goddamned witness I'll tear up your pissyassed sniveling little letter home to Momma, and nobody'll even
know where you died!"

Again Dref's chest moved, and once more.

"Come on, dickhead! You can do better than that! Breathe!"

Rad Dref lived, and was flying a Zhukov again within the year.

A soldier heard a sound, booted the door open, and flipped a grenade into the shanty. It went off, and the soldier heard the wail of a baby, then the tears of another child.

He forced himself to look inside, vomited, then started shouting for a medic.

"You know that goddamned Redruth's palace is like a damned *houm* warren," Maev Stiofan said.

Njangu didn't know exactly what a *houm* was, figured it out by context.

"I only learned about half of it," she went on. "Even Protector's Own weren't trusted a lot. But one thing I do know: Redruth's last hidey-hole isn't where you think it'd be, in the cellars. There's this passageway that we guarded that went somewhere. Nobody without the highest clearance—his top aides, a few *Leiters,* some unit commanders, not me, went through those doors."

"You remember where it is?"

"Surely," Maev said.

"Don't go and get killed on me 'til we get closer to that palace," Njangu said. "That might be interesting skinny, if things work out like they maybe are gonna."

"I don't like open land," Monique Lir whispered to Darod Montagna, peering out of a bomb crater toward the large, ornate building across the sweeping grounds that'd once been lawns. "Gimme a nice, crooked alley, anytime."

" 'Kay," Darod said. "I'll take the lead this time."

"Hell you will," Lir said. "I'll take Second Troop in a big fat wave. You gimme fire support when they try to level our heinies."

" 'Kay. Go."

Monique came to a crouch.

"Second Troop! Off your dead asses and on your dying feet! Let's go!"

The forty surviving Second Troop members came up in crouches and, waiting for the sky to fall, darted forward to the next cover.

Darod checked her sniper-modified blaster, took a deep breath.

"First Troop! In a rush!"

The rest of I&R zigged up, went on line with Second. Darod, panting hard, flopped behind a downed tree next to Lir.

"Why in hell," she said, "have they got us fighting like line slime?"

" 'Cause," Lir said, "they're running low on people with death wishes. Happens to I&R in every war. We start as elite, then they decide we're good enough to be line fillers, and then we get wiped out."

"Thanks for the history lesson," Montagna said. "But this is too easy," she said. "I really think—"

The artillery barrage came down, rounds crashing in a wave, on and on, endlessly. Montagna had her helmet buried in the dirt, trying to crawl up into it, when impossibly, she heard the incoming supersonic whine of the shell that was meant for her.

The shell hit on the other side of the tree, ten meters distant, and sent both officers tumbling.

Montagna realized with some surprise that she was still alive, lifted her head, opened an eye. Vision was blurred, and she wiped a hand across her face, and cleared blood away. She saw Monique Lir lying very still a few meters away.

"Sunnuvabitch," she managed. She'd always thought Lir was immortal.

Darod realized she didn't hurt that badly, and looked down at herself. Her camouflage uniform was dark-stained to her waist. Her hands came up, checked her breasts. They were still there. She cautiously ran fingers over her face. It hurt, but she didn't find any new holes. Shrapnel wounds, that was all, assuming she didn't have a big painless hole somewhere else.

First *Tweg* Huran was flat, next to her.

"You've got the company," Montagna managed. "How bad're we hit?"

"Not too. Three down, not moving, counting the boss. Maybe four wounded."

"Go take the frigging objective for me," Montagna said. "Anybody who can wiggle can give covering fire."

"But you're—"

"The medics'll be here when they're here," Montagna snapped. "You know the orders. Now move out!"

"Yes'm."

Montagna, feeling shock finger her system, pushed it away. She found a syrette in a pouch, shot half of it in her thigh, rolled over on her stomach as Huran shouted orders.

Lying almost next to her was her blaster. She dragged it over by the sling, found it didn't appear to be damaged. Montagna rolled into a shallow trench, winced in pain, and peered through the weapon's scope at the monolith ahead of them.

Nothing . . . nothing . . . nobody moving over there . . . oh there we are, down on the ground. Nope, not good enough to be the eye in the sky . . . go high . . . goddamned stone statues, wonder what this frigging place used to be . . . hard to make out if those are stones, or real people . . . ho-ho, gotcha, you sneaky little bastard, she thought, seeing a glint of light from an upper tower window that moved. *There's my artillery spotter.*

"Huran!" she shouted.

"Sir?"

"Get down! I got me the target that's causing the grief, I think."

Now, let's us see . . . range, no more'n 270 meters, pull it in tight, good buttweld, finger on the trigger . . . ouch, didn't know I got some shrapnel there, too, go away pain, come back later . . . hold on the glint, say it's some sort of spotting scope, about, oh, half a meter long, move your aim on back, should be a nice chubby goblin's head about there that I can't see . . . finger on trigger, tighten, tighten . . .

The blaster cracked. Darod brought the scope back on target, twisted the selector switch to AUTO, and let six rounds chatter into the room. The glint of light was gone.

"You're clear," she managed to shout, and let herself collapse over the stock of her blaster, hearing the yelps as I&R charged.

I'll just lie here and bleed a while, then rise on up and fight again came from somewhere. *The hell I will,* as pain washed over her.

She heard a moan, looked to the side, saw Monique Lir stir a little.

Blasters exploded ahead, and I&R swarmed into the building.

A turbine whined, and Montagna saw a Grierson land behind her. The ramps dropped, and men, women, medics by their paks, ran out. Neither ACV nor the medics wore distinctive insignia, since the Larissans found those an ideal target.

One medic slid down beside Darod.

"You're a mess," the woman said cheerfully.

"Thanks a lot. Where's your goddamned bedside manner?"

"Back at bedside," the medic said, opening her pak.

"I can wait a while. Everything's superficial, and I gave myself half a shot of painkiller," Montagna said. "Take care of my mother over there first, age preceding beauty and all that."

"Screw you and the *stobor* you rode in on," Monique Lir said weakly, and Darod Montagna knew everything would be all right.

Angara looked at the screen grimly. The Force was barely out of Agur's suburbs, and they'd taken almost 25 percent casualties.

"I don't like this, I don't like this at all," he muttered.

"Pardon, sir?" Erik Penwyth asked politely.

"I want *Caud* Hedley on a shackle connect."

"Sir." Penwyth nodded to one of the omnipresent com operators, who spoke into a mike, waited for an instant, then passed headset and mike to Angara.

"Sir, Hancock Six Actual."

Angara took the mike.

"Jon, I want you to send me your reserves. Then pull Second Brigade out of contact as quietly as you can. We'll have to take care of your targets later.

"We're going to need you over here to finish things off."

CHAPTER
28

"Is this the one who called himself Ab Yohns?"

Njangu keyed the mike.

"It is."

"A test," and Njangu could hear the cold amusement in Celidon's voice. "What do I prefer at my meals?"

"Barely cooked beef, and raw vegetables," Njangu answered.

"And what do I drink?"

"Ice water."

"You may be who you claim to be. What is your real name?"

"Uh-uh," Njangu said. "Not over a com. And for you, come to think about it, probably not ever."

A chill laugh came.

"You are definitely the double agent who fooled us. I shall continue, then, to use the name I knew you as.

"This must be brief, Yohns. I believe Protector Redruth has gone mad. He intends to destroy us all in his downfall. I am a mercenary, and have no particular desire to be devoured by his *suttee*."

"So you want to surrender?"

"Yes," Celidon said. "I'm arrogant enough to believe that, without me, your task will be far easier."

Njangu nodded agreement. Celidon was the closest thing Larix and Kura had for a practical tactician, even if he obviously wasn't as good as he thought at grand strategy.

"Tentatively, I'll agree with your call," Njangu said.

"If I come across, and I give you and your superiors the fullest cooperation, including the disposition of all our remaining units as well as access means to Protector Redruth's headquarters, I want an assurance there'll be no unpleasantries for me to face when the war is over."

"You mean, like a war-crimes trial?"

"Just so. Further, after a decent interval, I expect to have some sort of reward for my services. Perhaps some of the properties and valuables I've amassed here on Larix or on Kura, which might be better, being out of the limelight. I do not propose to starve in a garret."

Njangu looked at Angara. The *Dant* gnawed at his a lip, reluctantly nodded.

"Agreed," Njangu said, keeping the disgust out of his voice.

"Very good. The details can be worked out after I've reached safety. After all, we've all fought on the same side at one time or another," Celidon said. "As time passes, you might even want to avail yourselves of my services.

"But that shall be for the future. Listen closely. I propose to cross the fighting lines at coordinates five-six-eight-eight-slash-nine-eight-one-one at sixteen-thirty, this day. I shall be in a single Ayesha, and once I cross over Larissan positions will be flashing my landing lights yellow/blue/yellow at intervals."

"Hold," Njangu said, turned to his CO.

"We'll have him met," Angara said, "with two *velv* and two *aksai*. All of them will be repeating his signal. All of our ships will be armed and prepared to launch. If there are any problems from his side, any trickery, there'll be an instant response.

"God *damn*, but I hate some things about this frigging job."

Njangu repeated Angara's instructions, added, "you will not be fired at. I'll be in the lead ship and meet you when you ground."

"Good," Celidon said. "I anticipate a very successful partnership. Out."

The com went dead.

"I don't suppose," Njangu said, a little wistfully, "that you'd go back on your word, after the shooting stops, would you? There's a lot of accidents out here waiting to happen. Plus that son of a bitch thinks he's got better fighting moves than I do, which I wouldn't mind testing in a nice, quiet dojo with the doors locked.

"Sir?"

"You tempt me, Yoshitaro," Angara said heavily. "You tempt me greatly. But no. We'll play this as it lies. But get a squadron of destroyers to back you. Changing sides, I understand, gets easier the more you do it."

Celidon left his command bunker through a private tunnel that opened into a hidden garage, hurried toward his personal Ayesha.

He felt the blood racing, felt very alive. He'd not been one to stick around for the last part of a disaster, saw no reason to change his ways now. He'd never been on the losing side of a war, at least not for long.

His pilot, G'langer, who'd served him well, without questions, for five years, was waiting inside the ACV.

"Sir!" He saluted. Celidon returned the salute.

"This is a very special mission you and I are about to embark on," Celidon explained. "I've been ordered by the Protector to cross the lines and begin negotiations. The invaders wish a truce, and I'm to arrange the best possible terms. To make sure there's no problem with morale, you and I, and of course the Protector, are the only ones to know of these talks."

G'langer's eyes flickered, then he smiled.

"Great honors for you, sir."

"I hope so," Celidon said piously. "Then this terrible time will be over, and we'll be able to start rebuilding."

"Yessir." G'lander stepped aside, letting Celidon take his customary seat below the cupola.

"Sir?" he said.

Celidon noticed a change in his pilot's voice, turned, saw the man aiming a pistol.

"Protector's Own," G'langer said, voice gloating.

He shot Celidon four times in the chest as the *Leiter* scrabbled for his own pistol.

"Traitor's dues," the man Celidon had known as G'langer said, and went to the com to notify his superiors.

Njangu waited in the orbiting *velv* for an hour after the time Celidon had specified, then reported to Angara, and the operation was canceled.

Wonder what happened, he thought as his *velv* flew back toward its forward base. *Did the son of a bitch change his mind, or did he maybe fall downstairs, I hope, I hope?*

CHAPTER
29

Darod Montagna heard Lir's shouts of anger from the next hospital room, wondered what fools had dared to offend the dignity of the Lord of I&R. Monique's voice grew quieter, then there was silence.

There was a knock on her door.

"C'mon in," Darod said, eager for company, any company, even a goddamned nurse with the next shot.

Garvin Jaansma entered. He wore fighting uniform and combat harness, and had a thin black-leather case under his arm.

"Good afternoon, sir," Darod said.

"Darod. How come you're still laid up?" Garvin said. "I thought all you had was a face and chest full of shrapnel."

"That's it," Darod said. "But they said they wanted to do a reconstruct here and there."

"Why? You look like you."

"I am. Mostly. But here . . . here . . . and here are transplants." She made a face. "It feels weird, having part of you that's not part of you. They say, in a month or so, even I won't be able to tell the difference. I'd be happier believing them, if it didn't feel like plas stuck here and there in my face." She made a face. "And isn't that a lovely concept?"

"No," Garvin said. "So when's your discharge date? I&R needs a CO, and Monique's leg'll take another month to mend, plus she'll need another month of phystherapy."

"I'll probably be able to sneak out of here in another three or four days," Darod said. "Speaking of which, what was all that hollering about?"

Garvin made a face. "I've been put in charge of visiting the lame, halt, and malingering this week, not to mention passing out medals. Monique got a Silver Cross and another wound stripe. She started calling me all kinds of sons of bitches, saying she didn't deserve a frigging medal, all she did was get her ears leveled, and people dumb enough to get in the line of fire deserve to get busted, not awarded.

"She also told me that there was some shot-up Larissan in this hospital, who was lying there, and some officer from Second Brigade came by, doing the same medal parade I am, and gave this guy the Order of Merit. I don't believe her."

"I don't either," Darod said. "But that sounds like something Monique would pass along."

"Yeh," Garvin agreed. "You know Lir."

"I know Lir," Darod said. "And thanks for taking the time to come in and say hello, boss."

"It was Garvin, the last time, wasn't it?"

"Yeh," Montagna said. "But maybe I was getting a little too . . . brash, maybe?"

"You can leave it at Garvin."

"Oh. 'Kay. Sit down," Darod said, indicating a chair. "And what do you think of this hospital?"

"A little sterile," Garvin said. "Pun not intended."

"It used to be the Officers' Academy for this Protector's Own, somebody told me. I'm sure not sorry we grabbed it," Montagna said. "I&R butted heads with them twice before I got hit. Murderous bastards. But at least they're too damned dumb to do anything other than just keep charging the guns."

"So I understand," Garvin said. "We figure we've wiped out about half of them."

"I think I'll stay right here 'til you get the other half," Darod said. "A woman can get killed messing with those idiots. And why aren't you sitting down, like I asked?"

"Well," Garvin said, opening the case. "Like I said, I'm on the medal patrol. And you shouldn't do things like that sitting on your butt. There'll be more formal presentations when we're back at Camp Mahan."

He took out a small box, then a sheet of paper, and started reading.

"*Alt* Darod Montagna, Executive Officer of Infantry and Reconnaissance Company, First Brigade, Angara Force, is hereby awarded the Star of Gallantry—"

Montagna made a small noise.

"Don't interrupt," Garvin said, "for actions well above and beyond the call of duty, on whatever date it was, for a series of gallant actions against the Larissan enemy, including destroying two crew-served weapons single-handedly, killing thirteen and capturing twenty-seven of the enemy, and, later in the day, after being wounded, continuing to offer moral leadership to her men as they attacked an entrenched position, after her commanding officer had also been wounded. She further provided suppressing fire during their attack, single-handedly killing an enemy artillery observer who had her company pinned down.

"Such outstanding bravery is hereby recognized by the undersigned. For the Confederation, *Dant* Grig Angara.

"Stop snuffling, woman."

"I'll . . . I'll try," Montagna said, dabbing at her eyes with a sheet.

Garvin handed her the box, and sat down.

"Now, I'm just a visitor. It's nice to see you, Miss Montagna."

"Nice to still be seen," Darod said, looking at the medal in its case. "Thank you . . . Garvin. It's a very nice medal."

"Don't thank me," Jaansma said. "You were the one who was dumb enough to take on that artillery shell single-handed."

"Dumb me," Montagna agreed.

For some reason, Garvin reached out, took her free hand in his.

They sat in companionable silence for a long time, neither feeling the need to say anything.

The Larissan position had been designed to be untakable. Three gun turrets, heavy armor cast to look like boulders, had been positioned to be mutually supporting. Attack one, and the other two opened up on the attacker. Half a dozen bodies from two failed attacks still lay scattered nearby. The Legion hadn't been able to recover them, even by night.

The gun positions connected underground to crew dormitories, a small command center, ammo dumps, and a kitchen. There was also a tunnel, leading back to the palace, but that had been sealed, and the gunners told they were forbidden to retreat or surrender.

Something moved toward the turrets from the Cumbrian lines, then three more somethings, each smaller than a man. They crept forward, Larissan sensors not picking them up, until they were no more than fifty meters from the guns.

" 'Kay," Tanya Felder, now a *Tweg,* and in charge of ten of the fighting robots, said. "Keep on slithering, troops. Right up under their goddamned nose." She, and the other three operators were in their coffinlike stations in a forward outpost a few hundred meters away. Half a dozen I&R troops stood guard, in case the Larissans got cute and attacked the helpless robot drivers.

Felder was now operating Rumbles IV. The war had been as rough on robots as humans. Delicately, she moved Rumbles forward, and the turret was only a few meters away.

Suddenly a signal bleeped.

"We're blown," came in her headset from another operator.

One of the turrets swiveled, and its cannon fired.

"Missed me," an operator chortled.

The gun fired again.

"Aw crap," the last operator said. "I'm dead." She slid out of her coffin, blinking.

In the gouged terrain in front of the post, her robot lay, tracks up, smoking.

Felder paid no attention, easing Rumbles up to the turret that was her target, around it, finding cover in a small shellhole.

Someone must have seen the robot, because the turret swiveled back and forth, looking for a target. But Rumbles was well below the turret's sensors.

One of the robot's crab-claws reached out. Its claw had been modified with a high-speed drill. It touched the turret below the ring, and whined for a few seconds, then withdrew.

"I'm inside," Felder said.

"I'm in range," the operator of another robot said. "Whups. They spotted me. I'm hiding, pretty well pinned down."

"I'm at my target," the third said, sounding a little smug. "Drilling my way in."

Rumbles's other claw extended, and delicately inserted a small hose into the drilled hole.

Felder touched sensors, and an odorless gas sprayed into the turret. She waited, shifting impatiently, as the tank aboard Rumbles emptied. She changed the drill claw for another claw, this one holding a small tube, a detonator.

"I'm through," came in her headset, then, a few seconds later, "pumping."

EMPTY flashed on Felder's screen.

"I'm dry," the other operator reported.

"Now," Felder whispered for no known reason, "to get the hell out."

She keyed a mike.

"Assegai Arty Three, this is Sibyl Rossum Six. You can fire your diversion anytime."

Grounded Zhukovs behind the lines opened up,

lobbing twenty rounds per tube just behind the gun position.

Rumbles, claws prissily folded in front of it, scampered for a deep crater toward the Cumbrian lines, made it before the Larissan gun could shoot back.

"I'm clear," the other operator reported.

"Fire in the hole," Felder broadcast, touched another sensor, on a channel common to both detonators.

They exploded, setting off the extremely volatile gas. Flame swirled through the turrets, down into the sleeping, eating positions. Men screamed, danced, burning. Then the ammunition supply caught, and all three turrets blew, peeling back the land like giant trowels.

" 'Kay," said the *Tweg* now commanding the waiting assault company, "those *giptel*-screwers are gone. Let's g'wan over and see what else needs shooting."

The Force attacked. One infantryman ran close by Rumbles, and took a moment to reach down and pat the robot.

Four rockets slammed in, bracketing Njangu Yoshitaro and his two com operators. They'd been returning on foot to First Brigade Headquarters after Njangu insisted on having an eyes-on look at the positions the Force would be attacking the next day.

The blast hurled him through a destroyed storefront, and he landed amid bolts of dust-covered cloth. Njangu's ears rang unbearably, and he thought he was deaf.

He managed to get to his feet, saw his shattered blaster in the doorway, staggered out into the street, feeling as if he were on a ship in stormy seas.

Across the street was a woman soldier, staring at him in horror.

Yoshitaro was spattered with the brains, guts, and blood of one of his com operators, who must've been between the blast and Njangu. He looked around, very calmly, for the other, saw his head and trunk, sans arms, sans legs, impaled on a broken lamp standard nearby.

Njangu felt himself trembling uncontrollably. Something rose in his body, demanding that he scream, that he run, wildly, away from this insanity.

He took a few steps, slowly, then faster.

He felt as if a black pit yawned in front of him, wanted to throw himself in it, spin down and down, forgetting everything, forgetting blood, death, the wretched demands all these little men and women around him put on him, the smallest, most timid of them all.

A pit . . . no, not a pit. It was a monster, black, misshapen, trying to embrace him, and he must run, had to flee. . . .

Njangu willed his legs to fold up under him rather than flee and he went down hard, feeling the rasp of the curbstone against his cheek, and again he heard the rather contemptuous dismissal of *Mil* Liskeard,

"He used to be a tiger on roller skates . . ."

Used to be, used to be, used to be, his mind chanted. *Njangu Yoshitaro, used to be, used to be, used to be.*

Someone was turning him over, cradling him, and Njangu wanted to scream again, scream forever, life's blood in that scream.

His mouth opened and, very suddenly, there was no pit, no monster, just a scared *Striker,* saying "Sir? Sir? Are you all right, sir?"

Njangu's mouth opened and closed, like a fish drowning in air.

He put his hands down on the pavement, felt reassuring grit, and pushed himself up to a sitting position.

"Sir? Are you wounded? I can't see any wounds, sir."

Njangu took two very deep breaths, rolled until his legs were under him, came up. He almost fell, then the woman was holding him up, and they both almost went down again.

"I'm 'kay," he managed to mumble.

"That was really close, sir," the *Striker* said. "You look like you're in a little shock. Maybe you better lie back down? I'll call for the medics."

Njangu shook his head, knowing if he gave way, if he did lie down, that pit would open under him.

Luck, he thought. *All it was, all that brought me back was luck. If somebody hadn't been here, if I hadn't heard about Liskeard . . .*

He shuddered, knew he'd never feel anything but the deepest pity for anyone who broke in combat.

I can, you can, we all can. Maybe there's just so much we can take, and then we break like frigging twigs. Maybe . . .

"I'm all right," he said. "But maybe you could give me a hand back to Force Headquarters? I think I know somebody who has a bottle, and I'd like to buy you an extremely illegal drink."

The Force elements linked up. Now the city center, the Larissan headquarters, and Redruth's palace were surrounded.

But the Larissans showed no sign of giving up. Angara had PsyWar teams make 'casts to the troops, but only a handful surrendered. As often as not, when they tried to come across the lines, they were shot from behind by the Protector's Own, whom Redruth was using as a steel corset to keep his army together.

Other specialists tried to contact Redruth himself, wanting to talk about peace terms.

But no response came.

"The bastard," Jon Hedley said, probably with accuracy, "figures anybody who wants to flipping talk's a weakling, and about to fall apart.

"We're just going to have to keep pushing 'til our boot goes up his ass and comes out his flipping throat."

Njangu never told Garvin about almost breaking, but for some reason he did tell Maev Stiofan, one time when they were given an hour off duty at the same time.

He watched her closely, looking for a flicker, a flash of disdain. But none came.

"You know," she said when he was finished, "I think something like that happened to my father. His crew was loading chemicals, and there was an explosion in the 'ponics plant.

"It was, I guess, really messy, and only three or four of the crew lived. My mother went to the hospital, and came back very quiet, but said Father wasn't burned, didn't have any broken bones.

"The company moved him . . . and us . . . to what I think was a sanitarium. About a month later, they discharged him as 'kay, and found him a job at another plant, doing something different.

"He never talked about that day, but afterward, he was a little . . . different. Quieter. I even thought he was shorter."

Sure he was different, Njangu thought. *That black frigging monster took part of him away, and he could never get it back.* He shuddered.

"I'm not dumb enough to say forget about what happened," Maev said gently. "But time'll pass.

"Besides, the way this war is going, we're all going to get killed, and we won't have to worry about being psych cripples afterward.

"Come on. Both of us need a shower, and I just happen to know a chemical warfare company that's got one, even though they call it a decontamination unit. And I also know an abandoned hotel where there's a real bed that hasn't been shot full of holes. I found a big mother padlock and put it on the door myself."

The Larissan's Ayesha had been shot out of the sky a long time ago, smashing half through an office building. A month? A week? He didn't know. The man lay in his own stink, smelling his leg as it began to rot.

There was no food, but he had no appetite, anyway.

It rained once or twice, and water dribbled through a shellhole in the Ayesha, and he licked it.

He guessed the ACV had crashed between the lines, since he didn't see any of his own soldiers after the first day. He'd tried to call to them, but had been too weak.

Then there was nobody for a time.

He drifted, not unpleasantly, in and out of consciousness. But he didn't like that, tried to stay alert.

Then he heard voices, saw other soldiers. Enemy soldiers. They weren't what he wanted, so he waited longer. A day, another night passed.

He peered through the starred plas of the cupola, saw, coming along the street, a group of the enemy.

His vision was blurry, and he kept blinking.

Eight, maybe ten of them. Not enough. But then he saw the men with coms on their back, clustering around a man who held himself like a commander, carried what looked like a map board.

That would do.

He spun the control wheels of the turret, and slowly, laboriously, the cupola swung until the autocannon sights were on the officer. He could not miss.

He reached for the manual firing stud, and his hand fell limply, without strength. Again he stretched, lips moving in a prayer, a curse. One centimeter . . . two . . . five more.

Touch the button. You have enough strength. Then you can die. But touch the button first.

"All right," *Haut* Pol Trygve said firmly, pointing at the projection on his map board. "We're almost on the palace, and we'll take up new positions as soon as it's dark, and get ready for tomorrow. Put Rocket Company over here for the assault, which gives them adequate cover, and line of sight for support. Two assault companies will go in here, and—"

The machine cannon on the wrecked ACV blatted

half a dozen rounds, sweeping across the command group. Two 20mm rounds took Trygve in the body, killing him instantly. Others cut down a com operator and Second Regiment's III Section Commander.

Garvin Jaansma was bringing Trygve some replacement officers when the ACV opened fire. He saw Trygve's body convulse as the rounds tore it almost in half.

He was flat, blaster looking for a target, even as he realized where the rounds came from. Other soldiers were shooting, maneuvering toward the wreck. Grenades cascaded, then an infantry rocket launcher crashed into the Ayesha, exploded. Soldiers closed on the wreck, shooting as they went.

Somebody found a hole in the Ayesha, tossed grenades in.

Then there was silence.

Garvin was on his feet. He grabbed a mike from one of the surviving com operators, who'd stood in the middle of the firefight like a statue.

"Get me First Brigade Headquarters freq," he snapped.

"Huh?"

"Come on, man! Move."

"Oh. Yeh. I mean, yessir." The man touched buttons. "You're on their frequency, sir."

"Lance, this is Lance Seven Actual," Garvin said into the mike.

"Lance Seven Actual, this is Lance. Go ahead."

"Lance, this is Seven Actual. I shackle, uh . . ."

"Four Aleg One is the current code, sir," the operator said, now fully alert.

". . . Four Aleg One. Pilum Six Actual is down. Keld Ind Alf. Request orders, over."

There was a blurp of surprise from the other end, silence for a time, then:

"Lance Seven Actual, this is Lance Six Actual."

Caud Fitzgerald.

"Understand your message, Seven. Do you have a handle on Pilum's situation and its orders?"

Garvin thought hard, felt a hard flame of confidence roar up inside.

"That's affirmative," he said. "I was there for your briefing."

"Then continue the mission. Your call sign is now Pilum Six Actual until otherwise notified. This is Lance Six Actual, clear."

Garvin was now the Commanding Officer of Second Regiment, almost a thousand men at full strength. He tossed the microphone to the com operator.

"All right. You . . . Jenks it is, right? Stick on my ass. You're now my main voice. Call in my assault company commanders, and we'll get ready to take some real estate."

"Remember what you told me, a couple of days or centuries ago," Njangu asked Maev. "About that long passageway that went somewhere down to Redruth's rathole?"

"Surely."

"Well, I went and authorized some low-altitude, high-speed IR flights over the palace, without anybody getting dead, thankfully, and 'lookee what I got."

Maev examined the eerie hologram.

"Here's our lines, theirs, of course," Njangu said. "Here's the palace . . ."

"Shaddup," Maev said. "I'm a trained officer, too. I can read this projection as good, probably better, than you."

Her fingers touched places on the hologram not far from the palace.

"What looks like open country here, and here," she said, mocking Yoshitaro's delivery, "should not have any heat emanations like they do. That suggests there's something underground, with exhaust vents.

"Like maybe a bunker," she went on. "Like maybe

a very, very big bunker. A command center. Or maybe just a whole bunch of weapons pits."

"Nawp," Yoshitaro said smugly. "No guessing needed. Look at this. This is another infrared, from a Grierson, way up overhead, hovering, so you don't have the same detail. This is a nice time-delay series, every ten minutes or so for half a day.

"Now, you notice how the emissions from those spots you pointed out wax and wane regularly, like the poets say? Which means to me if they're weapons positions, all those regimented bastards cook at the same time, warm their little toesies at the same time, and so forth. Or else it's one big honkin' position with exhaust vents all linked together."

"I think you're right," Maev said. "And I think if we can get some backup and permission, it might be time to go exploring."

"Kinda thought you'd say that. But I'm not thrilled with that 'we' bit. I mean, this is dangerous, and all."

Maev gave him a look.

"Are *you* going?" she asked.

"Of course."

"Well, then."

Njangu started to say something, stopped.

" 'Kay. Lemme set some wheels turning."

Garvin led two attacks as Regimental Commander, taking moderate casualties. Each time, Second Regiment held a few dozen or hundred more meters.

He was scared spitless the first time, more confident the second. Nobody showed up to relieve him, so he guessed he was doing all right.

Other regiments attacked on their fronts, and the noose around Redruth tightened. Building by building, block by block, the brutal city fighting went on.

The ruined spires of Redruth's palace loomed. Death struck from its every spire, every hidden bunker, every innocent-seeming outbuilding.

Hastily trained replacements came in from D-Cumbre,

were fed into the combat formations and, as often as not, died before they understood how real war worked.

"Knock," Njangu said, peering into the round concrete pipe, half-buried in rubble, that was Garvin's private quarters. A dozen meters away was the culvert that was his headquarters. Garvin looked up from the map of the palace he'd been studying, saw Yoshitaro and Stiofan, crawled out.

"I'd ask you in for an aperitif," he said, "but it's a little cramped. Sorry."

"Congrats on the promotion," Njangu said.

"Yeh, well, it's a job," Garvin said, trying to keep the pride out of his voice. He cupped hands, shouted. A particularly filthy *Alt* stuck his head out of the culvert.

"What do you need, boss?"

"Valento, somebody shake me up some frigging caff for my guests, or I'm over there to beat butt!"

"Right, boss," the officer said. "Sorry. I should have seen 'em coming."

"Goddamned disrespectful swine," Garvin muttered. "If he wasn't so good at killing people, I'd probably do something drastic to him."

Njangu looked at Garvin's drawn face, at the lines of exhaustion, and decided not to say anything.

"Speaking of which," Jaansma said, "when're you going to get your ass back on the staff where you're supposed to be? Us field ossifers need guidance."

"Angara seems hell-bent to keep me forever," Njangu said. "I've been whining to come back to a place where a man can stand up and get kilt, but without results. And Fitzgerald isn't any happier than you are, either."

"Shit," Garvin said. "I've got an attack at dawn tomorrow, and don't have the froggiest on how to do anything except hit 'em again and keep getting slaughtered."

"Actually," Njangu said, "that's why we're here. Your orders have been changed."

"And Fitzgerald didn't bother telling me anything? What is this, some kind of supersecret that you've got to hand-carry the news? You sure this isn't one of your schemes, Njangu?"

"Well, actually it is," Yoshitaro said. "But mostly Maev's. Angara personally approved this one, and Fitzgerald said we should deploy through your sector. Sit down, gimme your goddamned map, and I'll show you how we're going to let you win the war."

Garvin moved four assault companies as far forward as he dared as soon as full dark came.

Now the palace was very, very close.

This is a good place to get killed, he thought. *But Njangu and Company stand a better chance in the corpse lottery.*

There were four of them: Njangu, Maev, *Tweg* Calafo, and *Striker* Fleam. Njangu thought of other names, other soldiers he might've preferred. But they were dead, wounded, or in another unit now.

There was very little left of the I&R Company he'd led. But that seemed the way of things.

The four wore light-absorbing clothes that should also reflect ground radar and IR, and their faces were blackened. They carried only a couple of energy bars and a single canteen each. They carried blast pistols, fighting knives, plus the antique suppressed single-shot projectile weapons. Fleam also had a short nail-studded club he swore was the best weapon of all on a night patrol.

Two hours before false dawn they crept out of the Force lines in an area that hadn't seen action in a couple of days, moving across the lines to the Larissan outposts.

The enemy troops were alert, but as exhausted as

their enemies, so the four infiltrators weren't ID'ed, didn't have to kill anyone.

They went on, past buried turrets, bunkers with gun barrels sticking out, pop-up cannon positions. No one was above ground. Being seen, even at night, was an invitation to death.

A fighting patrol or a night attack would have been discovered and wiped out. But no one allowed for a few skilled men, moving silently, which I&R had discovered on their various reconnaissances.

The ruins of the palace were around them, strange, jagged formations that'd once been logical constructs of men.

Njangu looked up at the ruins, remembering his promise to do a favor for the Universe's architects when he first saw the rococo nightmare, thought he hadn't meant to do the work personally.

A sentry hidden behind a broken statue saw movement and aimed. Yoshitaro's knife went home in his throat and he died. They dragged the body behind a pile of rubble and went on.

If they succeeded, they wouldn't come back this way. If they failed . . . it didn't matter.

They moved into the huge main entrance of the palace. The great doors had been blown in by airstrikes, and the tapestries were smoke-blackened, the art on the walls torn, ruined.

Maev led them down a long hall, toward the sound of voices. A door was open a crack, and light, the sound of voices came out.

She motioned them down, and they crawled silently past the room, went on.

Smaller halls opened, some still occupied, others bombed into rubble. Maev led them deeper into the palace, never being seen. Twice she stopped, realized she'd lost her way, and they went back, took another passage.

Again, light gleamed.

Maev took Njangu's arm, nodded, pointed. This was

where the passage she'd wondered about began. She drew her pistol, as did the others.

She'd said there would probably be only two sentries at the door.

Njangu held up one finger . . . then another . . . then a third, and the four jumped around the corner, weapons leveled.

Six Protector's Own gaped, then brought their blasters up. There were four dull clicks, and four Larissans were down, small projectile holes in their foreheads, under their helmets' bulge. Njangu was moving forward, snapkicked the fifth's blaster spinning up, knife strike going into the man's throat, spinning him, snapping his neck and letting him down as Fleam's bludgeon crushed the skull of the last.

They left the piled bodies where they'd fallen. If someone came, there'd be shouts and alarms when they saw the corpses. If the guard post was vacant, someone might look for the missing men quietly and surprise the raiders.

Njangu checked his watch finger. It was just about time. All they had to do was keep on creepy-crawling, grab somebody, and pull out their toenails until he or she told them where Redruth's quarters were, once Garvin's attack started and gave them some cover noise. Then they could go on to finish their mission with Redruth either kidnapped or, most likely, dead.

But it didn't quite happen that way.

CHAPTER
30

The artillery preceded Garvin's attack with a barrage that walked from the lines back to the palace, then came forward again. *Velv, aksai,* Zhukovs dived, firing missiles at any target that presented itself on any screen.

The palace grounds were worked over as thoroughly as any farmer's plowed field, not for the first nor the tenth time.

The Larissans held in their positions, knowing that fleeing, or even coming into the open until the artillery and aerial hells stopped would be utter suicide. They waited instead for the enemy infantry to attack, dark figures walking slowly toward them through the boiling haze.

Garvin's assault companies came out of their positions, went forward as the artillery gave the palace a final pounding, and a wave of aircraft dived in for a final strafing.

No one ever knew who fired the rocket. But it hit something delicate. A massive explosion shook the ground, and smoke boiled high, over the palace's tallest tower. For an instant, Garvin thought someone had set off a tactical nuke. But it wasn't that, something more conventional, perhaps a fairly small ammunition dump that'd been hit.

The ground was ripped open, revealing torn concrete that'd been laid, then concealed with meters of dirt.

The first Cumbrian to reach the smoking crater

looked down, saw the shatter of a room, and an open door.

"We got a way in!" he shouted. His platoon sergeant echoed the command, and infantrymen streamed toward the hole, dropped down, and the Force was inside Protector Redruth's command center.

Njangu and the other three heard the battle begin, opened the doors to the passage, and started down it. The sound of the artillery and bombing got louder as they got closer.

A huge explosion rocked the tunnel, sending them sprawling. Dust cascaded, and Njangu thought for a moment the passage had collapsed. They slowly picked themselves up, half-deafened, drew their blast pistols, since noise was clearly no longer a factor, and hurried on.

They heard shouts, saw two men, rather fat, technicians most likely, running toward them. The men didn't see the infiltrators, but were looking behind them, as they were being pursued. Then they spotted the four ahead. One shrieked in panic, the other tried to draw a tiny pistol, and both were shot down.

Someone invisible in the haze beyond shot at them, and Njangu and the others ducked into an alcove, and shot back.

Protector Redruth listened to the shouting, the slam of blaster bolts exploding, grenades blasting.

"You," he told his senior aide. "Take the rest of my Protectors and drive the Cumbrians out! Take any member of my staff you see with you."

"Yes, sir."

Calling for his men, the officer ran up stairs, boots clanging on the steel steps.

Redruth thought. Perhaps his soldiers would show their true mettle and destroy the invaders. Or perhaps not. He certainly had no intention of being taken prisoner, to be exhibited like a circus beast.

Nor did he intend to die stupidly in this hole like a rat. His destiny, and that of Larix and Kura, were inextricably entwined, and when he died, so would his empire.

He must escape, fight on.

Redruth went to a wall, pressed a hidden switch. The panel slid away, revealing a small elevator. He stepped inside, touched the top sensor.

The door closed, and the elevator hissed upward, past the Protector's Own barracks, mess halls, past the conference rooms, past the various computer-analysis spaces, the necessary chambers of a modern army.

It stopped, and the door opened into a bare concrete passage.

From here, he was minutes from the center of the palace. His staff thought it ruined, almost abandoned, but there were other tunnels he knew of, tunnels that led to the edges of the city, to hidden hangars with lifters, a way to escape and start again.

This is only the beginning, Redruth thought.

He heard the slam of blasters *ahead* of him, between him and the palace, between him and escape.

He was trapped.

Redruth always prided himself on being a pragmatist. If there was no other way out . . .

He saw a deep alcove, went into it. He took out his pistol, charged the chamber. He examined the weapon curiously, noting for the first time the fine engraving and the scrolled grips.

The weapon had only been fired once, at a range, when he'd been given it by . . . oh yes. By Celidon, damn his dark soul. No, twice. Yesterday, when that other fool had refused his orders.

Redruth snapped the safety off and lifted the pistol.

Njangu heard the single shot, crouched, waited for more.

Nothing came.

Far down the passage ahead, the battle roar grew.

"Let's see if we can't get in on the action," he said, and the team went forward.

Fleam saw the hand sticking out of the alcove, pointed, and they went down once more.

The hand didn't move.

Maev got up, and went around the corner of the alcove.

Protector Alena Redruth was sprawled in a pool of blood. Either his hand had slipped, or he'd had second thoughts at the last instant, for he was still alive, moving feebly, his jaw messily blown away.

His eyes were open, filled with agony. He stared up at Maev, seemed to recognize her.

She leveled the pistol.

"You can't do *anything* right can you, you sorry bastard?"

She pulled the trigger once, blowing a fist-sized hole in Redruth's chest.

Maev turned to the others.

"You sure know how to simplify life, don't you," was all Njangu Yoshitaro said with a shrug, not a trace of reproach in his voice.

CHAPTER
31

"To tell you the truth," Garvin said, "I didn't think we were going to live through this one."

Njangu thought of a wisecrack, changed his mind. "It got pretty grim out," he agreed.

He looked at the assembled Second Regiment, waiting for the transports to land. "The Force took a pretty big hit."

Garvin nodded. He'd heard, of the fifteen-thousand-plus in the two Brigades, about seven thousand were casualties, killed or wounded. I&R, for a known example, had fewer than sixty effectives.

"It'll be a while, rebuilding," he said.

"Are you sure 'we' want to? I mean, like you and me, not the editorial or collective-type 'we.'"

"What's the options?" Garvin asked.

"Well, I think we've got enough credits to buy our way out, if we want," Njangu said. "Unless you *like* being the youngest *Caud* in whatever history you're reading."

"It's not too bad," Garvin said carefully.

Caud Fitzgerald, with Angara's approval, had confirmed Jaansma as Commanding Officer of Second Regiment. She and *Dant* Angara had, grudgingly, let Njangu leave the Brigade staff to become Garvin's Executive Officer.

All other Regimental Commanders had been promoted *Caud* as well, the rank Angara had always considered proper for the responsibilities.

"Consider your options," Njangu said. "Hell, you

could be a rich lounger, considering Jasith's shall we
say material assets. Or you could even go to work.
Ex-*Cauds* probably can get hired on to be figureheads
at companies, can't they?"

Garvin thought about that, about being Garvin Mellusin. Then he thought about Darod Montagna, wondered what the hell was going to happen there, if
anything, if he even wanted something to happen.

"That doesn't sound like fun," he said.

"I'm starting to wonder if you still know what fun
is," Njangu grumbled. " 'Kay. Try another option. We
take discharges, come back here as part of the Civil
Government, trying to teach these robots how to be
human beings. There ought to be a *lot* of things worth
looting. Celidon said something about having some
serious goodies stashed on Kura. We could go looking
for those.

"Froude's already said he's mounting an expedition
to Kura Four, to try to find out what those goddamned
Womblies really are."

"Poor bastard," Garvin said. "Pity he and Ho
Kang . . ." Jaansma let his voice trail off.

"Yeh," Njangu said. "Pity a whole bunch of
things . . . and let's go back to where I was, talking
about illicitly enriching ourselves on the backs of these
downtrodden scumbuckets. That doesn't sound too
bad. Governor-General Jaansma. Real Governor-
General Behind the Arras Yoshitaro."

Then Njangu thought of Brythe, Pyder, Enida,
Karig, somewhere out there, and then of Maev. Before
Garvin could say anything, Njangu said:

"Naah. That doesn't sound like fun, either."

Garvin nodded. He looked around the spaceport.

"If I never see frigging Larix *or* Kura again, that's
twice too soon," he said firmly. "I wonder why we
didn't just nuke them and avoid all this hassle."

"Now, now," Njangu said. "Let's not be the blood-
thirsty uniformed barbarian we all know you to be. 'Kay.
You realize the options are getting a tad slender?"

"Njangu," Garvin said, "aren't you getting really curious to find out what happened to the goddamned Confederation?"

Before Yoshitaro could answer, a wave of transports came through the crowd cover, lowered toward the field.

"*Adj-Prem!*" Garvin shouted.

The regiment's senior noncom doubled toward him, snapped to attention.

"Sir!"

"Bring the regiment to attention and turn it over to its commanders. Order them to board ship."

Similar orders were being given to the other regiments at fields scattered around Agur.

"Sir!"

Shouts echoed around the field, and the ground trembled as the troopships grounded.

"Well?" Garvin asked. "So what about the goddamned Confederation?"

"Come to think about it," Njangu said, "that is a poser, isn't it?"

He clapped his friend on the shoulder.

"Come on. Let's get off this armpit, go home and see if some fool doesn't want to buy us a drink.

"*Then* we'll go sort out the frigging Confederation."